THE HOUSE ON
PARADISE STREET

SOFKA ZINOVIEFF

THE HOUSE ON
PARADISE
STREET

MARBLE ARCH
PRESS

MARBLE ARCH PRESS

Marble Arch Press
1230 Avenue of the Americas
New York, NY 10020

First Marble Arch Press trade paperback edition January 2013

Marble Arch Press is a publishing collaboration between Short Books, UK, and Atria Books, US.

Marble Arch Press and colophon are trademarks of Short Books.

For information about special discounts for bulk purchases, please contact Simon & Schuster Special Sales at 1-866-506-1949 or business@simonandschuster.com

Manufactured in the United States of America

10 9 8 7 6 5 4 3 2 1

Library of Congress Cataloging-in-Publication Data

ISBN 978-1-4767-1877-4
ISBN 978-1-4767-1879-8 (ebook)

For Anna and Lara

THE HOUSE ON
PARADISE
STREET

1

A polite stranger

MAUD

The day Nikitas died, his aunt came to speak to me in the evening. I was lying alone in my room as a muffled orange twilight gave way to darkness. The sounds of the Athenian night were familiar: neighbourhood dogs; mopeds whining up the hill; and the hum of traffic. Alexandra sat taut and upright on my rumpled bed, her tailored mourning clothes giving her the incongruous look of a raven landed in a laundry basket. I lay there, breathing in the naphthalene, watching her make automatic smoothing movements on the sheets. Her hand was speckled with age spots and a gold wedding ring held her husband's looser band in place. Now I was a widow too.

Alexandra took a breath before she spoke.

"There's something you need to do. You should contact your mother-in-law." I looked at her blankly, not understanding. *Petherá*: the very word sounded foreign, never used in relation to me before.

"Nikitas' mother. Antigone. She should learn what happened." Her speech emerged awkwardly, staccato. Aunt Alexandra normally succeeded in ignoring the existence of her younger sister, though occasionally, if she was particularly annoyed or upset by Nikitas, she would compare him to his mother.

"The apple falls under the apple tree. You can never get away from that." Too much time had gone by to speak of Antigone casually; it was almost sixty years since she had left. And she had never returned. Fixed in time as the young woman who had walked away and didn't look back, she had become in her absence the family's black hole, sucking emotions inwards and giving nothing back. The knowledge that she was still alive was worse than if she had died. It implied the continuation of insult and rejection.

When I first knew Nikitas, I was intrigued by the drama of his infancy. He showed me a framed photograph of his mother as a young woman. Taken from a low camera angle, the picture presents a heroine, with eyes gazing out to a victorious horizon. She is dressed in military uniform, but it is her face that is compelling: generous lips, resolutely straight eyebrows and long, dark hair falling unrestrained, like a contemporary teenager. There was undeniably a tragic grandeur in Antigone's appearance, but also in the lack of compromise in her life; what could bring someone to abandon her young child and leave her country for ever? Initially, as an outsider, a foreigner, in this family, I appreciated the idea of Antigone the rebel. Later, however, especially after Tig was born, I became enough of an insider to change my opinion. There could be no excuse for this stubborn old woman who had never cared enough to come back and see those she had left behind. Now that her son was dead, what could there be to say?

*   *   *

I imagine that many disastrous days start innocently enough, and the morning of October 29th 2008 was unremarkable. Later, trying to make sense of events, I looked for omens – some pattern or prediction. I tried to go over Nikitas' last days and weeks and even wondered about the invasion of ants in the kitchen that morning – a thick jagged line of them squeezing through a crack in the door frame and proceeding vigorously around the sink and into the cupboards. Their doggedness in the face of my attempts to annihilate them with washing-up liquid was almost touching, stumbling over each other to continue the progression, like disciplined soldiers taking up the front line. As I washed their crumpled black corpses down the sink, I thought about Nikitas, but I was not worried that he had failed to come home the night before.

When I had married Nikitas fifteen years earlier, I had known that I could not press him into a conventional home life, and in truth, our system usually suited me too. His job gave him the excuse to work unusual hours, and frequently, after writing late for a deadline or following a long evening out with friends, he would bed down at his "office" – a little *pied-a-terre* near Sophocles Street. Two ex-wives were only one of many indications that Nikitas' talk of liberty was not an abstract notion.

"I am a Greek," he'd announce as an explanation for needs that I, as an English person, could not be expected to have or to understand. Most Greeks discuss freedom as a theoretical measuring stick for their nation's history or for a person's quality of life, but in Nikitas' case, it was an urgent personal need. His desire to leave the house, to travel or to change his plans on impulse had the single-mindedness of the young child desperate to get out of the darkness and into the sunshine.

The previous day, October 28th, had been Nikitas' birthday as well as being a public holiday and, as usual, he had eschewed the "arsehole parades" that took place around the city and the birthday cakes and celebrations we sometimes organised at home. He had long ago encouraged Tig to boycott the school parade, so she had a lie-in rather than dress up in a blue skirt and sensible shoes and march the streets with her school mates, clutching blue and white flags.

"'No Day!' That's what we're good at in Greece, so let's say no, whether or not anyone listens," Nikitas told her. "You should say no to fascist-style marching – after all, we're celebrating our refusal to let a fascist Italian dictator invade our homeland in 1940. Not that it kept them away in the end."

I think Nikitas left on his birthday morning without saying goodbye, though I can't quite remember. Perhaps I just didn't hear him calling. I've gone over it many times in my head since then. Perhaps he hugged me and I've just forgotten.

As I made toast and encouraged Tig to prepare for school, I didn't contemplate calling Nikitas' mobile phone. If he had been working late he would be sleeping and, anyway, he usually had it switched off, resenting the intrusion implied by being permanently available. Tig had the outraged yet somnolent look of a hibernating animal that has been woken up in mid-winter, her long, almost black hair engulfing a pale face. She took a few dainty bites and threw the rest into the bin; Greeks don't eat breakfast – even those with foreign mothers.

Tig grabbed her school bag and I forgot to check if my mobile was in my jacket pocket. We left the back way, out of the kitchen door and down the wrought iron spiral staircase at the rear of the building. The sky was filled with a sickly yellow haze and a humid wind twisted the air. This disconcerting southerly appears from time to time, carrying Saharan sand all the way across the Mediterranean, depositing it throughout the centre of Athens as a layer of rusty powder. Our hands picked up the African dust on the handrail and the leaves on the lemon tree were tinted terracotta. The lemon tree dominates our yard. It was planted by Aunt Alexandra's father in the 1920s, when he built the house, and it now reaches to our first floor windows, the fruit ripening almost all year round. In the spring, the building is flooded with the blossom's intoxicating scent. The fire escape descends to the courtyard at the back of the house, alongside – almost inside – the tree, so you can reach out to pick a lemon or take a leaf to crush and sniff the citrus tang. Tig sometimes climbs onto the sturdy central branches and sits there, hiding. Aunt Alexandra makes a syrupy preserve from the lemon peel, offering it as a "spoon sweet" to visitors. Chryssa paints its trunk with lime-wash in springtime, to prevent disease and infestation. I have loved this tree since I first visited Paradise Street and in optimistic moments see it as a common point of reference for the disjointed family that I married into. Our totem.

The courtyard's familiar smell of cat piss and jasmine was overlaid with brewing coffee from Alexandra's ground floor apartment. Through the green grille on the kitchen window,

Chryssa was visible, stirring a pot of Greek coffee on a hissing camper-gas that she preferred to the electric cooker. She spotted us and waved, calling out through the window to Tig.

"Off to school, my Angel? May the Virgin go with you! Good progress!" She looked like a kindly country witch, in a worn, print dress, her grey hair twisted into a bun. Tig said good morning and waved back, more polite with Chryssa than with me or Nikitas, who were bearing the increasing brunt of adolescent wrath. I could see Chryssa's capable, knobbly hands pouring the coffee ("sweet and heavy", made in the traditional way) from the *bríki* into a cup and saucer. It would soon be carried through to Aunt Alexandra, with some cinnamon biscuits from the bakery. The two old women had the easy, unspoken companionship of people who take each other for granted, and while their official status was mistress and maid, decades of shared life had blurred the boundaries.

I loved being part of these routines – so regular, we could time ourselves in the morning by what stage the coffee was at, and whether *Kyria* Lambakis, our neighbour, was just leaving for her hairdresser's down the road ("Welcome to the girls! Good day to you both!"). It pleased me that Tig was rooted somewhere, in contrast to my childhood, with my absent parents and insecurities. If Nikitas yearned for freedom and found it within the confines of marriage, then I longed for familiarity and found it in a foreign culture. Strange how the same marriage can offer such different satisfactions to each participant.

The looming flank of Hymettus was covered with thick, phlegm-coloured clouds through which the sun emitted the sickly glow of a spotlight in a smoky room. As Tig and I walked up the hill to Athens' Thirteenth Secondary School, we were nagged and buffeted by the warm wind. Tig brushed away the tangles of dark hair that whipped across her face, obscuring large eyes smudged black with yesterday's liner and accumulated tiredness – going to bed on time had been abandoned years ago. She was neither child nor woman, but something fleeting, perfect and in-between and she slipped between confident worldliness and youthful vulnerability. The wound from a recent eyebrow piercing added a touch of drama; she was forbidden from wearing the small silver bolt at school and its daily removal was still a delicate manoeuvre. She had not asked permission for this "mutilation", as Nikitas described it, and he had tried unsuccessfully to hide his shock.

"I thought you approved of individual expression and questioning the system," Tig said, quoting him back as a challenge to counter disapproval.

"Nobody else's mother takes them to school, you know." Tig was wired up to an I-pod, whose tinny, pounding bass was just audible above the wind's bluster.

"I'm only coming for the walk. I know you can look after yourself."

Tig looked at me coolly and raised a disbelieving eyebrow. Before we reached the school gates she switched from English to Greek to say goodbye. I saw her notice and then not look at Kimon, a boy she likes but is too shy to speak to. She hurried away into the yard. I didn't stay and watch as I used to, waiting for the head teacher to make the call for prayers, and observing pupils from Albania, Bulgaria, Pakistan, China and the Philippines line up with everyone else to chant their way through *Our Father*, and cross themselves along with the Orthodox.

"Soon there won't be any 'little Greeks' in the school and they'll be teaching in Albanian," Aunt Alexandra had commented recently.

Nikitas' comment was acerbic: "She'd prefer things back to the good old days of the Colonels, with 'Hellas for Christian Hellenes'."

I had only just arrived home when I heard three brisk knocks on the door – Aunt Alexandra's code when she came up from her apartment on the ground floor. She usually called out: "It's me!"

"Don't open the door if you don't know who it is," she warned. "Athens has changed. There are so many foreigners now." I am very fond of Aunt Alexandra. She welcomed me into her family with generosity and despite the tensions between her and Nikitas, she has been like a grandmother to Tig. But there are times when I am reluctant to invite her in. That morning I didn't want to hear about her aches ("If you're above ground, you'll hurt"), or her fund-raising evening for her conservative New Democracy friends, or her latest gossip about Father Apostolos and his troubles. I was late with the last instalment of my research. This time it was a trawl through 1930s archives for a historian writing about Metaxas' dictatorship. Being a freelance researcher is not always easy, though I've built up quite a network of British and American academics who don't speak Greek or don't have the time and cunning to deal with the Greek civil servants who guard the material. I had planned on sending off the packet of photocopies and translations to Professor Stotter before the post office shut at 2pm. In truth though, the main reason I didn't want to open the door for Alexandra was that I didn't want her to notice that Nikitas had not come home. It left me feeling queasy when she drew me into an implied female conspiracy, where Nikitas was the "naughty boy" and I was conscripted into the ranks of sensible female stalwarts.

There was another knock, louder this time. I pictured her standing on the landing outside our door, her bluish, candy-floss hair moulded into a lacquered crash-helmet, the perfect painted fingernails and heels mildly skittish for an eighty-five-year-old. She would say:

"Good morning Maud", or more likely, she would use a diminutive for my name, and then add the possessive pronoun:

Kali sou méra, Mondouli mou – "A good morning to you, my little Maud." I was diminished then possessed, all in the name of affection and intimacy. Before opening the door, I picked up some papers to make myself look busy and back up my excuse. Alexandra looked awful and it was clear something was wrong. Her voice came out high-pitched. The police had rung her after failing to find me, she explained. Nikitas had been in a car crash on the coast road early this morning. Somewhere near Varkiza. She didn't know the details, but he was seriously injured. I was to go immediately to the Asklipieio Hospital in Voula. She had already rung Orestes in his studio upstairs and he was coming down.

My twenty-five-year-old stepson came jogging chaotically down the steps from the roof terrace.

"What the fuck happened? What's *Babas* gone and done?" Orestes looked bewildered, his features swollen from sleep, and he tugged at his crumpled T-shirt, as if attempting to bring some order in the face of disaster. Since I first met him fifteen years ago as a shy little boy, he had grown into an alluring, long-limbed man, whose dark hair reached his shoulders. "A real *palikári*," as Chryssa said, "strong and tall as a cypress." His gait was languid and almost shambolic, belying the lava of anger that lurked below the surface. He was normally unshaven, wearing the baggy, low-slung clothes favoured by his fellow students, but he still reminded me of the sweet ten-year-old boy who shook my hand and made us laugh the first time we were introduced.

"I'll take you to the hospital on my bike – that would be quickest." Orestes' spirits rose somewhat at the thought of his beloved motorbike, which he rode with verve, roaring and weaving through the city's traffic.

"No, we'll call a cab," I said, picking up the phone to dial and observing his features fall. The taxi sped down Syngrou Avenue towards the sallow sea and then south along the coast road. Orestes rolled a cigarette, opened his window and puffed the smoke out in an exaggerated sigh. His legs juddered nervously. I experienced a bizarre clarity of vision in my fear, as though I were seeing things for the first time: the pale lines in the dusty roadside oleander leaves, the mauve tint of an old woman's lips boarding the seaside tram at Faliro. I recognised adrenaline tingling through my skin; cold feet; an obstacle in the throat. The wind had produced a strange fog that drained the colour from everything, so you could hardly tell where the sea ended and the sky began, as though you might get lost in the greyness.

At the turning for the hospital we waited at some traffic lights where a slim tabby cat lay folded at an acrobatic angle in the gutter. Pink 1930s buildings and ornamental flowerbeds gave the hospital a seaside holiday atmosphere and the salty air was scented with pine and eucalyptus. At a window marked Enquiries, a garish blonde woman with purple nails was peeling an apple. I bent down to speak through the opened slot but the words came out curdled, as if I had forgotten my Greek.

"My husband, Nikitas Perifanis …" I paused, recognising how this language that had such a deep hold on me, and which I had started learning twenty years ago, could still retreat in moments of stress or exhaustion. It was not enough to be devoted to it, to read poetry, to dream in it, sing in it, fight in it and make love in it; Greek would never be my mother-tongue. She could become a faithless deserter in times of need.

We were sent to the Ward Sister's office, told to wait for the doctor, and stood hunched and trembling outside it by a row of patients drooped on orange plastic chairs. A medic in jeans and white coat appeared and led us a little way along the corridor, squeezing himself up against the wall in an attempt at privacy. He might have been only a few years older than Orestes, though it was obvious that he had already seen more ugliness and pain. His gaze of sympathy tempered by exhaustion was enough for me to grasp the gist of his announcement before he spoke.

"The news is not good." A distant buzzing sound of live wires touching. My body felt hollowed out then so heavy that my knees almost gave way.

Nikitas' car left the road at some point in the night. It rolled onto the rocks at the Limanakia – the Little Harbours – near Varkiza. A swimmer spotted the wreck from the sea in the morning. My husband was already dead. No other cars were involved, but there would have to be an enquiry, an autopsy.

The facts appeared quite simple, he said, but we should see the local police to give a statement. Orestes gripped my forearm too tightly, like a child who doesn't want to be left at the nursery. His skin was so white it was almost blue.

I had often imagined Nikitas' death; he was twenty years older and I knew the odds. But I had used his seniority like a shield as he took on the battles of age ahead of me. When I reached forty a couple of years earlier, it seemed gratifyingly youthful compared with his sixty. Although Nikitas took it for granted that I'd be the one left behind and enjoyed teasing me with "when I'm gone…", he did not appear old. I noticed the signs that his body was ageing (his solid torso slightly softer, his chest hair sprouting white), but his presence was as powerful and vigorous as it had been when we first met. And if Tig was sometimes embarrassed that people assumed he was her grandfather, he was not; he'd swing her up in the air, making her squeal.

"Don't care what others think – they're usually wrong."

I signed several pieces of paper without understanding what they were and was given the contact details of the police who were dealing with the case. I could not think of any reason why Nikitas would have been driving down that way at night. A man who might have been a nurse took us to the hospital's small morgue. He didn't speak, but his movements were deft as he pulled a lever down to open one of several metal doors and then slid out a long shelf. He peeled back a coarse white sheet and retreated discreetly. The dead man didn't look like Nikitas. It wasn't just the dark bruises on his face, but more the stillness. Nikitas was constantly moving. Even asleep, he sighed, rolled and twitched, letting out small yelping noises like a dog dreaming. When awake, his facial expressions were exaggerated, his gestures more expansive and voice louder or dramatically quieter than other people's. He ate more, drank more, embraced us all with hugs that expressed affection, but that also hinted at the potentially threatening strength of a bear. The only time he became still was when he was very angry; then he was the bear before the chase. Now he looked like a polite stranger. I put my hand on his chest until Orestes pulled at me.

"Can we leave? It stinks here."

We fled, leaving the nurse and the pungent smell of public swimming pools and school science labs. I said, "Thank you." I wasn't brought up in England for nothing.

Orestes strode ahead, out of the hospital doors and over to some bushes where he threw up. I put one hand on his back and the other on his forehead, as I did with Tig when she was sick. When he had finished, I led him slowly over to a bench under a canopy of jasmine by the hospital chapel. Nearby, two young nurses chatted as they ate cheese pies from paper bags. Pigeons danced at their feet, darting at the falling flakes.

2
Half my heart is Russian

ANTIGONE

Lately, when I sit in the chair by the window, I find that rather than looking out at the familiar grey towers of suburban Moscow, I am transported back to the Athens of my childhood. I have spent my life straining to look ahead, fighting for the future, for a better world. I believed in a new dawn that never came. Now that I am getting towards the end, where the only thing that is sure is the grave's dark night, I go backwards towards my own dawn. Mostly, I think of the good things, the early years, my parents and our house in Paradise Street before the war. I try to stop there, before everything else.

Russia has been good to me. Part of me belongs here as though there was never anything else. Half my heart is Russian. Even during recent years since Igor died, I find small pleasures and consolations. The apartment is not large but it is warm and comfortable. The view from the tenth floor allows me to see the vast Russian skies that are so different to the intimate landscapes of Greece. Moscow's ring road may not be the most beautiful place in this country, but I am able to see past the neighbouring apartment blocks to the woods. I used to go there for walks with Natalya until her legs got too bad. These days I don't see many people, but Natalya is like family – I have known her for longer than my own flesh and blood. We meet most days, and are close enough to be able to sit together drinking tea and not talking – not that she is often at a loss for words. My inclination is more towards the written word and I still write in a notebook most days. God only knows why. Perhaps it is to prove I am still here. Certainly there is quite a collection of them in the cupboard now.

When I first became friends with Natalya we were both in our late twenties. She had rosy apple cheeks and a voluptuous body that matched her generous character. These days she has put on so much weight that she rocks like a boat as she walks. Sometimes we still go for a steam at our local baths, and while we sit dripping in the fug, I take in the expanses of her flesh. Heavy breasts reaching to the sparse remnants of her pubic hair, calves solid and pink. In comparison, I feel like a fruit that someone forgot in the sun until the flesh became dried out and the skin hard and creased. My skeleton juts out where once it was invisible, reminding me that bones are all that will remain. Back in the changing rooms, Natalya puts on her capacious underpants and spreads out "a little snack": black bread, some left-over *bitki* wrapped in waxed paper, a lump of curd cheese. And, of course, a small bottle of vodka to toast one another's health with a cigarette or two. These small pleasures have become more significant with time.

Yesterday we sat together in my kitchen, watching the afternoon light wane until it was the colour of iron. Natalya's words washed over me like gentle waves and I only came out of my thoughts when she repeated a question.

"So, Antigone, what do you think? Should I go?" She slid another biscuit into her mouth and waited for my answer.

"Well, that depends." I searched for a platitude so as not to betray my absent-mindedness. "Going is the easy part... it's the return that is hard." Luckily, Natalya didn't notice and launched into a topic I have heard far too much of in recent times – her daughter, Lyuba.

Lyuba's husband is one of the new rich – a breed of men we saw appear out of nowhere in the 1990s, like the cockroaches from the rubbish chute by my kitchen. We always knew him as some kind of engineer and then one day he was driving a Mercedes, hiring bodyguards and going off for holidays in Italy. When the Soviet Union disintegrated around us, carrying all those ideals and sacrifices with it, we hoped something positive would emerge. Nobody thought it was perfect before, but we old-timers still spoke in terms of freedom and justice. But the new Russians weren't like that; they were nothing but cowboys. Now there are no convictions or principles, no aims but acquiring money. The rest of us have been left behind like flotsam washed high by the storm, our battles and beliefs useless. So, what with all the other cowboys and their gun battles, Lyuba's husband upped and offed to London, taking Lyuba and their daughter with him. Too many flying bullets for comfort.

"Lyuba has promised I'll have my own apartment next to hers with a maid just for me." Natalya tried to talk herself through her fears with the idea of a little luxury but didn't quite succeed. We didn't mention Lyuba's drink problem, her trips to the special clinic and her husband's temper. Problems. *Problemi. Provlímata.* They're all the same whatever the language. What can you do? It is what it is. Poor Natalya looked down and examined her hands – pudgy but always well cared-for. She still applies *Pearly Cloud* polish on her nails – the same colour for decades – convinced that a good manicure makes all the difference to a woman's appearance.

"I've never even been abroad."

I didn't answer this time and Natalya managed a small laugh.

"Lyuba said that so many Russians have moved to London they call it 'Moscow-on-Thames'."

I first met Natalya in April 1952 when I arrived in Moscow. So we've been discussing her problems for over half a century. She was the technical manager at the international radio station where I worked. On the morning of my first broadcast on *Moscow Here!* she saw how nervous I was and came up to me smiling.

"Beware of Greeks bearing gifts," she said, "but always accept one from a Russian." She offered a small glass of vodka and though I've never been a drinker, I downed it and accepted the lump of black bread – "so you don't get drunk". Then I read the news bulletin in Greek and tried not to think of who might be listening in Greece or, worse, of who could not listen because they were locked up or dead.

"You are a beacon, sending out light across the monarcho-fascist darkness," said the producer. So I thought of myself as a lighthouse, working on automatic, like a machine, and after that I was never nervous again. Onwards, upwards, tractors to plough for a better world, rockets to penetrate outer space, plans, strength, work. We were filled with optimism. I had two colleagues at the broadcasting centre whose parents had named them in honour of Soviet ambition and glory: Elektrifikatsia (Electrification) and Pyatiletka (Five-year-plan). Nobody thought that was ridiculous.

Natalya and I became friends. She took me out to walk in the birch woods at weekends and taught me about picking mushrooms ("never tell anyone where you find them" was rule number one). In good weather we'd take picnics and when we'd eaten, we'd lie about smoking Aurora cigarettes, which she liked for the picture of the laughing sailor on the box. Our conversations were often about her unsuitable boyfriends and whether she should sleep with them. We looked like two carefree young women with our lives ahead of us. I didn't speak about the past. I didn't tell Natalya anything more than the bare facts of our struggle in Greece, of defeat and our escape into the huge embrace of Uncle Jo and the Soviet Motherland. Stepmother-land? Why dig into the depths? You can't change what happened. It is what it is.

Although I had already been living in the Soviet Union for a while, Natalya was the first Russian I got to know well. The Greeks in Tashkent stayed close together. It was a reaction to what we had lost; when you lose your fight and your country you are afraid you will lose yourself and your past. We were exhausted from years of war and imprisonment and we were humiliated. But we clung to what we thought made us Greek. We might have been dropped down in the middle of Uzbekistan, but we made Greek newspapers, sang

Greek songs, cooked Greek food and soon we even had Greek weddings. The Russians liked watching us dance and recognised some of the Orthodox rituals they no longer used. But I didn't want to cling to the place I had left and to which I had promised I would never return. Not for me the dreams of going back. I was young and stubborn enough to want to forget the past and to keep looking ahead towards the promises of a better world. So it was a relief when the authorities chose me to go to Moscow to work at the radio station.

I had already been in Uzbekistan for nearly two years when they came to the factory. Many of us Greeks were employed there, manufacturing the machinery for hydroelectric energy – my early Russian lessons were dominated by technical terms that acquired a sort of poetry. "Turbine generator shaft, pumped storage, laminated steel stacks..." The unit manager said, "Please come with me, Antigona Petrovna," and I was taken into a room where a man and a woman from Moscow asked me to read a document aloud in Greek. They concluded that my voice was suitable and a week later I was on the train to Moscow. Although I said goodbye to people who had suffered in ways similar or worse to me, I was relieved. It was like winning the lottery – leaving the wind-lashed steppes and the sub-standard housing given to political immigrants who thought they'd find their dream made flesh in the Soviet Union. I could finally shut the door behind me and start afresh.

My friendship with Natalya helped me understand my adopted country. Although Russians have many things in common with Greeks, there is a dark, still well at their centre. We Greeks are all movement. When we have a problem we go away, we climb over the mountain, take a boat to foreign lands, search out the new. A Russian stays put, believing the problem will climb up the mountain with him if he tries to leave. He is convinced he is the butt of a huge joke in very poor taste. The whole world is against you anyway, so why bother? Greeks always suppose there's a way out. Like Odysseus, we are convinced we will outwit the Cyclops or sail past the deadly temptations of the Sirens. Of course we Greeks are also inseparable from our particular brand of nostalgia and grief at being far from home. We leave, but all the time we dream of returning, even if it is only to be buried in the same ground that ate our forebears' flesh. I was always determined that I would do no such thing.

It was through Natalya's circle that I met Igor. He was milky pale with blonde hair and a lanky, boy's body. "North and South" they used to call us, because I had the colouring of the Mediterranean, with almost black hair and a complexion that went brown the minute I went out in the sun. When I met Igor, he had recently started teaching at the secondary school where he would spend his entire working life. He taught literature and carried around a large shopping bag filled with dog-eared copies of Pushkin and Chekhov, and folders overflowing with students' essays. He was gentle and respected my silence about the past. In the early days, he still lived with his parents, so he would come to visit me in the apartment I shared with two girls from the radio station. We lay in my narrow bed under the wadded quilt, making love quietly so as not to disturb the others, listening to records, reading books, getting up to make an omelette, sleeping in a gentle embrace. We were companions from the start. Comrades. And that is as good a basis for a shared life as any.

After Natalya married Arkady, the four of us used to take holidays, often staying in the radio station's sanatorium near Sochi. The smell of the Black Sea reminded me of home, of day trips with my parents to Faliro. Salty rocks, hot, resinous pine trees, skin warming in the sun. Arkady was a joker, and he could make us laugh so much that we would cry. Then I would get sad because I hadn't laughed like that for so long, not since before the war. It made me think of Markos and how we would hide from our parents when we were small, letting them shout threats into the street, until we had to smother one another to prevent them hearing our giggles. By then, Arkady would be onto the next story, or would be squeezing Natalya until she screamed, and I would get up and walk away so they couldn't see my face.

"Ah, the tragic Greek heroine with the mysterious past," Arkady would say, in mock-theatrical tones.

When Lyuba was born, Igor wanted a baby too, but I didn't get pregnant. I didn't tell him about Nikitas. How could I? Where would I have started? What kind of woman leaves her child? Every time I saw Lyuba, the pain was so extreme I could hardly bear it. The creases on her chubby legs, the soft belly rising and falling like a puppy as she slept, the grunts and slurps while she fed – they opened up the wounds I hoped had closed. Natalya thought I was jealous and that all would be righted when I had my own "little darling", while Arkady gave humorous tips to Igor about what he should do to get me on my back and "knocked up."

Of course, Igor knew about my "women's troubles". I had

suffered since my time in the mountains. All the women did. Eventually, Igor insisted that we visit a doctor and when my excuses ran out, we went to Natalya's gynaecologist. She filled in the form about my medical history and one of the questions was "number of pregnancies". I replied "none", but after Olga Konstantinovna examined me, she was frank.

"If you are going to lie to me, Antigona Petrovna, I cannot help you."

Igor looked at me. They both waited for an answer. I focused on her white coat, the badge with her name, her hair in a tall bun.

"I did have a baby, but he died." After that I had to tell so many lies that I lost track of them and even Igor's patience dried up.

"I can't change the past, but we can leave it undisturbed," I told him. "It is what it is." Igor loved me, but after that he was more reserved.

Olga Konstantinovna gave me some medicines and sent me for a two-week rest-cure in Yalta. But I never did get pregnant. Igor became very attached to Lyuba and she called him "Uncle", asking him to read her stories over and over, as young children do. Sometimes he would take her out for an icecream or to a museum, and she would hold his hand. Lyuba came back from London for Igor's funeral and cried as much as she had at her own father's. As for me, I always kept my distance from Lyuba. Once she was over three, it didn't matter any more as there were no recollections of Nikitas to compare. Gradually, her podgy, dimpled limbs elongated and slimmed into those of a schoolgirl, and there was nothing to provoke the physical memories of holding Nikitas, of washing him or tempting him to eat. Naturally, I tried to imagine how he would be growing, what he would be doing.

When the pains came before Nikitas' birth, I was taken to the hospital in a closed lorry that stank of human waste. I knew why – intense fear provokes physical reactions. I added to the mess when my waters broke. The body has its own mysterious rhythms and it took a long time for Nikitas to be born. I entered a world of my own, pulled deep into spirals of pain as if I were diving into the sea until my lungs were bursting. Each time I emerged, I gathered my strength, preparing for the next descent, far away from what was going on around me. When I saw the baby, bluish, with one eye open and looking at me, he seemed like an ancient creature, more fish than human. An independent life for which I was the vessel. Nothing to do with what had gone before.

3
Privacy and solitude are not Greek words

MAUD

Orestes and I returned home from the hospital via the police station, where I signed various papers in triplicate and saw the statement from the swimmer who had spotted the wreck. During the brief time that elapsed after I called Aunt Alexandra to tell her the news, she had taken charge; she knew what had to be done. When Orestes and I came through the front door and into the communal hall, she opened the door to her apartment, already dressed entirely in black. She stretched her arms in a gesture of resigned sadness and embrace, pulling me to her, and including Orestes, who submitted, still pallid and queasy-looking. Chryssa came hurrying up behind, emitting a raw sound of misery. Her face was wet and her eyes red.

"Life to you, children. May God give him rest. May God forgive him."

I hugged Chryssa, bending down to hold onto her small

frame, feeling her tears on my face that was still dry from shock.

Tig was very brave. At 1.30, I walked up the hill for the second time that day and waited for her a little way from the school gates. By the time she spotted me, she and her friend, Eurydice, were already lighting up. Tig threw her cigarette in the gutter and stalked over, looking both angry and contrite.

"What are you doing here?" It was hard to answer. I had already taken a sedative from a packet Nikitas kept in the bathroom, and though it had passed its expiry date, it was effective in blurring the edges, rather as the pink Saharan sand was still dulling the city skylines.

I had previously imagined that if your husband died you ran into a storm of grief that would obliterate anything else. But it was not as simple as that. There were all the practical things to be done, and some of the time I was so emptied of emotion, I barely knew who I was – a cog in the machinery that surrounds a death. Then, unpredictably, the void would be filled with terror. I became like a cartoon character who runs over the edge of the cliff and suddenly realises there is nothing below them. Tumbling into the depths, I found myself letting out a groan, as though I was actually falling. Death seemed so close.

Throughout the afternoon, friends and relations rang up, wanting information; questions, disbelief, more questions. I telephoned my parents, who were shaken and sympathetic, but the distance that had characterised our dealings since childhood remained. I asked them not come to Greece and they didn't insist. They had never been close enough to understand my life and I wasn't interested in trying any more. Now was not the time to instigate change.

As the light drained away from the heavy clouds at the end of the day, I lay on my bed feeling paralysed, unable to move, as though a great weight was pressing down on me. It was then that I wondered whether I could just leave. Take Tig, go away, and it might be as though nothing had happened. I could erase Greece, make it an episode that was over, and return to a parallel ghost life – the one I would have had if I had not left England. That way, the disaster could be left behind. But even as I fantasised, I knew it was impossible. After all these years, Athens was home. It no longer mattered that I would always be a *xéni* – the word that used to haunt me when I heard it said of me in offices or shops. It always seemed an explanation of what I was not, what I lacked: a stranger, a foreigner and, above all, not Greek. I had struggled for a long time, trying to fit in, to do the right thing, to adapt, though eventually I preferred to embrace the freedom of existing on the margins. Still, in spite of everything, I loved Greece and I knew that going back to England could not be a solution. I had become an awkward hybrid who belonged nowhere – what an Italian friend called *ne carne, ne pesce* – neither fish nor fowl.

My decision to come to Greece twenty years ago was some-what chancy. I was embarking on a PhD in social anthropology and most of my contemporaries at Cambridge were planning to paddle up the Amazon to find lost swathes of rain forest or build their own mud hut in a forgotten African province. When I chose to examine "changing rites of passage on a Greek island", it looked tame in comparison. My fellow students enjoyed teasing me about what was evidently my intention to live the good life in the Mediterranean – beaches and buckets of bright pink taramasalata. There'd be moustachioed men dancing, the twang of bouzoukis playing *The Boys from Piraeus*, and a Kodachrome backdrop of the sun-drenched Acropolis.

I knew my decision irritated my grandfather. Desmond had been a classicist, teaching for many years at King's College, London and was a life-long scholar of ancient Greece. His obsession was Parmenides – Socrates' teacher and the so-called "father of Greek philosophy" – and he used to quote obscure phrases that meant little to me as a child. His favourite concerned the "wise mares" who were "straining at the chariot." He thought this was a good explanation of life; as charioteers, we need to give our horses enough freedom to run, but also to control them so they kept on track. "And maidens were leading the way," he would add, gnomically. When I became what he called "emotional," he would say: "Tighten the reins on the horses, Maud. Don't let them take control." If my grandmother, Lucy, heard, she'd add: "Let the bloody horses have a good time, that's what I say. Let them run wild."

My parents were not much in evidence. Having met at the Royal College of Music, they were just getting their first concerts with an ensemble that played early music on original instruments, when I was born. To add to my youthful resentment, they gave me a name I hated for its sturdy, old-fashioned quality. Nobody else of my age was called Maud, and it was no comfort that it cropped up through the generations on my mother's side. Her paternal grandmother was a Maud and her death soon before my birth (plus an inheritance of £5,000) had made the choice almost a moral obligation. My grandfather never tired of quoting Tennyson's poem *Maud* and *"Come into the garden, Maud"* was something I was sick of by the time I was five. Maud Thomas. It sounded solid and English, though my surname should have been Tomaszewski; my father's grandparents had tried to shed their Polish past as quickly as possible when they arrived in London before the First World War. Although I had often thought of getting rid of Maud in much the same way, I never quite managed. Later, as it was almost impossible for Greeks to pronounce, it was Hellenised. I was called Mad, Maood, Mood, Moody, but more often Mod or Mond – Μοντ – which in written Greek ends with "nt" because there is no single letter for the sound of "d". In practice, even Mond was frequently feminised to Mondy. At least it wasn't Maud.

My parents tried taking me on tour with them when I was very young, but in addition to their *viola da gamba* cases, I suppose I became one thing too many to carry onto aeroplanes and trains. It made more sense to leave me with my grandparents. So, although I spent some holidays with my mother and father, it was Desmond and Lucy who dealt with me on a daily basis, knew the names of my school teachers and what breakfast cereal I preferred. The remoteness remained, as I never became close to my parents. If they left me behind as a child, I left them behind as an adult. Tig has only seen them a handful of times.

As a teenager, my friends envied me my freedom. When I was sixteen, I was given the small, musty basement flat below my grandparents' house in Bayswater and largely came and went as I pleased. Desmond was too busy working to notice and Lucy was long past worrying about what I got up to in my "den". Desmond had visited Greece in his younger days and was clear that the virtues of the country's distant past were no longer to be found there. He felt the ancient philosophers, sculptors and politicians belonged to him and the British tradition, and he was dismissive of contemporary Greeks.

"They've spoiled the place. And you can't even say they're real Greeks. They have nothing to do with the ancients, though they'd like you to think that they are all Pericles' grandchildren. In actual fact they're Turks, Slavs, Albanians… a Balkan blend of former Ottoman subjects. And, of course, they never had the advantage of a Renaissance or an Enlightenment." He hoped I would study classics and dismissed my choice of social anthropology as "woolly as knitting". After I got a place to study it at Cambridge, he said: "A pity." Later, when I chose Greece as the country for my fieldwork, I knew it would annoy him. He quoted Byron to annoy me:

"Fair Greece! Sad relic of departed worth!" Later, it became a catchphrase that Nikitas and I used when we were annoyed or depressed by Greece: "Sad relic," we'd say, when a politician was accused of corruption or when a wooded slope outside Athens was burnt by arsonists and turned into prime real estate.

Tig came into my bedroom and we lay together, dry-eyed and stunned. We were soon joined by Orestes, who banged open the door, kicked off his tattered trainers, and lay down on the bed next to Tig. He was angry, still trembling slightly, processing the tragedy with masculine heat and noise, as his father probably would have done

"All he's done for me, all my life, is to leave me. Ever since I was two. It always has to be about him. And now he's really succeeded…" His voice broke awkwardly, almost like an adolescent's. "I think he did it on purpose."

"No. The police think it was an accident." I wanted to sound convincing for Tig, though my voice gave me away and

37

the flicker of her eyes in my direction showed me I was failing. "They'll give us the autopsy report tomorrow. It was just bad luck."

"Luck, like ants being trodden on? Or destiny?" Tig looked angry too, as if I should come up with an answer. I turned away, curling my body up as tight as I could, hoping I could hold myself together better like that.

Within minutes, Orestes jumped up, stretching his arms and putting his shoes on with jittery movements; he rarely remains in one place if he can move to another.

"Do you want to come up to my room?" He held out a hand to Tig. "Come on, doll." Orestes had moved in to the studio flat on our terrace at the age of sixteen, after yet another quarrel with his mother and step-father, and had never left. Appropriately, this sort of apartment is known in Greek as a *garsoniéra* – a bachelor pad – and that is what he made it. He painted it purple, though the colour had since been virtually obliterated by posters of savage-faced heroes and provocative graffiti. The curtains were only rarely opened, the windows mostly shut, and the room stank of stale marijuana smoke, half-eaten pizzas and the faint echoes of feminine perfumes.

From a young age, Tig became a mascot to Orestes and his school friends, charming them with her quirky, precocious questions. Later, Orestes' girlfriends sensed they must make Tig their ally if they were to hold on to their privileged position, though irrespective of their success in this, they never lasted long. Orestes was usually surrounded by girls, but the relationships invariably petered out as something more interesting appeared on the horizon. He stayed on good terms though, and there were countless pretty girls whom I had seen progress from bewildered tears at my kitchen table ("I don't understand what happened, *Kyria* Moody," they would sob) to becoming part of his loyal coterie.

That night, Tig slept with me, curling up on her father's side of the bed.

"The pillow smells of *Babas*," she said. "It's like he's still here." She cried at first but then fell asleep almost immediately from exhaustion. I lay next to her, breathing in warm hair that smelled of a fruity shampoo, like apples stored in hay. And beyond that, Nikitas. It was like an impossible riddle: how could he be dead, his body already turning into something else – a piece of meat in a metal drawer – when his cells were here, emitting his familiar, living scent? His physical self entered my nostrils – a vaporous spirit that would now fade away atom by atom. I wondered how I would bear this dreadful process.

❋ ❋ ❋

The following morning, Alexandra took me to Mr Katsaridis, the funeral director, in the next street. We walked slowly and she was curious to know whether I had called Nikitas' mother.

"Be careful," she warned, when she heard we had spoken. "My sister is one of those dangerous people who believe they are saving the world when they are really destroying it. If you speak with her again, don't take what she says too literally. I always say, beware of grand schemes and people who don't mind breaking eggs to make omelettes. Don't forget she found her home with Stalin." Alexandra already had one arm through mine, and she patted my sleeve with her other hand, as though she was closing the matter. "You are a strong woman, Mondy.

And you must stay strong for your daughter. Leave my sister alone, where she has chosen to make her life."

I had often passed Katsaridis' "Rituals' Office" but had never really noticed it. Living so close to Athens' most prominent cemetery, I had become accustomed to walking among death's trades: the ranks of florists, marble-carvers and confectioners of mourning sweets, with their mocked-up memorial cakes decorated with names. "Out of here!" people would often exclaim if the subject of death or cemeteries cropped up, but not in our neighbourhood. Greeks don't like cypresses in their gardens, for their association with graves, though their tall, almost human silhouettes grace the landscape. In our neighbourhood, however, it was normal to live below cypress trees, just as it was routine to see a black-clad woman wiping her cheek as she walked down the hill, couples going to tend a grave, or small groups of people waiting for memorials by the flower stalls. Quite often there were smiles as well as tears; it was a truism that funerals provoked both. I had previously held the mistaken belief that all this practicality removed some of death's mystique, as though you could outwit it merely by observing it long enough.

Kyrios Katsaridis was younger and kinder than I had expected, and supported me when I rejected Alexandra's suggestion of bringing Nikitas home for the night. I didn't want a wake. I couldn't bear the prospect of sitting up all night in a crowded room looking at Nikitas' dead body.

"These days most Athenians choose not to bring the deceased home," said *Kyrios* Katsaridis. His face was smooth, almost boyish, but he spoke with a deep and soothing voice. I wondered about this young man, what he drank at bars with his friends, how he had learned his trade. At his father's side, no doubt, in the Greek tradition. It's hardly a job you'd dream of training for.

There was no question that it would be an Orthodox funeral. Nikitas did not believe in God, he campaigned for the separation of Church and state in Greece and he wrote articles about how monks on Mount Athos lived the high life, wiring up expensive televisions in their cells and carrying out business deals on their mobile phones. The very sight of a priest's black robes on the street was taken as bad luck:

"Quick, touch your balls!" he'd whisper conspiratorially to Orestes. He despised the way that Aunt Alexandra, like most of the faithful, greeted a priest by kissing his hand, and his most heart-felt curses all included the figures of Christ and the Virgin. Yet like the vast majority of his compatriots, Nikitas didn't think twice about marking his way through life with a priest as master of ceremonies. The only reason he and I did not marry in a church – as he had with his first two weddings – was that I was not Orthodox. Tig, like Orestes before her, had been baptised when she was nine months old – slathered in oil, plunged under water, hair snipped, adorned with a cross. And she was given a name; you don't even have one until your godparent announces it to the priest.

We chose a coffin that looked like a glossed-up mahogany wardrobe with fancy handles. There weren't any hand-woven wicker baskets or biodegradable cocoons as found these days in England, and I didn't care.

"We found an excellent position in the cemetery. High up, in the part we call the artists' area. All sorts are there – singers, writers, actors. Nikos Xilouris, Viki Moscholiou…" *Kyrios*

Katsaridis looked pleased and I tried to be encouraging to the young man, nodding and smiling ridiculously. Later, I learned that it was Aunt Alexandra's widespread contacts and *savoir faire* that had procured the grave. Few but the most famous and influential are guaranteed a place in the First Cemetery these days and there had been at least one unofficial payment in addition to the hefty monthly rent we would pay for the plot. Freehold prices were mostly out of the question – pushing 100,000 euros.

As the day ground on, our sitting room filled with friends, acquaintances, colleagues from the newspaper, people I didn't even know, but who cared about Nikitas. Morena, Alexandra's Albanian maid, came in to help, taking time off from one of the other houses she cleaned, and brought her soothing presence to what became increasingly like what happened each September 15, on Saint Nikitas' day. No longer the nervous immigrant I had first met before I married Nikitas, she had become a solid family matriarch, with two sons who spoke Greek like natives.

The phone barely stopped ringing, the door was left open so people could walk in with sweets, flowers and presents and the whole thing usually went on late into the evening. Nikitas would cook and whip up the levels of *kéfi* ("there's no translation – you either feel the mood or keep quiet") with wine, stories, music and food until everyone was ready to dance or roar with laughter at his indiscreet tales about the politicians of the moment or his latest adventure abroad.

Nikitas was notoriously contradictory and could be awkward, but he had many friends who adored him, and even more people who were entertained by or interested in him. There were others who felt his influence in the media; the number of politicians of various persuasions who tried to keep close to him was remarkable. He had spent a lifetime with these people – talking, working, fighting and drinking. He used to tell me that he didn't care about these superficial relationships, but I saw they made him feel alive.

"Athens is a village," he said. "Wherever you go you find people you know." And it was true. It was impossible to walk down the street, let alone go out for dinner, without meeting someone from his vast social network. And in restaurants, Nikitas always had one eye on who was coming and going: a disgraced minister, a minor celebrity, an attractive woman passing – they all meant something to him and his solid yet mercurial presence seemed to act like a magnet. He enjoyed it when someone sent the waiter over with a bottle of wine as an offering, and he'd jump up to drink the health of the admirer who had arranged it, and then do the same too, shoring up fragile social ties with these drinking rituals. Now that Nikitas had gone, I should not have been surprised that so many people wanted to be there. A heavy middle-aged woman with thinning hair and brown clothes came up and embraced me. She told me she worked at the paper and rubbed her red eyes.

"How can he have gone?" she asked, as though I might provide the answer.

Several of Nikitas' distant cousins from the village arrived bearing food, and though I hardly knew them, they made themselves at home, making coffee for visitors, emptying ashtrays and answering the phone.

"The widow must not do anything," they insisted and the women made me sit, cosseting me as though I was physically incapable. Men wandered in and out of the apartment, smoking furiously and talking in low voices. Even in shock, I was impressed by the Greek tendency to gather together at difficult times. A private pain like illness or bereavement is public business. When someone dies, people come together, facing Charos, the personification of death, *en masse*, as if telling him he may have taken one, but we are all still here together. Solitude is only comprehensible as loneliness and isolation is unquestionably an evil. I used to complain to Nikitas in the old days that no one understood I might want to be alone.

"It's not chance that there's not even a word for privacy in Greek," I grumbled.

"There is a word but it has the same root as 'idiot'," he laughed. "In ancient Greece a private individual was an idiot because he didn't play a role in public life. In modern Greece you're an idiot if you want to be alone. Take us or leave us."

The news of Nikitas' death spread rapidly and people were ringing and coming over to the house in increasing numbers. Nikitas' first wife, Kiki, arrived looking grey-faced. I knew her only from the few occasions I had reluctantly attended exhibitions of her sculptures – mostly pale, elongated female forms inspired by Cycladic figures, though hers were often slashed with black markings that represented abuse or suffering. She held my hands for longer than I was comfortable with, her skin rough from handling clay and a collection of silver bangles jangling as she moved. Kiki and Nikitas had been married briefly in the early '70s when they were both "revolting students" (Nikitas' joke). Their enthusiasm for each other petered out after the end of the Junta that had provided the focus of so much passion and protest and a structure for their life together. But they had both remained friendly and met occasionally for coffee or lunch.

"She's so old," Nikitas had said last time he saw her, as though he was not also in his sixty-second year. Her wrinkles were a reminder of his own ageing and annoyed him; he preferred youth and beauty, treating them as though they rubbed off on him.

I had scarcely disentangled myself from Kiki, when Yiorgia, Nikitas' second wife and Orestes' mother, arrived. Yiorgia used to provoke in me an uncomfortable jealousy, and though in recent years it had diminished, I still saw her as everything I was not. A partner in a law firm, she had a magnetic beauty with classical features, silky hair and breasts, which Nikitas once, unwisely, told me were her finest feature. She was studying law when she got pregnant, and their marriage had smouldered fitfully for a decade, until she asked for a divorce and got remarried (to "another arsehole lawyer", as Nikitas said).

Yiorgia was crying when she came in. She hugged me extravagantly, her tears wetting my face and her musky-smelling hair smothering my nose. Her bosom pressed against me. Orestes came down from the studio, looking dazed and exuding a waft of marijuana.

"*Mama?*" He looked puzzled by our clinch and the unusual proximity of his father's three wives.

"My baby!" Yiorgia rushed to embrace her son, whose striking good looks matched hers. It was like a scene from a bad opera and I knew what Nikitas would have said, tongue in cheek: "Pray to Zeus – the god of family love." I left them, my extended Greek family, and went to my bedroom. For the first time, I became aware of an unfamiliar bitter taste in my mouth that stayed with me for weeks. However much I tried to get rid of it by drinking or cleaning my teeth, it always returned. Eventually I realised that what I had always thought to be a metaphor – bitterness in emotions – could be a physical reality; emotion translated into matter. Other clichés were made flesh too; my heart really ached. I felt it heavy and bloody in my chest, as if it were pumping the misery through me.

About an hour later, Orestes hurried in without knocking; he still clung to the privileges of a child.

"Are you OK?" He looked at me dubiously. "Can you come through? My godfather just rang. They are running some-thing about *Babas* on the news. Mega Channel. It's coming on now." I followed him back into the sitting room where the "party" showed no sign of ending. There were about twenty people crowded around to get a view of the television. Kiki and Yiorgia had arranged themselves in the best position on the sofa and I wondered whether they were also now widows of some sort. Aunt Alexandra hissed at everyone to be quiet from an armchair and Orestes and Tig sat on the floor. I stood, holding onto the door frame, the place you should go if there is no other protection in the case of an earthquake.

The eccentric broadcast that passes as "news" in Greece was well underway and the usual half-a-dozen journalist-inquisitor-commentators were shouting raucously from their own "little window" on the screen. There was too much noise to make out which particular Greek politician they were gossiping about, but one man was waving his arms, red in the face with anger, while several others laughed dismissively.

"Coffeehouse politics," was what Nikitas called it, though he was not averse to appearing himself from time to time. I sympathised more with the anonymous graffiti writer, who had sprayed a wall near our house with "Freedom to imprisoned TV viewers".

The news reader eventually made an announcement about the death of "our colleague, Nikitas Perifanis". Alexandra strained to listen, fiddling with her hearing aid, which hissed miserably. A young female reporter gave a brief résumé of Nikitas' life, describing him as "a child of the Left", who had battled against the Junta, showing him as a young man in the '70s with long hair and white bellbottoms and later, more grizzled and heavier, accepting a prize for his series, *Britain and Greece*. Then there was a brief interview with his old friend, and Orestes' godfather, Nikos Manousis, the poet. I could picture Nikitas shouting "Get the wanker out of here," as Nikos managed to emanate eloquent sadness while flirting with the female reporter, whose make-up could have graced the stage of a second-rate bouzouki club. Nikos was regularly approached to make statements on television as he had the right amount of vanity and gravitas and, like Nikitas, the pedigree of having been inside the Polytechnic in 1973, when the Junta's tanks rolled in. Both men had been studying law at the nearby School of Law, but joined the protests that turned a generation of Athenian students into heroes, martyrs and champions of the Left. Nikos' wavy white mane and dandyish linen suits embellished with silk handkerchiefs had become a trademark, while his honeyed bass voice produced reliably elegant sentences: "a man of integrity... child of the Civil War who fought for freedom and justice... award-winning journalist who was constantly searching..." The reporter looked flushed with pleasure as she thanked the poet for his contribution and announced that the funeral would take place tomorrow at 11 am at the First Cemetery.

There was a moment of silence in the room. The television had enchanted us with its reverse alchemy that transforms something rare or precious into something common or base; anyone can become an item slotted into the parallel world. I was glad when Orestes broke the spell.

"*Maláka!* Wanker! He's such a hypocrite. They're all wankers. They talk about their own heroism, how they fought against the Junta, how they saved Greece from tyranny. All we hear about is the 'Polytechnic generation', but they became the establishment. They're the ones ruling the country now – the politicians, the journalists, the professors. And look what they've done." Nobody answered for a while, as though the air had been sucked out of the room. A number of people present resembled exactly the type Orestes had attacked; men who had risen to powerful positions on the reputation of being freedom fighters. They were supposedly the latest example of a noble tradition of Greeks fighting Ottoman overlords for independence or Nazi occupiers during Second World War; all part of the same impulse, merging into one another, their portraits intermingling in the public consciousness, so that flag-waving school children were unable to remember whether the heroes of the Polytechnic were fighting the Turks or whether there were tanks in 1821.

Kiki answered first – as an artist, nobody could say that she had made a grab for power. Orestes was too young, she said, to appreciate what had been done so he could enjoy his freedom. But Orestes had answered that question during frequent arguments with his father.

"What freedom?" he replied, his cheeks reddening. "What

do you think my generation has got? Freedom to be unemployed after twenty years of learning set texts? Freedom to get a job earning 700 euros a month? You can keep your freedom – there's nothing I can do with it."

I hurried from the room, furious at them all for discussing politics when Nikitas was not yet even buried.

4
Penelope's cloth

ANTIGONE

The rains were terrible in October and Natalya and I didn't meet for several days due to the bad weather. When I finally managed to walk the hundred metres or so to her block and she opened the door to her apartment, I could tell immediately that she had something to say. The tang of cat hit me even before I entered and Misha sidled up and rubbed his long grey hairs onto my stockings. I make a point of appearing pleasant to him, though I never liked him and he knows it. If dogs can smell fear, then cats smell antipathy and Misha never fails to twist himself around my legs, growling under his breath.

Natalya said, "Look how he loves you." She has always been taken in by our performance. When her back was turned, the animal enjoyed sinking his claws into my ankle and running for cover before I could kick him.

Natalya blurted it out. "I'm going to London. Lyuba needs me. I've said I'll go for a while to see if it works out. Don't worry, I'll come back to visit, and maybe you can make a trip. I'll have my own maid to make us tea!" She tried to smile and looked away, ashamed. I had no difficulty in acting pleased for her. Burying my emotions is an old habit. I pretended to believe she'd be back, and agreed she was doing the right thing. But as I asked her practical questions about her travel plans, my thoughts were really on the prospect of dying alone in my apartment. I was losing the last person I had.

"Oh, and I have a favour to ask." Natalya's expression was uncomfortably apologetic. "Can you look after my darling Mishinka for me? My son-in-law is allergic to cats, so I can't take him. He'll be company for you."

After Natalya left, I was bereft. I tried to keep doing the things I did with my old friend, but even the steam sessions at the baths seemed pointless without her chatter and the fried titbits she brought. I now sit for hours in my chair, eyes blurring like the grey fog outside. Each day I retreat further within. Misha evidently shares my sense of abandonment and sits staring, flicking his ridiculous plumed tail with annoyance. In many ways, Natalya's departure is harder to bear than when Igor died. After his first stroke there was time to get used to him as half a presence. I cared for him as one would a baby, cleaning and feeding him, massaging his hands like the physiotherapist instructed. Sometimes I read to him from the books he loved, dog-eared and broken, their pages coming loose. I lost Igor bit by bit, and by the time we buried him, I had grown accustomed to the idea. Naturally I wept for a good man whose morning breath had mingled with mine for half a century, but life carried on. It is what it is. But it is different without Natalya.

I am haunted by all the people I have lost. When my mother died twenty years ago, I didn't even think of going back to Greece for her funeral. I had made a promise to myself. I remembered my father coughing out his last words, reduced to half his original size by Nazi humiliations. Then two years later, my brother, still only a boy despite his uniform and gun. Later there were so many others who died that their names pile up like heaps of rocks. Some went suddenly with a stray bullet and others went singing and dancing to their execution in the name of justice and freedom. We believed it was worth it with every cell in our body. I often wonder why I was saved from Charos' teeth. He had so many opportunities. I, too, could have found my "bridegroom" in the earth, and had a heavy "mother-in-law" of a tombstone weighing down on my chest.

There were other losses. When Stalin died, I had to read the report on the radio. It was 1953 – less than a year after I started the job – and we were all terrified. Stalin had been everything. At one point in the broadcast, my voice wavered and I had to stop to compose myself. I was worried that I might lose my job, but then I heard the sobs of other journalists on air and saw the mass mourning that took place. I realised it was only appropriate that we should weep. Nobody ever remarked on my lack of control. A few years later, when Khrushchev told us what Stalin had really done, it was even worse. I felt a huge bitterness, realising I hadn't even known that friends' and colleagues' parents or siblings were in the Gulag. Losing one's faith is the hardest thing of all, but it was too late to regret what I had done. I still know that what I believed in was right. How could it be wrong to fight for a world without war and hunger and exploitation?

What remained was comradeship and knowledge. I kept on with the broadcasts and paid lip service to the rules. Igor had the Russian's inherent pessimism and scepticism, so perhaps it was easier for him to bear another dose of disillusionment. I thought if I kept giving out the message on air every day it might help make it truer, though I knew I was sometimes helping the authorities weave a blanket of lies. At home, with Igor or with Natalya and Arkady, I would often unpick what I'd said, like Penelope dismantling her woven cloth at night.

Now I think the old flawed system was better than what came later. I try not to go out and witness the parody of America that the Muscovites are establishing in their city, with boutiques for millionaires and restaurants where most of us couldn't afford the bread. At this rate they'll soon be bringing back the Tsars and turning the rest of us into serfs. In my opinion, we'll all go back to Marx at some point and see what sense he wrote. As he said, we must doubt and question everything.

* * *

The first snows fell. The caretaker came to tape up the windows and told me they had forecast a bitter winter this year. I leave home only to take the bus for my twice-weekly shopping trips. I feed Misha the imported Finnish cat food that Natalya specified, but he has given up trying to provoke and ignores my presence. My only worry is what would happen if I died. My heart is no longer strong and though I take the tablets, I feel it flipping and pulsating like a trapped animal. I try not to imagine Misha eating me. I still read and I keep my notebook going, but mostly I just sit and stare out of the window at the rows of neighbouring apartments growing whiter. It is hard when nobody needs you.

My thoughts run through all the people who were important to me, but I am most preoccupied with my son. Every September I mark his name day in some way. Sometimes I baked a cake without explaining why. Igor would be pleased at this unusual burst of domesticity. I have some mementoes in a small suitcase – a lock of hair, a scribble Nikitas made when he learned to hold a pencil, a pair of babies' booties knitted by *Kyria* Frosso, the oldest prisoner. I take them out and sniff them, trying to recapture the scent I thought I could never forget, but it had been replaced by the neutral whiff of leather. I was always convinced I did the right thing in giving up Nikitas. The hardest sacrifice, but the right one. I decided from the beginning that I should have no contact with him – a clean cut is best. It would have been unfair to him to have held out some promise of maternal love when that was impossible. Better that he should have his own life, free from me. But after Natalya went, the decades of justification retreated. I am left with a bitter realisation that I abandoned the one person who needed me. And to what purpose? In support of ideals that I'm not sure I understand any more and that nobody else holds?

Alone in the apartment with Misha, I have begun to fantasise about going to my son. If Lyuba needed Natalya, perhaps Nikitas needed me too. You are still a mother, even if you don't see your child. At least that is what I always thought.

I have followed his progress from afar. Dora occasionally sends me news of Nikitas – she was the only person from my old life who kept in touch. She managed to maintain some contact with him, even when he was young and it had to be secret. She promised me that. Skinny as a scrawny fledgling, Dora had the strength of a buffalo. We met in the mountains, where she taught me how to share blankets when we slept out in the freezing cold.

"It's more important to have one underneath than on top," she explained, as we lay back-to-back to conserve body heat. She had married young and had borne two children by the time she was twenty. After her husband was killed by the Germans, she went to fight in his place, leaving her babies with her mother in Athens. She never made a fuss. When Nikitas began working as a journalist, Dora collected some of his articles and sent me the cuttings. Her letters described my son's progress, but she was never a great writer and I wanted to know much more. She didn't mention Alexandra; she knew I wouldn't want to hear about my sister. Or "Him", the monstrosity. Dora did tell me when "He" died, and though I used to imagine I would be pleased, too much time had gone by for that.

Occasionally there would be a photograph of Nikitas – dark haired and with the good looks of my father as a young man. I heard about his marriages – he is evidently a restless soul. He is on his third now. And he has two children, so I am a grandmother, though I wonder if they even know I exist. If not, I only have myself to blame. Sometimes, my mind rolls idly over an image I have of the children – one is already in his twenties – and I imagine sitting with them, telling stories about their father as a baby, about their great-grandfather and the house he built in Paradise Street.

* * *

It was nearly ten o'clock when the phone rang and I had long since fallen asleep in my armchair. I almost forgot I had a telephone, it went so rarely, and I jumped with fright at the unfamiliar sound. Perhaps it's Natalya, I thought, calling to tell me about London. Then I heard Greek words. A woman, but she didn't sound Greek.

"*Kyria* Antigone?"

"This is she."

"I am Mod. Nikitas' wife." Before she went any further I had already fantasised that she would ask me to stay, that Nikitas needed me, that they had a room ready for the children's grandmother. Then the news came out quickly. My son was dead. All these years when I thought I'd lost him, he was actually within reach. But now he was gone.

I stayed awake all night, pacing the small living room, trying to make a plan. I had no right to mourn, but I wept and raged. I smoked cigarette after cigarette and hit my fist against the table, until the cat hid under the bed. How had I been so stupid to wait until he was no longer there? By the time dawn arrived, I had made my decision. I had waited far too long. On the metro, a young woman gave up her seat so I could sit down and I spotted my reflection in the dark windows of the rattling train. What I saw was a skinny old Russian woman in a brown fur hat and mohair shawl, clutching an empty shopping bag from habit – in the old days you never knew what you might find and we always went out prepared to join a queue or snap up an opportunity. I got off at Arbat and walked steadily, so as not to slip on the ice.

I arrived in Leontiefsky Lane at nine o'clock and waited by the tall gate of the Greek Embassy and Consulate. It was not a place I had ever wanted to visit and, for most of the time I'd been in Moscow, this sentiment was perfectly reciprocated by those on the other side of the railings. A Greek communist was *persona non grata* for officials and diplomats. By the time the prejudices fizzled out in the 1980s, it was too late for reconciliation. I had made my decisions long before. I watched a caretaker inside the railings slowly sweeping the snow in the courtyard. When he stopped for a cigarette, he looked at me, sized me up and then came over, speaking in accented Russian.

"If you're wanting the consulate, Grandmother, it doesn't open till ten."

"I need a visa for Greece. I must have it today," I replied in Greek and he moved closer.

"Where were you born?" he asked, speaking his native Greek. "If you're Pontian, you need proof of your origins and then it's at least ten working days." When I told him I was born in Athens, he said then I wouldn't need a visa.

"I lost my Greek citizenship long before you were born," I told him. "Along with my home and the right to return. I will travel with the only passport I have, which is Russian."

"Ah, a political," he said, looking at me with mild curiosity. "Well, that's all long gone now. We don't see your kind these days. I thought most of you went back years ago." What with the cold, the sleepless night and the thoughts that were

5
A foreign country

MAUD

After the friends and relations drifted away I took a blanket up to the terrace and lay down on one of the old wicker recliners that were beginning to disintegrate, covering myself from the evening chill. It was something I often did with Nikitas, whose life was a constant movement towards the open air and away from the confines of a room or house. Whether it was to eat, talk or sleep, he considered it to be improved if he had the sky overhead instead of a ceiling. He enjoyed dragging a mattress onto the terrace so we could fall asleep under the stars, stumbling drowsily to our bedroom when the sun rose high enough to wake us. We both loved the terrace and though it was also Orestes' domain, next to his studio, we had turned it into a beautiful roof garden, full of plants. Each year, on Nikitas' name day, I gave him a tall olive tree in a pot and there were now fifteen up there, marking our life together, their trunks growing sturdier as my time in Greece lengthened. The oldest were starting to acquire what Seferis called "the wrinkles of our fathers" on their bark, while the newest was a spindly sapling still tied to a cane. The older trees produced a crop of large Kalamon olives each autumn. They fell, making wine-coloured stains on the floor, until Chryssa taught me how to preserve them and I gathered jarfuls each year.

Athens looked peaceful with its orange glow and rumble of traffic. I could see over the green expanses around the Zappeion and the National Garden to the looming mass of Lycabettus, with its white church on the summit. I was reassured by the familiarity of this scene, less ravaged by the terror that had gripped me earlier on. But it was hard to believe what some of the visitors had said, trying to be comforting, referring to their own, older griefs: "It will get better." "It will pass." Before long, Orestes came out of his studio smoking a joint, and tried to disguise his discomfort by offering it to me with a casual air. I suppose he assumed I would refuse – I had told him that the stuff didn't agree with me, and years ago, when Nikitas and I first noticed that Orestes was smoking, we tried arguing that weed is bad for the brain, in the hope of putting him off. This time however, I took the handmade cigarette from him and inhaled.

"My cousins brought it from the village today," said Orestes. "That's why it's so sweet. They've got plantations hidden in the fields – it's becoming quite a crop for them. They've found their 'medicine'." Blowing out the smoke, I tasted the bitterness on my tongue as warmth spread through my limbs and gravity weighted me down. Neither of us spoke. Orestes lay near me, his long hair spread across the dusty tiles, and we shared the joint until it was finished and I felt as immobile as the terra-cotta figures at the corners of the terrace.

Orestes reached his hand over and stroked my arm, then held it. I sensed his grasp as a sort of possessiveness in the vacuum left by Nikitas' death. The king is dead, long live the king. Nikitas adored Orestes, but he could not help trying to dominate him. He would never admit it, but he envied his son for his youth and freedom – the sound of Orestes' motorbike arriving at the back gate in the early hours of the morning was a provocation, the confrontation of the new to the old, the fast to the slow. If Nikitas liked to see himself as the anti-authoritarian rebel, he knew his son saw him as the system itself.

We stopped speaking and as I drifted in and out of sleep, I thought of myself twenty years earlier, like a foreign but well-known country. I was younger than Orestes when I first came to Greece. In 1988 Athens had been full of young men with wolfish expressions and black leather jackets, drinking Nescafé frappé and trying out their English on foreigners. "Europe" was thought to be a long way away. The city smelled of the *néphos* pollution cloud and Camel cigarettes. I had recently arrived and was preparing to go to the northern island of Thasos for my year of fieldwork.

I managed to acquire a room at the British School, an academic institution supporting British archaeological research in Greece, which also accepted a few anthropology students. The place was like a bizarre parallel universe. Outside the stone walls was fashionable Kolonaki, with its expensive boutiques and restaurants and the spill-out from the neighbouring Evangelismos Hospital – white-coated doctors smoking and groups of gypsies waiting on blankets by their vans. The school itself, however, was an Anglophone oasis with scented shrubberies, grand olive trees and tennis courts. Old stone buildings stood defiantly amidst the cement city's impermanence. Redolent of boiled vegetables and waxed parquet, the school was home to visiting scholars with tight, bookish features, who spent hours in the panelled library amongst busts of bewhiskered dead men. It felt like a cross between an English boarding school and a Greek convent, and was rumoured to be a hotbed of undercover agents – the glamorous Minister of Culture and former actress, Melina Mercouri, had called for it to be shut down.

My days were divided between reading in the library and attending Greek classes. One evening, having nothing better to do, I attended a lecture on an archaeological dig, followed by drinks at the director's house. I was introduced to a soignée Greek woman in her sixties, who spoke good English and wore pillar-box red lipstick that conjured up stars of the 1940s. She had a long association with the School, she explained. At the end of the party, she asked me to tea the next day and gave me a visiting card. *Alexandra Koftos*, it said, in swirling copperplate. *Odos Paradisou 17, Mets, Athina*. "I adore English tea." She smiled conspiratorially, as if admitting some more sinister vice.

The following day I arrived in Paradise Street at 5 o' clock as instructed. The road was quiet and tree-lined with pastel-coloured houses of varying ages and styles – quite different to the apartment blocks that dominate Athens. Number 17 was a solid, neo-classical building, painted cream, with dark green shutters, white pilasters and pretty terracotta roof decorations in the shapes of women's heads and two female figures at the corners. Alexandra greeted me like a friend, kissing me and asking me not to call her Mrs Koftos as it reminded her of her long-gone mother-in-law. She drew me in through a shadowy hallway and into the ground floor apartment. I looked around, admiring the spacious proportions and the combination of light and solidity. The floors were covered with shiny, dark-red stone containing the pale remains of fossils (that years later, fascinated Tig: "ammonites and belemnites" she learned to chant when she was small).

"My parents built this house," said Alexandra. "I've lived here all my life."

We sat in the formal sitting room, with windows shut and layers of beige curtains thwarting sunshine and curious passers-by. The furniture was an inconsistent mix of heavy wooden pieces that Alexandra had inherited from her parents and the gilded reproduction Louis XIV that she preferred. Silver ornaments shone from dust-free occasional tables and cut-glass bowls were filled with Gioconda chocolates. It is still the same, with its aroma of polish and floor cleaner mixed with lemon sauce and cinnamon. She told me how she liked the English, indeed had a little English blood herself, from a grandmother.

"We owe a great deal to the English," she said, as though I had contributed in some way. "After the war, they saved Greece. If it hadn't been for them, we'd have ended up under the thumb of the communists. We'd have become a Soviet satellite like Bulgaria – God forbid!"

Alexandra led me through to the kitchen by the back courtyard to help her prepare the tea. A round-faced woman in a dark cotton dress sat at the table crocheting, not watching the small television that blasted out a religious programme featuring an aged priest. Chryssa spoke in Greek and though I didn't understand very much, I thought I knew what she meant, with her kind expression and genuine smile. She brought out a syrupy lemon preserve, placed a thick coil of yellow peel on a saucer and poured me a glass of cold water from a bottle in the fridge. They seemed like eternal gestures of welcome to the stranger.

I carried the tray back to the sitting room and while Alexandra poured the tea, I looked at the silver-framed photographs placed here and there. One showed a family in what looked like the 1930s, with three children standing outside the house in Paradise Street. The father was sleek as a seal, in an elegant dark suit and waxed moustache; the mother graceful in pale silks, with hair styled into an angular bob. They looked content, though none smiled in the manner of modern photographs.

"This is me. The oldest." Alexandra pointed to a girl of about twelve in a white frock with curling, light-coloured hair. She had an authoritative air and was holding the hand of a pretty young boy in shorts and white ankle socks.

"My brother and sister were lost years ago. Markos was such a darling. He died so young. A terrible waste." She didn't tell me anything about the serious, dark-haired girl leaning at an angle on the other side of the parents.

I also met Alexandra's husband that first day. He came into the sitting room with the jaunty air and freshly combed hair of a man who has just woken from a long siesta. Taking in his sharp-creased trousers and slackening jowls, I guessed he was a well-preserved seventy.

"Spiros Koftos." He introduced himself and I caught a blast of his aftershave as he squeezed my hand too tightly, and leaned in towards me. Alexandra told him about me in Greek and he looked me up and down, nodding in approval, as though inspecting a prospective purchase.

"English? Very nice. Very good," he said to me in heavily accented English. "Welcome to Greece." Spiros told his wife he was going out and swung around, leaving in military fashion, not quite clicking his heels.

"He's going to the coffee shop," Alexandra explained. "All his friends go there – in the morning for coffee and news-papers and in the afternoon for a little whisky and cards. At least it keeps them out of trouble." She laughed, shaking her head slightly, as if the male sex were a conundrum it was not necessary to solve. Then she told me about her business – a clothes shop in Kolonaki called En Vogue (she pronounced it like "envog" and it was only much later that I realised what she meant). She was still involved, she said, though she no longer went in every day.

"I started off using my father's old premises. Perifanis was known for making the best women's clothes in Athens before the war and when we re-opened in the 1950s, it made sense to use the name, but in the '60s we started bringing in ready-to-wear from Milan and Paris and when we moved to a better location I changed the name. We have a loyal clientele and we're still making money."

I liked Alexandra, though I couldn't imagine what this *comme il faut* Athenian lady saw in a scruffy English student. With her tailored clothes, perfect manners and forthright opinions, she was not like anyone in my social circle. I was accustomed to doubt and questioning. Perhaps that is why I appreciated her certainties. She invited me to visit her several times, the last occasion being one morning shortly before I was due to leave for Thasos. Alexandra wanted to give me a tome about folklore in the Aegean written in the undecipherable formal Greek that was now defunct. It had fuzzy, grey photographs of men dressed up as goats with bells hanging from their clothes and women in headscarves gathered in circular threshing floors, performing obscure rituals.

Chryssa handed me a bulky, oily package containing pieces of cheese pie and a jar of sour cherry preserve, to keep me nourished in my island exile. She was just kissing me goodbye, when I saw a man's face looking in through the kitchen window. Alexandra did not quite gasp, but her features became rigid as Chryssa unlocked the back door and welcomed him. I guessed he was in his early 40s, thick-set, though not fat, with a solidity that looked as though it came through will-power rather than exercise. He moved with an incongruous lightness that made me imagine he had just crept into the courtyard like a cat or a burglar. His almost blue-black hair was broken with grey at the front and dark brows ran in straight lines, giving him a somewhat piratical aspect. I saw him focus on me as he hugged Chryssa and she rubbed his back as though soothing a nervous horse.

"Aunt. How are you?" he asked without feeling. "I just came to collect some things from the store room." Alexandra walked over and kissed the man on both cheeks, while he submitted to the greeting like a sullen boy. I was intrigued.

"Mond, this is my nephew Nikitas," said Alexandra, without enthusiasm. "He has the apartment upstairs, but he doesn't live there. He rents it out." I shook Nikitas' hand, finding the physical contact disturbing in a way I didn't immediately recognise. I felt young and awkward and to disguise the fact, started to give a slightly formal account of why I had come to Greece. Nikitas looked amused.

"So, you've come to study us. Well, don't believe anything they tell you and only half of what you see." He laughed and I blushed. "Whatever you think you understand, the opposite will also be true. We Greeks won't fit tidily into anybody's scheme. It's our nature. We're a mess." I wasn't sure if he was mocking me.

"I was just leaving," I said, wanting to get away from my confusion. He was close enough for me to smell him – something like cedar and green leaves.

"If you can give me five minutes, I'll give you a lift. I have the car outside."

"We could always call you a taxi if you prefer," said Alexandra, a little too eagerly. Chryssa, too, was looking at me as though I was making a decision that would have repercussions.

Nikitas bounded up the fire escape, which twanged and rattled, returning a few minutes later with some books from the store room.

"Are you ready?" He smiled at me as though he had won when I said goodbye and thanked Alexandra and Chryssa, and left from the back door with him. We passed under the lemon tree and through the yard, emerging into the alleyway, where two cats were locked in urgent thrusting. They paused, looked at us briefly and then continued, pulled by a far more powerful force of nature than fear. The male was pressing down the female's head with one paw and emitting a strange throaty sound. I avoided Nikitas' eye and he got out a packet of cigarettes and lit up. He was just unlocking his car – a beaten up Lada jeep – when he stopped.

"How about a walk first? Let me show you around the area."

We left my gifts from Chryssa and Alexandra in the car and continued on foot.

Nikitas took on the role of guide explaining Greek history to the ignorant foreigner. He told me why the area was known as Mets.

"It's all down to nineteenth-century Germans and their beer."

I wondered if he was teasing me.

"As soon as the Greeks were free from four hundred years of Turkish rule, the Great Powers wanted to find a king. So they located a teenager in Bavaria, who happened to be a prince, and they put young Otto on the throne." Athens was a two-horse town, "with shepherds herding their flocks on the Acropolis and not much else," when Otto's entourage of Bavarian advisers and architects decided to transform the new capital into their own fantasy of ancient Greece. According to Nikitas, they were also beer-drinkers and preferred it to Greek wine. Their solution was to build themselves a beer factory, and for some reason they named the area Mets, after Metz, the beer-making town in Alsace. Failing to find me sharing his outrage, Nikitas continued with his theme. "You can see this German influence all over Athens." He sounded as though they had done it to insult him. "They called it neo-classical and mixed 'Greek' columns with Germanic pitched roofs."

I told him I thought they were so pretty, these few remaining family houses, like his aunt's in Paradise Street, with their elegant facades.

"Yes," he admitted. "But my grandfather had a clever architect who understood about the Greek climate, about having terraces and courtyards for shade. Most of those Bavarians just ignored vernacular styles that had evolved over centuries. And we were left with a tradition that is both fake and foreign. Nobody knows what 'Greek' architecture means any more."

When we reached the First Cemetery Nikitas bought me a bunch of anemones from a stall. I didn't know how to react to the gallantry. Perhaps it was partly his age, which was about the same as my parents'. But it was also his gaze that made me feel he knew something about me that I didn't. I was pleased and intimidated, eager and wary.

"Are you hungry? Can I take you to lunch? We'll go somewhere nobody else will take you, however much time you stay in Athens." It was a challenge. I noticed the old woman who had sold him the flowers, observing the scene.

He led me through a monumental white entrance that was like something Mussolini might have built.

"I think you'll like this place – the best ouzo and *mezédes*." It sounded like a joke as we skirted a group of mourners waiting for a funeral and then turned sharp right along a covered marble walkway. At the end of the arcade was a diminutive café filled with cheerful, noisy customers who looked like cemetery workers – rough-handed grave-diggers and groundsmen, but also some pall-bearers in black trousers, white shirts and shiny shoes. The men were drinking ouzo, and eating plates of fried meatballs and other snacks. We sat on rush chairs at a table outside the door and Nikitas greeted the woman behind the bar by name, making a joke I didn't understand and ordering ouzo and a "selection". She laughed as she stirred something sizzling in a pan, while at the other end of the walkway, a funerary procession went by. It all looked intensely foreign to me. I was the outsider peering in, trying to understand.

Nikitas poured ouzo from a small bottle, clouding the clear spirit by adding ice and water.

"So, a toast to you. And to your research. I hope you find us very interesting and that you stay a long time." The aniseed taste was strong and unfamiliar on my tongue and the alcohol went straight to my head. I tried some of the *mezédes* – oily fried cheese cut with lemon, strips of cucumber, a few wrinkled black olives.

Nikitas drank much more than me and paid me what I took for alcohol-fuelled compliments.

"Did you always have those little flecks of brown in your eyes? It's the first time I've seen blue like that. And such pale skin – like a beautiful spirit from the woods that only emerges at night."

Nikitas told me parts of his story. Later, I often heard him recount it to other people, usually in Greek, but it always had the same tone it had that first time, when it was in English. He was droll, but distant, the phrases codified and fixed as flags strung on a far-off boat anchored in quarantine. He enjoyed the shock on people's faces when he said: "I was born in prison." And I remember the jolt it gave me the first time, imagining this man – so confident and physically powerful – as a small boy locked away.

"After the war, you only had to say the word 'communism' and they'd throw you in jail. My mother was sentenced to life. And that's how I came to be Greece's youngest prisoner in 1946. My greatest achievement."

Nikitas described his difficult relationship with his Aunt Alexandra, how she and Spiros adopted him when his mother went into exile – they couldn't have children, but they never managed to treat him as a son. They lied that Antigone was dead and it took years before he got the story straight. Even now there was much he didn't know. He never met his father, though he had discovered that his wartime name was Eagle – Captain Eagle – and that he had been killed during the Civil War.

I noticed how Nikitas' humour dissolved into acidity when he spoke of his Uncle Spiros.

"The worst sort of fascist. A policeman whose glory days were during the Junta. When I was young he would punish me and beat me. He'd come into my room and stare at me before he removed his belt. And he called me 'Little Bastard'."

By the time we had finished one small bottle of Plomari ouzo and eaten several plates of the snacks, the sun was lower in the sky and it was pleasant to wander: past the archbishops, with their mitre-topped tombstones, and the bronze sculpture of an emaciated mother clutching a limp baby – a monument to the suffering during the Nazi occupation. Progressing along shaded paths that snake beneath cypresses and pines there were large family vaults and tidy graves with flickering oil lamps and fresh flowers. Sculptures lined the way: languid maidens, portly matrons and satisfied old men, all with fixed marble stares. We laughed at the signs saying: "Don't steal flowers from the graves," and I pretended not to notice when Nikitas' arm brushed against mine, though I wanted to touch him. Stopping to admire the tomb of the Sleeping Maiden, he pulled my arm to make me stand with him.

"The long sleep. She makes it look quite pleasant."

I hadn't known that the English word cemetery comes from the Greek *kimitírion* – "sleeping place".

On our walk we saw the tomb of Nikitas' maternal grand-mother, who had died the previous year. Maria Perifanis, 1902–1987. Someone had planted rose geraniums in the earth and he picked a leaf, rubbing it for the scent.

"She lived on the floor above Alexandra, so after she died, I inherited her apartment," he said. "She was the best thing about my childhood. The bravest person I knew." He didn't tell me then that he had threatened to take his aunt to court to obtain his share in the freehold. But I sensed his strength next to me, with his bull-like sturdiness and broad shoulders that made people think he was shorter than he was. Oddly, people often think that I am taller than I am, and later, Nikitas was quick to point out that his height surpassed mine by at least half a centimetre.

We continued along the pathway to where a kink in the perimeter wall and a tall cypress tree created a corner that was hidden from view. Nikitas stopped and I hoped he would pull me to him and press me against the wall. There was a tension between us that I sensed could only be resolved that way. But he didn't do anything, and just leaned back, a hand outstretched, as if testing me. There was a moment of hesitation, like the seconds before deciding to jump into cold water, before I moved in closer. Our breaths tasted of ouzo and there was a warm, resinous smell from the russet tree trunk that prickled behind my back. He undid the buttons on my shirt and the sun warmed my skin as he stroked me. I had sized him up as a "pouncer", but he surprised me with his gentleness. Before we left, he smoothed my clothes into place and brushed the cypress needles from my back.

Two days later, I left for Thasos, and although I came back

to Athens several times during my year's fieldwork, I didn't see Nikitas. We hadn't even exchanged phone numbers and I certainly didn't want to ask his aunt. Even so, I loved my trips to the capital and embraced the freedom of the anonymous city. It might have been noisy and polluted (as the islanders repeatedly told me), but it was exciting and "erotic" (as Athenians were quick to point out). People looked into your face as you walked down the street, making a visual contact, however brief, that was not found in northern European cities. In Athens, I was able to drop the careful anthropologist's persona I nurtured in the all-observing island community. I'd go out with friends I'd kept in touch with from the language school. Phivos, the youngest and most handsome of the teachers, took me to drink and dance at the noisy bars that were just reaching the height of their fashion in the late '80s and that kept going until dawn. I enjoyed his good-natured warmth; his parents were justified in naming him after Phoebus, god of the sun. After our excesses, I'd stay in bed all morning and spend lazy days reading English newspapers and magazines, which were unobtainable on the island. Though my flirtation with Phivos was fun, it was Nikitas I thought more about, especially during my solitary winter evenings typing up notes and struggling over genealogical diagrams: matrilateral cross-cousins, patrilineal inheritance, agnatic lineage, affinal and consanguineous relations, spiritual kinship. I wasn't unhappy; it was interesting trying to transform messy reality into orderly columns and codes. But it was easy to find myself back in the cemetery, pressing against Nikitas, feeling his chin rough against my cheek.

6
Fly in the milk

ANTIGONE

I thought of calling back Nikitas' wife – no, his widow. My *nýfi* [bride, daughter-in-law]. Strange to use that word for the first time at this point in my life. But I couldn't manage it. I knew she lived at Paradise Street with Alexandra, but I threw a black stone behind me when I left; I could not go back, begging to be let in by a sister who had disowned me. However, I could count on Dora. Ever since we were able to make international phone calls from home, I have spoken to her once a year and she has filled me in on who is left at the meetings, on her children and grandchildren. She had just heard the news when I rang and was very upset. She said, "May God forgive him." She was always a good communist Christian. "I loved him very much."

I told her my plan and she spoke as though we had last seen each other the previous month.

"I'll be waiting at the airport. You can stay as long as you like."

I packed a small bag (I am perfectly capable of living with

one change of clothes) and took four old notebooks, the lock of my son's hair, wrapped in paper, and a couple of precious photographs I like to keep near me. The journey passed slowly. I was squeezed between the window and a large Muscovite who drank whisky from the moment he boarded the plane. His eyes were mostly squeezed shut and I had to shove him back into place when he leaned against me. As we approached, I looked down to see Greece for the first time in fifty-nine years. The colours were more subdued than I remembered, the sea greyer. There was a strange orange glow. Perhaps I had remembered it wrong.

I wondered whether I would recognise Dora, but there she was, tinier than ever, wrinkled, but basically the same as when we had said goodbye. She opened her skinny arms to me and though I am taller, I felt like a child going to its mother. We stood there a while, embracing, each taking a look at the old woman that stood before her. Passengers hurried past, some making disapproving noises that we were blocking the way, but we didn't care. That is one thing about having lived a communal existence – you learn to make your own space and to fight for it.

It was midday by the time we thought to check our watches, and the funeral was due to take place at one, so Dora hurried me out to get a taxi. As we waited in line, she looked at my luggage on the trolley and came in closer to examine a bag sitting on top.

"What have you got in there?" The bag was shuddering. I carefully unzipped the opening a fraction to reveal a mass of fur that was breathing heavily and hissing.

"Misha," I said. "I promised a friend to look after him.

What could I do? There was nobody I could leave him with."
I had given Misha a fraction of a sleeping pill before I put
him in his carrier and luckily he had snored peacefully all the
way through the journey at my feet. There were no customs
problems bringing him into Greece, but it looked as though
he had woken in a resentful mood. He flicked out a paw in an
attempt to scratch me, but I managed to zip him up before he
reached his target.

The main road into Athens looked more like Moscow
than anything I remembered from the 1940s, and it was
only when Dora pointed out the mountains that I began to
get some sense of orientation. Hymettus, Pendeli, Parnitha. I
understood where we were but I didn't recognise anything –
it was like arriving in a different city that had been dropped
onto a familiar landscape. Tall apartment blocks loomed like
strangers in the house.

"You can throw a black stone behind you, but sometimes
it calls you back rather than keeping you away." Dora understood why it had taken so long and why I had returned. The
day was warm and I was already sweating in my woollen
clothes and winter boots, but there was no time to go to
Dora's to change. The traffic was worse than Moscow and as
we edged along, the driver sounded his horn in frustration
and other drivers joined him until it sounded like a tuneless
band. Dora told me news of her children: Panos lives in France
and has lung cancer, and Evdokia is up in Thessaloniki and
has recently got divorced. Dora didn't complain. She looked
sprightly and said she was getting on with her life.

"I have my health, Glory to God. I'm still strong." Her hand
was light on my sleeve, but I could see it had strength.

As we approached the cemetery I recognised my old neighbourhood – the streets I had played in as a child. It was more built-up, but through the window there was even the smell of resin glue from the marble-cutters. The taxi stopped outside the cemetery and the driver agreed sullenly to wait for us with my luggage. I removed my thick cardigan and left it with my coat on the back seat by Misha, still in his bag. As we shuffled through the entrance, my heart began thudding as it used to when we were waiting for the fighting to start in the mountains. My breath came fast and shallow. This was my son's funeral.

We were late. Dora made enquiries and we were told to proceed straight to the grave. There was already another service taking place in the chapel. Dora led the way, but we made several wrong turns until we found ourselves at the back of a large crowd of people, most of whom were straining to get nearer to the grave. There must have been several hundred mourners – so many people who cared about my son. I looked at them, wondering what they had been to him. We were standing next to a smart young woman who was wiping tears from behind her dark glasses and two men who smoked furtively and muttered to each other.

"How many wives are there up there?"

"Not as many as there are girlfriends back here. The old fucker." I think I flinched and the first man noticed Dora and me. He coughed and nudged the second into silence.

The priest's chanting stopped, and after a pause came the sounds of earth hitting wood. Then the mourners parted and the priest came through, followed by a foreign-looking woman holding hands with a girl, who looked as I imagined my granddaughter might be – pretty but rebellious, with tangled dark hair and a powerful gaze that she turned on people who looked at her with pity. I backed away, holding on to the edge of a tall tombstone, just as I saw my sister coming, walking with an authoritative step. Alexandra saw me, but there was no glimmer of recognition and she kept walking. Why should she think that some old woman lurking in the shadows was the past returned to haunt her? I noticed that she was wearing my mother's earrings – the diamond rosettes from Constantinople. I could never forget them. Her hair that absurd shade of blue that certain old women make the mistake of thinking sophisticated. Why not make it purple? Or green?

Dora and I waited until everyone had left and then walked up some steps and along the path to the hole surrounded by wreaths and bouquets. A grave-digger was already shovelling the soil but stopped when we approached. I asked if I could throw in a handful and he held up a spade-load for me to take some, before stepping back respectfully. My offering had just scattered onto the coffin when I felt nauseous. My upper lip tingled and darkness descended.

When I awoke I was lying with my head on something soft yet lumpy.

"Are you all right?" Dora was sprinkling water on my forehead and lips. The grave-digger stood close by, looking down at me. I moved my fingers and felt the earth filled with small stones beneath me, and turning my head I saw that I was sprawled by Nikitas' grave on what appeared to be a mass of white roses. All around, heaps of flowers were emitting a sweet smell.

Dora said, "We put the wreath under your head as a pillow." She was always the practical one. "Just stay still for a few minutes. You're tired and I expect you haven't eaten much today." I admitted I hadn't and didn't mention my heart. Dora and the grave-digger were talking. The man was ready for conversation now the crisis was over.

"Last week we had a woman try to jump in. They caught her just in time and were pulling her up by her arms. There's not much we haven't seen in here. There are others who almost live here, they're so attached to the tomb. But I don't blame them." He asked Dora whether he should call an ambulance, but I insisted that I didn't need anything like that.

Dora said, "Here, have some chocolate." She brought out a small bar from her handbag, breaking off shards, like we used to do in the mountains when it was cold and we wanted to make it last. She fed them to me and the sharp fragments melted, sweet and smooth in my mouth.

When I got up, Dora dusted me off, and we sat on a wall to smoke. By the time we had dragged ourselves back the way we came, the funeral reception was long gone. I wouldn't have wanted to go anyway. "Like the fly in the milk", I'd have been – an old witch with dirt on her clothes and pollen in her hair. I only saw myself once we reached Dora's house and I looked a fright. Somewhere along the way back from the grave, a grey cat streaked past into the undergrowth, but I thought nothing of it. When we arrived at the taxi, however, the driver admitted that Misha had escaped. He said, "It was making a terrible racket, so I took a look inside and before I could do anything he'd leaped out of the window and run off into the cemetery. I spent ages looking for him, but there was no sign of the bloody animal."

Dora left me sitting on the back seat and went off to take a look. She was always someone who could catch birds in mid-air, as they say, but she returned empty-handed. She said, "We'll come back later with some food. But now we need to go home."

7
The solemn rhythm

MAUD

On the morning of the funeral, I woke with a jolt, crying out in fear. Bright daylight was coming in through the shutters. I had been awake much of the night and gone to sleep after 4am. My first thought was that I had overslept and missed the whole thing, but in fact, it was still before eight. Three more hours. Tig was lying next to me, breathing softly, her hair spread in dark tentacles across the pillow, one arm flung behind her head.

I moved along the corridor to the bathroom like a sleep-walker, slower and less balanced than usual. I assumed that this was some kind of hangover from Orestes' offering the night before, but like the bitter taste in my mouth and the aching heart, this clumsiness was to become a feature of the next days and even weeks, as I dropped things, bumped into furniture and stumbled over non-existent obstacles. Just as a shock can make the familiar take on a different aspect, so can it set the body off-kilter. I had a shower, drank coffee and got dressed, finding that, for the first time, I disliked wearing black – funeral black was not the same as chic black or arty black. "Nikitas' widow." The words went around in my head as I pictured my role in what I knew was a piece of theatre. It felt too soon and I wondered whether I would be able to play my part, or whether it was too much to do. Nikitas' death was still very raw and unprocessed for all this formality and ritual.

At 9.30 Alexandra came upstairs, having already corralled Chryssa and Orestes. They were all dressed in black too: Alexandra in a fitted suit, Chryssa in a thick woollen coat, and Orestes in black jeans and an unfamiliarly formal jacket, which I immediately realised Alexandra had pressed on him from what remained of Spiros' wardrobe. We were an odd little family: two old women, a foreigner, an anarchist student and a child-woman. As we passed through the front door, Chryssa passed me a large, green jug.

"Break it," she said, and I saw Tig looking at me, questioning what was going on.

"It's custom." I lifted the vessel, feeling a small chip in its lip with my thumb, and smashed it hard onto the stone steps. The jagged fragments were left there (Alexandra must have resisted a deeply instilled female instinct to clear up the mess) and we turned to walk up Paradise Street. I pictured us as a sad flock of crows, the older ones in front, plodding in dull solidarity. We were all quiet, numb, unable to share feelings that were too large and overwhelming to be tamed into conversation. Tig took Orestes' arm at the back, watching as some of the local shopkeepers came up: "Condolences. Life to you."

At the cemetery, we went to a small chapel-like room where Nikitas' coffin had already been placed by *Kyrios* Katsaridis and his dark-suited men. Propped up against the wall outside were several dozen wreaths made from white carnations. They were attached to tall sticks and draped with banners printed with the donor's name and a short message. Several wished *Kaló Taxídi* – Have a good journey. They reminded me of equipment for a protest. Nikitas would have appreciated the thought, as there were few public gatherings he liked as much as marches; he would often be seen at the front of a roaring sea of people, waving his banner in support of that month's injustice. We walked past them slowly, reading the words: there were wreaths from friends, colleagues in the media, a disconcerting number of well-known politicians and a few local businesses.

The open coffin rested on trestles in the middle of the room. I looked away rather than focus on the fixed white face. It was both strange and horrifically familiar, surrounded by a blur of flowers, white lace and polished wood. The air was heavy with lilies, sweet as fresh manure. There was incense too. Nausea arrived in a warm wave as my body tried to rebel. I put my arm around Tig, holding her tight, not wanting to imagine what she was going through. I asked if she would like to step up close.

"Not yet." She was looking away, her eyes too large, her skin almost green-white. We both shot glances across at Nikitas, as though looking at him full on would be too much; a look can turn a person to stone, to a pillar of salt, or like Orpheus, make you lose your beloved to the underworld for ever. We sat down on the chairs around the edge of the room, with the old women on the opposite side from Tig, Orestes and me. Chryssa was keening, talking to Nikitas, telling him how much she cared for him, how wrong it was that he should go before her, how he was like a son to her. Her speech took on a droning, musical quality, without becoming a song, and sometimes she got up and went over to the coffin, stroking Nikitas' hair. I wished I knew how to be like that, how to acquire the courage to navigate the storm of bereavement and face death with poetry. Alexandra sat without moving. She had the stoicism of the old in the face of a familiar enemy; death is no longer the unbelievably distant adversary of youth. I was grateful for her solid reliability, when everything else seemed treacherous and shifting.

Gradually, people started arriving for the funeral. Some milled about outside, talking, smoking, examining the wreaths, while others came in to say something to us or a last word to Nikitas. Nikos the poet, his old friend and *koumbáros*, was distraught. He clutched onto the edge of the coffin and cried like a child, berating Nikitas for leaving him. I didn't doubt that his feelings were genuine, though I remembered him flirting with the television reporter on the day of the accident. When, finally, the white-gloved, black-suited pall-bearers arrived, the scene became a kaleidoscope of images and sensations, dominated by emotion. Father Apostolos, Alexandra's friendly priest, led the way, with the coffin held high behind him, and we followed into the dark, hot chapel. Father Apostolos said the words as they had to be said, and the gestures were made – "the solemn rhythm of all their movements", Cavafy wrote. This unchanging ritual is carried out over and again, with words like spells, making order out of the chaos of death. Only the name of the deceased is inserted to the fixed form, as if individuality is almost irrelevant within the never-ending cycle.

It all happened quickly, in a dizzy blur: the walk to the open grave, the deep cuts of dry, stony ground; the throng of people squeezing in close to see the coffin lid being removed for a last look, and the banging of nails as it was closed. The priest chanted, "You shall sprinkle me with hyssop and I shall be clean. You shall wash me and I shall be whiter than snow." After that, the red earth: "You are dust, and to dust you will return." There's no escaping that fact, whatever language you say it in.

Once it was done, we pulled away like old-fashioned deep-sea divers with lead-weighted boots trudging through water, back along the paths to the bleak reception room. It looked like a school canteen; lines of wooden tables, laid with small cups of Greek coffee, glasses of brandy and bowls of sweet aniseed rusks. Aunt Alexandra took charge, putting me in first place in the row of chairs for the chief mourners. Tig was next, pulling the sleeves of her black jersey down over her hands, angrily wiping tears. Orestes sat hunched, as though he was too tall for the chair, awkward and out of place. Alexandra busied about, graciously not taking a seat. She put her hand on my shoulder several times and I knew she was not letting herself get upset. There had been about 200 people she thought, something that gratified her. "Impressive," she said later. Nobody stayed long. Having downed the drinks, they filed past us, shaking hands, kissing, murmuring over and over, "Condolences, condolences."

Phivos came, though I'd asked him not to when he rang. He had told me for so long that I should leave Nikitas – the last thing I needed was to confront his renewed attentions. He put his arms around me and I embraced him, taking in how youthful he still looked, twenty years after we were first friends, when all the females in the class got steamed up over his explanations of Greek verbs, declensions and cases. He was wearing a dark suit, something I was surprised to see he owned. He whispered in my ear, "Maud, you'll be OK. You'll see."

When everyone had gone, we emerged in silence, drained and exhausted. Orestes had his arm around Tig's shoulders. Across the way, I noticed the staff café where Nikitas and I had gone the day we met, almost exactly twenty years ago. The beginning and the end.

✻　✻　✻

After the funeral the periods of numbness evaporated and my body hurt all over. The tears that had only come sporadically began to flow, then continued in such quantities that my clothes became soggy and my eyes swelled into slits. Sometimes the sadness was replaced by fury and I raged at what fate had brought and at what Nikitas had done. The autopsy had come back indicating that he had been drunk. Hardly unexpected. There was no evidence of another vehicle, however, and with no reason to suspect suicide, the crash was deemed an accident. They seemed to think he had not died immediately, but were unable to tell whether he would have been conscious. I didn't tell anyone else that detail, but it haunted me, creating nightmares where I saw Nikitas injured, bleeding to death in the middle of the night, with nobody to help him. Afterwards, I would sit on the edge of the bed, dark misery clinging to me like tar. How could this have happened? Was there a reason? Why hadn't he told me? I wondered how I would get closer to the truth, but I also feared knowing

The next day was "the Third Day", when the first memorial is held by the grave, three days after a death. I told Alexandra that I had a migraine and could not come, but Tig joined in the preparations, making *kólyva* in our kitchen with Chryssa; boiling up wheat, mixing it with ground almonds, sugar and pomegranate seeds. Food for the dead, to be eaten by the living at the graveside. Its ingredients (all seeds and sweetness) evoke love, fertility and nourishment in the bitter face of death and decay – soul food made in Greece since ancient times. When it was ready and moulded on a tray, Tig brought it to show me – a large round mound, covered with white icing sugar and a silver plastic cross. They had placed silvery sugared almonds, slightly skewed, to form Nikitas' initials: N.Π. Outside the window, hundreds or even thousands of brown birds – starlings perhaps – were diving and swooping in the sky above the house, their manic chirping like magnified electronic beeps. They circled up over Ardittos hill, then back again, their white droppings splattering down on the roof tops and cars, leaving splotches for days to come.

While the family and a smaller group of friends and relations gathered again at Nikitas' grave, I did what my grandmother, Lucy, had done in times of trouble, and took to my bed. I had adopted it as a favourite tactic for coping with difficulties. From an early age, I'd taken advantage of its curative properties and Lucy would let me take the day off school without demur. Frequently, she would lie with me, remaining in her dressing gown, joined by Julian, her Jack Russell, and we would sprawl in or on her bed, reading, eating snacks and chatting. We also listened to music: Verdi's operas were a favourite (she adored Maria Callas and favoured a similarly dramatic style of eye make-up on good days). If we were particularly melancholic, we played recordings of my parents' viol music – "vile viols", as

Desmond remarked. Sometimes I still did that and would put on a CD of grinding baroque strings to match my gloom.

Over the next days, Tig went back to school and there were gestures towards creating a new kind of normality, but I stayed in my room, close to my bed. It was as though I was ill and my body was forcing me to accept its demands. Chryssa came to visit me at regular intervals, bringing soup or camomile tea, sitting with me while I drank it. She spoke slowly, almost hypnotically, not expecting an answer, talking about small, peaceful subjects, calling me her "sweet Mondy".

"I gathered this camomile in the village last spring. I always liked picking it – it was my job when I was a girl. I'd gather it from the fields, clean it, lay it out to dry. And it smelled so good. I used to enjoy all those jobs – putting the olives in brine, preparing *passatémpo* – salted pumpkin seeds – for the winter, making the cheese. I was the best at looking after the animals too. It was a beautiful life." She mumbled on and I half-listened to the descriptions of ceilings hung with quinces, pomegranates and melons, giving off their sweet aromas of home. It was almost as though she was singing to me as she used to with Tig – songs that droned in gentle rhythms like the sea on the shore.

Tig often came to join me too during those days, snuggling up as she did when she was little. The presence of her body was comforting to me and I could tell that she relaxed next to me, suddenly falling asleep, even during the day. "Sleep took her," as they say in Greek, as though it was someone abducting you, whether or not you desired it. At night, she stayed with me and woke with nightmares, calling out and grasping hold of me. I found her jerked upright, moaning, covered in sweat, and tried to soothe her, to explain where she was, until she came to. When I questioned her, she said she was trying to escape, that she had been trapped, locked up – the same sensations as when she was little and had night-frights. I gave her a glass of water and stroked her until she lay down and her breathing slowed as she relaxed back into sleep. I lay there thinking about Tig's Greek inheritance, worried that she was like a lightning conductor for the tensions running through the family, down the generations to the youngest and most tender. How were these unspeakable and unexpressed burdens passed on?

✳ ✳ ✳

About a week after the funeral I got up on a day of sparkling November sun. Tig wanted to go to see where the accident had happened and I agreed that she could take the day off school and we would go there together. Nikos had lent me his car for a few weeks while he was away in Paris, and we set off in his battered jeep that was littered with the evidence of bachelor life – newspapers, empty bottles, cigarette packets, a woman's scarf. The police had told me the exact location of the crash, and we drove along the coast road, past empty beach-clubs and gaudy open-air night-spots all closed up for winter. The palm trees had lost their frivolous demeanour and drooped with blackened fronds infested by African beetles that arrived with a special order for the Olympic Games a few years earlier. As we passed Glyfada and Voula, heading towards the open blue of the Saronic Gulf, I could see the dirty yellow haze that lurked over Athens retreating in the rear view mirror. At Vouliagmeni, with its roadside eucalyptus trees, stately but scarred from repeated crashes, we left the last of the city behind and the road snaked above a series of inlets, the Limanakia – Little Harbours – popular with boy racers at weekends.

As instructed, I turned off onto a short slip road, recognisable by a shrine shaped like a dolls' house-sized island church, complete with whitewashed walls and blue domes. Apparently Nikitas was not the only person who had died near here, as these "little churches" are usually placed by grieving relatives to mark the spot. This one looked fairly recent and a flame flickered from its oil lamp, nestling by a bottle of Jif. A postal van was parked close-by, its radio playing bouzouki hits at full volume. The driver sipped coffee from a polystyrene cup, and blew cigarette smoke out of the window as he gazed at the mauve silhouette of coastline leading down to Sounion.

Tig and I walked over to the edge, where a precipitous incline of rocks and undergrowth led down to a bay that had not been visible from the road. Flat, pale rocks sloped into a sea of glittering peacock blue and gulls squawked overhead. There was a steep footpath and we made our way down gingerly, trying not to slip. The recent rains had produced the flash of autumnal growth that is almost like a miniature version of spring, without the melodramatic excesses of the real thing. Fresh grass and white spears of sea squill emerged from soil still baked solid from the summer and fuchsia-pink cyclamen sprouted from rocks. Butterflies and dragonflies flitted around as though it was May not November. The policeman had said to look for a large pine tree and we found it about 150 metres down. Its trunk had a new cut in it and looking back up, we could see skid marks and disturbed ground leading from the slip road down the hill. This was obviously the place. Some partridges the same colour as the earth swept up into the air, trilling like skidding bikes. Tig sat down, picking at some grass and not catching my eye.

"Maybe this tree was the last thing he saw."

I hadn't told her that her father was apparently still alive after the crash. I hoped he had not been conscious; it would be a lonely place at night.

We sat without talking, warmed by the sun, inhaling the tang of sage and pine sap. The place reminded me of trips Nikitas and I used to make in the early years. He'd take the day off and we'd drive out somewhere down the coast with a picnic or end up eating a plate of fried anchovies in a beach taverna after a long swim. The water was his element.

"Shall we go for a swim?" I felt almost as surprised at my suggestion as Tig looked, but she followed me down until we reached the smooth expanses of grey marble that gave straight onto deep, clear water. The area was hidden from the road and I took off my clothes and dived in. The shock of the cold water was matched by incongruous elation as I felt the sun on my wet face and salt on my lips. I felt something close to liberation, even joy, in spite of all that had happened; contradictory opposites existing together, as they do even more frequently in Greece than elsewhere. I turned to see Tig jumping in, dressed in black pants and bra. She shrieked, twisting like a dolphin, diving deep, streaking back to the surface, thrashing out a few strokes of butterfly, then floating, eyes closed and hair spread on the surface.

❋ ❋ ❋

The next day I went to Nikitas' office. I needed to decide what to do with his stuff and whether to go on paying the rent there. But I also wanted to see his private place. I walked down Paradise Street, avoiding the bitter-orange trees that are planted in the middle of the pavements and whose branches and fruit are liable to slap you or scratch your face if you don't take care. The road was wet from the rain that had fallen early in the morning but bolts of sunshine now penetrated the clouds, gilding the puddles. There was a pungent odour like semen in the air, something that had disconcerted me the first time I came across it in Athens, but which now made me smile, remembering Nikitas' explanation.

"It's the carob trees," he said. "They flower in the autumn and give off this stink of sex. You can't deny that Athens is an erotic city when the whole place smells of sperm." Now this strangely human scent emanating from the trees' tiny flowers is a familiar olfactory accompaniment to autumnal decay, wet leaves, the end of the year. Sex and death, as usual.

As I waited to find a taxi, I looked across at the Acropolis. I was able to judge my mood by whether I was pleased by the sight or whether it annoyed me as a wearisome cliché. That day I felt happy to see the Parthenon, standing alone, creamy blonde and almost floating. Every Athenian has their own private Acropolis – a view from a bathroom window or a personal angle on that most public of places. Temple, church, mosque, weapons store room, provider of museum pieces, over-used tourist destination, and above all symbol, it is nothing if not adaptable to our fantasies. I like the way it's not perfect: the gashing hole caused by one of the many battles that have raged around it, and the familiar beige cranes used for restoration that protrude awkwardly like surgical forceps holding diseased bones in place. On a good day, this glimpse of the Acropolis after I walk Tig to school or as I wait for a bus, can be a reminder of my attachment to Greece's bare, salty landscape of rocks and ruins. Other times, the columns look like the bars on a window.

I flagged down a taxi that already contained two passengers. They were disagreeing with the driver about his support of LAOS, the extreme right-wing party.

"Greece is for the Greeks. I've nothing against foreigners, but they should go back to their own homes." The driver was enjoying his easy prejudices and I didn't have the heart to get into an argument as I usually did, asking whether or not his own parents or grandparents had not done a spell as immigrants in Germany, America or Australia (they usually had). I just thought: "Fair Greece! Sad relic..." and was relieved when he dropped me off on the corner of Sophocles Street. As I walked my spirits lifted a little. Nikitas had loved this area, where old Athens meets new; the town hall and the central fish and meat market, Pakistani cafés, Chinese clothes emporia, old men wheeling barrows piled high with cheap socks, bankers and businessmen striding along barking into mobile phones, East and West, forgetting and remembering. The streets are named after the ancients: Sophocles, Socrates, Euripides, Sappho, though they are now filled with groups of immigrants, cheap prostitutes and home-grown junkies. You don't really want to walk there at night any more, Nikitas advised.

Nikitas' office was in a modest version of the many arcades that snake under and between buildings in this part of town, each with a different character. The shops in this one looked too modest to stay in business, yet had remained there for years: the sign-engraver, with its dusty selection of bronze name plates and stick-on symbols for public toilet doors; the translation and photocopy office; the coin and stamp collectors' shop; the tiny key-cutting business, with its basil pot outside the door. I moved slowly, remembering how often I had come over here in the early years of our marriage. I usually met Nikitas down the road at *Diporto*, his favourite taverna – a smoky hole down some steep steps, with whitewashed walls, bare light bulbs hanging from the ceiling and a row of massive wooden barrels filled with pine-scented retsina. Fellow diners were mostly market workers who were offered a few simple dishes cooked in the corner – chickpea soup, salads with cracked olives and small fried fish; there was no menu. Nikitas talked to me about the significance of the classic Athenian basement taverna and how it represents the subconscious, the Dionysian celebrations of wine, food, music and open conversation, far from the constraints of work, family and logic.

"So long as the women are back home doing the real work," I'd snipe amiably.

"Maybe, but it's like Dostoevsky's *Notes from the Underground*, a dark place where emotions replace reason, where outsiders are welcome, where the normal rules are let go. It's where a simple, working man can feel moved to dance and is transformed into a god during that time. Nobody can stop him. To a people who have so often lost everything, this is important."

After lunch we would wander back to the arcade (a cool retreat from the baking afternoon streets), up the stairs and along to the end of the first floor walkway that overlooked the internal courtyard. Nikitas' office was dark and peaceful, despite its uncompromising mess of newspapers, ashtrays and unwashed coffee cups. He would draw the ugly orange curtains, inherited from the previous occupant, and undress me. We lay on the wooden-framed daybed, with its rough, village blanket. Nobody would disturb us.

I hesitated after fitting the key into the lock. I had never been inside alone before and even though Nikitas was gone, I did not want to spy. I often caught glimpses of his former life when I went there: the lengthy Before-Me era as opposed to the shorter With-Me one, was how I thought of it. Whatever our marriage was, I never doubted that I was loved. Nikitas retained an almost old-fashioned gallantry with me, complimenting me on my appearance, helping me negotiate the day-to-day problems of Athenian existence, buying me little presents from the stores selling hardware or herbs on Athenas Street. I was never ignored, but neither did I feel that these attentions were exclusive to me. He was interested in so many people and there had been so much experience before he met me. The two former wives revealed their presence in photographs, letters and small objects whose history I would never know. Sometimes I referred to myself as "Number Three", hoping to make Nikitas laugh. But it also made me realise how I was just one among all the other people who came and went through his life, leaving deposits, like water dropping silt along a river bank. It was all welcome to him. The more people you knew, the richer your life would be. But the longer we were together, the more I was aware of how little I knew of Nikitas' origins – the lake or spring at the source.

The air was musty, like coffee dregs growing mould. I went over to the daybed, gripping the worn wooden end, keeping steady, noticing the dent in the cushion that must have been left by Nikitas' head the last time he lay there. I sat for a moment, taking in the manly smells of wood and books, then opened the curtains, turned on the overhead light and went to the desk. It was swamped with papers that already looked old, as though the place had been abandoned long ago. The laptop was closed and dusty. Standing on top of it was a glass and an almost empty bottle of Cutty Sark whisky. There were several Greek books about the Civil War – thick paperbacks with grainy photographs of men with untamed beards and weapons slung across their backs. The dense texts were littered with acronyms like codes that might give answers: EAM, ELAS, KKE, EDES, EPON, OPLA, SOE, X…

Nikitas had been researching for a book about the relationship between the British and the Greeks through history, with a particular focus on the Civil War and its aftermath. He had been gathering material for ages, and had taken on an assistant who worked at the paper. I hadn't met her, but I knew that someone called Danae was helping stoke his anger about the contradictions that lay behind the famous British philhellenism and the country's involvement in Greece. He didn't have a title yet, but my nickname for his book was *Perfidious Albion*. He was annoyed that the British remained so ignorant about the Greek Civil War that they helped provoke.

"Even English school children know about the bombardment of Guernica and the horrors of the Spanish Civil War," he complained. "But nobody in England learns about the massacres of civilians in Greece a decade later. Sadly, we didn't get Picasso painting the English aerial attacks in Athens, or Orwell and Hemingway telling our story."

"Philhellenism, my arse," Nikitas liked to say. "In reality, the English have been just as much anti-Hellenes or mis-Hellenes. Even Shelley's old favourite, 'We are all Greeks', was a way of saying the English are better at being Greek than us. The English used Greece for their own fantasies and adventures, but trampled all over it when it suited. All Greeks know about Byron, the hero-poet who supported the Greek revolution. And maybe he did, but if it hadn't been in their interests, the English would never have backed us against the Turks in 1821. And then they spent the next 100 years trying to foist atrocious foreign kings on us. Oh, and don't forget the Ionian Isles were little English colonies for quite a time – they still play fucking cricket on Corfu."

I could almost hear Nikitas' voice as I tried to bring some order to the surface of the desk and heaped all the books together on a shelf, and made piles out of different papers. I find this occupation as soothing as other people find needle-point or knitting, and it is fitting that I have managed to place archives at the heart of my work. It was something my grand-father Desmond had taught me from a young age, when he got me to help organise his study. We would spend hours arranging the books alphabetically, sorting through index cards, tidying files and cleaning out drawers. Later, I brought this system to my own work, aware of how it made the world look better, bringing order to the chaos, just as it had given boundaries to my childhood, which so often seemed treacherously unstable.

One pile of folders was spread across a table and I found them filled with photocopies and pages of notes in unfamiliar handwriting I presumed was Danae's. There was a small, black lipstick lying close by. I opened it, twisting up the plum-coloured, pointed tip and examining the unwelcomely inti-mate object. It made me aware of how much I didn't know of Nikitas' life, of how I may have been loved, but I was also shut out. There was so much he chose to share with other people rather than me. I remembered overhearing Nikitas speaking with Danae on the phone not long before, and he was whipping himself up into a satisfying rant about his bête noir.

"The thing about the English," (Nikitas, like most Greeks, didn't say "the British") "is that what they like about themselves is all that crap about fair play, cricket, decency, moderation, and yet their whole history has been about oppressing other people with slavery, colonialism, and war. We are supposed to be taken in by their upright, perfect manners and their cups of tea, and we are all meant to love them as if they really were *tzéntlmen* and *milórdi*. But in fact they're the number one drunken hooligans – they invented football violence. And if you look at problem tourists in Greece, it's always them. Who else would create pub-crawls and open-air blow-job competitions in Greek tourist resorts? Not to mention their huge success with serial murderers back home. Have you ever wondered why we never had a Greek Jack the Ripper?"

I remember waiting in the room while he listened to Danae's answer, wondering what she was saying, until he shouted, "Exactly! Wherever you look in the world and pick a troubled place with civil war or terrorism, you'll often find the English had something to do with it. India and Pakistan, Israel and Palestine, Northern Ireland – and that's before we even look at Africa."

I picked up the whisky bottle from the desk and took a sip. It made me shudder, but then warmed my stomach and helped my breath go back to normal. I knew I shouldn't fill my mind with petty complaints at this point – Nikitas' obsessions and varied friendships were part of who he was. But I couldn't help feeling hurt. Why had he needed to keep these things from me? It was as if his death was the culmination of a collection of secrets, and possibly betrayals. I had never clung to him or nagged to know the details of his life, but I had always assumed I was honoured with the truth. Now I was beginning to wonder.

I sat down in the chair and began flicking through a pad of lined notepaper filled with jottings in Nikitas' handwriting. The uppermost page had only one word written in large capital letters: ΣΦΗΚΑ (*Sfíka* – WASP). It had been underlined several times, but meant nothing to me. On the other side of the desk was a large manila envelope marked with the initials J.F. Its bulging contents were held in by a thick rubber band, which I removed. I pulled out several letters, all addressed to Antigone Perifanis, Nikitas' mother. He had not told me anything about this material and I wondered where it could have come from.

As far as I could see, the letters were all sent from England by someone called John Fell, whose sharp, italic script scratched across the pages in black ink. I opened the first one, dated September, 1938. It was written on fragile, pale blue paper from Wadham College, Oxford and signed Johnny.

My dear Antigone,
Your letter was waiting for me when I got home and made me miss you and your family awfully. So much so, in fact, that I wanted to go straight back to Greece. England is as soggy and bland as the puddings they serve in college. I yearn for the intense colours and scents of the Mediterranean.

The tone was jovial and friendly. The writer recommended several English poets, including a number from the "Great War". I flicked through the envelopes, some of which were dated 1946 and later, and mainly sent from England. Several were addressed to Antigone at Averoff Prison and were stamped by the Greek censor. I opened them. The man evidently cared for Antigone, but despite the endearments, I could not gauge their relationship. It was not clear whether this was a lover. And if not, who was he? There were many practical details: "Shall I send more of the soap?" "Were the pencils the right ones?" But there were times when he became more thoughtful.

I arrived in Greece with clear ideas of right and wrong, of what we were fighting for. Now these absolutes have all faded into muted shades of grey. I feel much older, though not any wiser. It is unclear to me what history will make of this war and the world it has left in its wake.

I decided to read one more letter before stopping. It was dated 1947.

Since receiving your letter I have been choked with anger and frustration. It is utterly appalling about the Wasp. Why did you not tell me about this before? An impossible situation. Bloody.

I tried scanning some more pages to find another reference to Wasp, but with no luck. I replaced everything inside the envelope and put it in my bag.

Nikitas' office was almost as messy when I left as when I arrived, but my mind had come alive. The curiosity aroused by these letters dispersed some of the pain that was engulfing me. I was intrigued by the sense of Nikitas' mother as a young woman, and longed to know more of her life. As I walked along Panepistimiou (University Avenue), I started to make a plan. It was as if I had been offered some sort of way through the horrible chaos of mourning. By the time I passed the Parliament building, I had decided that I would do my own research into Nikitas' history. This would give me some answers, but it could also be my memorial to my husband. With luck, it might even provide an explanation for my daughter. Tig would need to know at some point; it was her history too.

I turned off Amalia Avenue, with its traffic fumes, tram terminus and peanut barrows, and walked into the muffled green of the National Garden. Formerly the Royal Garden, the park was planted by Greece's first Queen, Amalia, in the 1830s and its rows of spindly palms look as though they date back to then. Signs warn of the danger of things falling from the ageing trees. Old men and tired migrants sat slumped on benches and a couple of late-season tourists in shorts trudged by, looking like incongruous birds left behind after the flock migrated. I slowed down, thinking I would have to speak with Antigone. She was the only person who could help me under-stand more about Nikitas' origins. Now that I was no longer able to speak with Nikitas or ask him questions, it would be a kind of communication. I would try to find his answers as well as my own.

When I got home I wrote a short letter on the off-chance that John Fell was still alive and still lived at the address given on some of the letters from the 1940s: Corner House, Claywell, Sussex. There seemed little more chance of it reaching its target

and lemon for me and took the bus to the cemetery twice to search for Misha. She also made three trips to her brother to take him food and clean his apartment. Dora is better than a saint because she is noisy and still shouts with a voice too big for her tiny frame and tells terrible jokes even after all these years.

I wanted to call Mod (I must check my daughter-in-law's name) to talk to somebody about Nikitas, but I was paralysed. I kept thinking about the one time I saw my son as an adult – something I never told anyone about. Another burden of guilt. It happened over twenty years ago, in the 1980s, so I suppose he was about forty. He had written. He said he was travelling to Moscow for work and would like to see me. I replied, giving a time to meet outside the hotel where he was staying – the Rossiya. When the day arrived I set off from home and I don't think I have ever been so afraid – not even in the war. I can admit that now. I walked down through Red Square and from some way off, I saw him. I suppose I would not have recognised him but for a photo in a newspaper that Dora had sent me. He was smoking and stamping his feet in the snow, his breath puffing out plumes of tobacco into the freezing air. He wore a fur hat with earflaps hanging down. I cannot explain why I hid behind a parked car. There are no good excuses. I just stayed there for some time, taking sidelong looks so he wouldn't notice me, knowing that there was nothing I could do to make up for so many decades. Yet I wanted to watch my son, to take in every detail. I knew it was too late to become a mother. After about an hour, my jaw was shuddering and my feet numb despite the lined boots I wore. I watched as he looked around him and into the distance for a last time and walked through the revolving doors into the hotel. I waited a moment before turning to go, aware that there was still the opportunity to change this story. When I arrived home, I didn't tell Igor about Nikitas' letter or about what happened. I wondered whether my son might turn up at our apartment, as he knew the address, but he obviously decided against it. Who would want a mother who let you down all over again? That night in bed, I heard my mother's voice: "Antigone, you deserve your fate. You have brought all this on yourself." And it's true.

> Son, my flesh and blood. marrow of my bones, heart of my own heart, sparrow of my tiny courtyard, flower of my loneliness.

Yiannis Ritsos wrote that. A comrade during the war, he also knew about being locked up for your beliefs.

* * *

When I eventually called Mod she sounded pleased.

"Antigone!" She called me by my name and used the intimate form of address as though I were a friend or relation. She said, "I've been trying to ring you. Where have you been?" I could tell she was surprised I was in Athens, which was strangely gratifying, as though I was part of her life. I told her about Dora and her house in Patissia and how I had been unwell. She said, "I would really like to see you. I would like to talk." She invited me to go to Paradise Street, but I suggested we meet in a café. I was not yet ready to face all the ghosts, let alone my sister. I said, "Somewhere simple. Somewhere I can find easily," and she suggested a little place on Anapafseos. I remembered it as a shady, sloping road full of marble monument workers, whose name made you picture the peaceful rest that could be found at its summit in the First Cemetery. And when I arrived, that was what it still was, though motorbikes streaked up and down more than in my day.

I arrived early at Cafe 13 and a woman who must have been as old as me, gestured at a dozen empty tables from which I could take my pick. Mod had said that the place was quiet. I sat towards the back of a room that reeked of bleach and contained only two elderly men, who gawked at me as though I were an intruder. I stared back at them, not intimidated. Mod arrived exactly on time and my impression was of a slim body and a cloud of curling, almost red hair – the woman I had seen at the funeral. Her face was gaunt – you could tell she was grieving – but her eyes were beady with curiosity as she approached. I stood up and offered my hand but she moved in close and kissed me, holding onto my hand and examining me. She appeared to be looking for some kind of answer. She said, "You have Nikitas' eyes, but I can also see my daughter's mouth and chin. We named her after you, but I call her Tig." I was never one for small talk so I liked her directness, though it was quite overwhelming being turned into the matriarch of a family I didn't know. We both sat down and I offered her a cigarette, which she refused. I lit one myself, taking my time so as to pull myself together, drawing the blessed smoke in deep.

My daughter-in-law said she wanted to find out more about my son. She would like to talk to me and write some things down.

"Research," she said.

I said, "Perhaps I'm not the best person to help you. After all, I last knew Nikitas when he was three."

I could see the thought pass across her face: "Aah, a difficult old woman." And perhaps I am, but I had nothing to prove. Why should I open myself up to a stranger in this way? She said, "But you could tell me about yourself and explain what happened, why you left him. I need to understand more. You could do it for my daughter – your grand-daughter."

I did not answer, but sipped my coffee, pondering. Then I asked her how her name was spelled, which made her laugh and her whole face altered and became quite beautiful and lively. I saw for the first time what my son might have seen in this woman.

Mod tried a new approach. She said, "I wanted to ask you about John Fell. Who was he?"

"A family friend. Dead and gone, I should imagine." I wanted to say: "What's it to you, my girl?" What did she want, my curious daughter-in-law, with her insistent ways? What kind of interrogation was this? She told me she had found a letter to me from England and looked at me closely as I answered. I turned the questioning back and asked her what the letter had said. And where did she find it? Mod paused, as though we were talking about her private correspondence, not mine. Then she said, "It was from before the war – you must have been a schoolgirl. And it was sent from Oxford." Mod had that terrier-like tendency I've seen in other English people, including Johnny. Once they've picked up a bone they won't drop it. That's their strength and their weakness; they didn't hold onto their colonies all that time without having strong teeth and a belief that whatever anyone else says, the bone is theirs.

I told her briefly that Johnny had been a student of classics before the war, and that he came to Greece two years running to study inscriptions on the tombs in Keramikos. He taught English to me and my siblings. Then, to my surprise, Mod suggested we visit Nikitas' grave and we left the café as a group of mourners were pushing through the door like a herd of sheep. At the entrance to the First Cemetery, she bought two bunches of anemones from a flower stall and gave me one. The earth over the grave was still raw and there was no stone yet, but we sat for a few minutes on a wall, looking at the scene. She spoke very softly, not looking at me.

"I loved him, your son." I could not come up with the right answer ("I'm pleased", "so did I", "what difference does that make?") and remained silent. I was never one for the quick retort or the easy chat – I've left that to others, like Natalya or Dora. My answers come to me later, when I'm alone.

As we walked back in silence along the paths, I spotted a cat hiding under a shrub. I bent down, saying Misha's name, trying to coax him out with Russian endearments.

"Ksssss, ksssss," I called. I saw Mod looking at me as though I was mad but she said nothing.

"Ksssss, ksssss. Mishinka, come here." Eventually a skinny tabby bearing no resemblance to Misha got up and slunk off and I couldn't face explaining the whole story. Mod's expression revealed how disturbing she found my behaviour, but I didn't mind. I have nothing to prove. Still, when she kissed me goodbye and helped me into a taxi, she appeared disappointed. And who can blame her? I have made a habit of letting people down.

It took almost an hour to get back to Patissia, as the centre had been blocked off for a demonstration. We got stuck in traffic and, crawling along, I had plentiful opportunity to reflect on my mistakes. Why was I keeping my distance from the English girl? What was my problem with talking about the past? I would soon be gone anyway, so why not tell some stories? Now that I had my very own family I should make the most of them – I had to admit I was curious to meet my grandchildren, my own flesh and blood.

Several Somali children were playing on Dora's front steps when I arrived and they laughed at me as I made my way into the hall. The lift eventually arrived with one of the Ukrainian women carrying a shopping bag and I greeted her in Russian. She answered dully, as though everyone spoke Russian in Athens. Dora was out and I sat at her kitchen table with a new pad of lined paper. In front of me I placed a lock of hair, a button and a photograph. They would help bring the memories. I didn't feel like speaking to anyone about my past – perhaps my silence has been kept too long to break it – but I decided to write down my own version of events. Perhaps my granddaughter will read it one day. I will start at the beginning, as one should.

❋ ❋ ❋

My childhood

When I was a child, my parents appeared like demi-gods. They towered above us and their past was our family mythology.

I would ask them over and over to tell me their stories– so different from one another. My father, Petros, was born in 1897, in Perivoli, a village near Lamia, right in the middle of Greece. His father had been a tailor, but died when Petros was four and his mother took her only son to Athens. They rented a room in Kalithea and the young widow set up as a seamstress. Petros left school at twelve but he was ambitious and helped his mother expand her business. They brought in one employee, then another and Petros got hold of fashion magazines so they could copy the latest ideas from France. They moved to a larger workshop, eventually acquiring an atelier in Psyrri, where smart Athenian ladies came to be measured up and to choose fabrics and patterns. My father was too young to fight in the Balkan Wars and managed to avoid being called up during the First World War. Instead, he continued his own battle to make Perifanis a name in the city. By 1920, he had succeeded. He was rich enough to buy a car and a house where they had a cook and a maid. By this time, my paternal grandmother was dressing in silks and furs, and helped oversee a workforce of eight seamstresses.

The story of how my parents met was my favourite part of the legend. I heard it countless times and still recall how my father described his first sight of my mother. In October 1922, when Petros was 25, a beautiful young woman walked into the atelier. She asked, in educated Greek, whether he needed a secretary, adding that she had plenty of experience. Petros did not know she was lying, and that Maria had only arrived in Greece the previous month. He too lied – that he had just been about to advertise for someone to help with the accounts. Petros already knew what he wanted.

My mother was among the first wave of refugees from Smyrna. For us children, there was a sort of glamour in the enormity of the disaster. We heard about mythological scenes of destruction: the city flaming in the night sky, rampaging Turkish soldiers spearing babies on bayonets, bodies floating in the water. It was as though their screams reverberated through our childhood. For my mother, however, "Catastrophe" was a word that followed her around like an ugly dog. With a combination of luck and determination, she managed to get onto a crowded boat in Smyrna's harbour with her mother and younger brother. Her father had been taken away – like many thousands of adult male Greeks, he just disappeared.

They arrived in Athens with a few bundles and no money, joining a deluge of uprooted people with nowhere to go. Some were given tents on the empty slopes of Hymettus, others camped by the Hephaestus Temple at Thisio. Maria and her family were taken to the Municipal Theatre in Kotzia Square, where each family was allowed to occupy a box, rigging up blankets for a little privacy. It was a beautiful place – designed by the famous German architect, Ziller – but that was little comfort to its devastated occupants. Maria's mother, Sylvia, cried all day. And my grandmother was not even Greek, so she did not have the debatable satisfaction of arriving in her fatherland. She had been born into an English family in Smyrna. They had lived in a villa and owned a business exporting dried fruits. Her parents had warned her about marrying a Greek and she had never even learned his language properly – everyone she conversed with in Smyrna knew French, English and Turkish as a matter of course. Then in 1922, on account of her Greek surname, she had been sent away from the only country she ever knew. When I was young my grandmother still lamented those painful times. She'd say, 'We were like beggars. We had lost everything and knew nobody'."

Naturally they were not alone in their troubles. Within a year there were over a million Asia Minor refugees. They were classified as "Greeks" because they were Christians and sent "home" to a country they had never seen. Many didn't even speak Greek. They were just numbers, little people, pawns for political ambitions and international treaties. As usual it was down to the whims of the Great Powers – the British (of course), the French, the Americans. One day they told the Greek army to invade Turkey, saying they'd be there to help, the next they had disappeared. The foundations of a tragedy were set.

My mother and her young brother, Diamantis, had been brought up in the kind of sophisticated, cosmopolitan milieu that did not exist in Greece. Life was as gay and cultured as in Paris, they said, but with a better climate. As a girl, Maria had attended the *Kentrikon Parthenogogeion* [Greek Girls' School], had taken lessons in dance, piano, botany and drawing with private tutors, and had gone to the latest charity concerts. She was a keen amateur actress and singer and belonged to an acting society, so when they set up home in an Athenian theatre she was young enough, at twenty, to be amused. During her explorations backstage, Maria came across some costumes and extracted a suit. She still had it in her wardrobe when I was a child – a reminder, she said. It was made of grey striped wool and had a matching hat. My father liked describing it in later years, as absurdly out of fashion, but, with its close-fitted cut, deeply flattering.

Realising that she was the only person who could do something to help her family in its dire situation, Maria decided to find work. This was something she knew nothing about, but she pinned a flower to the actress's suit, cleaned her boots and set off to an address in Psyrri. Inside her bag was an advertisement from a magazine that someone had left on one of the seats in the theatre. The half-page spread had a picture of an elegant woman and proclaimed that Perifanis [a name related to the word for pride] was the only place for a lady to go to be proudly well-dressed. *Perifanis: yia perifano styl.*

My father fell immediately and deeply in love, and although he was not educated as she was, I can see why my mother was attracted to him. He was confident and full of energy. And he was a good man. He took her for a drive in his motorcar and she lost her hat when it flew off. They had lunch in Faliro at a restaurant overlooking the sea – it became a family favourite and we always heard about their first meal there with the best, most orange red mullet that had ever swum in the sea. Within a month they had married. The wedding photographs showed Maria holding orange blossom and lace, and Petros so proud by her side. Next to them were the two widowed mothers. I remember them as life-long friends, despite their different backgrounds. Each recognised the other's suffering.

My father instructed an architect and by the time Maria gave birth to their first child in the winter of 1923, the new house in Paradise Street was ready. Alexandra was the first, blonde and blue eyed, followed a year later by me and finally by Markos. We sang English nursery rhymes with our Smyrna grandmother (who lived up in Kaisariani with our Uncle Diamantis) and heard village tales of evil spirits and mountain brigands from the other.

When we were young my father was determined to give us everything he lacked as a child. We were proof of how far he had come. He loved that my mother wanted Alexandra and me to be proper bourgeois young ladies, with music lessons and dancing and French. In the evenings my mother used to light the candles on the piano – an upright Imperial – and she'd sing Italian songs she learned as a girl with her teacher, Signor Robini. We all thought she was the most beautiful woman in the world.

My father had our clothes made up by his seamstresses – white sailor suits in summer and blue in the winter. And he made sure that the table was overflowing. In those days if you had meat twice a week you were a *pashá*, and we always did, although my mother used to tease my father because he still loved the plain Greek cooking of his childhood, especially *bobóta* [maize porridge], which he insisted must still find a place on the table. My mother thought it was tasteless "peasant food", but she loved him and went along with his wishes.

"*My Bobóta* ," she used to call him, and he didn't mind. He'd call her his Smyrnian girl.

On Saturdays, my father went to the patisserie and bought a huge basket of chocolates and sweets that would sit on the hall table all week and we could take whatever we liked. On Sundays we went to church down the road at Agia Photini, where the Judas trees flowered bright pink in the spring. I was afraid of the pigeons that gathered to peck at crumbs from the sweet holy bread that was often handed out. The birds fluttering sent me into a panic, made worse by people's laughter. Perhaps I was allowed to be too sensitive, but I was also always the rebel, the middle child caught between Alexandra's haughty ways and Markos, the baby. I was much closer to my brother – we were almost like twins. Neighbours called us the little gypsies, for our dark complexions and also for our wild streak. While Alexandra used to sit and listen to the grown-ups or read a book, Markos and I would play in the street and climb trees on Ardittos hill. We rubbed dirt on our faces, put leaves in our hair and picked the gluey scabs of resin off the pine trees, coming home like "wild creatures". But nobody was really angry. We were just taken out to the washroom and bathed, then given clean clothes and a bowl of warm *trachanás* porridge.

Markos and I both wanted adventure. Sometimes we would follow the Ice Man after he left the daily lump for the ice box on our front door step. He had a large, beaked nose and smelled of sweat. But we liked him for the frightening stories he told us in a hoarse voice. From him we heard of murders and missing children and he handed out small pieces of ice for us to suck. Or we would visit Kyrios Yiorgos at the bakery, hoping for a piece of steaming bread fresh from the oven or a misshapen sesame ring. Everyone liked Markos for his wide-open dark-brown eyes and easy smile that got us out of trouble so many times. He never lost that shimmer of innocence, whereas people assumed that I was leading him into trouble.

When we were quite young, my paternal grandmother

gave me and my siblings three small icons. She had bought them on a trip to Tinos, at the shrine to the All-Holy Virgin, after climbing the steps to the church on her knees. "Till they bled," she said. "Nothing without sacrifice." We children obediently kissed the silver-plated haloes of the *Panayia* and *Christouli*, curled asleep in her arms. We said our prayers as instructed and placed the wooden icons under our pillows to protect us from harm. I liked the solid outline of mother and babe jutting into the soft pillow. I suppose I always appreciated the absence of doubt.

Later, Uncle Diamantis began to talk to me about injustice. He taught me about workers' rights and hungry children, about capitalism's inevitable demise, and I swapped the icon for a copy of *Rizospastis*, the communist paper that I bought in secret. It cost one drachma. It was made illegal under Metaxas, at the time when the dictator began rounding up the communists. But it only went under-ground. Diamantis took me to the shacks and shanty towns where it was still available. Most of his friends were people like him, who had come over in 1922 as young refugees. They had moved from tents into huts and gradually into small, mud-bricked houses on dirt roads. There were whole new neighbourhoods like New Smyrna and New Philadelphia. These places were chaotic and the people were shockingly poor, but the houses I visited with my uncle were always clean and well kept. Naturally, most did not have bathrooms or what we would now see as minimal necessities, but they turned them into homes. Oil cans with basil and geraniums made miniature gardens, and fences and walls were whitewashed each year in time for Easter. The older generation clung to dreams of going back, or politicians' empty promises of compensation, but the younger ones saw there was no return. They knew it was up to them to fight for their future.

Diamantis and several of his comrades were sent to prison during Metaxas' petty fascist regime for being communists (the law against "communists and subversives" had been in place since the '20s). But I went on buying *Rizospastis* on the quiet – my parents would have been horrified. I was a youthful but committed convert, and when Diamantis was released he fed my faith with certainties. He showed me suffering that was so obviously wrong that it was impossible not to adopt his belief in an earthly, socialist paradise. Diamantis often took me out "for ice-cream" and we'd attend meetings with his union friends from the Papastratos cigarette factory where many of them worked. They were hardened by relentless work, strikes, arrests and imprisonment, and they laughed at my pretty dresses and teased me for my "bourgeois manners". Still, they welcomed me to the basement off Piraeus Street where they met and made their leaflets on a rusting printing press. Diamantis wanted me to learn. He showed me his worn copy of *Das Kapital* and a small bust of Lenin, kept in his bedroom. And he sang with his guitar – romances from Asia Minor and stirring socialist anthems, including a few in Russian. It was from him that I learned the *Internationale*:

So comrades, come rally,
And the last fight let us face.
The Internationale,
Unites the human race.

When he took me home, Diamantis often made ironic comments: "Run off now, back to Paradise."

I knew better than to tell the family about what went on during my outings. Neither of my parents was interested in politics, though my mother, like many Asia Minor refugees, had been a keen supporter of Venizelos. She still viewed the old liberal statesman as the greatest hope Greece ever had. My father put his business first, preferring to stay on good terms with everyone ("They're all the same, just looking to line their pockets like everyone else"). As for Alexandra, her alliances were with the adults and, as first-born, she took her responsibilities extremely seriously. She was determined to keep me and Markos under control and was as aloof and certain of her authority as an officer with his troops. If she found us younger ones up to no good, she would report us without hesitation. Once, Despina, our maid, found my stash of *Rizospastis*. But I swore her to secrecy. It helped that she knew I'd seen her kissing the baker's son in the alleyway.

❋   ❋   ❋

Johnny Fell. Strange that Mod wants to know about him. I wonder about that letter and about what happened to the rest of them. I look at my picture of Johnny – one of the few things that made the journey into exile. It sat for decades in one of Igor's old school files that I used for my papers. The photograph is a shiny black and white one, with scalloped edges and "Ilissos, 1938" written in pencil on the back. He is tall and slim, with shirt sleeves rolled up. His hair is neatly parted. Behind him is a wall of massive stone and he is smiling at the photographer

– me. I loved him. But then we all loved him. He was only about twenty when we met him in 1937, but to a thirteen-year-old he seemed quite old. My mother thought him the perfect English gentleman, like the ones she'd known in Smyrna. I think my father appreciated that Johnny was masculine without being competitive – he learned demotic Greek and drank retsina with the workmen at the archaeological digs. What started as a social friendship quickly became something more like family, and after my parents asked him to give us some English conversation lessons, he moved into the house for several months over the summer and again the next year.

Johnny brought out the best in all of us; we felt brighter under his gaze. We often had lessons outside, walking over to Hadrian's Arch, or up to the top of Philopappos hill. We'd sit under a tree and listen to him talk. I liked the way he pronounced my name in the English way: "Antígony", with the stress on the second syllable, as opposed to the Greek "Antigóny", which emphasized the penultimate one. It made me special, to be someone else in English, unlike Alexandra, who was the same whichever language you said it in. Johnny got us to learn English poems by heart. I wanted to be the best, his favourite. I loved reciting Byron – "*Where'er we tread 'tis haunted, holy ground.*" I sensed the romance of Greece through Johnny's eyes, the lure of a pure, ancient world. We learned quotes from Milton:

Athens, the eye of Greece, mother of arts
And eloquence.

I still remember so much. When you're young, it sticks.

Johnny taught me the word "philhellene" and I felt lucky to be a Hellene, lucky to have been born in this special place. We Greeks were able to appreciate ourselves more because we saw our past reflected in foreigners' admiring eyes. I believed that the English were philhellenes. That's partly why it was so hard when they turned against us. In the end they wanted to dominate us like everyone else.

When Johnny returned the following year in 1938, I had changed. I was taller, my breasts had grown – I had become a young lady. And I was in love with him. I had absurd dreams that I would go to England, that I would marry him. Of course I was still a child. I knew nothing. But there was something that passed between us. Or so it seemed to me. I kept the memory close and secret. I called it by the code name "Ilissos", after the day we sat by what remained of the ancient river.

It was early September, some days before Johnny was due to leave for England and I had not yet started school. I persuaded him to come on a picnic with me, knowing that Alexandra was visiting a friend and conveniently forgetting about Markos. Naturally, I would not have been allowed out with a boy on my own, but because Johnny counted as a teacher, somehow nobody noticed. It was the first time I had walked on the street with a man and I felt both proud and afraid. After all, at school there was even a special children's supervisor, whose job it was to prevent the sexes mixing, tracking pupils if they went over to the park, checking their identities. This was one of the charming details of the petty fascist state that Metaxas was trying to impose on the country. Another was the weekly session of "national education" at the National Youth Organisation – personal hygiene and sanitising toilets. That's what they thought was important. It was all uniforms, badges, documents with numbers. Even our black school pinafores had the school number on it, to help the snitches that backed up the regime.

The unforgiving heat of August had given way to September storms, but the day we went down to the Ilissos was warm with a sea breeze blowing up from the Saronic Gulf. The ancient river was Johnny's idea.

"A fair resting place, full of summer sounds and scents," he said, quoting Plato. "This is what Greece gives – we can sit in the same place that Socrates went with his pupils. We can hear the same cicadas he did." The ancients thought that cicadas were given the gift of song from the Muses, he said. They appreciated their music so much that they would catch them and weave little cages out of grasses and asphodels in which to keep them.

It is true that in springtime the area around the Ilissos was lush and green, if unkempt. I remember seeing irises, dragon-flies and, once, the turquoise flash of a kingfisher. But it was never the verdant bank described by Plato and dreamed of by Johnny. By summer, the river was a smelly trickle of mud, the grass was like desiccated straw – it was hardly "a fair resting place" for even the most forgiving person. However, I realised that we needed to match untidy reality to a fantasy – Johnny wanted the place to fit his image of nature in ancient Athens. So, we persuaded ourselves that we were in the most charming place, rather as Athenians like to think they are direct descendants of the philosophers and sculptors who walked these places in the distant past.

We went a little way up from the Ilissos near the gigantic

Roman walls that enclose the Temple of Olympian Zeus. There were olives, cypresses and figs as well as wild undergrowth and we stopped by a plane tree, whose branches grew broad and low. I spread a rug on the ground and laid the picnic out: courgette pie baked by Aspasia that morning, bread, fresh curd cheese, peaches and lemonade. I watched Johnny as he lay in the shade after we had eaten. His eyes were closed, topped by eyebrows bleached blonde by the summer sun that had also burnt his face brown. He looked content. I lay down too, pretending to sleep, but looking at him between my eyelashes. The hard, warm ground below me seemed to be the centre of the universe, and I thought I could feel the planet spinning. I edged my arm closer to Johnny, not quite touching, but tingling, almost aching from sensations I did not comprehend. A romantic ballad of the times went round in my head – "Take me, take me", though it did not speak to me of physical love but of going away with Johnny, of going to England. I pictured him in a study, surrounded by books and shards engraved with mysterious sayings. And me by his side. Neither of us said anything, but I saw him look at me and I knew he cared. That was enough. After that, the word Ilissos became my secret reference to pure happiness. Nothing was ever so simple again.

The evening before Johnny left, my parents organised a farewell dinner. Aspasia, our cook, prepared the food all day, creating the Asia Minor delicacies that she, like my mother, had grown up with. Both women knew that some of our neighbours referred to them as Turks and commented on the spicy cooking smells emerging from the kitchen. But neither cared. In fact I think that my mother liked to provoke them.

She encouraged Aspasia to add more cumin, more garlic.

"If they call us 'baptised-in-yogurt', then throw the yogurt in! And make sure you add plenty of spearmint to the *keftedákia*." She was convinced that the smell of these little fried meatballs was guaranteed to drive the neighbours mad with longing. I remember the menu that evening: giant tomatoes stuffed with rice, raisins and parsley; blackened, smoky aubergines on the grill; lamb fricassée, fava bean purée with capers. The memories of these tastes are like ghosts.

The best dinner service and linen was laid, and my father made a small speech to our dear friend *Yiannis*, as they usually called him. My mother wore her diamond earrings from Constantinople and they sparkled in the candlelight. Johnny said he would return the following summer to the best people he had ever met. Afterwards, I sat up all night looking out of my bedroom window at the night sky, imagining England.

9

The unspeakable name

MAUD

When I told Tig and Orestes that I had met Antigone, they were only mildly interested.

"Did she explain why she never came back to see *Babas*?" Tig was sitting in the kitchen, eating pieces of bread dripping with honey and carefully avoiding the crusts, which she placed around the edge of the plate. Her fingernails were bitten short and streaked black with the remnants of varnish.

"She wasn't allowed to come back by the arsehole fascists who ran this country," said Orestes, using the tone of an irritable teacher with an indolent pupil. He was standing slumped against the open doorway that led to the spiral stairs, one arm stretched up the door frame with almost balletic grace.

"She didn't really explain why, but we did talk about *Babas*," I said, replying to Tig's question. "You could tell that she is his mother – she looks like him. And she is very stubborn. But interesting. Unusual. Would you like to meet her?"

"*Eh*," said Tig, using the non-committal Greek sound that leaves everything hanging.

"*Eh*," echoed Orestes. "If she wants to meet us. But I don't know what the point is. You can't just show up after sixty years and expect a ready-made family. It's not McDonald's: two grandchildren with French fries and a Coca-Cola please."

Tig looked exhausted and smelled of cigarettes and stale clothing. She had spent the night "on guard" at her school, which was under student occupation for the second time in the two years since she had moved there. The change from her private school in the smart suburb of Psychiko to the local one near home had involved much more than just meeting a wider social and ethnic group of children; she had discovered the delights of dissent. The move had occurred after both Tig and Orestes harangued Nikitas about his hypocrisy in claiming to be left-wing yet educating his offspring privately.

"Even the hard-line communist politicians in Greece send their kids to private schools," said Orestes. "None of you have any principles – it's all just theory."

It didn't take much to make Nikitas flip.

"OK, go to the state school," he said to Tig. "Why not? I was educated there and turned out fine." I raised no objections and the following September, Tig stopped taking the school bus up to Psychiko and began walking through the neighbourhood to Athens' Thirteenth Secondary School.

Although Orestes had only ever attended private schools, he advised Tig about how to make a success of the occupation and was well versed in the language of protest. I imagined that he was behind the school children's most provocative slogans, though some were more charming than angry. I particularly liked, *Walls have Ears and Ears have Walls*. Banners were painted and hung from the windows, classrooms were smashed and adults were forbidden to enter the grounds. A milder version of the repeated student occupations that paralysed universities throughout the year, they were a peculiarly Greek hybrid, combining the pleasure of a rave, the anger of a protest march and the satisfaction of a riot. I had given up asking why; the children's "demands" were normally a pretext – a "lack of facilities" or "lack of teaching staff", but I suspected they were mostly a vent for pubescent anger.

Most parents I spoke to viewed these rebellions indulgently; the young are expected to rebel in the name of freedom; it's almost like a rite of passage. And it never entirely goes away. Protestors who regularly block the city's main arteries are quite often elderly men and women concerned about their pensions. Nikitas was pleased that his children were rebelling, but he criticised their lack of organisation.

"Yours is a soft generation," he said to Tig and Orestes last year, when they were making plans for breaking into the school at night. "You haven't been up against the tanks or beaten by the Junta's police. You must get organised – you need aims and demands." He explained over and again the significance of the asylum law and its origins in the massacre of students at the Polytechnic. The law forbidding police from entering universities had become a basic tenet of young people's freedom after the Junta's downfall in 1974. It went along with the referendum to get rid of the monarchy and the end of right-wing rule. As a consequence, when adolescents took over their schools around the country and placed new padlocks on the gates, they had little fear that their gatherings would be forcibly broken up. All sorts joined in. Tig told me that friends arrived with pizzas and drinks and then rough elements would smash the place up, until the party eventually fizzled out. And then school started up again, much as it had been before. It was one of those customs that was now almost as accepted as the official parades for national holidays that forced pupils to march through the streets to military music carrying the Greek flag. Two sides of the same coin.

The truth was that this year, Tig's absorption in school politics suited me. Her distance allowed me to leave behind the weight of grieving and busy myself with ideas of research and writing – this time for myself and not some demanding academic who needed statistics on Greek abortion rates or archive work on nineteenth-century poets. But now, seeing my daughter at the kitchen table, she looked terribly young and vulnerable. I was reminded of her as a toddler – eating her bread and honey in much the same way, with fastidious delicacy. She was still a child.

Aunt Alexandra's reaction to Antigone's return was completely different. I went down to her apartment after 5.30, knowing she would have finished her regular two-hour nap – a non-negotiable habit to which she attributed her lasting health and beauty (though she didn't put it like that).

"Here? Back in Greece? She can't be." Her breath came loud and scratchy. She had already applied her regulation powder and lipstick – the bold red of her youth – but her lips now looked livid against a chalky face.

"Wait," she said, removing her hearing aids from both ears, thus becoming almost entirely deaf and unable to hear any more of the undesirable news. It was a useful ploy that often gave her time to think. She adjusted something on the pink, snail-like devices that produced a squeal, and then fitted them back into place. She patted her bouffant hair as though checking it was still all there and tucked her hands into the waistband of her skirt – an unusual but characteristic gesture of hers that I associated with intransigence.

"She can't just come back. I made a promise that my sister will never enter my house again. I cannot let down Spiros. Before he died, he reminded me of that." Alexandra's face had sagged from shock.

"I won't go back on my word." She looked at me severely. "Antigone destroyed our family. She led my brother Markos to his fate and she wanted to destroy Greece. Before she left, she sent a burnt letter to me and Spiros."

"What's that?"

"It's the worst thing you can do to your family. I'll never forget opening the envelope and pulling out the letter. It was charred ash around the edges. Pieces came off in my hand and left marks on my clothes. She wrote that she would never see us again. Spiros said it was black magic, a curse, and that my sister was a witch."

Gradually, as I filled her in on the details of Antigone's return, Alexandra regained some of her control and poise. She asked about her sister with a formality that came of using a word that is normally taboo: Antigone, the unspeakable name, the disgraced person. I understood better why it had been such a bitter experience for Alexandra when Nikitas and I named our daughter after her younger sister. Looking back, it was perhaps an uncharacteristic decision to follow the conventions of Greek naming, where grandparents are honoured in their grandchildren's names (paternal side first), but I liked the name and Nikitas apparently wanted to commemorate his missing mother. Despite Alexandra's love of propriety she had been appalled. Even after fourteen years, she was still unable to bring herself to call Tig by her baptismal name, preferring *Beba* – Baby – or any number of endearments (my gold, my eyes, my lamb, my love, my bud) rather than pay tribute to her sister in this way. She had always been *Yiayia* Alexandra– Granny Alexandra. And in spite of the tension that persisted between her and Nikitas, it was Granny Alexandra who had taken Tig out for walks around the neighbourhood when she was little, who had had her to stay when Nikitas and I went away for a few days, and who had provided a solid sense of extended family for our trio.

"There are many things you should understand about Nikitas' mother." Aunt Alexandra was pulling herself back into control. "She betrayed us. First, the family, and then her country. She joined a band of brigands that was ruled from Moscow and wanted to turn us into a miniature Soviet Union. We've all seen what happened in Albania." She was getting into her stride now and drew herself up straight. "You'd think they'd been saints from the way they talk about themselves, but they were bullies and thugs. They've even admitted it themselves. There are those on the Left who regret provoking the civil war and destroying Greece. There's a book called *Luckily We Were Defeated, Comrades*, by Lazaridis, and he was a friend and fellow prisoner of Beloyiannis. I suppose you know who he was?" I confessed I didn't and Alexandra explained about Beloyiannis being "the great martyr of the Left", who was executed in 1952 as a traitor.

"They were wrong." Alexandra sounded stronger as she lined

up her arguments in impregnable rows. "You can't believe what they did – the killings, the brutality, how ruthless they were. They were even worse than the Turks, with their 'gathering of the children'." *Paidomazoma* – the very word was chilling, conjuring up centuries of Ottoman domination and cruelty, when the best of the empire's children were forcibly plucked out and sent for lifelong military service as Janissaries in Constantinople. During the Civil War, the communists had "saved" vulnerable children from warfare by taking them to the eastern bloc or "stolen" them from their parents in order to indoctrinate them abroad. It all depended which side you believed.

"They didn't care about Greece, about their fatherland, and they saw the Allies as enemies because they were 'Imperialists'. Such nonsense. They just wanted power. That's all there is to it. And thank God, they lost."

"I know both sides did lots of bad things," I said, trying to appease Aunt Alexandra. "But I've never really understood why the family took it so personally that Antigone had different beliefs. She was still a daughter and a sister."

"She took Markos." The intransigence was clear in her tone. "He was still a schoolboy when she made him leave everything and go with her. He wasn't even shaving yet – a baby, but they gave him a gun and he was dead before his nineteenth birthday. He didn't deserve that. My mother begged and pleaded, but Antigone was pig-headed. She could do anything she liked with Markos and she didn't understand that certain things come before ideals and grand plans. I don't want to make a list of accusations." Aunt Alexandra smiled at me. "I know we can't live in the past. But you must be careful. You can knock all you like on the deaf man's door. My sister will never change."

I told Alexandra I'd see myself out by the kitchen door, planning to say hello to Chryssa in the kitchen. Morena was there with her, preparing green beans for a stew, older now, like all of us.

"That's nice, you'll meet your mother-in-law," said Morena, straightforwardly and not suspecting the degree of trouble this visit might entail after I announced the news.

"Tell me what you remember about Antigone," I asked Chryssa.

"Antigone was a good kid. They were all good kids." Chryssa said she remembered playing with all three of the Perifanis children during the long summers up in the village. Her father had worked for Petros, their father, caring for the old stone house when they were away, and tending their large orchard and vegetable garden. Each week he had sent a box of vegetables, seasonal fruits and fresh eggs to Athens, taking it down to the train station at Lianokladi, and it had been collected at Larissis station in Athens by one of Petros' employees.

"There is nothing for Antigone to be ashamed of. In a civil war, everybody loses. And Greeks know better than anyone how to put out their own eyes. We don't need help with that."

*　*　*

The next day, I rang the newspaper and asked to speak to Danae. I wanted to know what she had discovered and was curious to find out more about her. I couldn't help a touch of envy creeping through me as I dialled. Who was this woman who had known so much about Nikitas and his preoccupations? Why had he confided in her and not me?

"Surname?" they asked at the switchboard.

"I don't know. She's a sub-editor, I think."

"Ah, Danae Glykofridis, I'll put you through." Her surname – Sweetbrow – was gratingly charming.

She didn't sound pleased to hear from me. "How are you, *Kyria* Perifanis? My condolences, once again. I didn't have an opportunity to speak with you at the funeral."

So she had been there. I wondered if I'd seen her. "I would like to meet you if you had time. I'm trying to gather up Nikitas' research and I know you were helping him." I tried to stop my voice sounding too spiky, though Danae did not.

"Things are very busy at the paper. I'm not sure what I could tell you."

I rose to the challenge, not wanting to let her get away so easily. "It wouldn't take long."

"What sort of thing are you interested in?" Her tone was neutral now, if wary.

"I'm just sorting through Nikitas' papers, doing a bit of my own investigation into his life. I wondered whether you could tell me something about the direction he was taking his book."

"I didn't do that much." I heard her lighting up and exhaling smoke that sounded like exasperation. "He wanted me to find out more about the beginning of the Civil War. I've been going through the archives, especially at the Communist Party, and also what's left of the police records. So much was burnt after the end of the Junta."

"What about his personal story? I know he wanted to investigate that."

"He told me I must never talk to anyone about that," she

said. "I'm really sorry, but I can't discuss it. Not even with you."

I was so surprised, I laughed. A horrible, distressed sound.

"He made me promise." She was making it even worse.

What were these promises I didn't know about?

"I could tell you what I've found out about the British interest in Greece in the 1940s," she continued. "About *Tsortsil*" (I always used to find the Greek pronunciation of Churchill amusing). "That's what I've been doing most work on recently."

I didn't want a history lesson from this woman. I was sure she would have learned all the best lines from Nikitas about how dreadful my *sympátriotes* – my fellow countrymen – were. "What about the Wasp?"

She paused. "I'm very sorry. Really. But I always keep my word."

Later, I thought of sarcastic remarks I could have made about the mistaken idealism of youth, but I just said, "OK, I'll call you again if I have some specific questions." I put the phone down and banged my desk so loudly that Alexandra rang from below to ask if I was all right.

10
I dreamed that Greece might still be free

Antigone

"How long will you be staying in Athens? Will you go back to Moscow?" She was full of personal questions, this English girl. And she had an unnerving way of turning to look at me while she was driving, and swerving in and out of the traffic like a Muscovite taxi driver. She may be quiet but she is not timid. The truth is her curiosity has helped me escape a prison of loneliness. I never thought I would, but I have come home. I once believed I had created a life in Russia, but it evaporated like breath on an icy day. I have so little to show for those decades – only a bolt hole on the tenth floor that I don't care if I never see again. Not even my books. Ideals and dreams are all very well for the young, but at the end we yearn for the soil and roots from which we came. I realised this very late.

Her questions caught me off guard.

"I want to make sense of Nikitas' life and I can only do that with your help. Will you tell me what happened to your brother? And Johnny? And what about Nikitas' father? I hardly know anything. Who was this man Nikitas told me about – *Kapetan Aitos*? Did Captain Eagle have a family? Is there someone left?"

I told her that was all history. "Leave it," I said. "You can't bring back *Kapetan* Eagle and I have no idea about his family. Let the dead rest and get on with your life. "

Mod looked at me with frustration and opened all the car windows abruptly when I lit a cigarette. I don't know what to tell her.

When I arrived back in Patissia, Dora was with the young daughter of one of the Ukrainian prostitutes.

"I'm just helping Sveta with her homework. There's stuffed cabbage leaves in the kitchen. Help yourself while we finish."

I wasn't hungry and went straight to my bedroom, lying down on the narrow bed. It was covered with a lumpy, crocheted blanket that dug into my back and smelled of the village – sacks of wool in our store room, ready for spinning. Markos and I used to hide in there, underneath the main house in Perivoli. It was where I first smoked, aged ten. I had stolen some cigarettes from Uncle Diamantis, whose supplies from the Papastratos factory were endless. Markos watched me, as though admiring my daring, then took the cigarette between his thumb and forefinger and inhaled like a real old professional from the coffee shop.

❋ ❋ ❋

When I think about the war I sometimes forget how proud we were in the beginning. That was when our tired old dictator, Metaxas, pronounced his famous "No!" to the Italians. No, they would not be allowed to come and trample all over Greece. Our defeat of Mussolini's macaroni-eaters up in the snowy mountains of Albania was a triumph against all the odds. The names of Koritsa, Ayioi Saranta and Argyrokastro became famous across the world. They gave hope at a time when only the Greeks and the British were holding out against the fascists. But then the Germans joined in, bombarding Athens, flying in over the docks at Piraeus and across the city. A siren was set up near our house and when it started, we'd run next door to the Lambakis house which had a shelter in the basement. I always tried to take my dog, Irma, which annoyed *Kyria* and *Kyrios* Lambakis.

"Leave the dirty dog outside," *Kyria* Katina said each time, and I refused to go in without her. My mother called Irma my "lady-in-waiting", for her loyalty. I'd found her as a muddy, black puppy, roaming around on Arditos hill several years earlier and though of uncertain ancestry, she had turned into a well-behaved highly intelligent dog. Whenever the siren rang Irma howled with fear, like a second warning. "A devil's hound," *Kyria* Katina said. But in the shelter Irma was quiet, keeping one eye on me and the other on *Kyria* Katina who whispered prayers. They always lit the oil lamp under the icon that *Kyrios* Kostas had hung for extra protection.

Gradually, our boys started returning from the Albanian front and my school became a reception station for the wounded. You'd see lines and lines of soldiers arriving on foot, having walked all the way. Their faces were blank with disappointment and shock. Many came without boots, their feet bound in cloths, with gangrene and frostbite. Some were ill, others had lost arms and legs. Uncle Diamantis returned missing a toe, and two fingers from his left hand. Although he'd been a political prisoner on Aegina before the war, they allowed him to fight for his country. After that he always walked with a limp and he never played his guitar again. But the worst thing for everybody was not the injuries, but the disillusionment and humiliation.

The Germans arrived in Athens in Holy Week of spring 1941. By then, there was nothing left of the British army stationed in Greece – they'd moved to Egypt, along with the Greek forces and a provisional Greek government. The Greeks stayed there, under the thumb of the English, until the Germans left. My father called us all inside and we sat in the drawing room with the shutters closed. Everyone had shut their windows as though in mourning and the entire city was quiet. The only noise was the tanks rumbling like a distant storm. It was one of the few times I saw my father weep. For him it was a dishonour; he was deeply ashamed. And he wasn't the only one. Koryzis, our Prime Minister, shot himself. But shame was just the beginning. By the winter there was practically no food as the Nazis took away what we had. The English naval blockade meant that food was not getting through at all. It was better to let us starve than help the Germans. Even with money and ration cards, there was barely anything to buy. Our weekly crate of fruit and vegetables from the village could not be loaded on the train any more. It was the first time I ever felt hunger as something more than just the pleasant prelude to a meal. And we were among the lucky people. We tried to sell off things from the house, but money became almost worthless. You couldn't eat it. Father had to lay off all but one of the seamstresses at his atelier – she did repairs in exchange for bread or beans.

People started dying of starvation. It became common to see them collapse on the street, but I still remember the first time I ever saw a dead person. It was my seventeenth birthday, in November 1941. A school friend and I were walking along Hermes Street, looking at what remained in the shop windows, checking for a bargain. I bought some wild greens from a woman who said she gathered them on Hymettus. Later, however, my mother said they were not edible and threw the lot away. It was just after the barrow with the greens that we saw the corpse. He looked about forty, dressed in a suit and hat – an educated type. His body lay curled on the pavement and I noticed the slightly yellow teeth protruding from his open mouth. After that, we got used to it. Every day we saw the carts and trucks filled with bodies. Our lives moved so quickly away from privilege. That's what war teaches – the order we take for granted can just vanish like theatrical scenery. Our everyday existence is a fragile facade. Behind it lurks violence and chaos.

Soon, the only people flourishing were the black-market-eers. In our neighbourhood there was one man who profited from hunger – Dimitris Koftos, Alexandra's future father-in-law, though we didn't know that at the time. He had a grocer's shop in Archimedes Street from before the war, but during the occupation he lived like a *pashà*. *Kyrios* Dimitris got fatter when everyone else was losing weight. He had big moustaches like a nineteenth-century brigand and tiny piggy eyes. Soon he was buying up houses from people who were forced to sell them to survive, and he acted like the local boss.

Everyone knew *Kyrios* Dimitris had links with the Germans and Italians. He closed his shop and stuffed his cellar with sacks and tins, and things that you couldn't get – not just flour, beans and oil, but chocolate and sugar. And sometimes good bread – not the dreadful black German stuff with potato flour. *Kyrios* Dimitris only sold food if he knew you as he was frightened of getting caught. My mother used to send Alexandra over to get some black-eyed beans or lentils because she always came back with something extra in the bag – a few biscuits or some eggs. She was very pretty when she was young, with her blue eyes and light coloured, curled hair, and Spiros, the oldest of the three Koftos sons, had his eye on her. I can't imagine why she let someone like him pay court to her. I'd have thrown the eggs back at his head.

The Koftos boys were handsome bullies. Even when we were small I remember Spiros kicking younger children or getting his brothers to hold a boy so he could punch him. During the occupation all three became informers, like their father. They went to Flocca's café, where the Germans gathered, and where people sent anonymous letters denouncing their fellow Greeks. I once passed and saw Spiros talking to an officer. Who knows what he said and who was arrested or killed because of him – the prisons were full and there was news of executions almost every day. The Germans began using the *blóko*, rounding up all the men in certain areas and gathering them in the square. Then informers came in, wearing hoods, and pointed out who was left-wing or who belonged to the resistance or just someone they didn't like. And those people were taken away as hostages, or shot without further ado. I know Spiros wore a hood at least once as he boasted about it on the street. It was a way of feeling powerful for weak people.

Just as when we were young children, Markos was usually by my side and we were always outside. Whereas Alexandra was a "home-cat", we were street kids, "dirty dogs" like Irma. Markos looked innocent, but he wasn't. He didn't know what fear was and I became more daring with him. We got to know the Italian soldiers in Pangrati. They weren't as bad as the Germans, though they were no saints – they were fascist oppressors too. Markos would swap cigarettes or an orna-ment from our house for bread, coming home triumphant with the prize inside his jacket. He looked so sweet, with his black, curly hair, big, brown eyes and short trousers, even the soldiers liked him, though when they couldn't see him, he'd taunt them like the rest of us. We'd shout out "Air", the Greek battle-cry, to remind them of their humiliation in Albania. Markos believed in resistance as much as I did. It was as clear as black and white. Anyone could see the fascists were wrong and resistance was right.

My school friends and I used to paint slogans in the street: "Down with the fascist occupiers!" or "Freedom or Death!" It was a risky enterprise and youth was no guarantee of safety if they caught you. One evening, I took Markos with me to keep watch while I painted AIR in tall red capitals on our school wall. On the way home Spiros stopped us in the street. He looked excited, his blue eyes were lit up and his hair was greased flat. He was tall and strong and he held onto the strap of my bag as though to stop me running away, which I might have done. I prayed he would not notice the tip of the paintbrush sticking out; inside was a small tin of red paint that could only have one purpose. I could hardly speak. I never doubted that, whatever his feelings for my sister, he would have reported me. It was Markos who kept his head and tried to distract Spiros by asking him questions.

"Did you see a German moved into our street?" Markos jumped around like a clown, making Spiros look in his direction and away from me. He was quick-witted like that. "He's an officer, billeted with *Kyrios* and *Kyria* Panopoulos. They had to move out of their bedroom for him and now they're sleeping on a sofa. But they're hoping he'll bring in some food." Spiros looked impatient. He said, "Yes, yes", and waved his hands as though wanting to swat a fly. There was something he had for Alexandra, he said. "Tell her to come to the shop in the morning." He walked away and I had to sit down on the pavement to recover.

Alexandra came home the next day with a lump of meat wrapped in paper – an unbelievable luxury at a time when the ducks had gone from the Royal Garden and the numbers of cats and dogs on the streets was noticeably dwindling. We all stood around staring as though it was the first time we'd seen meat. Then Aspasia chopped it into tiny pieces and made a stew with beans. It wasn't long after this time that Irma, my dog, disappeared. There was no evidence to suspect Spiros, but I had a strong feeling that he was connected. He was heartless enough to do that and nobody was fussy about the provenance of meat in those days.

During that first winter of the occupation my father fell

ill with tuberculosis. I believe he couldn't bear to see all his achievements melting away and that he felt he was nothing without his success. As the provider for his family, it pained him to see us hungry and he often gave us part of his rations, which made him even weaker. He became terribly thin. My mother barely ate, but seemed to survive on will power. She never mentioned her needs and discouraged us from talking about food: "Just ignore it," she said, when we complained or dreamed up fantasy recipes. "You are stronger than hunger. God will provide." She became increasingly devout during the war, spending hours at church, but she was always a practical person and one of the first things she did was set up a soup kitchen with some local women, to help the children of the parish. Those families who could contribute something did and for dozens of children it was the only food they got. Sometimes Alexandra and I helped ladle out the boiled macaroni or lentils, and cut the horrible bread made from lupine – the stuff they normally feed to pigs. And you'd see these little kids with swollen bellies from malnutrition, queuing up with their tins. Many were orphans who had recently lost their parents and their silence was the worst thing – they'd forgotten how to play or to make a noise. They looked like tiny old people.

Sometimes the English planes would fly over and we were happy even when they dropped their bombs – it was a sign that someone cared about us. But it was a black time for the Greeks. We felt we were being gradually exterminated.

※　※　※

Johnny. Writing his name now reminds me of how I used to write it over and over. You might think the war would destroy the childish dreams, but in fact it was the reverse; the fantasy was my escape. I went down to the Ilissos and sat on the broad branches of our plane tree, picturing his long limbs and intelligent eyes, imagining how his kisses might be – I had never kissed a boy. My reveries were bourgeois stories of marriage "and they lived well and we lived better" as the fairy tales finish. I knew nothing else.

Winter 1942. Cold rain was splattering down in the darkness when the doorbell rang. It wasn't late, but nobody liked it when a visitor came after nightfall. Your immediate thought was that something bad had happened – a death, news of another group execution, German soldiers with an order to search the house. If there was a worst point in the war, this was it. Hope had become too elusive and slippery to grasp. When I opened the door, I did not recognise the man standing before me. His face was unshaven, his hair dripping beneath a sodden hat. It was only when he asked to come in that I heard his voice, with its English accent, and realised it was Johnny. We all gathered around him in the drawing room. Even my father got out of bed and lay on a sofa, directing my mother to open the bottle of brandy they kept for emergencies.

"Welcome to our old friend!" my parents said in the hushed tones we used instinctively.

Johnny replied with the correct formula, "Well found!" He remembered his Greek even though it had been four years since his last visit. I could barely speak from nerves and pleasure. His hair was dyed black and his skin tanned from months in Egypt. He had just come from there, he said – a captain now and working for a secret agency called Force 133. I later learned that this was a code name for the SOE, Churchill's solution for undermining the Nazi grip on Europe. Sabotage, parachute drops, gold sovereigns. Words like incantations.

My father was upset that we didn't have food to offer. It is dishonourable if you can't feed a guest: "Shame!" My mother dug out a small bag of lentils and made a soup with some onion. And later in the evening, we all sat at the dining table where we had been four years earlier at Johnny's farewell dinner. My mother used a silver tureen, which looked ridiculous with the khaki slush not even half-filling it. There wasn't even any bread to have with it. I felt awkward because I saw us all through Johnny's eyes, diminished and altered from the family he had known. The contrast between our hollowed, thin-skinned faces and Johnny's well-nourished cheerfulness was shocking. My father, slumped and feverish from tuberculosis, was half the man he had been. My mother had turned grey from this second great disaster of her life, her beauty threatened by malnourishment and anxiety. Nevertheless, that evening she put on her favourite diamond earrings from Constantinople (all her other jewellery had been sold) and a little lipstick as a gesture to the occasion. We three teenagers were scrawny and taut with anticipation. Even Alexandra, who still liked to refer to me and Markos as "the kids," was excited by the development.

Johnny refused the offer of a bed that night. He knew the penalty for us if he was discovered. The following day he was leaving for the mountains somewhere near Lamia, but he needed somebody to take money to a safe house in Athens in three days' time.

"I was wondering whether Antigone might do it. A schoolgirl would be unlikely to be suspected." He looked at my father, who paused as though he hadn't heard and then nodded slowly. I was so excited Johnny wanted me that I ignored the insulting implication that he thought I was still at school. I said, "But, you know I have started my first year at the university. I don't wear a school pinafore any more. I'm studying law." The truth is there was not much studying going on at the university, but I was proud to be there.

"My dear girl, that's marvellous." He patted my shoulder and I was paralysed with joy.

That was the moment when I realised we could refuse to be crushed. I could fight back. I was "in". It was like the old saying: "If the first cog catches you, you can't escape" – you are caught up in the machinery. Both Markos and I pleaded with Johnny to go with him to Lamia. We knew the area – we had the house in Perivoli. But he insisted we would be more useful in Athens. He needed people who spoke English and Greek to liaise between British agents and the runners. Later I learned that all this was part of a plan code-named *Animals*. Its intention was to create a diversion, to distract the Germans so they would think the Allies were going to invade Greece rather than Sicily. Markos and I immediately sensed the excitement. We'd beat the Germans this way. It was perfect. When he left, Johnny shook hands with my father and Markos and kissed my mother, sister and me. I felt wild. I was burning.

Three days after Johnny's visit, Markos and I took a tram to the centre. We walked to the stop separately, pretending not to know one another.

"Don't speak to me. Don't even look at me," I warned.

"I don't want to look at you, dim-wit. I'll just make sure you are safe." He was younger than me by sixteen months, but he liked to look after me. I put the letter and a pack of fifty gold sovereigns given to me by Johnny in my leather school satchel underneath some text books. I had a key in my pocket and had memorised the address. While we were waiting at the tram stop, one of the Germans billeted in our street walked up and, when the tram arrived, he went to sit opposite me. The soldier stared at me as though preparing to speak and my heart started beating with such violence that I feared he would see my chest moving. I pictured the developments, the search, my arrest, and the pain of letting Johnny down. I averted my gaze, but every time I raised my eyes he was focusing on me. There was little doubt about my fate if I was caught; being a girl was no help. I knew there were drops of sweat on my upper lip.

Finally, the German got up and I prepared myself for the worst, hoping Markos would save himself when I was taken away. The man leaned in, so I could smell the foreign cigarette on his breath and see the blonde bristles on his chin.

"Lovely eyes," he said in heavily accented Greek, smiling and revealing shining white teeth. I almost burst into tears from relief and shame. Markos' cheeks were red and he stared at the floor until we got off from different doors at the next stop.

The apartment was just off Queen Sophia Street, near Evangelismos Hospital. Markos waited for me further along the road, while I let myself in and went up to an apartment on the fourth floor. As arranged, the bell rang sometime later and an Englishman arrived at the door. He was stocky and pink-skinned and he laughed a lot.

"Billy Hicks," he said, taking my hand and squeezing it too hard. "But everyone calls me Basher." Basher spoke ancient Greek, and I wondered how he would get on trying to pass himself off as a native, but he was full of confidence and he never did get caught. I handed over the letter and the money and he explained where the next meeting would be, with one of the runners who would travel between Athens and the mountains. They had links with the partisans, he said, and they were working together on an important plan. I told him my Uncle Diamantis was with ELAS [Greek People's Liberation Army], and how that was the armed wing of EAM, the biggest resistance movement.

"Ah, the Commies, eh?" Basher raised an eyebrow.

"No. They are patriotic Greeks who want freedom and peace," I said. "We all want the same thing." We didn't continue the conversation and Basher gave me a bar of English chocolate, which I shared with Markos in the small park near the hospital. It was the creamiest, sweetest thing we had ever tasted and I licked the crumbs from the paper.

After that, Markos and I helped run three safe-houses in Athens. They were bases for the Greek runners who needed somewhere to stay between journeys, and occasionally for British agents. Markos' school had closed down and lectures had been suspended at the university, so we had plenty of time. I have to admit that beyond the satisfaction of helping the resistance, there was great pleasure in knowing I was doing something for Johnny. I thought of him obsessively, imagining how I would join him in the mountains, how I would help him, how we would be together after the war. I was very serious and very innocent. When Basher was in Athens, he enjoyed living the high life, bringing girls to the apartment and getting hold of perfume and whisky. To him, the war was a game and he annoyed me. I didn't like the reckless lack of discipline. Now I understand it better – the close companionship of death can provoke all sorts of reactions. And though at twenty-five, he seemed old to me, we were all very young. It was Basher who often handed me money and instructions, and once, a note from Johnny. I kept it with me for the rest of the war until it disintegrated after I fell in a river. I knew it by heart.

> *Dear Girl,*
> *I often think of you. It rains so much up here that I have forgotten what it is to be warm and dry. I remember the old days in Athens, before the war, as being always sunny. As distant now as ancient Hellas. Thank you for everything you are doing. All this will end, you know.*
> *"I dreamed that Greece might still be free."*
> *Please send my greetings to your family.*
> *With love,*
> *J*
> *p.s. best to destroy this*

Just before Easter 1943, my father died. He was forty-six.

We knew it was coming, but it was as though the roof had been ripped off our house – we lost our protection from the outside world. We felt like orphans. When his body was laid out in the drawing room he looked so small, as though he had shrunk. The bells were tolling for Maundy Thursday and Christ's death and I never wanted to celebrate Easter after that. My mother's desolation was increased because she could not fulfil his final wish to be buried in the village. It was impossible to find transport to Perivoli; it was hard enough to enlist a man with a cart to take the coffin to the First Cemetery. Our neighbour, Kostas Lambakis, was a grave-digger there and he helped us with the practicalities. My paternal grandmother died less than a month later, unable to bear the loss of her only son. Death had become so commonplace that their passing didn't provoke the shock in the neighbourhood that it would once have done.

Our family split into two camps after my father's death. My mother worked tirelessly with the church to help people in the neighbourhood, and Alexandra often joined her. There were so many women whose husbands and sons had died or been injured in Albania or who had been imprisoned or executed, and they had little way of caring for their families. My mother's soup kitchen expanded and she even gave lessons to the children, many of whom lived like street dogs – scavenging and filthy. Spiros moved in closer, making himself useful to Alexandra, bringing her little presents and smirking knowingly. He supplied the sugar and almonds for the *kólyva* at my father's memorials, so he managed to endear himself to my mother too.

I cannot criticise what my mother and sister did – it

was an honourable thing to help the weak, but Markos and I were different. We wanted to fight – although, so far, our protests had been more symbolic than practical. We had already joined the youth resistance group EPON [the United Panhellenic Organisation of Youth], which was growing by the day. It showed that even children could stand up to the fascist occupiers. Then there were the youngest of all – the "Little Eagles". On one huge march, we carried black flags all the way through the city. It felt right to do something after the mass executions and to protest against the proposal that Greeks be sent off to work in German factories.

We may have been young, but we became organised, electing delegates, making pamphlets. And on national days, we visited the memorials to the heroes of '21 – Kolokotronis, Bouboulina, Karaiskakis... those great men and women who had freed Greece from slavery over a century before. We were their heirs and we wanted to be worthy of them. We took flowers and danced to a gramophone by their statues. They were terrible times, but the truth is that for us young ones, it was exhilarating. It wasn't to do with politics – for most of us there was no choice but to resist. We weren't afraid, and going to the mountains seemed the most honourable thing to do. Our problem was how to get there.

In the winter of 1943, a year after Johnny's appearance at our house, I found a way. Uncle Diamantis sent me a message to go to the old cellar in Piraeus Street. I had not seen him since the start of the occupation, but we had heard rumours of his rise in the resistance. He seemed larger and tougher than I remembered, his face sunburnt and bearded from two years in the mountains. I smelled wood smoke when he embraced me and noticed his strong hand with the two missing fingers grip my shoulder.

"Look at you, my little Antigone. A beautiful woman!" He stared at me as though he had imagined I was still the little girl who wanted ice-cream. He was now a captain in ELAS. *Kapetan Fotias*. He took the name Fire. They all took a *nom de guerre* to protect their families, he said.

"The whole country is joining us – it's the only way forward, to get rid of the fascists, to be free." His eyes were shadowed with tiredness but didn't lack fervour.

"But we are doing much more than that. We're bringing freedom and education to the oppressed and ignorant. We're setting up schools in villages where nobody can read, we're making people's courts so the villagers themselves can decide what justice is. We can't go back to the old kings and dictators. This is a new way forward. We are making a new world." Uncle Diamantis spoke urgently. He told me about Aris Velouchiotis, their leader, who rode from village to village, recruiting men to the cause, and he told me the ELAS partisan's oath:

> *I, Child of the Greek people, swear to fight faithfully from the ranks of ELAS, spilling even the last drop of my blood, as a genuine patriot, for the removal of the enemy from our land, for the freedom of our people...*

"We need educated people like you." It sounded like more than just a suggestion. When I told Uncle Diamantis about Johnny and the safe-houses he was dismissive.

"They say they're our allies, but the English are playing

their own games. They use us, but they don't like us. Aris is right when he says they are spies and agents. Now they're giving money and arms to smaller resistance groups that are against us. Leave your English spy and come with your own people."

Uncle Diamantis knew nothing of my affections for Johnny, but he saw the disappointment on my face.

"What about the sabotage?" I asked. We had all been encouraged by the destruction of the Gorgopotamos bridge the previous year, when ELAS and other partisans had joined the English. "I thought we were fighting the fascists together."

"Of course Gorgopotamos was a triumph! But the English wouldn't have managed anything without Aris and without our help. We cut off the German connection for weeks, so Rommel couldn't get his supplies in the Egyptian desert. Listen to me, Antigone – the English are not to be trusted. They are not here to help us. They want to be ready to dominate us when the time comes. It's the old imperialist method of divide and rule – they encourage us to kill each other so they can stay on top."

Before I left the cellar, I helped my uncle print some leaflets on the old press, which was still functioning after all these years. There was a picture of Aris with a couple of his black-capped men. He sat proud and rotund on a horse, his big beard like a youthful version of Father Christmas, a face both kind and ambitious. He looked avuncular and trustworthy. I could fight for him, I thought.

When I got home, I heard Alexandra's voice from the back yard. I paused at the kitchen door, realising she was arguing with Markos.

"You follow her around like a dog, believing she must be right, but she's wrong. Go back to your studies – ignore the propaganda."

"So you'd prefer I was a fascist collaborator like your boyfriend?" I had never heard Markos angry like that. He was always the one who eschewed conflict; the easy-going baby of the family, whose smile was "a blessing" (as our grandmother said).

"Spiros is trying to help his country. He's a patriot who wants freedom for Greece. He just doesn't want it on Stalin's terms." Alexandra had put on a coaxing voice. "That doesn't make him bad. Can't you see you're taking the wrong decision? Father would have told you that – Greeks aren't cut out to be Bolsheviks."

I waited, expecting that Markos would find a compromise and appease his older sister, but he sounded furious.

"Take his shitty soap back. I'd rather be dirty than use it." I heard a door bang and then I came into the kitchen – a place no longer filled with tempting smells, but cold and empty. Alexandra was standing rigid, glaring at a bar of soap that lay on the bare wooden table. Without looking at me, she said, "Spiros sent that for you. He said it might help wash away some of your communist filth."

I found Markos in his room, his face feverish with fury. When I told him about Uncle Diamantis, he wanted to leave for the mountains that very day, something that was impossible as we had to wait for instructions. Markos explained what had happened with our older sister, who had suggested that he follow Spiros' example and join the so-called Security Battalions. That way, he could don the traditional and prestigious Evzone uniform and become a puppet for Hitler. *Yermanotsoliades* [German Evzones] we called them. Their job was to betray their own people, to track down the resistance and hand them over to their fascist masters; the lowest, most repellent form of collaboration. Like the partisans in ELAS, they also swore an oath, though it was somewhat different:

> *I swear by God this sacred oath, that I will obey absolutely the orders of the Supreme Commander of the German Army, Adolf Hitler.*

Later that evening we heard banging on the front door. When my mother opened it, Spiros came pushing his way in, panting and clearly terrified.

"Quickly, I need to hide. They're going to kill me." We could hear noises in the street – boots hammering, excited male voices. My mother spoke calmly, like a doctor taking charge at an accident.

"Antigone, take Spiros up to the store room on the terrace. And stay there. Nobody should know that you are here either." Spiros was already running up the stairs and I followed him up two flights until we reached the roof terrace. As I unlocked the metal door I heard more knocking at the front of the house. I removed the key and locked it quietly from the other side. We both ran across to the store room and pulled the door shut. Spiros flinched as it creaked.

We sat on two rusting metal chairs, getting back our breath. I had not seen Spiros for a while and he had changed. His skinny adolescent limbs had thickened and he had grown a moustache, clipped and sooty black. I noticed his smell – sweat mixed with a pungent cologne. It reminded me of the nutmeg Aspasia used to grate into the sauce for *pastítsio*. His eyes were wide open and fearful. He was very proud of those blue eyes.

"Who's chasing you?" I was almost sure what the answer would be.

"It's those arsehole communists," Spiros hissed, leaning in too close. "We know who they are and they won't last long. If you do the right thing, Antigone, I'll make sure you're OK. We know about Diamantis. You're on the wrong side." He stopped and listened, still as a frightened hare in the hills near Perivoli.

We remained in the dark store room some time, until Alexandra knocked gently on the door and whispered Spiros' name. She had been out when the incident occurred and now stretched out her arms towards him like a cinema diva. She said, "My Spiros. They were kicking at our door.Luckily Mother calmed them down. You must be careful. They are animals, these communists."

11
Wise mares

MAUD

Sometimes I feared that this digging around would not help anything. I thought about how Antigone had sat in the café, smoking avidly, watching me with beady eyes, apparently worrying about what I was trying to unearth. Nikitas used to say that, like Orpheus, you look back at your peril. The old or dead objects of your desire will not come back – Eurydice was never really going to make it out of Hades, even if Orpheus' curiosity had not made him turn around to check whether his beloved wife was following him back to the land of light and life and music. There is a danger in chasing after the past; you neglect the present and the future is no longer interesting. Like Eurydice, who was bitten by a snake on the banks of a river, Nikitas' death had come suddenly and shockingly, but perhaps the living should not look too much towards the land of the dead.

After our first meeting in Paradise Street, over four years passed before I saw Nikitas again. By 1993 I was in my late twenties, living in London, and my fieldwork on Thasos was long behind me. The constipated pages of my thesis were filed away in the bowels of the university library and my contact with Alexandra was limited to the occasional card. I had taken on a junior fellowship at University College and was living an existence that was not unhappy. I only occasionally saw my parents, who had divorced, and were living in neighbouring streets in Twickenham (each having married colleagues from their early music milieu). My grandfather, Desmond, had recently died of pancreatic cancer, a couple of years after Lucy's death from a stroke. I watched him wither and shrink till he was a light husk, barely inhabited.

"The mares are taking my chariot away," he whispered from his hospital pillow the afternoon before he died. "And the maidens are leading the way." Over the next hours, he went so slowly that it was hard to tell the point at which he was not there.

I ran into Nikitas at a symposium on the fate of the Elgin Marbles, or what we now called the Parthenon Marbles – after all, how could you name these precious sculptures after a syphilitic Lord who had stolen them, sawed them off the temple walls, sunk them in a boat, hauled them up from the depths, stored them in his Scottish mansion and then sold them to the British Museum? There was a noisy delegation from Greece that included the Minister of Culture and a group of tight-lipped British government and museum spokesmen. Impassioned speeches from the Greek side claimed the Marbles were their rightful inheritance and they would make Greece complete in a way that nothing else could. The British speakers were cautious and weasel-worded, hinting at Greek irresponsibility and mentioning pollution in Athens, world heritage and how all museum collections would be doomed if the Marbles went home. Among the audience were many British supporters like me, calling for the restitution of the treasures. We basked in the warm light of certainty, up on the moral high ground, able to discuss how the famous frieze was sawn off by aristocratic vandals, why the *firman* that was issued to Elgin in Constantinople was not valid, and why the Greeks deserve a national symbol that has not been desecrated and plundered.

I spotted Nikitas at the reception that followed and, like the first time I saw him in Paradise Street, my initial reaction was apprehension – only this time I recognised it more quickly as the fear of attraction. He was drinking red wine and appeared to be telling a story to some people at the other end of the hall; they were all laughing as he waved his hands. His face was tanned, his white shirt crumpled and he had a restless expression. I made for the door and walked out of the building into needles of November rain. I had spotted my bus coming along the street, when I heard him say my name. I turned, greeting him with fake surprise, answering in rusty Greek. He kissed my cheeks and held onto my shoulders, looking at me as though I were a young child who had grown taller since last time. I noted that he looked older, his hair more streaked with grey and his face heavier. But his evident pleasure was disarming and I found myself struggling unsuccessfully to keep my distance.

"Let's get away from here." There did not seem to be any question that we were leaving together. "I need to escape from the organised dinner." Nikitas explained that he had come over from Athens with the Minister and his entourage, to cover this conference for his newspaper.

"Let the wankers get on with the banquet without me." He was already bored with this latest campaign to retake Greece's missing national treasure.

"Who gives a shit about those old rocks locked up in the British Museum?" he smiled, pleased at his own subversion. "The English approach is to tell us to 'stop making a fuss'. They say we're 'crying over spilt milk'. I love their expressions. But making a fuss is what we are best at. Don't think that the Greeks who visit London care about seeing the sculptures – they are far more interested in going to Selfridges. And imagine if we did ever take them back, what would we have to complain about then? It would be like Cavafy's poem about the barbarians: what would we do if the problem disappeared? We need the barbarians."

Later I realised that Nikitas was provoking me and that he could argue the Greek case with equally passionate eloquence, but at the time I took him seriously enough to launch into arguments about the sculptures needing to be seen under Greek light, about the central symbolism of the Parthenon with its missing pieces, and the unjustness of the whole story. Nikitas laughed even more.

"They should get you to fill in for poor old Melina Mercouri," he said. "You could take over from our ageing goddess of cinema and politics and fire us up with rhetoric."

We walked through the rain to a small Japanese restaurant, where we ate sushi and drank sake. Nikitas assumed an intimacy with me, speaking as though he knew me, recounting the latest news from Paradise Street.

"It's as you left it. Everyone a little older. You'll see when you come." He said it as though he was sure I would and I could not think of the right response. "Aunt Alexandra is still the perfect lady, though she can't quite manage it with me. I'm still the fly in the milk for her and Spiros. I have always spoiled their tidy life. Spiros hates me as much as ever and when I see him I feel the rage of a small boy who can't stand up to a bully."

"Surely he doesn't bully you now?"

"Of course not. He may even be afraid of me. But whenever I see him it's as though I lose my strength, as though I become a child again. I feel the same pain in my stomach that I felt when he came to my room when I was young." I asked Nikitas to tell me what happened, but he was reticent.

"Spiros was careful not to go too far, not to leave bruises – it was more what he said. He enjoyed the power of provoking fear. Once, he caught a large fly in my room and pulled its wings off. Then he placed it on my desk, on top of my open grammar book and gripped my wrist till it hurt. He said, 'Watch out, my boy, and you'll be fine. You don't want to lose your wings, do you?' After that I had visions of myself growing wings, of flying and falling, of Spiros with a knife. It was a twisted sort of sadism."

Nikitas swigged his sake with enthusiasm, ordered another bottle and changed the subject. He was travelling a great deal, he said, writing pieces for his newspaper, and had made a couple of documentaries for television. Yiorgia had asked for a divorce – something he'd been expecting. He showed me a photograph of his young son, Orestes. I told him about the university, and mentioned Austin, attempting to give my boyfriend's presence in my life more weight than it had. I mentioned his job at an advertising agency, his science fiction film-script and his family home in New York. I didn't mention the evenings of ready-made meals or sex as impersonally athletic as Austin's daily work-outs at the gym. In any case, Nikitas didn't look very impressed. His smell was familiar, and now mixed with the steam from our drenched coats and damp hair.

I agreed to meet Nikitas the next day. We walked by the grey Thames and took refuge from the cold in a pub where we drank Guinness and had lunch. He drank much more than me and became voluble, speaking a tone louder than usual. Later, I realised he was proud of being "a strong glass" – a drinker who could hold his alcohol. That day was the first time I noticed his need for an audience and how he took the time to tell a joke to a group of men at the bar while he ordered more drinks. They roared with laughter and he returned looking satisfied, as though these London men were proof of the excitement and pleasure he provoked wherever he went. I realised it was a performance, but at that stage I thought it was for me. In the afternoon we visited the British Museum, almost as a joke, walking through the echoing halls to inspect "our looted past", as Nikitas put it. His cynicism peeled away as we stood before the extraordinary sculptures; furious centaurs, draped goddesses and naked warriors fighting to the death.

Over the next days, Nikitas' persistence was steady, as though he had made up his mind that he would be with me and it was just a matter of waiting for me to realise it. My resistance had the frailty of a besieged city whose walls are being breached on every side. I lied to Austin the evening I invited Nikitas to my flat, saying I had to work, and Nikitas arrived like an old-fashioned admirer with flowers and wine (he had managed to find some heavy, red Nemea – "what Hercules would have drunk before he strangled the lion"). We talked until dawn and, when we did end up in bed, it was as inevitable as if there had never been any choice or question. While the light of the London morning slunk its way in through the window, I lay in the crook of his arm as he slept. My cheek rested against his chest, where a solid bass drum thudded reassuringly, like something eternal.

Nikitas took this night to be the sealing of a pact.

"Come back to Athens. Come and live with me." Later, he said it had been very clear to him. He enjoyed how my calm exterior masked the complexities below, my earnestness about establishing the truth, and how I didn't know I was beautiful (I didn't). I thought he might be mocking me when he said that with me it was like making love for the first time. As to my own feelings, I would not admit to myself how much I wanted him; I could not imagine that we had a future. At forty-seven he was "old", he lived at the other end of Europe, and he dragged around the legacies of former marriages, disappeared parents, and any number of family feuds.

A few weeks later I went out to Athens for the Christmas holidays. We stayed at the small house Nikitas rented in Plaka. I knew my grandfather would have told me to "watch the horses" at this point. Once, when I was telling my grandmother about the charms of a teenage boyfriend, my grandfather butted in, "If you get on like a house on fire, it'll probably burn down and all that's left is ash. Mind how you go, Maud." Nikitas gave himself over to making sure I would find it hard to leave or at least that I would soon be back, making his country my suitor as much as he was himself. And he succeeded; while I had felt affection for Greece when I had lived there as a student, this time it became the only place I wanted to be. My grandfather's pessimistic warnings were irrelevant – a damp, English blanket of gloom, to be shrugged off in favour of bright Mediterranean skies. We drove to the sea and lay in the wintry sunshine on a beach made of tiny pebbles, then went to a shack where they served small pink cockles called 'shinies' – which we ate raw, followed by fried red mullet and retsina that tasted of summer pine trees. We visited a *Rembetika* club in Piraeus, where the young musicians sat in a row on the stage, singing songs from the 1930s and '40s. They told of prisons, oppression and painful addiction to love and drugs, as though they had lived those lives themselves.

Nikitas became like a teacher, determined to inspire me and make me love his subject. I saw the pleasure he took at his success.

"It's as though I'm seeing things from a new perspective – from your eyes. It makes everything fresh and new," he said. We went up to the hills that hem Athens in on three sides, and from where you understand that the city seethes and boils in a cauldron, bubbling up the mountain slopes and spilling down to the sea.

"You think the buildings are white, but when you see them from here they're creamy, like piles of old bones," he said. On Penteli, we picked up pieces of its famous marble and on Hymettus, we gathered wild greens as the old women do, using a kitchen knife and a plastic bag. Afterwards, we sat among the trees near Kaisariani Monastery, on slopes where the best honey in Greece was produced for millennia, and watched the sun go down over the Saronic Gulf.

"This is the most perfect light in the world," said Nikitas. "There is something about Attica that produces all the right ingredients for the light to create beauty. It is the catalyst that transforms whatever it touches." We looked across at the gilded mountains and the wide expanse of gleaming sea.

"You can see why people needed to create the concept of the divine in these circumstances – even humans can seem like gods in this light. And the best thing is that it cannot be spoiled, however hard we Greeks try." Whether it was the luminosity or not, we both felt like gods, at one remove from the rest of humanity, obsessed with one another so that everything else appeared mundane.

I had not thought that I would be the sort of woman to give up her job and home to go and live with a much older, twice-divorced man in another country. My life had not been characterised by recklessness. Nevertheless, that is what I did. I gave my notice to the university, agreed to finish the academic year, and ended things with Austin. He was what my grandfather would have called "a good sport" about it and kept in touch, asking my advice about his subsequent girlfriends and later on, sending me email jokes.

When I returned to Greece for Easter, Athens was being ravaged by an amorous spring – like a plain bride made beautiful with flowers and veils. Drifts of camomile sprang up on waste ground, producing visible clouds of scent. The bitter-orange trees lining the pavements exploded with outrageously perfumed blossoms, and house-martins and swallows returned to their nests among the city's human inhabitants. Nikitas took me to see his village, in central Greece: Perivoli, the place he associated with the greatest happiness of his childhood. His grandmother, Maria, used to take him there for the summer holidays and she rebuilt the family house after the war. She told her grandson she had always loved the place because it reminded her of where her family summered in the hills near Smyrna – both places had mulberries, plane trees and mountain breezes that cooled you even in August. For Nikitas, the rural pleasures of his youth were amplified because they were enjoyed without Alexandra and Spiros.

"They used to go to the village of Spiros' forebears near Tripoli – a dreary flea-pit full of fascists," Nikitas said. Perivoli was firmly left-wing and the Koftos couple did not feel welcome there. However, Chryssa used to go with Maria and Nikitas, keeping house for them and visiting her many relatives.

In Perivoli, Nikitas showed me where he ran wild, unwittingly using the same paths his mother had as a child and revelling in the same kinds of freedom. He made friends with the local boys, who showed him how to kill snakes, milk goats, steal fruit from orchards, and the fastest way to get up to the remote church of Prophet Ilias, where they masturbated together on a rocky promontory with views across the whole valley. In the village *kafeneío* Nikitas introduced me to some big-bellied men, whom he remembered as skinny, sunburnt boys, and they slapped his back and bought him drinks. I felt like the foreign "chick" along for the ride. But I saw how Perivoli had become Nikitas' Eden. It was the place he dreamed about and yearned for in a way that could not even be assuaged by visiting it; an abstract ideal of home and ancestry.

Visiting his old haunts, we bathed in the hot springs that form pools down in the valley and afterwards sprawled on powdery, sulphurous rocks that smell like the bowels of the earth. On a stroll through some olive groves, Nikitas presented me with a lacy white flower resembling cow parsley, saying it was *kónio*.

"Don't eat it!" he warned. "That's what Socrates drank after he was sentenced to death. It paralyses the nervous system so first you lose all feeling in your toes, then the numbness spreads up your legs and when it reaches your heart you've gone." They used it all over ancient Greece, he said. On the island of Kea, when old people were unable to cope with life any more, they had a big party and then went out to sea in a small boat with a cup of *kónio*.

"No degrading homes for the dying and demented in those days. A way to leave with dignity." Later, I looked up the word *kónio* in a dictionary: hemlock. It occurred to me how knowing the name of something in your own language can make it slot into a comfortably familiar category, while learning a word like a child who sees something for the first time, allows it to be fresh and fascinating.

So determined was Nikitas that I should join him in Greece that he even found me work with a historian friend who needed some archive research. I agreed I would start as soon as I arrived in June. It was also at this point that I was introduced to Orestes, during Holy Week, when everyone was preparing for the great celebration – whitewashing, spring cleaning, buying new clothes, fasting, going to church, dyeing batches of hardboiled eggs red, and slaughtering lambs for the paschal feast. Orestes was dropped off by his mother and came in to Nikitas' place looking pale, tense and younger than his ten years. Nikitas and I made the mistake of laughing at his formality when he said:

"Pleased to meet you," and shook my hand ceremoniously. His eyes sparkled with suppressed tears as though we were mocking him, and it was too late when I replied, "I'm very pleased to meet you too." Nikitas picked his son up, misjudging the moment, as he tried to decrease the tension with rough though affectionate playfulness.

"What a son I have, *eh*? A fine fellow." Orestes' seriousness and sensitivity touched me and we developed an unlikely rapport that sometimes bewildered his father. Later, even during his most difficult teenage phase, when he stopped talking to his parents, Orestes would come to me. I know that Nikitas was sometimes resentful.

❋ ❋ ❋

Nikitas and I got married that winter, in December 1993. I was six months pregnant and was already undergoing a complete transformation: linguistic (Nikitas started talking to me in Greek rather than English); physical (my breasts swelled, my stomach grew hard as a drum and I was devouring platefuls of olives); and emotional (I had left everything else behind). There was a song Nikitas knew from his paternal grandmother and he used to sing it to me and his unborn child, the restless 5/8 rhythm rolling on as though it would never stop. It spoke of a girl – a "little partridge" – garlanded with myrtle, with breasts like pomegranates. Tears in the well, spirits in the wood, mountain churches, threshing floors… I was the bride and I never doubted that while Nikitas was in his late forties, he was the *palikári*, the courageous, upright young man of the song who plants the seed that grows the tree and wins the girl of his dreams.

I went to see Alexandra several times after arriving back in Athens, but I always felt awkward; she was evidently not pleased at my relationship with Nikitas and I felt guilty, as though I had betrayed her in some way. Nevertheless, she was polite and gracious and, when she learned we were getting married, she invited me over to Paradise Street one morning. Alexandra had just been to the hairdresser and her hair was lacquered into a solid lilac-grey cap. She looked as well turned out as ever – her seventy-year old legs shapely in high court shoes. She was wearing a navy blue dress that looked expensive. Spiros made a show of greeting me, though I could tell he didn't feel comfortable. He probably suspected that Nikitas had told me all sorts of stories about him, and it was true that when I now saw Spiros, I thought of his cruelty to his adopted son and how he had mocked and beaten the "little bastard".

"Welcome to the lovely bride! How is our little Mondy?" I kissed him hello with reluctance, feeling his moustache brush my cheeks. "Third time lucky for the groom, *eh*? He's still a strong man, our Nikitas," he said with an off-putting wink. I thanked him stiffly, recoiling from the "snake", which was how my future husband referred to his uncle. To regain my composure, I pretended to examine a formal studio photograph of Alexandra and Spiros on their engagement. They made a handsome couple; she was curvaceous in a tightly fitting skirt suit, with curled hair and dark lipstick, while he exuded masculine power, holding her hand and glaring slightly at the camera, under his lustrous brilliantined hair.

Alexandra wanted us to take coffee in the sitting room as though I was an honoured guest, but I asked to see Chryssa first. She seemed smaller than ever and I stooped so she could hug me "May you live, may you live!" she repeated with obvious pleasure. She saw me notice a woman sweeping the tiled pathways out in the courtyard and called through the window, "Morena, come and meet our bride." An attractive, round-faced young woman came in and shook my hand shyly, looking down at the floor.

"Morena is from Albania," announced Alexandra. "She's a good girl. She's helping us out with some of the heavier jobs as none of us is getting any younger, you know."

"So we're both foreigners here," I said, hoping to put Morena at ease, but she just fingered a gold chain at her neck and looked even more nervous. It was only later I learned how she had walked over the Albanian-Greek border through the snow, in order to join her husband in the Athenian basement he shared with seven compatriots. I had little appreciation then of what traumas the hundreds of thousands of recently-arrived Albanians had to go through to make it to what they hoped would be a new life.

After we had drunk our coffee, Aunt Alexandra said she had something for me.

"I have no daughter of my own and there are things I would like to pass on before I go." Beckoning to me, she walked over to a table at the side of the room that was covered with a pile of linen. She unfolded an exquisite crocheted cotton bedcover, all in white, with flowers and zigzag edges hung with white pompoms.

"This is from the trousseau my mother prepared for me. There are embroidered cloths made by my grandmother, and various sheets and pillowcases I don't use. You won't find things like this anymore – they're hand stitched. I always cared about you, Mondy. Now you will be part of our family and I hope you will be happy. And if you have a daughter, you can pass these on to her." The bundle of delicate lace and finely sewn tablecloths that I walked away with were like the sealing of a pact of female cooperation between me and Aunt Alexandra. She wanted me on her side.

The idea was to do something quiet and I didn't invite my parents or friends from England to my wedding. On a freezing day we bought our rings at the last minute from a cheap jewellery shop off Athena Street and went to the Town Hall. I'd been expecting a few of Nikitas' friends but in the end there were several dozen. Nobody came specifically for me except Phivos, who was shocked that I had returned to Athens and was getting married to "this old tough-guy" (as he put it). I noticed Phivos throwing rice at Nikitas with extra vehemence at the end of the brief ceremony, as everyone called out the usual greetings:

"May you live!" A few added the traditional wish to a pregnant woman: "Good Freedom!" We moved slowly down Sophocles Street, the entourage holding up the traffic and creating its own commotion – there's no celebration in Greece without noise and disruption. Even traffic lights changing colour provoke a chorus of honking. Nikitas told a joke about the English man on his first trip to Athens who remarked: "How convenient that when the lights go green they make a sound to let you know."

The nuptial lunch was at *Díporto*, Nikitas' favourite basement taverna. We took over the place for the afternoon, waving at passers-by who peered down from the street and called out "May you live!" After we had eaten, musicians arrived with an accordion, a bouzouki and its miniature relation, the *baglamá*. Tables were pushed aside, and soon people were dancing and singing. Underneath my dress (a capacious and brightly embroidered antique that Nikitas had bought in an Istanbul junk shop with the idea of hanging it on the wall), the baby kicked and bucked as though joining in the festivities.

I was pleased to shed my own surname and become "Mond Perifanis" as a reflection of my new, Greek life, but perhaps I should have worried a bit more about becoming part of this particular family. For some time I believed that my move to Greece was a way of creating a simple, pared-down persona – a clever trick, as though leaving behind my old existence physically would therefore slice through the roots that tied me to place, family, and above all, memory. At that stage – the phase I later recognised as my "Hellenic Idyll" – I abandoned myself to the worn but nonetheless charming cliché of the cool northerner being bathed in the warm water of Mediterranean delights. Perhaps it is no more of a cliché than falling in love; both are limited in duration and may be followed by pain or disappointment, but while they last are as real as anything that alters a person's perceptions.

In later years, after the idyll faded, I began to see the experience as a fantasy. I compared my delusion to those lovers of the ancient Greek world who believe the smooth columns and elegant sculptures were always pure white with uncontaminated simplicity. They forget, or don't know, that most of those creations were originally painted with gaudy colours, the sculptures dressed in fashionable robes, their eyes flashy and provocative, the columns bright with circus zigzags and seaside stripes. I might have left behind the location of my past, but it was hubris to believe that a new life with Nikitas would be characterised by clean-cut minimalism. Gradually, I began to experience the alienation of being an outsider. "Where are you from?" became the defining question of each new encounter, where I tried to resist being stereotyped with my nation's characteristics. In the beginning I felt like a character in a novel, recreated each time I revealed my country of birth, but unhampered by my personal history: when nobody knew you as a child, or disliked your parents, or approved of your school, you are potentially something new. But increasingly, I sensed I was being defined by my first answer – put into a box from which I was not then allowed to emerge. Also, although my command of Greek was constantly improving, I became frustrated by my limitations, at not understanding all the jokes and references to personalities, events or films that everyone else had grown up with. I saw the missing parts as my deficiencies.

The third stage, after Idyll and Disillusion is Pragmatism. Ultimately, my status as an outsider became another form of liberation – to hell with other people's preconceptions. I thought of England without disdain, even indulging in occasional bouts of nostalgia for rolling green fields, London's cultural life, tea in a pot and other miscellaneous delights. But I was clear that I was wedded to Greece. And it is in this phase that I have tried to remain.

* * *

Tig was born in the spring with shapely limbs and questioning eyes. Previously, I found other people's babies to be entirely without interest so I was shocked by the ferocity of my love for and fascination with this child. Nikitas, too, was inordinately proud of his daughter, and as we walked about our neighbourhood in Plaka, we were made to stop every other minute for neighbours and shopkeepers to scoop her up and make a fuss: Greeks have no doubt about the delights of other people's offspring – "May she live!" rang in our ears like a signature tune. Tig's first walks were around the slopes of the Acropolis, through the cat-filled alleys of Anafiotika and past the persuasive calls of taverna owners and souvenir sellers. When Nikitas was out, I often walked over to Paradise Street and sat with Aunt Alexandra, who insisted on being called *Yiayia* – Granny – and dandled, fussed, sang nursery rhymes and offered advice as though she had brought up legions of babies. Chryssa made nourishing purées for Tig and loaded me with containers of whatever else she had cooked to take home for me and Nikitas. Even Orestes, aged eleven, appeared charmed by his little half-sister. And maybe because she had an older brother, Tig grew up with the rebellious independence and confidence of a younger sibling, combined with the observant nature and ability to converse with adults that is more typical of only children.

When Tig was a few weeks old, our courtyard was dug up by the Athens and Piraeus Water Board, which was replacing the narrow, frequently blocked drains in our area. The street had a deep ditch opened along one side and cuts were being made at right angles into certain buildings that required updating to a more modern drainage system. As with any project that goes below one metre in the city, the workmen from the water board were accompanied by an archaeological foreman. A dour, middle-aged man, he stood around smoking, with a worried expression.

"You always hope they won't find something special," he said on the day the noisy team of workers took over our shady yard, pulling away the large paving stones, shovelling out the earth, and dragging the pots containing herbs and flowers out of the way. "If you make a discovery, then you have to call in the archaeologists. And then there's no stopping them, with their measuring and note-taking, and the whole job goes on hold and everyone's annoyed. It's a nightmare. You dig any little hole in Athens and you're immediately inside the ancient world." The foreman explained about time-consuming permissions granted from the ministry, about warehouses filled with boxes of finds that nobody has time to examine, because all the archaeologists are busy with new digs and are constantly pressurised by architects, landowners and citizens who need to get on with their lives.

"Every time anything is built or dug in Athens there has to be an excavation first. Someone who wants to build himself a house can wait ten years before something happens, unless he pays for the archaeologists himself. Then, when the study is over, the foundations are laid and a great big concrete apartment block is put over the top. And it's onto the next one."

The water board men completed their day's work and left at 2pm, chucking the last of their Nescafé frappés and cigarette butts into the trench. After checking that they had gone out onto the street, the foreman took me over and pointed to one edge of the cut that had a smooth surface, like a slab of stone.

"It might be a tomb," he said gloomily. "I've had to call the archaeological service and they're sending someone to take a look. Let's hope it's nothing too interesting, *eh*? Or you'll have guests in your yard for rather a long time." Almost as soon as he left, a woman arrived. She was about my age, skinny with short hair, a sunburnt face and dressed in boyish clothes and lace-up boots. She shook my hand in a professional manner.

"Hmmm, let's see what we have here," she said, like a doctor examining a patient. I stood under the large vine that was covered with brand-new, lime-green leaves, and sniffed the black hair on Tig's head as she slept on my breast in a sling.

The archaeologist used a brush and small fork, revealing more of the stone surface and then gently coaxing the red earth around the top edge. Quite unexpectedly, something dropped into her hands, rather as a baby falls into the midwife's grasp, and she held up a delicate, ceramic vase with a narrow neck and a curved belly, on which was engraved a parade of geese and ducks, showing red through the black glaze.

"It's the sort of offering that was normally left on a child's grave," announced the woman, blowing particles of soil from the perfectly formed object in a matter-of-fact way. "When a baby died in ancient Athens, they'd often bury it right by the house. So we have a good indication that this marble is the side of a tomb and I'd say it dates back about two and a half thousand years. The child and its parents almost certainly lived here and the vessel would have contained oil or sacred water. They would have placed it on the sarcophagus at the funeral."

"Aren't you going to examine the tomb?" I looked at the earth-stained side of marble. The archaeologist raised her eyebrows in the silent Greek "No". For a short time, we gazed at the sweeping lines of the geese necks and chubby ducks' wings that were like the illustrations in a children's book, then she rolled up the funerary urn in a plastic bag, and placed it gently but not reverentially in her rucksack.

"I'd be grateful if you don't tell the workmen or they might want to explore it themselves and they'd just destroy it. We're not allowed to dig any further than the work-in-hand requires. Even if the drains are being dug up near a king's grave, you just leave it alone and make a note of it. It's illegal to proceed beyond what is strictly necessary. If we went ahead for something like this, we'd never stop. We already have more than enough material for several lifetimes of work. It's not the digging we want; it's the research and study."

I had always been secretly bored by archaeology, with its painstaking techniques and perplexing terminology, but here in our courtyard were the remains of a child or a baby, whose mother had slept somewhere near where I slept and had suckled her infant where I fed Tig. The palimpsest of centuries upon centuries of human existence was made startlingly real. A manuscript written and re-written, lived and re-lived, wiped out and started over again. My baby was just the latest version. I felt the link by blood that a child can give you when you are an outsider; my own roots in this contradictory city.

"We'll never know," she said with a gesture towards the vertical marble slab. "That will be for future generations to discover. Maybe your daughter's daughter…" She looked down at Tig's sleeping face.

"May she live!"

"Stay a while." I couldn't bear to let her go. "Let me make you a sandwich. Please tell me some more." This buried secret filled me with an intense curiosity and the prospect that it would exist, unexplored, below our feet was deeply frustrating. She hesitated, looking at her watch, then relented, taking off her rucksack again and introducing herself more officially:

"OK. Just for a little while. Amalia Potamitis. Pleased to meet you." She shook my hand. We both went into the kitchen and I prepared some bread and cheese and sliced some tomatoes with basil into a salad, while trying to draw her out about her work.

"Couldn't we just take a quick look at the tomb and then re-cover it?" I asked.

"Where are you from?" she countered, hardening slightly. When I told her England, she smiled a bit too politely.

"The English have had some wonderful excavations in Greece. You're lucky that you have the money for research and proper academic investigation." We took our food out into the courtyard and sat at the table.

"The problem for us Greek archaeologists is that we're so few." She sounded weary. "There's never the funding for proper studies. And there's constant pressure to finish excavations so that construction work can begin. We just don't have the opportunity to uncover our own history – that's done by foreigners – the Americans, the British, French, Germans... they're the ones who have the upper hand, even if on paper they need our permission."

I didn't try pushing Amalia again, but then Nikitas returned and the atmosphere changed.

"I read your articles. I'm a great admirer of your writing," said Amalia, blushing slightly after he introduced himself. We went over to have a look at the side of the sarcophagus with Nikitas, and Amalia obligingly unwrapped the vase with the birds for him. He was captivated and I saw he had the same longing I had to discover more. Amalia explained again why we could not.

"You know the meaning of sarcophagus?" Nikitas asked me. "It's from the Greek *sarx* – flesh, and *phagein* – to eat. Flesh-eating. That's what awaits us all."

We returned to the table and Nikitas brought out more food, turning my modest offering into something more impressive. He offered Amalia *avgotáracho* – the salty fish row preserved in yellow wax, which he sliced into thin, red slivers.

"The people who buried that child would have eaten something like this too," Nikitas said as he put slices on Amalia's plate. "Amazing that we've been trading *avgotáracho* around the Mediterranean for millennia." Nikitas also produced two bottles of beer, which he and Amalia drank while I fed Tig, who had woken up and was starting to grumble. After we had eaten, Nikitas made coffee and brought out three tiny cups of espresso with a bitter-orange syrup sweet made by Chryssa.

"How about if we remove enough of the top soil to just take a look at the lid?" Nikitas put on his warmest smile: he had lost none of his ability to charm women of any age. "Nobody would have to know. We'd put the paving stones back afterwards and it would be our secret."

Amalia paused, then without saying anything, smiled quickly, brought out her tools again and began more of the gentle brushing and scraping I had witnessed earlier. While she worked, Nikitas drank small glasses of mastic liqueur, icily viscous from the freezer, and became increasingly excited. He put his arm around my waist and whispered,

"It'll be full of treasure. *Jewel-studded bracelets, and rings magnificent with sparkling emeralds.*" He was getting on to Cavafy. "Maybe it will be a major discovery. Like Schliemann at Troy. We'll place the golden diadem on your head, Maud, my love…" Once the lid was exposed, it didn't take too much to persuade Amalia to push it slightly to one side so we could peep into its darkness. She produced a torch and pointed its white laser beam onto a jumble of bones and a pitifully small skull.

"It looks like a child of about two or three, I'd say."

"Is that an egg?" asked Nikitas, pointing to a dented white object.

"Something for the journey to the underworld," nodded Amalia. "It's the high alkaline soil that preserves calcium so well. And look over there in the corner. Those little sculptures are toys – a dog and the one with wheels is probably a horse. These were the things the kid would have played with."

Nikitas helped Amalia pull the lid back on the sarcophagus, and they shovelled the earth, laid the paving stones on top and swept away the excess dirt to disguise what we had done. The archaeologist looked solemn as she took her leave.

"Never tell anyone, OK? Grave-robbing and archaeological crime is a huge problem in Greece. I don't want to be part of anything like that."

"*Amalia mou*" (he was already calling her "his" Amalia), "this will be our secret. We'll die with our lips as sealed as the tomb." He held one of her hands between his. "Thank you a thousand times."

* * *

Over the subsequent years, we established certain routines, though that word was anathema to Nikitas, who continued to come and go according to mood. It is true that from the start, our attitudes to time and our body-clocks divided us, though we never discussed that explicitly. Nikitas appreciated the night in the best Greek tradition, believing that life gets going in the evening, reaches a crescendo in the small hours, and that mornings are ideally given over to sleep. This schedule fitted a journalist's hours, and when he had to get up early, there was always siesta time from around 2.30 to 5.30, those appealing "hours of public quiet", when noise must cease, phone calls are kept to a minimum and anyone who can takes to a darkened room for a rest. One of Nikitas' complaints about how Greece was deteriorating was that there was no longer much respect for this quiet time.

There was a time when I used to join Nikitas at night, going out to dinner at eleven, proceeding to a small music club or sitting on a roof terrace with friends till the darkest hours before sunrise. I have even taken dawn coffee near the central market before going home with Nikitas griping contentedly over the early newspapers. After Tig was born, Morena sometimes babysat, and we'd find her lying asleep, open-mouthed on the sofa in the small hours, but gradually I reverted to my northern ways, reneging on the all-nighters. By the time Tig was attending nursery school, I was "sleeping with the chickens" (as Greeks call the wimps who go to bed early), before waking with her at seven. Nikitas didn't complain – there were many who would sit out the night with him – not only journalists and artists, who eschewed early starts, but people with office jobs, who willingly renounced the vacuum of sleep for something more exciting.

"It's the Greek way," Nikitas said. And it was. It was all about grasping life and never mind if your day is tainted with exhaustion. Even children are put into training from a tender age. Was this also why so many Greeks were poets, I wondered. It was so usual to discover that a doctor, a taxi driver or a school teacher was pouring out private poems or had published something somewhere, I had come to expect it – a national habit, like smoking or loyalty to the village.

During my early years in Athens, I had a couple of foreign friends – women who had also married Greek men and were bringing up children. Caroline and I had the same gynaecologist and we bonded over complaints about Greek hospitals, patronising doctors and interfering old women who tell you how to bring up your child. Later, our conversations would inevitably deteriorate into ex-pat grumbling (the chaos, the traffic, the way nobody used seatbelts, even for their children, the smoking…), as though there was little else for us to discuss. So when she and her husband moved to Rhodes to open a hotel, it was something of a relief. I turned instead to a few Greek women I liked, but my favourite, Lydia, turned out to be an old girlfriend of Nikitas' – something they had neglected to tell me. I ended up, if not exactly a hermit, then somebody without a large group of friends, who was absorbed into my husband's impressive collection of comrades, admirers, companions, allies, hangers-on and ex-lovers.

The exception to this pattern was Phivos, who kept in touch over the years and, though Nikitas made enough disparaging remarks about him to indicate he sensed the threat of the younger man, he tolerated our friendship.

"Come out for a drink this evening. Let's go dancing," Phivos would say with a laugh so there were no hard feelings when I refused. "We're still young. Leave the old man and have some fun." We regularly met for coffee, or, as Tig grew older, for early films at the large old cinemas in the centre. He told me the latest gossip from the language school, which he now managed, and about his parents, whom he visited every Sunday for a family gathering.

"I love them and I worry now they're getting older," he said, reminding me that there were families without deep springs of discontent and misery at their core. His relaxed boyishness was strikingly different to Nikitas, who engulfed me with his intensity or, when he was absent, left me bereft in the vacuum. Phivos revealed no dark shadows. He made me laugh. And he made it clear that he still wanted me. I have to admit that there were times when I wanted him, but then I imagined the progression of our affair, its inevitable end, and I knew that I would quickly lose his friendship. I tried to keep things light, giving him advice on girlfriends, who were usually beautiful and impossible.

"You're the only girl for me, Maud," he half-joked, when yet another relationship was on the rocks. "It's obvious," he said. "I mean, what goes *miaow-miaow* on the roof tiles?" He liked that expression, perhaps because things were often clear to him. It's something like asking "Is the Pope Catholic?"

Sometimes I talked to Nikitas about the possibility of moving into the first floor apartment in Paradise Street; it would have been very convenient for me to have family support with Tig. When I was working on a research project, I'd often drop Tig off with Alexandra and Chryssa, who doted on her until I picked her up some hours later. And after all, I argued, the place in Mets was his, unlike the rented house in Plaka, where the picturesque facade and charming courtyard could not disguise the cramped interior that was damp in the winter.

"Given all the battles you fought with your aunt after your grandmother died, it's a pity not to be able to enjoy the place."

"I won't even consider it if Spiros is there," he said. "The man is poison."

In the end we didn't have to wait long for things to change. It was a warm day in early September 1999, when Tig was five and Nikitas had been writing all night at his office. He showed up in the late morning, tired and unshaven, but triumphantly bearing several bags of vegetables and a large red fish.

"I got it at the market and want to cook it straight away while it's fresh," he announced. "I've already called Nikos, who is bringing a couple of friends. I'll set up the barbecue."

I had left Tig at Paradise Street earlier that morning and was finishing off some notes for an English academic, having waded through piles of documents relating to the policies of Eleftherios Venizelos. Wafts of burning charcoal and roasting fish made their way in the first-floor window as Nikitas got to work on vast quantities of food; there was always too much – even if he was cooking for two, he would fill a baking tray for ten.

"That's the Greek way," he'd say if I questioned it. I heard him singing snatches of dissident songs from his heyday, by Theodorakis or Savopoulos, then forgetting the words and humming to himself.

By the time I came down, Nikitas was in his element – at the centre of a small but enthusiastic group of people who didn't have to be at work on a Tuesday afternoon: two journalists, one poet, a university lecturer and a young woman with waist-length hair who didn't speak. Nikitas was engulfed in smoke and garlic fumes, making toasts, hugging new arrivals, and distributing pieces of a rare Cretan *graviéra* cheese and glasses of eye-watering *tsípouro* from the village. The big fish spluttered and spat on the grill.

I noticed Nikitas stumble before I felt the paving stones in the courtyard tremble. In the time it took for a jug to fall from the table and shatter, I felt regret that Nikitas must have drunk too much – again. But then there was a noise like an approaching army of stomping boots and our guests were quick to recognise what was happening.

"The gods are sending their greetings!" said Nikos, the poet, with bravado. But an unfamiliar subterranean roaring was soon accompanied by the disconcerting sound of roof tiles smashing onto the road and distant screams. Car alarms began wailing as we stood frozen. When the juddering stopped and it was obvious that we had not been swallowed up by the earth, the guests began calling their family and friends on mobiles ("Where are you? Yes, we're fine"). A thin crack now snaked its way down the front of our house.

We quickly established that everyone at Paradise Street was unhurt and Nikitas went over to collect Tig. However, a couple of hours later we received a phone call from Chryssa. It seemed that Spiros was dead, though he had not yet been formally identified. At that stage, it was unclear what had happened. He had been out when the earthquake struck and seemed to have had a fall. To be fair to Nikitas, he showed nothing but concern for Aunt Alexandra following her husband's death. But gradually, as the details emerged, he became obsessed by Spiros' demise, intensely gratified by what he saw as its natural justice. He dined out on it for years.

"First we heard that Spiros had fallen down some steps," Nikitas would say, grinning. "Then it turned out that he'd fallen from a window somewhere in Metaxourgeio ("Silkworks") – not exactly a neighbourhood you'd expect his sort to frequent. 'Business' was what my aunt said, but I soon found out what sort of business when I went to the address and found a light bulb hanging outside the door. Apparently my uncle was a regular. I drank coffee with his favourite – a Bulgarian called Franka, with a motherly manner and enormous tits. They'd been together in a room on the first floor when the earthquake struck and the ceiling collapsed, along with a chandelier. It turned out that the plaster ceiling had been rotten, but Spiros thought the whole building was collapsing. So he rushed to the window and jumped.

"It vasn't zo far down. I sought he'd be OK." Nikitas provoked hysterical laughter with his increasingly outrageous imitations of Franka's imperfect Greek, as she crossed herself, saying "God forgive him." For Nikitas it was the perfect end, that someone as pompous and uptight as Spiros should breathe his last outside a brothel on an insalubrious street in Metaxourgeio, surrounded by a group of prostitutes in dishabille. To add the final touch, he impersonated the curious Chinese men from the cheap clothes shop next door, who lingered in groups on the pavement, observing their neighbours, making comments in their own language. It became Nikitas' party piece – cruel, but sweet in its vengefulness.

After the earthquake, our place in Plaka needed extensive repairs and Nikitas gave notice to his tenants in Paradise Street. Within a month we had moved in. It suited me. There was more space, a roof terrace, the magical lemon tree and two

12

To the mountains

ANTIGONE

Dora woke me before dawn and for a moment I thought I was back in the mountains and jolted with a fright. But no, it was November 2008, my son was dead and Dora wanted me to go on a day-trip with a bunch of old has-beens.

"We go to Gorgopotamos every year for the commemoration," she said the day before in reply to my grumbles. "It's important to remember anniversaries – you keep the events alive. And there'll be people you knew." I didn't want to see people I had known but, while Dora may be small, she doesn't accept a "no" without a fight. She said, "It was only in the 1980s that they recognised the fact that we fought in the resistance. Now they've actually admitted we did something positive for our country, we can't go letting them forget. *Eh*, Antigone?" So we drank a first coffee and took a bus through the quiet Sunday streets down to Omonia. It was chilly and we had our coats buttoned up and bags hung across our chests like school satchels. We didn't speak much.

Neither Dora nor I had yet joined up in 1942 when the *andártes* helped the English blow up the Gorgopotamos train bridge, but it had marked a point for everyone in the war. The joy was indescribable. It was the first success in fighting back at the Germans and our youth groups organised various events to celebrate. We were shown the pictures of huge viaduct arches collapsed in the valley, and felt the intoxication of having stopped the Nazis in some way – that they were not unbeatable. Sixty-six years later, those who had fought the fascist occupiers were still celebrating, even Dora and her friends, who were not members of the Communist Party any more. Like many of my Greek comrades, they'd left the Party after 1956 and Khrushchev's revelations, but they remained committed socialists, part of the Left until death.

A chilly November sunrise had lit up the city by the time we found the coach parked at Kotzia Square, apparently now re-named National Resistance.

White-haired comrades were murmuring in groups on the pavement, or hauling themselves slowly up the steps and into their seats. Several people came up to me.

"Welcome back, Antigone. It's me, Dimitra Papakonstantinou, from Volos. Do you remember?"

I didn't.

"We listened to you on the radio all those years. You were our secret – 'the voice of truth'. You kept us going." So many secrets, so many truths.

"Condolences, Antigone. You never lacked courage." What a shock to see beautiful Artemis as a heavy granny with wobbling jowls and dentures that clicked. She had been sent away from the mountains on account of her looks. We called her Beauty, but she never did anything to provoke. Of course that made her all the more attractive. They said she distracted the men just by being there. The ELAS ethics were very strict – a Spartan code, with relationships strictly forbidden. There was no place for romancing, let alone pregnancy. Normality was suspended.

Mod had said she might come and arrived with a teenage girl I realised must be my granddaughter. They both looked exhausted and I marvelled at this woman's persistence. She said, "I thought you would both like to meet. After all, this is her history too." The mother presented the child, who looked at me suspiciously, with large, black eyes, and kicked her shoe against the kerb. I say child, but I could see she already had a woman's body. I didn't know how to greet her and was saved by Dora, who rushed in saying, "Welcome to *Antigonaki* – you look just as your grandmother did." It was true that she had the same unruly black hair I had, and her direct eyes were familiar. You could see that we were family. Dora kissed her and cooed and fussed as though the girl were her own grand-daughter, which allowed me time to gather myself and do the right thing. I wanted to be like Dora but I am not. I'm out of practice with family matters. I said, "I am very, very pleased to meet you," and gave her a kiss on each cheek, which didn't feel enough. A piece of metal pierced her eyebrow – an unnerving contrast with her lovely face.

Just before the bus set off we took our places, with "the young ones" in front of me and Dora. I looked through the gap in the seats at their heads – young Antigone's tangled lengths of black next to her mother's reddish brown curls. I imagined how it would be to stroke it, but didn't. Twice,

189

my granddaughter turned to take a quick look at me, trying not to catch my eye. A tape of Greek and international revolutionary songs was playing too loudly through speakers. A large, laminated photograph of Aris had been stuck to the coach's windscreen. He looked just as I remembered him, with his clever gaze and black beard. He was wearing a leather jerkin, a bandolier and a surprisingly ornamental sword. Aris Velouchiotis was tubby and shorter than many of the girls, and he was never very polite to us – in fact he was a bit of a misogynist. But he commanded respect and was strict with everyone in ELAS. Nobody doubted that the punishment for disobedience would be harsh. He was from my father's parts and though he took the name Aris from the god of war, his surname honoured Velouchi, the snow-capped peak that dominates the landscape. He was like a prince of the mountains with his guard of *Mavroskoufides* [Black Caps]. The story was that their black sheepskin hats were taken from Vlach collaborators up in the north after Aris and his men destroyed them. Whatever his failings, Aris was the right man to lead us and, like an archbishop, he inspired us to take the oath and to hold no doubts.

Across the aisle, some comrades were complaining.

"Why is it that there are so many roads and squares around the country dedicated to other resistance leaders like Zervas, but not for Aris? We should have a Velouchiotis Street in every town." And so on. Having seen all the recent changes of street names in Russia and the tumbled statues of Lenin and Stalin, I have seen how meaningless these cycles of history and memory can be.

After about an hour on the coach we stopped at a large

service station and were told to be back at the bus in ten minutes, but my granddaughter disappeared. We all sat waiting while Mod ran around the place calling "Tig, Tig," until she returned saying that her daughter had finally answered her mobile phone. The girl announced that she had walked over the Autogrill foot-bridge to the other side of the National Road, found a bus heading back to Athens, and was now on it. Mod looked shattered.

She told me and Dora that she'd been trying to keep her daughter away from her older brother, Orestes, and his friends. She said, "Orestes is getting her involved in things she is much too young for." Apparently my grandson belongs to an anarchist group. Someone saw him taking Tig into the Polytechnic, which has become like a headquarters where they meet, and plan their fights with the police. They even make petrol bombs there. I watched Mod through the gap in the seats, weeping as the bus set off again towards the north. So much for any rapport with my namesake. It seems she was not so impressed by her long-lost grandmother.

The rest of the comrades were in a good mood and didn't notice the small family drama. They shouted jokey comments across the aisles.

"The English Ambassador is going to be at the ceremony. He'll give us all a gold sovereign!" How ironic that even though blowing up the Gorgopotamos bridge was the most successful of Anglo-Greek collaborations, we still feel betrayed by the English. Later we learned that Churchill had forbidden the BBC from even mentioning Aris and his *andártes*. So when they reported the triumph on the radio, nobody heard that we had been there, let alone that ELAS boys had been in the majority. We were useful to the English – they let us help them – but they were against us from early in the war. That sense of injustice never goes away. It is true what they say about the victors writing history, but those who win have the luxury of forgetting. It's the losers who remember – those who experienced the humiliation of defeat.

*　*　*

The day-trip to Gorgopotamos shunted me back in time and the soothing grumble of the coach's engine coaxed out memories. We sped along a large, new road, which I presume followed the same route I had taken sixty-five years earlier, when Markos and I went to the mountains. "To the mountains" – that was our dream, as it was for so many who dreamed of freedom. The landscape felt familiar, though as children we used to travel from Athens by train, rumbling slowly northwards to Lianokladi, on the plain outside Lamia. There was no road up to the village then, and one of my earliest memories was being in my mother's arms as we rode up the winding track by mule. It was dark, and she had pointed into the distance.

"Can you see the lights up there? That's Perivoli."

When Markos and I went to those parts, in 1943, we had hidden in the back of a transport lorry driven by a friend of Uncle Diamantis. We couldn't see anything as we were pressed in among a load of canvas rolls. Icy rain rattled like stones on the metal roof and I leaned against my brother. I remember noticing how wiry and strong he had become, even though he still looked young for his age. He put his arm around my shoulder and his hands were grimy from the floor of the truck. His breath smelled of lemon – we had brought one from our tree to suck against the travel sickness we both suffered from. We didn't think about our mother. We had left her a note saying: "We have gone to do our duty as Greeks." Markos said: "If I see a German I'll kill him." He showed me his knife in its leather sheath. We were both fuelled by youth and hatred of the enemy that was destroying our country.

There was a German checkpoint at Thermopylae, where the mountain cuts down steeply to the road and where Ephialtes betrayed his fellow Greeks to the Persians. Interesting that his treachery should be memorialised by using his name as the word for nightmare. Is there a perverse pleasure in remembering our traitors? Why else should we burn effigies of Judas each year before Easter? Fortunately for us, the weather was abysmal (it was raining chair legs, as the driver commented), and there was not a thorough search, so the truck was soon on its way again. After a few kilometres, the driver turned off the road onto a track that ran through trees. He stopped and came round to the back. He said, "Kids, this is where you get out. You can make your way to Perivoli – it shouldn't be more than a few hours. Keep in among the trees. This is your area, you must know the way."

Markos did know and he led me like an agile goat, passing the sulphurous thermal springs and up into the oaks and firs that cover these slopes. We both loved this area, where Mount Iti looms dark indigo and the Sperchios valley opens out green and fertile down to the sea. Markos had walked and bicycled all over it. Already, he had changed on this journey from a boy who follows his older sister, to a young man of almost eighteen who leads her. Sometimes he waited, playing the gallant, holding out his hand to help me up a difficult slope, or pressing back the branches of a tree so I could pass. We don't always change gradually in life; some-times it happens all at once, like a chrysalis opening or an egg hatching. Markos' metamorphosis was like that.

As you travel away from the sea in Greece, you enter a more solid, darker, rougher landscape, peopled by quieter, more serious characters. Our father used to tell us that we should be proud to be *Roumeliotes*, from Roumeli – central Greece. We were children of the mountains, who meant what they said, who had their feet on the ground, but were always independent. The contrast was with the instability of the sea and its influence; frivolous, dancing islanders who were as unreliable as their weather, or the Asia Minor Greeks with their cosmopolitan ways ("except your mother, of course"). My father instilled in us a love of this forested terrain, so we felt we belonged there, "in the mountains", even though we lived in Athens. He used to say, "This earth is made up of the bones of our ancestors and we have this earth in our bones." Over the years, Father had given back to his small village, paying for the restructuring of the main square, and helping many of its families with financial and other prob-lems. Whenever he returned to Perivoli he was feted as "one of ours", and though he was dressed in fashionable suits and town shoes, he was as comfortable sitting in the coffee shop with the shepherds and smallholders as though he had never left their ranks.

By the time Markos and I arrived at Perivoli we were wet

through, but happy to be in our beloved village. I always liked its winter scent of wood smoke, distant snow and sheep shit and the last chrysanthemums wilting in gardens. We had been instructed not to go to our house, but to the next-door building, where the Kallos family lived. Christos Kallos took care of our property and tended the vegetables and fruit trees. The tallest man in the village, with a slow, booming voice and clear grey eyes, he welcomed us into the house, calling for his wife, *Kyria* Lukia, who was much smaller but equally forceful a character. "Give the guest food and a bed, and then ask who he is" was their policy and in any case, we were welcomed like family. *Kyria* Lukia took us to the fireplace and told us to undress, giving us blankets to wrap up in. Chryssa, their golden-haired daughter, who had her father's eyes and her mother's stature, brought us mountain tea. A little younger than Markos, she had played with us every summer when we were children, but she had turned into a woman since our last visit. I could tell that Markos was awed by the mysterious transformation, taking her in with quick glances. Chryssa's two older brothers, Panayiotis and Theodoros, were the village's most handsome bachelors, known for their dancing. They had fought up in Albania, walked all the way back and were now signed up with ELAS. They said, "There are lots of girls now. Soon everyone will have joined."

Kyria Lukia dried our clothes and cooked *bobóta* in the outdoor oven. After the meagre city rations, the cornmeal baked with goat's cheese and the wild greens in olive oil were the most delicious tastes. There was no bread as all the wheat had been taken by the Germans and the villagers had to make do with a sludge of acorns and potatoes. Afterwards, we cracked walnuts by the fire. I slept for a few hours in Chryssa's bed before being woken by her brothers, whispering that we must leave. Panayiotis and Theodoros walked Markos and me all the way up to Karpenisi. We travelled only after nightfall, stopping at Palaiovracha and several safe villages along the way. It was a difficult journey, walking through wet woods and along goat tracks obscured by snow, avoiding dogs and people. We tried not to slip or trip in the darkness. Even the crackle of fallen oak leaves was a possible danger. In this region where Aris was loved, there were still those who would hand you over to the Germans. It was the same when people had betrayed the old klepht bands to the Turks – the *andártes* used some of their old hiding places, as well as a few of their techniques. By day, we hid – once in a shepherd's hut and once making a shelter from branches in a wood.

While we waited for darkness, Panayiotis and Theodoros told us stories about Albania, the amazing triumph when little Greece had beaten back the Italians. Then the subsequent disillusionment when defeat by the Germans became inescapable. On their way to the front they had had an extraordinary experience that still haunted them. Some months before the two young men had left for war, the family's horse, Bebis, had been forcibly taken away by the army to be employed as a pack animal. He was only a few years old and much loved. His mother had died giving birth to him and the family had brought him up themselves, feeding him by dipping their fingers into a bucket of milk and letting him suck. That's why they called him Baby. Naturally, they thought they had seen the last of their horse. However, when the brothers were transported up into the snowy mountains that link Greece and Albania, their truck slowed as they reached an encampment. And there, tied to a tree, was Bebis. Identifying him immediately by his characteristic dappled grey colouring and white muzzle, they called his name from the truck. The horse whinnied, recognising them. Then it reared up on his hind-legs and collapsed. Panayiotis and Theodoros rushed over but the horse was breathing its last. It died shortly afterwards from heart failure. They were tough village boys, these brothers, who thought nothing of slaughtering animals, but they were shocked by this episode. "Fate brought us together again," lamented Theodoros, "only to take him away for ever."

Once in Karpenisi, Markos and I were signed up into the 13th Division of ELAS and given uniforms. I was told, "You're educated. You've been to university, so you'll be a captain." I explained that there hadn't been any lessons at the university but I was just told to choose a name. Our *nom de guerre* was supposed to protect our families, but it did something just as important – it turned us into fighters, made us new people. I chose Victory and, as *Kapetanissa* Niki, I was put in charge of a girls' platoon. Markos became Wind. We had finally arrived "in the mountains" – a term which had become synonymous with the resistance movement. People would not only say "we're going to the mountains" when they joined the partisans, the newspapers would report that "the mountains have decided to take part in negotiations with the British" or "the mountains are fighting back at the Nazis". Needless to say, it often later became "the mountains are extremists whose intentions are dangerous".

They gave me a week's training and I was looked after by Storm, whose real name was Anastasia Alexiou. At twenty-four, she was the oldest woman in our division, and we showed her the respect we felt her age deserved. She was short and stocky, with the strength of two men and the determination of thirty.

"Better one hour of freedom than forty years of slavery and prison," she repeated as often as possible. "If they could fight and die for that in 1821, it's good enough for me now." We really did see ourselves as the descendants of the War of Independence. We felt we had wings. That is very pleasing to the young.

Storm had killed a German soldier and for some strange reason, she had taken his trousers. Other people took guns, perhaps a watch, but Storm had removed the dead Nazi's muddy khakis, taken up the hems and now wore them herself. We couldn't understand her distasteful attachment to these spoils of war, but we had to admire her bravery and determination. Eventually, when she was ordered to remove the Nazi uniform, she folded up her trophy and carried it around in her knapsack, as though the trousers had become a lucky charm.

My lucky charm was a rifle – a Mauser, given to me by Captain Eagle. I suppose it had come from a German too. I carried the gun with me all day and slept with it close at night, its metallic smell strangely soothing. Eagle was a fighter, a committed *andártis* with arms hard as iron. He had a set look to his face, but his brown eyes reminded me of a calf. I knew he liked me, though, of course, he could do nothing about it. It was all in the angle of a glance or the tone of voice, and he was kind to me. I have often thought about how things might have ended up, if we had lived in another place or time. At that point, love was an irrelevance to be put on hold until the world had changed. And the truth is that, even if we had been free, I was still thinking about Johnny. I never mentioned my Englishman – already there was a suspicion that the English were only in Greece for their own gain. But at night when I stood on guard, it was Johnny's face I saw. And when we trudged through the snow, I imagined him warming my hands in his. I spoke English words over and over in my mind like incantations. "Freedom" seemed a different thing to "*Eleftheria*" – more theoretical, but equally profound. In my dreams I saw things I could not admit to myself.

Most of the time, my girls' platoon was far from the ambushes and skirmishes with the Germans, though the threat was always there. Our main task was going to the villages, persuading people to join our movement and organising cultural performances, with songs, dances and small theatre pieces. We were "preparing the ground" so that once the war ended the people could run their own lives. *Laokratia*. Rule by the people. Women alongside men. Liberty would bring equality. *Laokratia* – in "our" villages, our banners proclaimed it with bright red paint on old sheets, hung from bedroom windows as they used to do with bridal sheets the morning after, as proof of virginity.

"Justice is in your hands now," we explained. We helped them set up people's courts, organised classes for adult literacy and opened schools that had been closed and, had never taught children beyond the age of twelve. I realised for the first time how people lived in the villages, where hunger and isolation kept them weak and oppressed, and where the man of the house was a dictator. Girls and women were finally throwing down their headscarves and walking with heads uncovered.

Our "government of the mountains" was ushering in a new era of justice and hope.

The physical side of life was hard. I don't remember ever having enough sleep or being completely dry. We were continually drenched, marching through streams, sleeping outside. When we lit fires, we gave off steam. Our legs were red and sore from the rough woollen trousers, but when we could, we'd take them off at night and press them under our packs so they'd get creases. We were still women. We cared about our appearance. And at our time of the month, we just had to cope. We washed our towels in the rivers – we always kept clean. And when we had no toothpaste, we used charcoal from the fire to clean our teeth. As to our hair, we tied it in plaits, and made a promise to each other to leave it uncut until we were rid of the occupiers.

❋   ❋   ❋

After my training was over and I had learned something about life in the mountains, Storm and I were instructed to take some supplies and a message to a camp high up on Mount Iti. It was early spring and down in the valley the blossom was out. At the last minute, Captain Eagle told Markos to go with us as a guide, and it was lucky he did, as I don't think we would have found the place otherwise. Markos was also the only one who could keep our mule going. Storm started out by teasing me and my brother for being "bourgeois butter-babies" who wouldn't have known the mule's arse from its face if she hadn't been there to help. But she had to eat her words when, half-way up the mountain, the mule refused to budge. It just stopped and stared at us as though it had had enough and whatever Storm or I did, we couldn't change its mind. Strangely, though, Markos spoke to it, as if he was explaining something to a child, and stroked its neck. Gradually we realised it was going to move for him and it did. After that the animal would only proceed for Markos, who patted and praised it as we walked up towards the sky above the clouds. My brother was a privileged city boy, but he had absorbed the practical skills of a villager – he knew how to make things, how to chop wood or help with the animals. I saw Storm's attitude change along with the mule's, as Markos won them over.

It was night when we reached the cave. It had been used as a hide-out since the Turkish occupation, and probably ever since men had first needed to disappear from the authorities. We saw flickering flames from the darkness within and, tethering our mule to the other animals near the entrance, we made our way in. We were like Odysseus' men entering the Cyclops' lair – in this case, a large rocky chamber, lit by a few oil lamps and a fire. A hefty, wild-eyed *Kapetánios* known as Jason greeted us.

"Welcome, comrades! We're expecting you." He opened his arms as though this was his palace and he was the *pashá*. "Come and get warm, and then we'll feed you." About twenty-five bearded men were sprawled around a blazing fire, while others lay on make-shift beds of branches and leaves or sat cleaning their guns. They were dressed in a bizarre mix of clothes that included the official ELAS uniform, but also items acquired from Italians. Some men were dressed like the old klepht brigands, in the *foustanélla*. These kilts had 400 pleats to mark each year of slavery under the Turks. There was also a priest, his black robes spattered with mud and crossed with a double bandolier of bullets beneath a wooden crucifix. Of all the partisans in the cave, Papakarabinas was the most imposing. Father Rifle had a sonorous voice and slow-moving eyes that seemed to read your mind. He wore a stovepipe hat but kept a cutlass in his belt. Though I later heard him preach God's love, it was clear that God meant us to kill Germans however we could.

As we went towards the fire, two men rose to greet us. The first was Uncle Diamantis, who took me and Markos in his arms. He quickly wiped his eyes to prevent anyone seeing his tears of pleasure – despite his theoretical principles and belief in control, he was an emotional man who was quick to cry or be overwhelmed by anger. Beyond him I saw the other man, wrapped in a long cloak. It was his movement and the apologetic hunch of the shoulders that helped me recognise him– a loping movement of loosely jointed limbs.

"Antigone! Markos!" The voice was unmistakable and, when our uncle released us, Johnny took our hands, then changed his mind and embraced us in turn. Numerous pairs of eyes were on this unlikely reunion. As Johnny's dark-blonde beard rubbed against my face I thought I might faint. Perhaps it was the warmth of the cave after the cold outside. Luckily Johnny and Markos started asking each other questions, the *andártes* became animated and *Kapetan* Iasonas ordered a bottle of *tsípouro* to be passed around in celebration. We all took swigs of the burning spirit, and my shock was lost in the confusion and darkness. My uncle made a toast to the brave Greeks who were living on the mountain where Achilles was born. This was where klephts had hidden from the Turks and where history was once more being made.

When we had eaten there was music and singing – they had a couple of instruments. When the men began to dance, Markos pulled me and Johnny up and we joined them, making our way around the fire. Johnny stumbled as he tried to make up the steps and our boots pounded on the earth floor. Afterwards, when there were some quieter songs, Markos and I sat with Johnny and Uncle Diamantis and talked. Our clothes dried and our faces reddened from the fire. They were both there to prepare for an operation against a German convoy down in the valley. Negotiations were taking place. Johnny said, "The Nazis are finished and they know it. It's just a matter of time now and they'll be gone."

Uncle Diamantis rubbed the stumps of his missing fingers. He said, "He's right. The Germans will go, and then the English must leave us to our own freedom." He patted Johnny a little too heavily on the shoulder, and addressed Markos and me. "This young man is a good person. I know he gave you culture and education when you were young. But he must tell his people that the time has come to let us Greeks make our own future without interference. We don't want any more of their kings and we don't want to be an English colony. He's a good man, but he and his people must let us run our country." Johnny looked ill-at-ease, nodding and half-agreeing. "We'll soon be off," he said, managing a short laugh.

Then he changed the subject, turning to mythology. Here we were up on Mount Iti, which was not only Achilles' patch but the place where Hercules died, he said. After all his struggles, the strong man of myth had submitted, gathering trees and building his own funeral pyre. When he was ready, he had placed his lion's skin over his body, laid his head on his club and commanded Philoctetes to light the fire.

When Johnny thought the three of us were no longer being closely scrutinised, he told us in English that we had made a mistake by joining ELAS, that we had "backed the wrong horse". Naturally, we were right to resist, "but not with the communists. You won't get anywhere with them." Markos grew angry. He asked Johnny, "So what are you doing here?" We began to get a sense of the "English games" that the *andártes* had told us about – how, while we were trying to build a new society, they always felt they knew better.

Johnny said, "I'm on your side. I only want the best for you and Greece. I know the problems your kings have brought – of course there should be a referendum. But you won't succeed with the Stalinists." We asked him many questions and most of his answers have faded, though I will never forget how strange it was to hear his description of his recent stay in Egypt. The glamour of cocktails at the officers' club, men in white uniforms and beautiful women in evening gowns. We heard about boat trips on the Nile, rumours, spies. I was like a child listening to a fairy story. There, in the darkness of the cave, with its strong aroma of unwashed men, horses and smoke, these images were scarcely credible.

Before we settled down for the night, I went out of the cave and walked a little way to relieve myself. The clouds had cleared and the sky was bright with stars. The still, cold silence was overwhelmingly beautiful, as though the world had been left behind. When I went back, I saw Johnny and Markos standing by the entrance. Johnny had his arm around my brother's shoulder. Then he held out his hand, gesturing at me and murmuring in English:

"And the beautiful sister, the warrior Antigone." By the time we went in again, most of the men had lain down and there was already some of the snoring and grunting that continued through the night. I lay back-to-back with Storm – it was the usual way of keeping warm – and Markos did the same with Johnny, whose eyes I spotted wide open and thoughtful in the darkness. It was a strange night, where my happiness at finding myself with the man I had longed for was countered by misgivings about what he had told us. As though to bring me down to earth, we all became infested with fleas, and by morning I was covered with small, intensely itchy bumps.

My memories return like snapshots – isolated scenes, though the faces are often missing. I can't properly remember what my brother looked like. I know he smiled a lot, but I can't picture his features. Two days later, Markos left with most of the men to set up the ambush and Johnny made his own way – he didn't say where he was heading. Storm and I stayed in the cave with a wounded man who couldn't walk. We tried to make ourselves useful; we darned socks, cooked bean soup and tidied the branches into bed-shaped piles. There was nothing else to do except pick fleas from our clothes and throw them to crackle in the fire. I felt bereft.

After the ambush, in which four Germans were killed and several vehicles destroyed, Storm and I were due to meet our platoon in Perivoli. My father's birthplace was part of the cultural programme that had been set in motion, with a view to improving the deprivations of village life. We had staged theatre performances there and the villagers' people's court had been very successful. It was a still, hazy dusk when we approached Perivoli and even before we saw anything we smelled the stink. However, we didn't notice the last plumes of smoke that were still twisting up skywards until we were close enough to see the horror. The whole village had been destroyed. The houses were blackened ruins with collapsed roofs. The streets were covered in ash. An old woman came up to us moaning in shock, her face filthy with soot.

"The Germans came just after dawn." She said she had been on the hill with her sheep. She watched it all. She could do nothing.

"First they took the men and shot them. Afterwards they put whoever they found inside the school." We trudged with her through the charred rubble to the main square. A few bodies lay in the street, but there was a sinister silence – the pile of smoking stones and timbers which had been a school was filled with dead villagers. The murder location became a funeral pyre. Easy revenge for the ambush the day before.

I felt utterly helpless in the face of the atrocity. Even Storm appeared paralysed, and she had developed a thick skin from witnessing death in many forms. We sat on a wall and smoked in silence. Then Storm shook herself into movement and addressed me formally as though she was giving orders to dismantle camp.

"*Kapetanissa* Victory, we will search for survivors. After that, we'll gather up the dead and wait for the rest of our platoon." We didn't find anyone alive apart from the old woman. Those who had escaped were up in the hills. Some returned the next day and moved about like ghosts, unable even to grieve properly. The tragedy was too great.

Storm and I allocated an area near the destroyed school for laying out the bodies and we carried the murdered villagers there. My nostrils filled with ash and the awful stench of scorched flesh. Many of the blackened corpses were people I had known since childhood, though I was unable to identify most of them. The only thing that made it possible for me to carry out the job without breaking down was the hatred I felt against those who had perpetrated the atrocity. It brought an element of coldness to my panic. In one house we found a mother with four children, all of whom had been shot, except the baby, whose head was smashed against the wall. His brains were spilt on the floor. His woollen booties had come off and I put them back on his feet and swaddled him in a rug. That is something you can never forget. Or forgive.

My clothes and hair became impregnated with the stink of smoke and burnt bodies and I couldn't get rid of it for weeks. After some days, I washed my hair, but our thick woollen uniforms were too heavy to wash and dry in the cold winter weather, during constant changes of camp. Every time I lay down to sleep I felt nauseous from the lingering smell of people burnt to death.

Our platoon arrived with some of the men from the cave, including Father Rifle. Storm took charge of our girls, forbidding them to give in to their emotions.

"You are fighters," she shouted. "Now let's get on with it." So we spent our time burying the people of Perivoli. We carried them to the cemetery and dug graves, though the bodies from the school were in such a bad state we placed them in one pit. The roots from a row of cypresses made it hard to extract the earth, but they stood by like dark guards of mourning. Father Rifle performed brief funerary rites – nobody had the heart for more. The subdued ceremonies were nothing like the funerals for *andártes*, where we had sung the *Internationale*, wrapped the body in a Greek flag and fired a gun in the air.

During the quiet after the warrior-priest's chanting, I heard a noise coming from inside the ossuary – a moaning like an animal in pain. I opened the wooden door and saw someone curled up on the floor. She was emitting awful sounds. I thought it was an old woman – her hair was grey and matted and she was filthy. But then I saw it was Chryssa. Her fair hair was covered with soot. Initially I imagined she was wounded, but we found no injury. The damage was emotional. She was unable to speak or fully understand what we were saying, but we discovered later that her entire family had been killed. Her brothers, Panayiotis and Theodoros, had been taken off with their father and shot. Her mother had been burnt alive in the school with the others. We never found out exactly how Chryssa had escaped – her family's house was now little more than four blackened walls. Some of the girls made her mountain tea and wrapped her in blankets, and while we buried the dead, golden-haired Chryssa lay in the ossuary among piles of boxes filled with the bones of her forebears.

The following day Markos arrived with more men. He was so shocked he could not speak. I saw him leaning against the gaping mouth that had been Chryssa's front door, trying not to let anyone see that he had vomited. Before we left Perivoli, Markos made me promise that one day we would rebuild our house there and that wherever he died, he should be buried in the village or at least end up in the ossuary. I would break both promises. Perivoli became one more name on the list of places that were annihilated – the hundreds of villages torched and ransacked, their ruins inhabited by grieving, black-ragged survivors.

13
English alien

MAUD

"Am I allowed to go now?" Tig spoke like a rebel mocking a tin-pot dictator. She looked the part too, having cut off her long hair the day she ran away from the Gorgopotamos trip. I presumed this act was to mark something as, after all, the choices were many: rebellion, teenage provocation, not to mention the hackneyed "stage of grief" devoted to anger. She looked younger, the roughly hacked locks giving her the painfully vulnerable look of a prisoner or a mental patient.

"I was so worried. You should have told me you were going back to Athens before you just walked off." She looked at me without pity.

"As if you'd have let me." She scraped the kitchen table with her fingernail.

I had expected the expedition to Gorgopotamos to be a way of introducing Tig to her grandmother, while conveniently keeping her apart from Orestes and his anarchist cronies for at least a day. But it had turned into a debacle. I heard my voice rise as I asked her again what she was doing when she went out with Orestes and his friends. The tone of Tig's reply was a lugubrious contralto.

"Nothing. We just talk." She looked away, as though preoccupied with more important thoughts, and when I told her she was grounded for a week with no leaving the house except for school, she barely reacted.

"You can lock someone up but you can't change their beliefs." It sounded like a quote from her father.

During the week of Tig's punishment she avoided me. I recalled the same feelings of rejection when she had been about nine and she stopped speaking English. Sometime later she had reverted, saying it embarrassed her to hear me talking in Greek. Her refusal to speak her mother tongue seemed to be a way of allying herself to her father – in effect, he was her *patrída,* her fatherland.

"I hate English, it's stupid," she had said, as though seeking her father's approval in a conspiracy against the outsider. Someone suggested it was an Oedipal phase that would pass.

"Electra complex," Nikitas corrected.

"Female Oedipal complex?" suggested a friend with years of psychoanalysis to draw on. I knew consciously that it was only a stage, but Tig's youthful dismissal of me through my language upset me. I was alienated from my own child. I wept when I could not be seen – in the shower, hot tears of frustration washed away by the jets of water. It came with a realisation that there would always be things I could not understand in Greece – that I was doomed to remain at the margins.

It only gradually dawned on me that my marginality and my lack of interest in politics was a significant lacuna in my character for my husband. After all, I was assimilated in numerous ways and Nikitas had wanted me to come to Greece and live with him when I was far more ignorant of his world. Had my innocence worn thin, I wondered. I had always been aware that like most of his fellow Greeks, Nikitas assessed someone on the basis of what he sensed or knew their politics to be. He was far from unusual in stating that he could not imagine liking, let alone being friends with someone who was right-wing. I knew theoretically that in Greece everyone cares about politics in a way that you don't have to in England – all Greeks have a political position, probably that of their family, which determines the students' groups they join, the newspaper they read, the coffee shop or taverna they patronise and whose company they keep. I assumed that, as a foreigner, I was exempt from this framework, though my declaration to new acquaintances that I was "apolitical" drew a blank. There was so much that was good in our marriage that for a long time it had not been obvious to me how hard it was to be a part of Nikitas' life and not be part of this game.

I understood that the Civil War had left Greece wrenched apart, so that allegiance to one side or the other was still often based on wounds inflicted almost a lifetime before. However, it was impossible for me to feel that pain. I sometimes wondered why Nikitas had chosen a wife who cared so little about things he believed to be crucial. I would never experience what it meant to be born into such a small, powerless population that had suffered so much but whose members knew they belonged right at the centre of the universe. It took me a long time to realise that it also helped him that I was an outsider, that I did not belong and therefore did not have to become part of the mess. Nikitas' own conversion from the highly conservative milieu in which Alexandra and Spiros had brought him up was like a religious rebirth. It had gone along with the discovery of what had happened to his mother – she was the martyr at the heart of the story. And simultaneously, it was the most effective rejection of his adoptive parents he could have made.

By the time Tig was nine she was already imbued with a sense of political values I would never have. It had come as naturally as the ability to cross herself when she passed a church – a habit instilled by Alexandra and Chryssa when she was two and that had shocked me when I had first witnessed her pudgy, pink hand make the movements from her pushchair; she had only dropped the habit in recent years. But Tig's reaction against me went further than customs. I wondered whether she had overheard Nikitas' increasingly frequent and negative comments about the English, ostensibly due to the research for his documentary series. He had even included a section about British anthropologists who travelled "in the footsteps of their colonial forebears". These "so-called scholars" objectified and patronised the Greeks as they did the Africans or the Papuans of New Guinea.

"Greece was hardly a British colony," I retorted. But that seemed to be beside the point. I still smarted from what I had taken as a lightly veiled insult to my own well-intentioned research on Thasos. I might not have inherited the suffering of generations as Nikitas (and presumably Orestes and Tig) had merely by being Greek. But I was far from immune to feeling wounded by my husband's slights. I remembered his words exactly.

"These anthropologists generally avoid the complexities and

contradictions of Greece's more sophisticated urban populations. They focus instead on remote rural communities, which conform more easily to ready-made clichés of simplicity and tradition."

During the week after Tig cut off her hair, I noticed that she was sneaking out with Orestes, but I didn't even try to question her. Several times, she returned late in the evening, pretending she had been up in his room on the terrace, though her breezy manner and cool cheeks indicated otherwise. I began to realise that it was not only my daughter who appeared to be avoiding me. Orestes rarely came into the apartment and didn't pause to wave any more from outside the kitchen window when he bounded down the external spiral stairs, or come in with a lemon blossom he had picked on the way up. Even Antigone announced that for the next days she was going to stay in at Dora's house and write. I started to think that maybe she knew I had not told her the truth about the packet of Johnny's letters. I wasn't even sure why I had lied and said I only saw one. One evening, overwhelmed by loneliness, I decided to go and see if Orestes was in his studio. Pausing at the top of the metal staircase, where it joins the terrace, I took in the ambient sounds – two dogs barking, the Lambakis' television blaring bouzouki songs from next door and some teenage boys I could see smoking and muttering in the back alley. Approaching Orestes' studio, I stopped again, making out the unmistakable noise of people making love – a rhythmic beat of hushed voices and the bed or something hard tapping softly against a wall. I stayed a few seconds more than I would have done if someone had been watching me, wondering who was in there with my stepson, then crept down the metal stairs, trying not to make them creak too much.

Later, as I prepared to go to bed, I saw the shadow of an unknown woman letting herself out of the back gate into the alley. It brought on a wave of envy and grief that, at forty-two, I was no longer young, that I was left on my own, that I had nobody to hold me. I pictured the frightful image of Nikitas' body that I knew so well, disintegrating in the earth. My awareness that Phivos might be waiting, choosing his moment to move in, like the inevitable hero of a story, only made me feel worse. I thought again about the point, some years ago, when something might have developed between us. I had been miserable, suspecting that Nikitas was involved with someone else. Instead of confronting my husband, I had turned to my old friend and, one evening, Phivos and I had gone out to dinner and drunk too much. I was tempted. And in different ways, we both said things we regretted. It was hard to forget some of his phrases: Nikitas was "a fake, who used the superficial charms of a Zorba to pull the girls," Phivos had said. I'd be better off with someone my own age. I can't remember if he said: "someone like me," but the implication was obvious. Although I was still close to Phivos, I could not get involved in the way he wanted. It was too late.

"It must have been very hard for you, losing Spiros," I said the next morning when I encountered Aunt Alexandra collecting her mail from the post box outside the front door. "Did you feel lonely?" I didn't say that I had not slept all night, pierced by the sharpest, most overwhelming loneliness I had ever experienced.

"My girl, the only thing left for me is prayer," she said. I had noticed her frequent visits to church and the meetings with

Father Apostolos. "We all suffer, but I know God is looking after me. I've always known that he will protect me. Faith is what matters in the end. Faith and love, and I have plenty of both." She didn't add, "Unlike some people," but it was there in her tone. The return of the prodigal sister had been a huge shock to her habitual confidence.

Even Chryssa seemed to have lost her usual equanimity and moved about in a daze.

"Nikitas was like a son to me," she repeated, wiping her eyes with the back of her arthritic hands. "Who'd have thought it? God forgive him. And now Antigone back home. It's true what they say: 'Another person's soul is an abyss'; you can never see down to the depths."

After a decade living at Paradise Street, I had become accustomed to the bustle and intimacy of our irregular extended family. We may not have been a "normal" Greek family, but we had many of their normal characteristics. These included living with relations in close proximity; countless Athenian apartment blocks have half the doorbells with the same surname, as children and grandchildren establish their households as close together as possible or even own the whole building. In the beginning I was sometimes annoyed by the interruptions, especially on the days when Aunt Alexandra popped up to visit me three times, stayed for coffee at least once and sent Chryssa up with food. Now, with each person treading their path in isolation, I missed their company. I understood better why Greeks want noise, why they shout, play music loud enough for everyone to hear and why the television is always on like another voice added to those already raised in constant conversation. When Nikitas gave up smoking for a while, he took to using his grandfather's worry beads – beautiful, worn pearls of amber, threaded on olive green silk with a tired tassel at the end. Nikitas tried to conquer the symptoms of nicotine withdrawal with their movement and noise, just as generations of Greek men fill pauses and silence with the incessant swirling and knocking. Worry beads mark the tick-tock of life passing, like prayer beads, though they accompany street banter and coffee shop drinks rather than communication with God and blessed wine. The implication is that you will get all the peace and silence you need in the grave; until then clamour and commotion mean life.

I spent many days in Nikitas' office, flicking through his books, sorting his papers and filing them chronologically. It was a strangely satisfying task, though it was also poignant and disorienting to sit in Nikitas' chair. There were times when I could hardly bear the task I had set myself, as it only emphasised how much my husband had chosen not to tell me. It was like witnessing my own betrayal, and made me wonder whether the marriage had been a sham and if I was the only one who hadn't seen it. Perhaps Phivos had been right all along. Occasionally, my anger made me hate Nikitas; he had left me in the way he had lived with me, with distance and secrets. And I had been too stupid to realise it.

As well as the more disturbing pointers to Nikitas' hidden interior, there were the miscellaneous objects and photographs in his desk's drawers that took on the loaded value of relics. It is as though the elements of physical detritus we leave behind are imbued with meaning beyond themselves. I fingered the talismans, only some of whose histories I knew: a white stone we found on a beach many years before that resembled an ancient Cycladic fertility offering; the amber worry beads and two large keys, one for the old Perivoli house that burnt down during the war and the other from Maria's house in Smyrna, that her mother had always hoped they would reclaim.

Nikitas and I had loved going to the village together in the early years, but that was another of our joint pleasures that altered with time. Partly it was Nikitas' tendency to go there on all-male winter weekends that consisted of roasting meat on the fire, playing cards all night and boozing; women and children were surplus to requirements. I'm not sure whether the distance between Nikitas and me was something I provoked, though I found it increasingly hard to go to Perivoli. I would arrive there in the early days expecting bucolic peace and encounter a constant stream of visitors with time on their hands and a winter's worth of bottled-up stories to recount. They'd bring biscuits and eggs and home-grown vegetables, along with requests that Nikitas help them find a job for a nephew or take a stand on some dubious local intrigue.

"Bring out the *tsípouro*, wife!" Nikitas would half-joke each time another villager knocked on our door and if I didn't, he would pour the drinks himself, and put some cheese and olives on a plate to go with them. I felt he wasn't sure whether he wanted me to be a classic *Kyria* Katina housewife or whether he already saw me as "an English alien", as he said in jest. It didn't help when he discovered that my name, Maud, means "mighty in battle".

There were moments in Nikitas' office that were agonising for other reasons, when my rage at him mutated into pure sadness. One day, I found a file innocently labelled Notes 1999, in which Nikitas had described some of the torments he suffered with Spiros. The pages were handwritten.

As a boy, what was hardest was not being able to predict how Spiros would behave. One day he would ruffle my hair and give me money to buy sweets and the next he would slap my head and look at me with hatred. I was constantly tense, worrying about the next blow. There were times, as a young child, when I feared he might kill me. I believed that because he was a policeman, nobody would be able to do anything about it. Spiros' obsession with bringing me up "with discipline" was relentless. Every misdemeanour had its particular penalty – he was quick to take off his belt when I broke one of his ridiculous, petty rules. My preferred punishment was being locked in the store room on the terrace. There, I would spend the time rummaging in boxes and flicking through books. I dreamed of a future without him. I was waiting for the moment I could leave my aunt's household for ever. If there is a legacy from my uncle, it is a dread that can well up inside me from nowhere. I am taken back to the sense of helplessness and terror I had as a very young child. What my doctor classified as a "breakdown" was the worst example of this returning trauma, but it was not the only one.

I remembered clearly how, soon after Nikitas' documentaries were broadcast, he had this "breakdown", though that is such a polite, contained label. I found him in the middle of the night lying naked on the bathroom floor, sobbing and unable to speak. He had been drinking heavily recently, and waking before dawn, but this time I could tell it was more serious. Afterwards, he could hardly speak for days. When he did talk, he told me how he had once tried to see his mother in Moscow, on a work trip. It had been some years before I met him. She had not turned up to their rendezvous, and it was after this that he had his first "collapse" of the sort that I had witnessed.

"Perhaps something happened to prevent her. Maybe she was ill?" I had suggested, realising that this maternal rejection in adulthood had been a deeply painful experience. "Did you not try to contact her to see why she didn't come?"

"You can't imagine what the Soviet Union was like then," he said. "We had KGB minders, and there wasn't the opportunity to go hunting for mothers. Anyway, there wasn't any point. I got the message – it was too late for both of us." A psychiatrist gave him some pills and Nikitas kept a stash of tranquillisers "for emergencies". He didn't want to discuss it further with me and rejected the idea of therapy ("My story would be much too stimulating for the psycho-analyst," he joked bitterly). I never saw Nikitas like that again, but after he died I was tormented by wishing I had taken the event more seriously.

I went over to the wooden-framed sofa and lay down, pulling one of the scratchy blankets over me against the November chill. Holding the two keys in my hands, I tried to imagine Nikitas' last hours here in his office: drinking the whisky, making the decision to drive somewhere. Why did he go to the sea? What was troubling him? I was unable to make sense of it. There was so much I wanted to ask him now and the frustration and misery at not being able to felt like a raw wound that would never heal.

14
With bloodshed if necessary

ANTIGONE

After the Germans left we walked from Lamia to Athens and I was given time off to go home. My brother was in a separate unit and we had not yet met up when I hobbled into Paradise Street on blistered feet. My hair was cut short – like many of the girls in the mountains, I had left it untouched until the Germans left. Then we had celebrated with scissors. The old woman who opened the back door didn't recognise me, nor I her. Then my mother let out a small cry and we embraced. But she hardly spoke, apart from asking where my brother was. Behind her came Alexandra, who greeted me coldly, kissing me with distaste.

Alexandra filled the space with her hostility and it was very clear which of the two women now had the upper hand. Laying down the law came naturally to my sister. I was informed that she was now engaged to Spiros Koftos, who was back in Athens after his stint with the "German-Evzones". He had given up his *foustanélla* for the uniform of the Athens police force and was helping the British army on the streets of Athens.

In other liberated countries like France and Holland they were rewarding the members of resistance groups and punishing the collaborators. In Greece it was the reverse – the British appeared perfectly happy to arm those who had sided with the Nazis. Each night there were fights as our boys tried to locate traitors like my future brother-in-law, and fascist louts hunted down anyone associated with the resistance movement. The city resounded with guns each night as skirmishes and ambushes took place – Greek against Greek.

Alexandra said, "Either you renounce your links with the Stalinists or you find another home." She sounded as though she had prepared her ultimatum. Naturally there was no choice. I was given the time to collect a few things from my room, and it was Chryssa who came to help me. She had been living at Paradise Street for the previous six months, since we sent her there from the mountains. After her traumatic experiences in Perivoli, we had taken her with us to begin with. She didn't speak but made herself useful, helping with chores, and marching with the rest of us when we were on the move. However, we saw that she was too disturbed to remain close to the fighting, and as she had nobody to care for her, we arranged for her to go to Athens with a message for my mother. From what I saw, she had become a part of the family that was now rejecting me.

My mother's parting words were harsh.

"You can come home when you bring me my son." That is what she said. As though I wasn't her daughter. Grief changes people. The tree in the courtyard was covered with unripe green lemons.

It was unlikely that I would run into Johnny in this surreal and dangerous atmosphere, but I did. We came across one another by chance at Zonar's and though I thought of ignoring him and leaving, he came to speak to me. It was early evening and he offered to take me to dinner, as though that were a quite normal thing to do. The city was once more almost starving. You had to fill bags with billions in paper money to pay for a loaf of bread, and they kept devaluing the currency so that one drachma had become the equivalent of 50,000,000,000 old ones. Johnny had heard of a small restaurant in Kolonaki that had previously been popular with the occupying forces. He thought you could eat well there if you paid in gold sovereigns, and he was one of the lucky people in the city to have this reliable currency. I think Johnny was as shocked as I was by the experience of choosing food from a menu in French and then eating fillet steak and meringues with cream. I have never felt greed and revulsion in such equal measure and Johnny admitted that he too felt nauseous from the meal.

"I suppose this is how the Kolonaki 'fireplaces' still eat?" I said to Johnny, referring to the powerful families of that area, who seemed to have survived better than anyone else. "They're terrified that 'the mountains' are bringing revolution to Athens." I tried to explain that up in the mountains, we had seen how much better Greece could be – better than before the war – and what freedom could mean. We couldn't return to a past which could no longer exist. Half a million Greek deaths should not be in vain. But I don't think Johnny really understood. He asked about Markos and what we were going to do now we were liberated, as though he didn't understand that our fight for liberty had to continue. Afterwards, we walked through streets where worthless bank notes lay in the gutter like waste paper. I was unhappy at the realisation that I was now fraternising with the enemy and I think we both grasped that it was impossible to be friends.

Soon after this inappropriate dinner, the December Events began. However, when I arranged to meet my brother on December 3rd, nobody could imagine that the terrible *Dekemvriana* were about to happen. The winter of 1944 was cold and wet, but weeks of bad weather now gave way to sunshine. It felt like a blessing for a day that would later be called "Bloody Sunday". We had organised a demonstration, maybe the largest that had ever taken place in Athens – at least 60,000 of us protesting for justice. We wanted democracy and to play a part in creating it. I found Markos at the entrance to the Royal Garden and we walked with the crowd along Amalia Avenue to Syntagma Square. People were arriving from every direction, carrying banners and placards: 'No to another occupation.' 'People's Rule not the King.' We were shouting along with the rest – proud as well as angry – and people were singing and dancing in front of the Parliament building. Markos and I were close to the Grande Bretagne Hotel when the shooting started. I couldn't tell where it was coming from, but I heard machine-guns and screaming. Later they said it was from the police station. There were three people near me, just turning to leave and then they were flying – flung up and onto the road.

There was a spray of blood across my coat.

I heard shouts: "They're killing us."

We pressed ourselves into an angle in the wall of the hotel, protected from the direction of the guns, but as people ran past, Markos got pulled into the crowd and I was knocked to the ground. I would have been trampled to death if it hadn't been for two young men who grabbed me. Then we were swept along together. It was like being in strong waves – you couldn't push against the power of the crowd.

By the time I found my brother in Stadium Street, the protestors were slowly making their way back towards the now silent guns and the victims. Corpses lay in the road and dark pools of blood stained the marble in front of the Parliament. Nobody knew how many victims there were, though some said thirty-two dead and 148 injured. We stood with a crowd before the Grande Bretagne. The bodies were spread out all around, but we went back to where we had been – where I had seen the three people killed – a girl and two men of about my age. They were dressed respectably, their shoes clean. The girl's skirt had ridden up her legs and someone pulled it down for modesty. British officers and journalists were looking down on us from the balconies of the Grande Bretagne.

They say that nobody knows who fired the guns into the crowd. Perhaps it was the police, perhaps the English. People have argued ever since about this spark which lit the terrible fire of our Civil War. But the truth is that nothing was done without the support of the English. I saw young girls making shrines of twigs and flowers around the patches of blood into which people dipped their handkerchiefs. Later, these were used as flags and banners by the crowd to confront the murderers.

That evening, I was among a number of ELAS girls who shouted messages and announcements across the streets using a megaphone. We called members of ELAS to their barracks and the following day, we organised attacks on police stations across the city. There was also a general strike. We marched into the centre again – this time with hundreds of thousands. I helped two other girls carry a banner reading: "When the people are in danger from tyranny they choose either chains or arms." After the funerals, the crowd was fired on again by supporters of the fascist X group. More citizens were killed. The sense of betrayal was physical – like being savaged by an old friend.

Later, we learned what Churchill had said to General Scobie, holed up in the Grande Bretagne: "Do not hesitate to act as if you were in a conquered city where a local rebellion is in progress." Churchill wanted control "without bloodshed if possible," though he added, "with bloodshed if necessary". If it seems long ago or unbelievable, just look at Afghanistan or Iraq.

15
December events

MAUD

The next time I met Antigone was at Zonar's, the recently reopened, historic café in University Avenue that used to be a gathering place for so many Athenians. Gone were the dark corners, the intellectuals, the retired men in hats and hand-made suits and the mix of seedy, old-time glamour that I remembered from my first visit to Greece in the late '80s. Now the bright, plate-glass-fronted space was filled with women of a certain age with expensive suits and hairdos, and businessmen with mobile phones at the ready. I put my arm around Antigone when kissing her hello and for a brief moment she looked quite flustered and pleased – so much so that she then spent more time than necessary digging about in her bag to find her cigarettes. She asked me to go and borrow a lighter for her and I watched as she sighed in pleasure with the first inhalation and thanked me.

"I don't remember it like this," she said, as though the rest of the city had remained the same. She drank a "Greek coffee" [*varý-glykó* – heavy-sweet], which had been "Turkish coffee" when she was young.

Antigone was more expansive than at our previous meeting and without my even asking, she began talking about the war. She said she was writing her story every day and had even brought me a few pages to read.

"It was here that I met Johnny Fell after I arrived in Athens in late October. There were English soldiers drinking beer, laughing like donkeys. They liked to say that they liberated us, and people welcomed them as if they had." If she had to choose the point where her life changed irrevocably, it was not the outbreak of war, she said, nor the German occupation. "It was after we were supposedly free. Do you know about the *Dekemvriana* – the December Events?"

I told her I had heard of them. You can hardly live in Greece without knowing something about those harrowing weeks in December 1944, when the Civil War became inevitable.

"You know, Mond, there are points in life when you realise you are living history. Normally, history only exists with hindsight – at the time it's just things happening, rumour, news."

After our coffee, Antigone and I walked out of Zonar's and along into Syntagma – the square named after a constitution that has so often been lacking in Greece. The sun was breaking through the low-hanging clouds producing a golden glow on the stone facade of the Parliament building. The former royal palace looked as two-dimensional as theatre scenery – a backdrop for the white-stockinged Evzones who were changing the guard with slow-motion leg swings, observed by a group of Japanese tourists. Antigone walked slowly but deliberately, peering around her as though trying to see into her own past. We stood for a moment in front of the renovated Grande Bretagne Hotel, next to a row of large cars and uniformed doormen, before crossing over into the centre of the square. Choosing a bench by some trees filled with bitter-oranges, we sat in the precarious sunshine. Crowds were spilling out from the metro station and a group of tall, slim African men were gathering up their pavement wares of fake Louis Vuitton bags into sheets and hurrying towards Hermes Street to avoid the police.

Antigone was opening up to me at last and I took advantage of this to ask her about her brother. She spoke about him warmly, retreating back into her memories of when they had been together in this very square in 1944.

"Markos had grown up so much since we left Athens the previous winter," she said. "He had become a man – taller and stronger. He was starting to grow a beard. He had always been brave, but he had acquired opinions and dreams. He could have done so much."

I smiled, encouragingly, but Antigone broke off and stood up.

"I can't stand the pigeons. Can we move over there?" She shuddered within her sensible, tweedy coat and tried unsuccessfully to laugh, admitting that she had always hated these birds. It was a fear that went back to childhood – something about their pink claws and the way they flapped. Encouraged by the crack of vulnerability she had allowed to show in her thick carapace of theory and principle, I felt a wave of affection for my mother-in-law. I liked how this brave fighter had admitted a foolish phobia and pictured her walking around this square as a child, holding her parents' hands, squeezing her eyes shut at the pigeons.

When we had found another bench, I continued my questioning.

"How did Markos die?"

She replied without facing me, looking instead at the splashing fountain in front.

"The English killed him," she said quietly. "And after that, I had no family. It was the end of hope." She turned to face me. "I need your help with something, Mond. I made a promise to my brother and I wish to keep it. I went to the place where he was buried but there is another tomb there now. He has gone and I want very much to find him." She paused, weighing up my reaction. "I am sorry to mix you up in this, but I think my sister must know. And I can't ask her myself. I know it sounds like the myth all over again." She gave a grim attempt at a smile.

We parted in the square and I walked down into the metro station, past the displays of amphorae and archaeological finds that had been unearthed during the building of the underground. There is even an ancient skeleton, lying in its opened tomb, preserved behind glass like a museum exhibit. If nothing else, it provides a momentary reflection on the brevity of life for the passengers that hurry past.

When I got home, I looked up the story of Antigone in my battered copy of Robert Graves that often supplied me with the background to an obscure god or a myth I wasn't sure about. I couldn't remember the name of the unburied brother, but soon found all the tragic details.

Antigone didn't have the best start in life: Oedipus' youngest daughter, her mother was Jocasta, who was also her grandmother. After Oedipus discovers that his marriage was based on murdering his father and committing incest with his mother, he puts out his eyes and leaves Thebes. He orders Antigone's two brothers, Eteocles and Polynices, to share the throne in his place, but Eteocles exiles his brother, who then returns to attack the city. Both brothers are killed. The new King Creon orders that while Eteocles should be buried with full honours, Polynices is a "traitor" and should be left unburied and unmourned. This is the point where Antigone steps in, refusing to leave her brother's body like carrion. She goes against Creon and the laws of the state and performs the proper funerary rites to honour Polynices. When Creon finds out, she is sentenced to death by being buried alive, but Antigone hangs herself before the punishment is carried out. Creon's son kills himself for love of Antigone, and is followed by his mother, Eurydice.

What a miserable story it is, I thought, even if it does have a strong young woman standing up to male authority. What sort of triumph is it, when you kill yourself? Is there some kind of moral to this tale, I wondered in what I realise was an absurdly Anglo-Saxon approach to its interpretation.

* * *

I decided to contact Danae again. She might just spout anti-British history at me, but I hoped to pick up something about Nikitas' preoccupations. Now that Antigone was starting to open up to me, I wanted to get closer to what my husband had been thinking about. Danae still sounded reluctant on the phone, but agreed to meet me the next day at the small garden café behind the Numismatic Museum – Schliemann's old house on University Street. I got there early, intending to take up my position and to spot her as she arrived, but as I walked through the garden, a young woman motioned to me. She was sitting in dappled sunshine, speaking on the phone, and mouthed "sorry!" pointing to her mobile. I sat down and watched her talking and smoking. She was about Orestes' age. Tall, slender, and somehow both scruffy and elegant. Sun-tanned legs showed through the holes in her jeans. Her shiny, dark hair was clipped up in an artfully messy arrangement. She wasn't wearing much make-up but her lips were definitely a glossy plum-colour. I should have brought the lipstick from Nikitas' office with me. It was obviously hers.

"Sorry," she repeated, when she got off the phone. She shook my hand, spoke to me in the formal plural and asked if I'd like a coffee. She had a double espresso with lots of sugar. I had green tea. I felt pinched, old and unable to express myself.

"So how can I help you?" She was self-assured.

I couldn't answer at first. A horrible realisation was dawning that her involvement with Nikitas had gone beyond reading old Communist Party records for him. She was just the sort of girl he liked – intelligent and cultured as well as attractive. And there was an intensity about her expression that spoke of experience as well as youth.

"Anything you can tell me about what Nikitas was searching for is relevant." I tried to sound unconcerned.

She didn't reply at first and I realised she was finding a way of giving me something without betraying her promise to my husband. Throw a scrap to the dog and it'll leave you alone.

"I know that he felt very angry about how the English behaved at the end of the war," she said. "He took it personally,

I suppose, because of his mother. But basically, I did lots of archive work for him."

"What sort of thing?"

She looked relieved and proceeded to tell me about Churchill and Stalin's meeting in Moscow in 1944. I let her talk.

"When it was clear that the Germans would lose, *Tsortsil* went to see Stalin so they could divide up south-eastern Europe between them. It was like children swapping sweets. The piece of paper Churchill used to jot down his ideas still exists. It shows his suggestions for percentages of 'influence' in each country, and Stalin ticked them in agreement." Danae looked at me to assess my reaction.

"I suppose that's how politicians work," I replied, un-impressed. "The strong always take advantage."

"Yes, and that's how the lives of millions of the 'little men and women' around the world are decided on. The two 'great men' divided Yugoslavia 50:50, the USSR was given ninety per cent in Romania, and Britain got ninety per cent of Greece." She sounded quite passionate about these percentages.

"And the other ten per cent of Greece?" I said it flippantly, but she answered seriously.

"That went to so-called 'others'. And the interesting thing is that Stalin kept his word. He never helped the Left in Greece, even though they were desperate and thought he would. He let the British and then the Americans do whatever they liked."

I heard Nikitas' voice emerging through this pretty young woman. And she was managing to keep everything so imper-sonal. I wondered what they'd had together. Did she love him? Danae lit another cigarette and went banging on about *Tsortsil*. Apparently Churchill had asked Stalin whether they should destroy the piece of paper, which was evidence of their power games. Stalin replied: 'That was God's first mistake – he didn't ask us when he created the world.'

"They were playing at God, and enjoying it," said Danae.

How enjoyable for her to feel so self-righteous, I thought. I said, "Do you think Nikitas was upset by something in particular? What about his father? Did you find out anything about *Kapetan* Eagle? He was killed during the Civil War wasn't he?"

"Yes. I think I could send you the details about that. After all, it's in the public domain. I'll send you an email, if that's OK. He died in 1947."

Danae said she should be getting back to the office and signalled to the waiter for the bill. I insisted on paying and we had the ritualised little argument that is a matter of Greek honour before she submitted and allowed me to get the upper hand. It felt like a very small victory.

sons – were locked up. My Uncle Diamantis was shipped to a concentration camp in Egypt, along with thousands of his comrades.

It was an upside-down world, where right had been turned to wrong. We had no doubts about the justice of our fight, though anyone could see we were losing. English tanks ploughed through our road blocks like a car crushing toys. We were reduced to making our own weapons: Molotov cocktails using old bottles, or tin cans filled with nails. Sometimes our boys put dynamite inside a street tram and sent it rolling down a hill, hoping to damage our enemies. No-Man's land was up by Omonia square.

We became accustomed to seeing death. Corpses littered the streets like grotesque caricatures of the living. Passers-by stepped around them without a second glance. Each day was like a throwing of the dice for whether Charos would take you or pass by this time. Perversely, as defeat loomed, the weather was perfect and the ravaged city was bathed in sunshine. Nature remained oblivious to the woes of human beings. Our company was staying in a house in Kaisariani and had been there long enough to establish a few routines – cooking and washing clothes. One fine, luminous morning, several men went outside into the yard to bathe themselves and smoke a cigarette in the sunshine. The sudden attack was far from being the first I had witnessed, but the contrast with the domestic scene was shocking. An English plane flew low, spitting bullets into the streets and, though it didn't hit the house, several men were killed. *Kapetan* Iasonas whom I had known since our days in the cave, was split nearly in two. His skull opened up and his entrails spilt on the ground like an Easter lamb's. We gathered him up as best we could and cursed the monarcho-fascist English. I thought of Johnny – he was definitely the enemy now.

In the middle of this bloody December, who should arrive in time for Christmas but Mr Churchill himself? He had become obsessed with "the Greek problem" and thought he could come over and sort us out. But by now we realised the English had gone from ally to occupier. It was clear that Churchill's arrival was an opportunity for us; killing the fat old man with his cigar at the headquarters of the occupying forces, in the Grande Bretagne Hotel, would be a triumph. Markos was involved in the attempted assassination.

I was at the house in Kaisariani the night before they left for the operation. My brother was as excited as a small child and the two of us talked through much of the night, sitting wrapped in blankets in what had been the kitchen but was now a bare room with a marble sink and two broken chairs. We spoke about *Kapetan* Iasonas and mourned him, then turned to our childhood, and ended up playing the masochistic game that should never be played when you are hungry, of imagining food. Markos described the smell of the sweet bread that our mother baked for Christmas. Then I joined in with the taste of the roast pork that marked the end of the fast before Christ's birthday. We always gorged ourselves and then lay full and sated like snakes. In the cold and dark, we even whispered the Christmas *kálanda* we used to go around singing on the streets, banging our triangles and knocking on doors where they'd give us sweets or a few coins:

Good evening, my lords, if it is your wish – of Christ's divine birth I shall tell the tale.

Markos and his comrades left the house in the unwelcoming hour before dawn. We had only slept a couple of hours and it was freezing – there was snow on the mountains surrounding Athens. Dressed in civilian attire, the boys looked pale and thin – they needed no disguise to look like most other Athenians. Inside their clothes and in a couple of workman's bags they were carrying explosives. All day I was tense with fear, imagining them crawling through the sewage tunnels underneath University Avenue, making their way along to Syntagma and the nerve centre of the English in their smart hotel. Luckily, I was busy myself that day, as I had to walk down Syngrou Avenue to meet with a group of families in Kalithea that was preparing to leave Athens. I was to give them instructions for their exodus and prepare them for the march to Elefsina. On my way back, I was unable to resist the temptation of taking a walk around my neighbourhood, though I didn't go to Paradise Street, passing instead by the cemetery. Small boys were begging, holding bowls out to the mourners to receive a spoonful of *kólyva*. It was a shock to notice Spiros among the people lingering outside the gate. He was talking with two men and I looked away, lowering my head. I had heard about how Spiros' brothers and father ended up and, though every death should be regretted, I can't say I was sorry that at least a few collaborators faced justice. And then several seconds later, I realised who the other men were: Johnny and Basher Hicks, his old colleague from the early days of the resistance. Perhaps I should not have been surprised, but I was filled with loathing. My fear made me rigid as bone.

None of the men gave any sign of having noticed me, though I later came to believe they knew the game better than me. I didn't observe anything as I walked back up the hill to our base in Kaisariani; but the truth is that I didn't take as much care as I should have. I knew the rules: how to double back and wait, to use the back ways. So why did I lead our enemies as though giving them a gift? I have run through that small hour so many times over the years. I have tried to give myself the comfort of believing there was nothing I could have done. But I am never convinced. I have even tried to persuade myself that it was chance some hours later, when I spotted Spiros walking in the road by our base. Anything, but the likelihood that I led him there. It was not an area someone like him would go to by chance – a fascist would be likely to "disappear" if he went for a stroll in "Little Stalingrad". I only saw him from behind, moving slowly in the dimming light, leaning into the wall, his hat pulled low. Perhaps it was just someone who resembled him. That comforting thought has come and gone, but the diabolical image has stayed.

Before I left the house again early that evening, Markos arrived exhausted and stinking like the sewers he had been working in throughout the day. I embraced him, feeling his clothes damp and his hair caked to his head. We scarcely spoke. He nodded as though to say that all was well – that they had succeeded in leaving the explosives in the sewers under University Avenue, near the Grande Bretagne. We assumed that the following day Churchill would be dead. I didn't tell him about Spiros and Johnny. There is always plenty of time for regrets – you can keep them as long as you like. Of course, the bombing attempt failed. They found the dynamite and Churchill survived, as we all know. But by the time I learned that, there were far worse things to deal with.

I returned to Kalithea to help the families on their night march to Elefsina. A mass departure from Athens was taking place and anyone associated with the Left was advised to leave before they were arrested or worse. I was to go with them as far as Kokkinia, an Asia Minor refugees' quarter, where other comrades would take over. It was slow going – mothers were carrying babies as well as bags, children were exhausted, with blisters on their feet. Everyone was afraid. English planes were slaughtering groups like these – they made easy targets during the day – but we made it to Kokkinia without mishap. It was a strange sort of Christmas – it made us think of the *Panayia* and her arrival with Joseph in Bethlehem.

"We're just missing the wise men," someone quipped, in the chill of a moonless night. "And a warm stable."

I slept for much of the day and it was evening by the time I got back to Kaisariani. I was worrying about how I must warn Markos about Johnny and Spiros and I strode along the dirt road, trying to avoid the potholes and puddles, but mud stuck to my shoes, making them heavy and slowing my pace. I was wearing civilian clothes – a thin dress, a coat that was too large and as I had no stockings, a pair of short socks that did nothing to stop the cold creeping up my legs. As soon as I came around the curve in the road, I saw that something terrible had happened. The solid, two-storey house where we'd been staying looked different. At first I thought my eyes had tricked me in the darkness, but then I saw that there was no wall on the street side. It lay gaping like a doll's house from which the hinged front had been torn off. I could see furniture on the floors above, but the deep silence made it clear nobody was there. Nothing moved. I tried to make my way through the garden to where the back door had been, but it was filled with rubble and burnt rafters.

"*Despinís* – Miss," a voice whispered. "Over here." An old man was standing hunched by the remains of the outer wall on the road, tapping his forefinger to his lips, indicating he had something to say.

"What happened? Where did they go?" I held onto his arm. He looked ready to drop.

"The English came. Just after dawn. We couldn't believe the noise. Planes and tanks. There were dozens of dead. And not just in this house – the families across the street are grieving their own this evening." The survivors had been taken away as prisoners and were probably already on a boat for the Middle East.

"There's no room for patriots in Greece any more."

"What happened to the dead?" I asked.

"Sometimes they take them to the Royal Garden. It's become the city's unofficial morgue. The authorities just dump them there. And families go to search for their own."

I didn't know what to do. It was impossible to go home. But sometimes, in the face of terror, a strange calm descends and your body behaves like an obedient pack animal. I made my way down the hill from Kaisariani, across the Ilissos and into the lower part of the Royal Garden by the Zappeion. It was after the curfew, maybe about 10 o'clock by then, but nobody spotted me. I was a ghost in a deserted city. I thought about Spiros – that he must have betrayed us to the English. And it was already dawning on me that I had possibly played my part in provoking this disaster. I could not bear to think that Johnny was involved. When I heard voices, I edged cautiously towards them, along pathways where families and lovers used to wander on Sundays. In an opening, some people were standing next to row after row of corpses. There was a sickening stench.

The voices belonged to two men who were guarding the makeshift mortuary and they turned at the noise of my footsteps.

"Who are you? What are you doing here?" Rough voices. I didn't want to give away too much.

"I'm looking for a friend."

"What sort of friend? What happened?" I only had to mention Kaisariani for him to understand.

"Ah, the Reds up in Little Stalingrad? Well, your boys aren't doing so well now are they?" I was not among friends, it was clear. I persevered and asked whether the dead from that day's fighting had arrived. He gestured with his head as he lit a cigarette.

"Over there. That's the new batch. There aren't any names."

"Do you want to smoke?" asked another man with a kinder face. "It helps with the stink."

The bodies were covered with sacking and in the dark it was almost impossible to identify anyone. I pulled back the rough fabric at random and just made out a face blackened with dried blood. I could tell from the hair that it was not my brother. I went back and asked the kinder man if I could borrow his matches and, by the flickering flames that went out too soon and burnt my fingers, I eventually found several comrades from the house in Kaisariani. Each time I lifted the hessian I prayed that it would not be Markos. I pictured him escaped and in hiding, or arrested but safe, even injured and in hospital. Anything that would make him not be there. I made silent promises about what I would give. And then I saw him. I didn't make a noise. I sat down next to him on the dirt path, and held his hand. It was stiff and cold. I felt scratchy dirt on it. His eyes were open and I saw no obvious wound, no blood.

"Is that him?" said the kinder man. "Condolences. May God forgive him." He offered me another cigarette, but I didn't take it. My body was shaking. He said, "You should get out of here. If they find you, they won't hesitate to take you in. Mourning doesn't grant amnesty, my girl."

"How can I take him?"

"That's for the family to arrange, not for us. Some even bury their own here in the park until they can do something better."

I left and made my way automatically to my old haunt by the Ilissos – where Markos and I had played as children and where I had gone with Johnny. It was very cold. My dress snagged on plants and nettles stung my legs. When I located the plane tree, I laid myself across the branches as I had done in what felt like another life. Animals passed by – foxes perhaps. They made unrecognisable sounds. I wished it was me lying under the sack in the Royal Garden. I knew I couldn't go home. They had said I should never return unless I brought my brother, and they did not mean in a coffin. The lines had been drawn. It was obviously impossible to fulfil Markos' wish of ending up in Perivoli. His desire to be buried "with Hercules", on the slopes of Iti was a childish dream. But he could not be left "unburied, unwept, a feast of flesh for keen-eyed carrion birds" – in those days I knew most of Sophocles' *Antigone* by heart. As the first signs of light emerged behind the shadows of Hymettus, I made a plan.

I was waiting outside the First Cemetery at 7.30 and, when I saw our neighbour, Kostas Lambakis, arrive, I followed at a distance. I thought of him as old, since he had teenage children not much younger than me, but I suppose he was not even forty. His wife, *Kyria* Katina, was a vinegary woman – she always found something to complain about. But they were not bad people. *Kyrios* Kostas' hefty body had diminished during the war, so he looked deflated and creased, but his expression was kind. He was a comrade – he was friendly with my Uncle Diamantis, though he had never joined the cause. I believed I could trust him. I approached him when he was some way from the cemetery's offices and could not be seen by anyone.

"Antigone?" He wasn't sure if it was me, though he'd known me since birth. I realised I looked terrible. Having heard me out, he agreed to help, but I had to wait till he got off work. I followed him to a tool shed by the Protestant graves, where he said I could wait, and sat shivering on the floor. I could smell the rust and earth on the spades.

Kyrios Kostas said, "We'll take the handcart. Then we'll bury him somewhere temporary – maybe here with the foreigners – until we can do the right thing." I asked him not to tell my mother because of Alexandra, who would inform

Spiros. I didn't want to give my future brother-in-law the satisfaction or the idea of hunting me as he had Markos. In the middle of the day, we set off with the cart in the direction of the Royal Garden. As *Kyrios* Kostas bumped it through muddy potholes and over debris from bombed houses, he told me nightmarish stories. In order to spread propaganda about leftist brutality, he said, criminals were hired to remove the corpses of civilians from the Garden and mutilate them. They were slashed and sliced and had their eyes gouged out before being delivered to the police stations. Some perverted types even managed to gather so many eyes that they filled a bucket. Then they paraded them around for all to see, as evidence of what the "communist bandits" were capable of. Naturally, misinformation as vile as this was extremely effective and attracted the attention of the international press.

We entered the Garden without trouble and wheeled the cart along the overgrown paths to where I had been the night before. I could now see exactly where this impromptu morgue was – the part that used to be filled with flowerbeds planted in colourful patterns. It was where my parents used to bring us for walks when we were children. There had been a kiosk for drinks in those days, and a few tables and chairs. All that had gone and the metamorphosis was grotesque. The place where Athenians once took strolls had turned into the only place available to lay out their dead. The area was quite busy with people trying to identify their relatives. One family was huddled around a body, their dark clothes covered with dust from sitting on the ground. I found Markos easily the second time and we stood for a moment looking down at him.

"God forgive him. May you remember him, always." The

17
Wild greens and cold water

MAUD

Antigone rang me twice to ask if I had found out anything about Markos' grave, but I was reluctant to get involved in a row over someone who had died in 1944. I had enough of my own problems and a more recent grave to worry about. Antigone insisted however, telling me details about their grave-digger neighbour, Kostas Lambakis, who had buried Markos secretly. He had rightly surmised that nobody would look for the boy among the British and Germans, who kept their Protestant corner separate from the Orthodox Greeks.

"It was over in the corner of the foreign part," Antigone said. "*Kyrios* Kostas put a small temporary plaque with his initials – M.P. Nothing else." Now there was no sign of the grave, she explained. Antigone had walked up and down with Dora to no avail. After examining every plot, the two old women went to the Lambakis house – still the next-door building in Paradise

Street, but *Kyrios* Kostas had died years ago. His son, Babis, had no knowledge of the matter.

"I very much want to find him." Antigone's voice was insistent and I could tell that she was not going to forget about it. "It has stayed with me as a regret during a lifetime in Moscow. I'm not called Antigone for nothing." What a strange myth, that celebrates a young woman standing up to the authorities and preferring to die rather than leave her dead brother unburied.

"Who cares what happens to rotten bones?" Tig said after I explained.

"He's your Great Uncle," I said, unconvinced by the title I was giving this boy who was only a few years older than my daughter when he died.

"Why can't these old grannies just get on with their lives? They're obviously using you as a go-between." It was late afternoon and we were sitting in the kitchen while I cooked lentils in Nikitas' way, with pureed red peppers, bay leaves, plentiful wine and extra garlic for the sauce. The windows were fogged up and a gentle rain seeped from the dark sky. From where she sat on the kitchen table, Tig swung her legs – clad in black leggings and heavy boys' boots. I wished we could get back to the camaraderie that we had from the time when she had stopped rejecting the English language (aged about eleven) and the time when anything parental was automatically off-putting (aged about thirteen). During that happy period we had got on so well, enjoying our insider-outsider status, and playing games with the two household languages, taking Greek expressions and translating them literally into English. We'd trade mock insults and threats: "You don't know from where the chicken farts" – you're so ignorant; "You're going to eat wood" – I'm going to beat you (accompanied by a threatening hand slicing the air); "You made them sea" – you messed up; and "pumpkins" – rubbish. When I found Tig wide awake hours after her bedtime, I would say "your eye is a prawn", but over the last couple of years it had stopped being funny. Even Tig's favourite, "so what the eggs" (so what?) had been abandoned like an outdated nursery rhyme.

"I'm planning to go and see *Yiayia* Alexandra," I said. "Do you want to come? She loves you more than anyone."

"I can't be bothered." Tig's thumbs tapped away on her mobile phone keys like a virtuoso, a smile flashing across her lips as she read a message, her face illuminated by the blue light. "And I'm going out soon. Anyway, you're a big girl, you can manage by yourself." She enjoyed throwing my own clichés back at me. She made a rapid, fake smile and jumped off the table. "Orestes and I thought we'd go and see our real grandmother." She was trying to gauge my reaction. "We rang her and said we might drop by."

"That's nice." I felt an unreasonable twinge of jealousy and hoped it wasn't obvious. "What time will you be back?"

"Nine or ten," she said, her hand passing over the still unfamiliar surface of her shorn hair as though she was stroking an animal. "I've got my mobile."

I thought of Nikitas' injunction to pray to Zeus, the god of family love, and wondered how you do it. Libations and roasted oxen, presumably.

Once the lentils had cooked and sat steaming aromatically, like a picture of the homeliness that was missing from our family, I rang Aunt Alexandra and asked when would be a good time to drop in.

"Come now, my child. I'm always happy to see you." I felt the affection in her voice. She may not have been the best mother substitute to Nikitas, but she had always been good to me.

"Come down and I'll make some tea. And you can try my new lemon sweet. I've made ten jars." The tree in the back yard was weighed down with yellow fruit, like Christmas decorations. I had picked enough to fill a large bowl in the kitchen and they lay there, slowly rotting, developing pretty patches of blue and green.

"Let me kiss you." Alexandra welcomed me as though I was a visitor she had not seen for some time, rather than someone who had just come down the stairs. I breathed in her lady-like scent of powder, hairspray and polished leather, soothed by the familiarity, by how everything about her and her home was the same as always. I didn't care that she was right-wing. I never had.

"You just don't understand," Nikitas said to me during one of our discussions about how political orientation defined a person to their core. "It's not just where you place your cross at the ballot box, it's who you are. But an English person doesn't have that awareness. You can't imagine it. You English never experienced the fear of waiting for the police to knock on the door at night because of your political beliefs. You don't know about jails overflowing with political prisoners." His face would go red with annoyance and each time I experienced it as a complaint about who I was, about my Englishness.

"Ah, poor *Mondouly mou*." Alexandra looked freshly coiffed and was dressed in a sharp-collared white shirt and grey skirt. She was back in her normal outfits after a couple of weeks sticking to dark mourning clothes and gestured to them.

"It's what you feel inside, not what you wear," she announced, as though I might have argued otherwise. She had worn black for a year after Spiros died and, although she was a staunch supporter of custom, she knew that these prescriptions had become far more flexible than in her youth; her mother had been in widow's weeds until she died.

"This is a hard time, but it will pass. God will look after you."

I reflected how that comment would have been enough to set Nikitas off on an anti-clerical diatribe whereas, for me, Alexandra's certainty was comforting, even if I didn't share it (more of my "liberal English bullshit", I thought, conversing with Nikitas in my head). She had been good to me since my student days and had provided steady, reliable love for Tig throughout her life. The older I got, the more I valued these quiet, less glamorous virtues.

We sat in the sitting room and she poured tea into her guest cups and saucers and made small-talk – how Chryssa was feeling her age and was asleep at the moment (as if she herself was not in her eighties too), and how there was a big pan of *spanakórizo* in the kitchen and I should take some for my supper ("does my little granddaughter eat spinach yet?"). Then she paused, adjusted her hearing aids, sighed deeply, tucked her hands inside the waistband of her skirt and said:

"I suppose my sister has been feeding you her old propaganda. I hope you can see through it. They were always good at telling stories that flattered them. But you can't hide behind your finger – the horrible facts of what they did are still facts."

I got straight to the point and explained that Antigone was

trying to locate their brother's grave. I asked whether she knew what had happened.

"So, she has finally come begging," she said, looking angrier but more confident than before. "*Mondy mou*, we should call things by their name. Markos was my brother, too. Can you imagine what it was like when we learned he was dead? We had nothing to grieve over, no body to bury, no memorials to offer to his soul. Did she not think of her mother's suffering? She only ever thought about herself. Well, now it's her turn. Why should I help her?"

My suggestion that it might be helpful to let the quarrel remain in the distant past and make peace was not taken well.

"Ask her what happened when those wicked communists saw they were losing. Ask her about how they went around houses dragging entire families out of their beds to kill them. I expect she has conveniently forgotten whatever doesn't fit with the picture of her as a holy martyr to the hammer and sickle. Ask her about the forced marches." Although I had picked up a certain amount of information about the Civil War over the years, I had not heard about these. Alexandra looked gratified. "You don't hear them talking about those things, eh? It was a nightmare – shattering for Spiros and me. You never forget something like that."

Alexandra mentioned OPLA (Organisation for the Protection of the People's Struggle), the communist secret police, who had murdered Spiros' father and brothers.

"They'd arrive at houses before dawn and take anyone they thought was not on their side. 'Enemies of the People,' they said, but weren't we people? *Kyrios* Dimitris was always kind to us, and Spiros' two brothers, those wonderful lads…

so handsome and strong. They were pulled half-dressed from their house like criminals." Alexandra spoke calmly but with disgust in her voice, describing how later, after the bodies were found, Spiros went to identify them. They had been thrown on some wasteland, their hands tied behind their backs with wire and it was obvious they had been beaten and tortured before they were killed with a bullet in the head. She said that Spiros' mother lost her mind and had left Athens to stay with her sister in Sparta and Spiros – "virtually an orphan" – was taken in at Paradise Street.

Two weeks later, armed men burst into the house.

"You can imagine what we thought." Alexandra was getting into her stride and I sensed her weighing up my reactions, fighting to gain ground over her sister.

"We were sure they were going to kill us, like Spiros' father and brothers. They pointed guns at us and kicked Spiros as we went down the street."

"It must have been terrifying," I said.

"The strange thing is that I was so angry that this would be the end of my life and that I would miss my wedding, that I lost my fear. I told our abductors that we were Greeks and patriots and not afraid to die for our country."

The engaged couple were taken to a house filled with similarly disoriented people and told they were hostages. Alexandra was locked in a room with dozens of other women while Spiros was taken somewhere else. She stayed there for two days, sitting on the floor and waiting to be shot.

"I hope you will never be in a situation like that – women of all ages crying and moaning. Some were ill. It was bitterly cold and we were not dressed properly. There were grandmothers and babies – nobody was safe. There was no toilet and no food, so you can imagine the state of the room. We all thought we were going to be killed by those savages."

In the chaos before the hostages were taken out of Athens, Alexandra somehow managed to get released. She didn't explain how, but that was how things worked – you lived or died on a whim or by chance acquaintance. Spiros, however, was forced to go on the long march. As a policeman, it was surprising that they let him live at all, as they were among the most hated groups. His coat and shoes were taken away and he had to wrap rags around his feet and join a straggling line of exhausted, war-weary and terrified Athenians, who were made to walk out of the city towards the north under armed escort. In total, they numbered about twenty thousand, including around a thousand British prisoners-of-war.

"They were like sheep, herded along the road and beaten if they lagged behind," said Alexandra. "They didn't have food, except a few wild greens and cold water, so of course people began to collapse. When they couldn't walk, they were killed and their corpses left by the side of the road." She described a dreadful situation; there was snow on the hills and the hostages were made to walk without shoes. There were families with children and old people, and at night they slept outside with no protection. Each day they became weaker.

"The communist bullies took away their clothes and many of them froze to death. They were beaten for having lived in a nice house. And what was all that for? For being 'bourgeois'?' Ask your Antigone about that. She knows very well what happened. Ask my sister about that glorious episode. She was there, with her gun and her slogans. Spiros begged her to let him go and she refused – her sister's fiancé, whom she had known since childhood. Well after that, it's hardly surprising that I disowned her. From then on, I didn't have a sister."

Alexandra told me that after twelve days, the march was stopped near Arachova. Those who had survived were suddenly released and had to make their own way back to Athens and some, including Spiros, were transported by the Red Cross. Later that winter, mass graves were discovered outside Athens.

"The communists took whoever they didn't like and murdered them," she said. "And don't imagine they did it *nicely*. Tin can lids for slitting throats – that was their style. Or bullets to the back of the head. You can imagine that by then, not many Athenians felt like letting the Reds run the country. They had shown their true colours. Thank God we had the English helping us, or we'd have become a satellite of the Soviet Union. It was due to the English and then the Americans that Greece was saved. I've never forgotten that."

Alexandra paused, looking exhausted by the memories. I had always thought of her as the perfect lady who would never lose control, whose emotions were carefully measured; rather "English" in fact, or at least what the Greeks call English. But here, I could see someone who had been traumatised and whose husband might have been a brute, but was also brutalised.

"You think a strong man will recover, but those things don't ever leave you." She got up slowly from her armchair and picked up a framed photograph of her husband, aged perhaps thirty-five. She brought it across, holding it reverentially, like an icon or a relic and showed me what looked like a perfectly healthy man with a carefully groomed, black moustache and a patronising smile animating his features. However, Alexandra said that Spiros was tormented by nightmares about his family's murders and he was permanently affected by the march. He was hospitalised for pneumonia immediately afterwards, and then suffered from a chronic weak chest.

"And later, after Nikitas was born?" I wanted to ask Alexandra how it was possible that she and Spiros had taken in her hated sister's child as their own, after all that happened.

"A child is an innocent creature of God," she said, and I sensed the answer was one she had used before. "I couldn't let my own nephew go to an orphanage. And Mondy, you know, I loved him. I wasn't able to have children – we'd been to doctors. Later, it's true that Spiros and I sometimes wondered whether we'd made a mistake. Nikitas was trouble, right from the beginning. There are some things that are passed on in the blood. You could tell that he had inherited certain traits. But we gave him a chance in life."

After we cleared up the tea things, I returned to the sitting room and moved slowly around, looking at the familiar photographs in their frames. I now noticed other details in the 1930s picture of the Perifanis family outside their house in Paradise Street. As a girl, Antigone had a stubborn, tight-lipped expression that I noticed still appearing regularly on her wrinkled, octogenarian face, whereas the teenage Alexandra stood upright and sure about herself, as though there could be no questions, just as she did now. Markos was holding his oldest sister's hand, but I saw that his gaze was directed towards Antigone. The divisions and alliances were already in place.

Before I left, Aunt Alexandra told me that Markos was "safe" and that I could pass that message onto her sister.

"You know that for us Orthodox, a person's remains are

sacred. That's why we don't have cremation. That's why we keep the bones. But it's also why my sister made such a big mistake, even a crime, by not letting us know what happened to my brother after he died. Don't worry, *Mondy mou*." She patted my hand. "I will tell you where my brother is resting. I am not a bad person. And you are my family now. There is nobody else who will mourn me when I'm gone, just you and my beloved grandchildren."

I returned to my empty apartment clutching a plastic container of the rice and spinach and a jar of Alexandra's lemon "spoon sweet" – thick coils of yellow peel covered in syrup. I fished one out with a fork, letting the sticky liquid drip down, and ate it, my mouth filling with aching, acid sweetness.

✻   ✻   ✻

The following day was November 17th, the anniversary of the students' uprising at the Polytechnic in 1973. Schools were shut, so Tig and I slept in – she didn't appear until midday. Due to the annual march through the centre of Athens, the commemoration has become a general holiday and I was accustomed to the celebrations. It was strange being at home without Nikitas there to press his point, to rally the children and to play recordings of rousing marching songs by Theodorakis that still had the allure of something forbidden, as they had been during the Colonels' Junta.

When Orestes and Tig were younger, Nikitas always took them to the Polytechnic and then all the way through the centre of Athens on the march to the US Embassy. The children liked the part where everyone chanted angry slogans at the Americans, accusing them of having supported the Junta; I recall Tig returning aged six and chanting: "Down with the Americans!" with a grin on her face. There were a couple of times when I went, but I found it hard to relate to the enthusiasm, even if Nikitas did explain to me over and over how significant the student occupation of the Polytechnic had been and how their deaths beneath the Colonels' tanks had led to the end of the seven-year dictatorship. Spiros had made sure that his nephew was arrested and beaten up frequently during this period, and though his threats of exile on Makronisos were never fulfilled, Nikitas felt he had suffered for his beliefs.

Some years ago, Orestes refused to go to the Polytechnic with Nikitas and Tig. He drew battle-lines with his father across sensitive, almost sacred ground by attacking the very concept of the commemoration.

"I don't want to hear your ancient arguments with their stale slogans. Blue pricks! They don't mean anything any more. That's all over. The world is a different place." Orestes had become a young warrior when he laid into Nikitas. His eyes were even darker and more direct than his father's and the pair looked like stags sizing each other up, one an old alpha male, the other younger and less powerful but faster and with the future on his side.

"Why should we have to carry your burdens?" Orestes said, as the tension increased. "Why should we fight for you? You should leave us alone to live our youth and solve our own problems." In the end, Nikitas backed down by feigning nonchalance.

"It's your loss if you don't understand that we made the

world better for you. Stay home and have a wank. I'll go with your sister."

The discussion got worse when Nikitas sneered at his son's choice of communications and media studies at university.

"It's not a real subject," he said. However, Orestes was equally capable of the verbal put-down.

"Just look what your studies have done. You and your friends have destroyed Athens. You've all become rich, you've ruined the environment and you've created a corrupt system based on cronies with contacts. If yours is the model, God help us." Later in the day, Orestes had told me he would "pass by the march" to check it out, and in subsequent years, he had gone with his own friends from university. However, each year he became angrier about the self-congratulatory style of his father's generation and the way they gloried in their exploits.

This year, I ignored the anniversary – a small stab of revenge towards Nikitas by showing I didn't care. Instead, I stayed at my desk, working on a translation I had been failing to concentrate on since the accident. Tig went out and, yet again, I found myself alone in a still house, with the particular quiet of a city abandoned by most people except the protestors and police. In the evening, I took a bowl of lentils and sat down in front of the television. The news was filled with reports of the march. As usual, hooligans and anarchists had turned the more sober proceedings into chaos. Hooded youths threw petrol bombs and ripped up pieces of paving stones as missiles to throw at the lines of gas-masked riot police, who sprayed canisters of tear gas into the crowd. Lines of orderly protestors marched along, chanting slogans and ignoring the war-like conditions they left in their wake. The camera zoomed in on some elderly marchers and among the rows of respectable pensioners, I spotted a familiar face. At first I could not believe it, but there was no doubting it was Antigone. And next to her was Dora. They were holding banners that read *Americans, Murderers of Peoples*. I laughed aloud at the absurdity of these elderly women up to their old tricks, pacing stolidly against a backdrop of riotous youths in black balaclavas lobbing Molotov cocktails at reinforced police vans.

After the news, I switched channels, changing from a talent show, with half-naked teenage girls writhing to Greek rap, to a talk show hosted in a mocked-up taverna, with jugs of wine, plates of food and re-hashed *rembétika* songs. I ended up with something called *Great Greeks*, where the audience had to choose between a surreal mix of twentieth century politicians and ancient philosophers: Sophocles or Karamanlis, Papanikolaou of the smear test or Alexander the Great, Socrates or Eleftherios Venizelos?

"The new opium of the people." I could hear Nikitas' voice as though he were there. "They want us to be dazed and anaesthetised, so we don't think about more important subjects." It was true – the longer I sat there, the more frozen I became. I was alone, trapped between the fossilised fights of the older generation and the equally unfathomable battles of the young, in a country that was not even my own.

❊　❊　❊

Although I was intrigued by having spotted Antigone and her friend on television, I didn't feel like seeing my mother-in-law – and still hesitated to use the title. I was sickened by Alexandra's stories and I didn't want to be dragged too deep into their feud. However, Antigone was surprisingly insistent. She rang me several times and wanted to find out if I had discovered anything about Markos' bones. Eventually, I agreed to visit her at Dora's house. Perhaps I had subconsciously been expecting a partisan's lair, but in fact it had the familiarly feminine touches of so many Greek homes – hand-made doilies on the television set, kitsch china ornaments, old, framed photographs. Dora brought out a choice of spoon sweets on dainty saucers and then went to prepare coffee, which she served with "dipping biscuits" from the bakery.

"My sister always wanted to have the upper hand," Antigone said, after I mentioned that Alexandra had spoken about the marches and abductions. She handed me a thin plastic folder with some handwritten pages. "This will show you the story from my viewpoint." Antigone looked well, and though her clothes were as indifferently combined as Alexandra's were elegant, she had evidently had a haircut and her eyes were bright. When she spoke, her strong features were animated like someone much younger.

"It will also give you an idea of why I am so busy."

I flicked through the sheets that were covered with a tidy, if slightly shaky Greek script in blue biro.

"Of course bad things happened," she replied, when I told her the gist of her sister's revelations. "It was a war. We were desperate. And the other side had superior weapons and manpower. There were 70,000 English killing us with their Spitfires and tanks. And they were taking *our* people as hostages. They transported them all the way to prison camps in Egypt. What could we do?" I could tell she had worked out the justifications long ago, just as Alexandra had for what "her side" did. As for Spiros' suffering, Antigone had little sympathy. Dehumanising the other side had always been the first rule of war.

"Spiros should have been shot, or at least imprisoned, for being in the Security Battalions and for collaborating with the Germans. I suppose my sister didn't mention that I arranged her release before the marches. She was allowed to go home. As the fiancée of Spiros Koftos, she was seen in a very bad light – everyone knew what the Koftos family had been up to all those years – but they agreed to let her go because of me."

According to Antigone, Spiros was not treated so badly and Alexandra was exaggerating the case. It was true that nobody had much food, and that those "gangsters of the air" (the British) had strafed them at one point, believing them to be a column of communist families leaving Athens. However, she herself had got Spiros a pair of boots from somebody who died and, she claimed, she had persuaded the *Kapetánios* in command not to have him executed.

"I told them that, as a policeman, he was more useful to us as a bargaining chip. We saw a different man, a coward, once he was away from his cronies and henchmen. He wept and moaned and begged me to help him. And I did – not that he would have ever revealed it. Didn't he return to Alexandra and get married, then live happily ever after?" Antigone's tone was acid. "It was the rest of us whose lives were ruined."

Before I left, Antigone said she had something for me. She examined my face as she returned from her bedroom with something small wrapped in tissue paper.

"Thank you. What is it?"

"It is something important to me but I think you should have it."

I began unrolling the paper until a slender lock of dark hair was revealed.

"It was cut from my son's head when he was three years old – the last time I saw him. I kept it during all my years in Russia but maybe it is of more use to you now? A link to the past perhaps?"

I looked at the child's curl and managed not to cry. I didn't want this to turn into one of those drenched female scenes that Nikitas had found so trying.

"Try to think how he would have laughed at this," I thought.

"Bravo Maud," he would have said. "You've got my stubborn old mother right in your pocket – just where you wanted her."

18
Dirty Bulgarian whores

ANTIGONE

I didn't see Markos' grave until long after he was buried. When I was arrested at the Royal Garden they took me to a police station, just off Syntagma. There were so many people inside that, in the chaos, I managed to escape. It wasn't a glorious achievement, climbing over rooftops or fighting the policemen, but a question of seizing the moment when nobody was looking. A group of us were waiting to give our details to a police clerk and the policeman guarding us went off somewhere. I stood up and walked away, waiting to be stopped, but nothing was said. I wasn't handcuffed. I walked down some stairs to a back entrance and was soon out on the street. I didn't look back. I hurried on, into Stadiou [Stadium] Street, cutting off past the old Parliament building and into the winding side roads. Each moment I expected to hear a shout and to be caught, yet nothing happened. I went on, head down, trembling with cold and fear, feeling more alone than I have ever felt. I had lost my brother and we had lost the fight.

Athens was in the hands of the English and their stooges. I didn't know where to go, but I realised I had to leave.

There was a safe house somewhere near Larissis Station and I made my way there. Then I was helped to leave the city – there was no point in staying. We had been defeated and the choice was now chains or weapons. It was only natural to choose the latter. "The mountains are accustomed to snow", as they say. So there was a weary familiarity to life when a small band of us travelled on foot, by truck and with mules along old country tracks. After several days, we arrived back at the mountains near Lamia where I had begun, so full of hope, just over a year before. The button from my brother's jacket was still in my pocket – a greyish, two-holed circle of horn. I kept fingering it. I liked taking it out to stroke the ridged edge.

I met up with what was left of my battalion, including Dora, who had been to see her two small children at her parents' house outside Athens, but left them again to continue the fight. What fight? At this point we were a sad collection of people whose hopes had been drowned like kittens in the river. It was cold and wet. Bands of fascists were on the hunt for us. Then, in February there was Varkiza – the so-called Peace Agreement, where ELAS leaders agreed to turn in their fighters' weapons on condition that they would play a part in Greece's politics. It is hard to imagine the shame felt by any partisan who gave up his or her weapon. Your gun was your honour and your life. Many of the men had acquired their weapons in battle with the Germans and Italians – they were their most precious belonging, something for which they had risked their lives. I thought of the beloved

Mauser that *Kapetan* Eagle had given me the previous winter, with its smell of oiled metal. It had kept me company day and night until it was lost in the fighting when Markos was killed. Another loss. I'll never forget seeing the toughest men I knew crying like babies when they threw their guns down on a pile. Some even committed suicide. We all wept for what might have been. Of course, we were never allowed to join in the political process. We were tricked into helping our enemies defeat us. If you are unjust to someone, you wound his soul, and that doesn't go away, however many years pass. The bitterness always remains.

After Varkiza we had the White Terror. Colonel Grivas and his X-boys rampaged through the streets of Athens, while gangs of right-wing thugs terrorised the villages, beating, killing and raping with impunity. Our enemies called us brigands, but they were the ones supporting these fascist bands. In the countryside we dreaded the ferocious *Sourlides* from Volos, who wore their hair long and greasy, with beards divided in two like devil's horns. Sourlas was their leader, and they rode on horseback, dressed in black waistcoats, hung with bells, pistols and knives. The police gave them a free hand to do what they liked in villages that were known to support our cause and their brutality was notorious. They liked to torture their victims before they murdered them. And they were also useful for handing over live leftists to the police, who would then be sent off in their thousands to jails and island camps. The constantly growing population of prisoners was almost all made up of former partisans – people of conscience who had done nothing wrong. At a time when we were all exhausted by years of violence and war, the horror just kept going. We tried to keep our discipline and our rules continued as rigorous as ever, but they were black days.

That summer was dry and baking hot. In June, we heard the news of Aris' death. I had met him several times, but I had not known him well. To tell the truth, he was always a bit dismissive of us girls – he was a man's man, with his Black Caps around him, filling everyone with awe. But he was a great leader. His voice was urgent yet gentle, inspiring us all to keep going. He didn't deserve to be treated like that – hunted down and murdered, though some say he managed to finish himself off before they got him. They chopped off his head, along with that of Tzavelas, his deputy, and strung them up on a lamp post in Trikkala's central square. The pictures were in all the newspapers – the hero who had fought the Nazis and brought justice and freedom to the villages, mutilated and humiliated in death. I was horrified by the grotesque photograph. It took me straight back to the cellar in Piraeus Street, and memories of Uncle Diamantis and the hidden press. It had been Aris' picture, still wet and black, that originally summoned me to join the fight. That seemed so long ago.

After the summer it became harder than ever to survive. The English occupation of Greece meant that they distributed food aid and supplies around the country, but nothing reached the mountain villages where we still had support. The villagers could not feed themselves, let alone give us anything, and the drought that year added to the desperate situation. We moved around in smaller groups, but it was becoming almost impossible. Occasionally, we took a sheep or goat from a herd and had a feast, but mostly we didn't even have enough beans or grains to make a soup. Once we we even reach Athens," she warned, as Dora and I applied unfamiliar lipstick before a mirror.

We met a contact near the port in Piraeus and were taken to a house in the refugee neighbourhood of Kokkinia, near where I had stayed during the *Dekemvriana*, the previous winter. The weather was awful and we spent hours in a tiny house, boiling up the mountain tea we had brought with us, and listening to the rhythms of the rain hitting the tin roof. The elderly couple who owned the place gave us a large package of cigarettes that they had acquired in exchange for something, at a time when barter and the black market were the commonest forms of commerce. Neither of them smoked, so we three sat puffing away almost without stopping, lighting the next cigarette from the last. We had a passion for Comrade Tobacco that never left us. Smoking was a pleasure and, above all, companionship, however lonely you felt. And after the conditions we had been used to in the mountains, it was a luxury to sit in a dry room blowing smoke rings. We had been told to wait for instructions, but when nothing happened on the second day and the rain stopped, I left my comrades and went in search of my brother's grave. I walked over to Mets in my high-heeled shoes, and arrived at the First Cemetery exhausted and with blistered feet.

I found our old neighbour, *Kyrios* Kostas, gathering up withered wreaths and burning them. Like the previous time, he did not recognise me. I spoke quietly.

"It's me, Antigone, your neighbour." He crossed himself several times as he looked me up and down.

"*Antigonaki*, you've become a lady," he said with approval. I didn't feel like a lady but a ridiculous fake, with my lightened hair and agonising shoes. *Kyrios* Kostas led me to the Protestant Cemetery, the walled-off part for foreigners. And there, over in one corner, next to the tomb of a German couple who had died in the 1920s, there was a grave marked by a small, horizontal stone. It was engraved with my brother's initials, М.П. *Kyrios* Kostas said, "I didn't want to put any more than that in case of trouble. I know you'll do the right thing by the boy when you can. We'll get a nice stone and a proper plot, and you'll bring a priest. Naturally, you must let your poor mother know. I don't want to make trouble in your family, but she is suffering." I sat down and tidied the grave, as I'd seen women do in every graveyard I'd ever been in. But I had never understood before. It was as though I was stroking my brother as I brushed the dried leaves away and, when I whispered to him, I felt he could hear.

By the time I returned to the house in Kokkinia, I was unwell. I had a cough and recognised the light-head and heavy limbs that mark the beginning of illness. I went straight to bed and slipped into uneasy and hallucinating dreams. It was another nightmare when, a few hours later, there was a loud banging on the door and several men pushed their way into the house, shouting in the darkness. They were the police. Using torches (there was no electricity in the place), they dragged me out of bed along with Dora and Storm, and told us we were under arrest. There was no time to do anything. They pointed guns at us while we pulled on clothes and followed them out to a van. The old couple had been sleeping in the kitchen and they were taken along too. We were driven to a police station in Piraeus, where our hosts were put in one cell and the three of us in another. We had shown the police our false identity cards, but they seemed to know we were partisans.

"Dirty Bulgarian whores!" they said. "Filthy communist traitors! You betrayed your country, you deserve to die." Storm was never at a loss for a reply and said, "If we're Bulgarians, you're Turks! We are Greek patriots who love our country."

"What you need is a good Greek man to knock some sense into you." One of the policemen leaned in and squeezed Storm's cheek as though she were a child. He twisted it until there was a red welt. "If you were a patriot, you'd be at home with your family. You made your choices and now you're going to pay for them." He spat a gob of phlegm on the floor by our feet.

There was no bed in the cell, and the two blankets they brought us were so soiled that we threw them in the corner and sat on the floor, leaning against the wall. Later, however, it became so cold that we put one of the greasy, blood-en-crusted rags on the floor to lie on and pulled the other on top of us so that at least our backs were covered. I was sweating and shivering from the worsening fever and none of us slept. As the sun came up and the concrete floor of the cell was lit up with a thin line of light, I watched lice crawling on the blanket. They seemed like monstrous creatures. I was so weak, I felt powerless to protect myself but, when Dora woke, she crushed them one by one: "before they make us their breakfast". She smiled at me and her mouth looked enormous, then distant, and her teeth white and sharp. I didn't know where I was and can't remember anything of the next day or so. Eventually, I was seen by a doctor and was put in a cell by myself, which had a bed and a pile of similarly disgusting blankets. It was more comfortable, but I felt utter loneliness of a sort I had never experienced before nor have since. Nobody spoke to me, except the guard who brought watery soups and stale bread twice a day. He wasn't unkind, but something even worse – uninterested.

After my illness passed, I was moved to a police station near Omonia. At my first interrogation I was told they knew exactly who I was, so there was no point in denying it. They even knew about my family.

"Why couldn't you have behaved like your sister?" Naturally they wanted to learn about my comrades, but I was nothing if not stubborn. The more they tried, the more I refused. They used to take me up to the top floor of the building, to a room where the policemen rested, which contained several beds. They would remove a mattress from one and tell me to take my clothes off down to my underwear. Then I was told to lie face down on the wooden base of the bed. Four policemen held me by my wrists and ankles, while another one beat me with a truncheon. They grunted like animals and shouted as though it was good entertainment. I didn't tell them anything. Even when I was covered with black and purple bruises I refused to speak to those pigs. I lost count of the times they took me there.

One day, a guard came to my cell and said I had visitors. Before I could ready myself, two people walked in. When you are not prepared, it is harder to be in control. I had never cried or even called out in pain while I was being thrashed by the policemen, but when I realised who the man and woman in front of me were, I crumpled onto my bed and wept like a child. The woman, hunched and thin, staring into my face without speaking, was my mother. Next to her, in the pristine khaki uniform of our English conquerors, was Johnny. I was both relieved and angry, comforted and hurt. My mother sat down next to me and took me in her arms, as she had when I was younger. She kissed my forehead and stroked my hair, making the soothing noises that had always calmed me as a child.

Johnny was talking, though it was hard to take in what he was saying. "Article 125 of the Penal Code... Instigation of civil war and the formation of armed bands... crimes of high treason." He looked very clean and pink, his skin close-shaven and his hair combed. He spoke in English to keep the conversation more private from the guard lurking outside the door. "It's serious, Antigone. But I want to help you. Don't forget, you have a brother-in-law who is a senior police officer. If you do the right thing, Spiros will help you too. He is family now." I looked at the man I thought I'd loved and hated him. I detested the English and their hypocrisy. As to Spiros, he was beneath contempt.

"I have always done what I consider to be the right thing. If you really want to help, you can leave." I spoke calmly, surprised at myself. "And you can tell that to your fellow countrymen," I said to Johnny. "You have 'helped' us enough. We're not part of your empire and we don't want to be a British colony." My mother left some food, kissed me goodbye and went out after Johnny.

My trial was a farce, but there was no laughter. There was only one punishment for high treason: execution. I was expecting it, and yet when I heard the judge say the words, there was a strange sensation in my intestines, like lead pipes

19
The incurable necrophilia of radical patriotism

MAUD

When Nikitas and I moved into Paradise Street with Tig, I was happy with our new existence. I loved the house, which somehow managed to be both solid and decorative: floors of grey marble, filled with small fossils that Tig traced with her fingers; the sturdy terracotta sculptures of Athena, standing sentry at the corners of the terrace and gazing out across the city; the heavy green shutters, which filtered strips of light into the bedroom; the old bath with 1930s French chrome taps. The whole place was redolent of Petros, Nikitas' grandfather and the journey he made from village boy to self-made businessman; it was his monument to a successful life. I liked being part of the continuation of the Perifanis family. Practically too, it was good to have Alexandra and Chryssa, the two "grandmothers", downstairs, and I appreciated their company.

Having been brought up by people whose formative years

had been during the Second World War, I found it easy to relate to the two old women. I remembered how my grandparents had valued peace for its own sake, and how careful they were with food (half a tomato saved on a plate in the fridge, leftovers recycled into new meals). Chryssa often cooked for us and both she and Alexandra were happy to take Tig for hours on end if I was busy. I enjoyed sitting with Chryssa in the kitchen, taking the role of *sous-chef*, cleaning vegetables or cutting onions (Greek style, in one's hand rather than on a board) and talking with her while she rolled out feta pies with scalloped edges or made *dolmades* –vine leaves stuffed with rice, onions and pine nuts.

"It's like embroidery," she said, as she folded them into parcels, like small presents, and then smothered them in egg and lemon sauce.

Despite my hopes for a domestic idyll, I admit that this was when Nikitas and I began to have problems. Or rather, the problems began to show. Nikitas was plagued by nightmares about earthquakes. I would wake to find him dragging me from the bed so we could escape from the collapsing house. Sometimes he'd shout for Tig, until I soothed him into waking properly and then going back to sleep. Perhaps the return to a childhood home associated with unhappiness was harder for him than I realised. Spiros cast a long shadow even after his demise and Nikitas continued to belittle his uncle whenever possible, mocking and criticising him, and harping on about his last moments. He argued that the manner of a person's death changes the perspective of their life.

"When I think of how Spiros spent a lifetime lecturing me about the value of the family, of Christianity, of telling the truth… all a great pile of shit in the end. If you die in a ridiculous way, you will be remembered for that. It reveals your essence, much as dying resolutely makes you a hero. Imagine if Jesus hadn't ended up on the cross, but had died of flu – maybe the world would have turned out quite differently. Or take our King Alexander, who died from a monkey bite that got infected. Almost a hundred years later he still isn't remembered for anything else."

Now that Nikitas was gone, I recalled his words, pondering on what his death revealed about him. The fact that he had died alone, in the small hours and away from his family, holding onto secrets, was a bleak reminder of how the gap between us had been widening. The shift in tone started gradually, like an invisible disease working its way through the body. It's not that we didn't love each other, but that certain things started to rankle. I began to believe that at least part of his veiled hostility was due to my nationality. When he made his documentaries about Greece's relationship with Britain, each new scandal he uncovered was like a black mark against me personally. I began to feel shamed and humiliated, as though I was being smeared with mud and cinders, as the Byzantines used to do to miscreants, after parading them sitting backwards on a donkey. I understood better why the Greek *moúntza* gesture of splaying the hand (as though to smear) has, ever since those times, been the nastiest insult in this country. The outstretched palm of the hand, sometimes paired with the other hand for emphasis, goes beyond the power of curses and offends an individual's honour.

"Do you know what you English did to the resistance fighters after the end of the Second World War?" he asked, using the second person plural when speaking about British politicians who had been in power decades before my birth.

"And don't forget Cyprus – your handy little colony in the Mediterranean. Of course, it was such a useful stop-over on the way to India, but even after the Indians were given their freedom, England clung on to Cyprus. Who in England remembers that long after India became independent, you went on executing Cypriot Greek freedom fighters for being terrorists?" Nikitas' film on Cyprus had interviews with old men in village coffee houses, who spoke of the British as unjust oppressors. They were still haunted by their lost comrades and convinced that their cause was just. Two of the respectable-looking pensioners stood up to recite the oath they took in the 1950s:

I shall work with all my power for the liberation of Cyprus from the British yoke, sacrificing for this even my life.

"Naturally, the English tourists who fill the charter planes and go to sweat like pigs on Cyprus' beaches have absolutely no idea," Nikitas said, revelling in his outrage. "They're like the Germans who drive past Cretan villages, ignoring the signs listing how many civilians were shot there by the Nazis. Forgetting is very useful when you've committed atrocities."

I had not known these things, or at least not in detail. And, to tell the truth, I felt aggrieved by what felt like wrongful accusations, rather than remorse – these episodes had occurred well before I was born. I suppose my outsider's innocence ceased to be refreshing to Nikitas. I believed that I was not part of any grand plan, mass political movement or colonial conquest; I was an individual, a human, who happened to have been born in one place and lived in another. That didn't convince him.

"Our history is inside us," he said. "It's in our cells, just as our grandparents and ancestors live on in our DNA. We cannot escape from what went before, from what our countries have experienced."

The more Nikitas laid into me as though I were to blame for Churchill or the brutality of British troops in Cyprus, the more I began to find fault with my adopted country. What had previously been exotic became annoying, starting with the details of daily life. What sort of country expects people to put their shitty toilet paper in baskets instead of down the drains? Why couldn't they install normal drain pipes like everywhere else? Why is it considered normal to have power cuts for hours on end during summer heat-waves and winter storms, as though we were living in Gaza and not twenty-first century Europe? Why are seatbelts seen as an infringement of liberty (even for children), when they know that the roads are the most dangerous in Europe? Why is the Greeks' idea of freedom interpreted as the freedom to park across the pavement, blocking women with pushchairs and pensioners, or the freedom to smoke incessantly, everywhere? Of course, once I started down this slippery slope, the questions came faster and more furiously. Why was it considered normal when we handed the surgeon a "small envelope" containing 3,000 euros cash when Nikitas had a minor operation in a state hospital?

There are times, especially after a roasting hot night in summer, when even a cotton sheet seems to burn the skin and the whine of dive-bombing mosquitoes drives you mad, that I long for the soothing North, the subtle shadows of grey London light and cool summer nights where you sleep with a duvet. "Moaning Maud" – that is what I am, or at least what I became. Even worse than "Bored Maud", as an old boyfriend used to say. At least I wasn't "Maudlin" or "Mordant", as Desmond, my grandfather, called me affectionately. He would make up limericks that made use of all the words that rhymed with my name. *There was a young lady called Maud, who was always incredibly bored...* I remember flawed and ignored, but there was also roared, gnawed, clawed.

Above all, the thing I had tired of was the Greeks' obsession with themselves, with the nature of Greekness, with how they are viewed and how unfairly they are judged. Beware of saying even the slightest critical thing about Greece to a Greek as they will take it as though you have said their mother is a whore and their father her pimp.

"Everything has to revolve around your suffering," I once told Nikitas in frustration. "You *like* being the victims. You blame the Turks for keeping you as slaves for four centuries, the British for their political meddling, the Americans for supporting the Junta – anyone but yourself for the mess."

Looking back on my disillusionment with Greece, I realise that I had forgotten to place it alongside the extremes that mark so much of life there – a ratcheting up of intensity so that each experience takes you further than it might elsewhere. It starts with the senses. Colours, sounds, smells and tastes are richer in Greece (the tang of lemons off the tree or spearmint in salad, tomatoes or figs that taste of the sun). But these extremes continue so that emotions are stretched to breaking point in all directions. The lack of safety precautions is all part of the thrill; political correctness will never catch on. After Nikitas' death, I had started to see these things more clearly. And now, it seemed not only obvious but understandable that the Greeks have a tendency to create tragic myths out of their experiences, with the Civil War being one of the most powerful and long-lasting. The almost magnetic lure of calamity here was simply the other end of a spectrum on which the closeness of family and community has bound people together so tightly.

While I was clearing and sorting things in Nikitas' office, I had come across a book called *The Incurable Necrophilia of Radical Patriotism.* The title alone was enough to make me take it home. It was filled with comments Nikitas had written in the margin – angry disagreements (*Ochi!*) and scorings-out in heavy biro. One day, Orestes came in to find me lying on the sofa reading what turned out to be a critique of the left-wing Greek obsession with the glory of defeat, especially in relation to the Civil War. He laughed so much when I showed him the book that I feared he was going to cry. It was as if the spasms of laughter had drawn out emotions prompted by his father's death that he had been successfully controlling. When he quietened down, he sat on the arm of the sofa beside me.

"It's true – we love our martyrs in Greece," he said. "It's better to lose in the name of honour than to win. *Babas* and his cronies clung onto the resistance story for so long because they got off on that masochistic shit. It excites the wankers – the pleasure is knowing they held the moral high ground. It applies even more to his mother's generation, which was practically wiped out. It doesn't matter if everyone was imprisoned or killed. As long as it was in a good cause. What a fucking mess." Orestes groaned in contentment. "Incurable necrophiliacs! That's what they are."

20
Farewell poor world,
farewell sweet life

Antigone

When my son was born, he did not cry. He just looked at me as though he knew something. His body was like that of a tiny, wrinkled monkey, with black down over his back and a thick head of hair. They washed him, swaddled him tightly and handed him to me like a package ready for posting. I had no idea what to do. I had never seen a newborn or cared for a baby. Ironically, my life in the mountains meant that I was more, not less, innocent about the functions of the female body than my contemporaries in the city or the countryside. I knew how to clean a gun and gut a hare, and I was not afraid to walk up a mountain at night. But I had not really known what was involved in childbirth and had no idea how to change a nappy or hold an infant. Confronted with this new life, I was bewildered. Thankfully, babies are efficient teachers and I submitted to the powerful urges of nature.

The staff in the Elena Hospital were not unkind, though they did whisper and stare. After all, I had come in wearing handcuffs. They made jokes.

"He's a patriot," one nurse said.

He had certainly chosen a triumphant day. He arrived on October 28th, when we all remember our "No" to the Italians.

"This boy won't let anyone trample over him," the nurse went on. "He'll be a fighter."

I often thought of those words over the years, hoping they would be a form of blessing for my son.

Although I had haemorrhaged badly and there were complications I didn't understand at the time, I went back to jail after three days. But instead of being returned to Kallithea, I was taken to Averoff Prison, entering through the front door on Alexandra Avenue. The sun burnt my face and a Cyclops eye peered through a hole in the door. Bolts and bars screeched and I passed through several doors, before I was stopped and searched by a hag. She pawed at my clothes and thrust her hand between my legs.

"Careful, I'm bleeding," I said. "I have given birth."

She muttered, "May it live for you!" as though it was a curse. Then she led me out to the courtyard. Hundreds of women were gathered like a flock of crows, in black and grey clothes and dark headscarves. There were old crones and teenagers, virgins and widows, strong village mothers and pale city intellectuals. Over by a large palm tree and the prison chapel, dozens of little children were shouting and playing. From the other side of the high walls came men's voices from the male section. My head spun from the sun and from some lingering weakness, and I looked for somewhere to sit. Before I could find a space, familiar voices called my name and Dora almost knocked me down with her embraces. Behind her was Storm. My old comrades shouted over the noise of the people who had gathered around to watch.

"What happened? The baby? Are you all right?" Storm and Dora had been transferred to the Averoff a couple of months before and had heard nothing of me since then. They both looked well – Dora as small and springy as a rubber ball and Storm standing solid and dignified.

"I have a son. He is well." My voice was like somebody else's. "They say they'll bring him." I swayed, ready to pass out, and Dora sat me down on a step. She placed a hand on my forehead, while Storm fetched water.

"Not as good as the springs on Mount Iti." Storm handed me a tin cup. "The fight continues, wherever we are. Your health, Antigone."

Dora said, "May your son live for you. May he have health, happiness and be a brave revolutionary. He'll get a good training in here with all his aunties. But the godmother has to be me or Storm. You'll be with me in the mother-and-baby dormitory. It's noisy and crowded but it's all right." Dora glanced at Storm and paused.

"Don't worry – it's no secret." There was never any compromising with Storm. "I call figs, figs and troughs, troughs," she liked to say. "I'm down in the dungeons – on death row. I can't say it's cheerful – we're in single cells without windows, but we manage. We sing together, even if we're twenty steps underground. It's good practice for the time we'll soon be spending beneath the earth."

Two small children ran up to Dora and pulled at her

clothes. She told them, "Give a kiss to your Aunt Antigone." Then she introduced me to Panos, her three-year-old, who jumped and shouted and refused to come near me. His sister, Evdokia, who was quiet and serious, kissed my cheek with such sadness that I felt faint all over again. Later, I met *Kyria* Tina, Dora's mother, a woman even smaller and more energetic than Dora. *Kyria* Tina had been imprisoned for supporting her daughter and supplying other "bandits" with food and shelter. So, with nobody else to care for Dora's children, the "poor mites" – as their granny called them – had been brought into prison too.

A few hours after I arrived at Averoff, my baby was brought from the hospital. They told me to feed him and the older children gathered around to stare at the tiny creature. When I changed him, they pointed and laughed at his "fur". After the feed, the nurse took him away. Three hours later, he was back again. This rigmarole continued for eight days, after which they said he could stay – I was allowed to keep my parcel. By then, my son had changed from the silent, questioning infant he had been at first. He wailed like a demon for hours on end. The only person who could help was Dora, who took him in her arms and calmed his raging. She boiled up camomile and fed him from a spoon when he had stomach pains. And she sang him songs to distract him.

If it wasn't Nikitas crying, it was another child – we were at least a hundred mothers and children in the special dormitory. Averoff had been built for two hundred inmates and now housed about twelve hundred. We were almost all "politicals" (criminals were kept separately) and we were locked up for nineteen hours of the day. There was nowhere to go but the triple-layered bunks in which the children were squeezed, two to a bed. Washing was strung along the bars over the high windows and a large bucket in the corner was used when the guards would not come to take us to the toilet. The smell of physical life was overwhelming – hair, skin, feet, and all that flows from women's and babies' bodies: dried milk gone sour; infant vomit; menstrual blood seeping onto rags; urine darkening in the bucket and soaking into nappies; and sweat from the constant struggle to keep ourselves and our offspring clean.

Our confined existence settled into a regular pattern that contained all the joy and sorrow of life anywhere else. We all believed in the same thing so, if anything, we became more determined to keep our fight going by becoming better organised. We instituted morning gymnastics, and anyone with a profession or talent used it: there were four doctors, several lawyers and various teachers and artists. The seamstresses were the only ones who didn't do general housework as they were so busy. Although there were restrictions on books and paper, we started reading and writing lessons. Some of the older children attended these, including Elpida, the youngest prisoner. At the age of twelve she was a political enemy, who had been through a court martial and been convicted of high treason. Her crime was handing out pamphlets – others were in for painting slogans on walls. She was a good girl, Elpida. She helped look after the babies and did her lessons, and as her name [Hope] suggests, she helped us stay optimistic with her sweet nature.

We had a special programme for the "black cloud" – the group of old grandmothers who normally dressed in mourning clothes. Many were illiterate and we taught them to write so they could send letters to their families. I particularly liked *Kyria* Frosso, an ancient crone with a kind, wrinkled face, who must have been in her 80s – I never imagined I would reach that great age myself. Sometimes she would hold the baby for me when I was busy and I would write letters for her when she was too tired to spell out each word by herself. Of course, much of our day was spent dealing with the practicalities of living in cramped quarters with so many people. Apart from trying to keep ourselves and our children clean, we had rotas for chores. There were the "floor Marias", "corridor Marias", "canteen Marias" and so on. The "yard Marias" had to scrub the whole courtyard and the "washroom Marias" made the fires to heat cauldrons filled with water, which they then distributed: first to mothers and babies, then to death row prisoners so they would be clean if they were taken for execution, then to grandmothers and those with TB, and finally to the remaining inmates. Then the "canteen Marias" took the cauldrons and used them to cook food for over a thousand mouths. We had songs for different chores. The "washroom Marias" sang the *Kalamatiano*, *Three boys from Volos*. We were determined not to let the system beat us.

Naturally, it was never quiet. Everyone wore wooden clogs and clattered up and down the stairs and stamped across the concrete yard like charging cavalry. Women calling, singing, arguing, children playing and crying. The noisiest person of all was *Kyria* Tina, Dora's mother. I loved her like family and she became an honorary grandmother to Nikitas, despite being in a different dormitory to us. You could hear her voice all over the prison. In fact, she was chosen as the primary "caller", who shouted out our names when there was a roll call or when we had visitors. At night, things were quieter, but the noises were more upsetting. Not so much the babies, but the women weeping, many of them crying out from nightmares, remembering the horrors that they had been through. Everyone had a story to tell about how they had been beaten or tortured. *Kyria* Tina had had salt put in her wounds and Storm had several fingernails pulled out. Dora told me how they took boiled eggs from the pan and pressed them under her arms. Her armpits were left scalded and weeks later, they were still tender. We all had worries that grew worse in the dark hours.

Sometimes I envied the death row women down in their dungeons for the peace they had – I yearned for some relief from the constant swirl of humanity. The only time there was a moment of sudden quiet was when men from the isolation cells started singing before they were taken away for execution. Whenever we heard them we froze – we would stop dressing a child or mopping the floor, listening out for the sounds of their departure.

In the darkest, coldest part of the year, when Nikitas was still only a few months old, I had a visitor. It was raining and I had been with the "cauldron Marias" that morning, so I was wet and dirty. I heard *Kyria* Tina yelling out my name for the visitors' room. Prisoners went in ten at a time and had five minutes in which to exchange news and to get what we called "free air" from the outside. I had never been before, as nobody from my family had visited. I knew they would not be impressed by the arrival of a bastard – plenty of babies were pushed through the hatch at the foundling hospital for lesser crimes. It was dark and I couldn't see well in the small room, though I did notice two windows covered in bars and wire mesh. The guard motioned me over to the far window and I peered through, wondering who had come for me.

When I saw Johnny on the other side of the bars, I almost walked back into the rain. This was the second time he had come to stare at me as if I was a caged animal and I hated him for it. There was no place for an English oppressor in my country or my life. But I couldn't turn around. I was weak.

"How good of you to come." I hoped I sounded like my mother at her haughtiest. He didn't answer, but stood close to the bars, looking at me. I felt ashamed that he should see me with my hair like rats' tails. I knew my face was red from the steam and I noticed how shabby my clothes were. Johnny was in uniform, his hair slicked down and his face so closely shaved it was like a boy's.

He said, "I am going home. I can't stay in Greece any longer." He paused and I waited in silence until he found his voice. "Markos... I'm so sorry." He struggled with the words.

I said, "You are a murderer, Johnny. Why did Markos have to die?"

It was evident that he wanted me to believe him. He said, "You can't hold me responsible. I wasn't there. I only found out later. I loved Markos." His face contracted and I wondered whether he was going to cry. "I'm leaving, but I would like to help you. I know you have a son. There must be so much he needs." Time passed as slowly as water turning to ice while I stood there, hearing Johnny's words but saying nothing. I shut out the memories of the joy we had experienced before all this – the Ilissos river, the poems and picnics. Another life. The bell rang and the guard shouted for prisoners to withdraw. The five minutes had passed.

"Send me soap," I said, thinking of my son. "And wool, for knitting." Johnny nodded, but said nothing.

"Everyone needs paper and pencils, so anything like that is useful."

He put his hand up to the window, but the wire between us prevented any contact even if I had reciprocated.

"Goodbye, Antigone. I hope your country's misery will soon end."

I nodded and left the room with the other prisoners. I was disoriented by the visit, but my friends were delighted when, on the next visiting day, a large parcel arrived. The guards confiscated the coffee and cigarettes, but we were left with generous quantities of tea, sugar, soap, dozens of balls of wool (blue for a boy), and twenty notebooks and pencils.

"Ask your Englishman to come again," they begged. "Ask if he can send more. Never mind if they are royalist, colonialist pigs." And he did. I must give him credit for that.

❊   ❊   ❊

We baptised my son just after Easter. Storm insisted she should be godmother. She said, "I will die a virgin and never have a child of my own. At least let me have a godchild." She teased me that, when the priest asked her for the name, she would say "Anaximandros" after her beloved father. But when the moment came, she called out "Nikitas", so that even the crowds in the courtyard heard her from the chapel. We all understood she was talking of victory and hope. The baby watched quietly as Storm held him, wrapped in a towel, and the elderly Father Philippos got on with the service.

"Out with the Devil, out with him." He repeated the phrase over and over, making the spitting motions and looking pointedly at Storm. Needless to say, the prison's priest was no lover of communists and we never enjoyed his visits. He pressed us to repent of our political sins and renounce the Party: "Sign the statement," he'd say, "and go home to your families like good Christian Greek women. Stop wasting your time with godless criminals. You are lost children who can be saved by Christ and by yourselves."

When Nikitas' towel was removed and he was covered from head to toe in olive oil, he became uneasy and then angry. I watched in dismay from the required distance as Father Philippos grabbed my screaming child around the midriff and made for the font. His grey beard was scratching the seven-month-old's back. As he made to plunge Nikitas into the water, the baby started to slip from his grip. Dora and I lurched forward, but we were too far away to help. I glimpsed Storm's face as she registered the danger and dived for him. Afterwards, we realised it was a movement like she had made so many times to escape bullets on the mountains. She caught my son just as his arms slithered from the priest's hands and godmother and child landed together on the tiled floor. A small pause followed, as Nikitas stopped crying in surprise. Then his voice reverberated around the prison walls – lungfuls of air forced into screams. On and on. We established that he was not hurt, but the chapel was filled with noise. Dora's children started crying and there was muttering from the hundreds of prisoners, who were crammed into the chapel and pressing around the entrance.

It took some time before Father Philippos regained enough composure to continue, and then he didn't have the heart to put Nikitas all the way under the water. Instead, he gave a hurried version of the rite, dipping my son in three times up to his waist. He handed the baby back to Storm.

"Silly old goat," she whispered, as we dressed Nikitas in beautiful blue woollen shorts and jacket, knitted by *Kyria* Tina. Of course, we had no *boubouniéres* to hand out – where would you get sugared almonds? But there were flowers left over from Good Friday, the only day of the year when visitors were allowed give them to prisoners, to decorate Christ's bier: clove-scented carnations, white calla lilies, and some roses that had dropped their red petals everywhere and left smears all over the tiles.

It was only a few hours later that they announced there would be executions the next morning. Storm and three other women were among those to be taken to Goudi, along with a group of men from the neighbouring part of the prison.

Storm said, "We didn't enter this fight to live, but to die." Her face was grey, but she wouldn't admit that this was more than any other battle.

"Death will take us all, so it's the same whether it's now or later. The important thing is how you live and how you die." The other women were equally brave, like early Christians going to their deaths, charged up with faith. They tried to comfort the rest of us but it was hard to stay calm. They also wrote letters for their families and prepared themselves. Dora and I helped Storm wash and fix her clothes, and I brushed her hair, braiding it into a thick rope. Dora cleaned her shoes, wiping away the dust that got everywhere and making them shine. It was important to go to your death in a dignified way, looking as good as possible and with your head held high. When the call went for us to return to our cells and dormitories, the girls on death row went away singing and even after they were locked into their tiny dungeons, they continued. We could hear their voices all through the night, singing until they were hoarse.

> *Farewell poor world,*
> *Farewell sweet life,*
> *And you, my poor country,*
> *Farewell for ever.*

They sang the dance of Zalongo, remembering the women of Souli, who had sung and danced along the edge of the cliffs, choosing death and honour over slavery under the Turks. As Ali Pasha's troops came to capture them, the mothers threw their children off the cliff and then danced themselves over the edge, leaving the soldiers looking down at their bodies on the rocks below.

As dawn came, the singing grew louder and we realised that the prisoners had come into the courtyard. We got out of bed, leaving the children sleeping, and climbed up to the windows, so we could see our friends for the last time.

"Go to the good, Storm! Farewell! Take a good bullet!" Dora's voice was steady.

I called to the godmother my son would never know, "Goodbye, friends! Goodbye, my *koumbára.*" Storm waved and kept on singing, pulling her three comrades into a dance. The guards let them go and the four women danced the *syrtós* hand-in-hand around the palm tree, like the women of Souli. The sun came up, bringing rosy threads to the sky.

As they were finally led away, Storm shouted, "Death is nothing. Better one hour of free life."

"Don't give in. Don't sign the statement," called Evanthia, one of the other condemned prisoners. "Don't lose your honour, don't betray the Party."

After they had left, we slowly climbed down from the windows, unable to talk, but loath to go back to bed. We heard the lorry set off along Alexandra Avenue and turn right onto Mesogeia Avenue. Then the sound of crows taking to the skies with a harsh "kra, kra". The birds had learned that if the prison lorries turned up towards Goudi they were bringing food. When the execution was over, the crows would fly down and peck warm flesh from the bodies before they were gathered up and taken away. We returned to our bunks in silence. I watched my child as he slept in the narrow bed we shared. His face was still and peaceful, and his belly rose and fell like a measure of time passing. If it had not been for him, I would probably have been in that lorry too.

"Kra, kra, kra." On and on they called in the distance.

Several hours later Evanthia returned. We were in the yard doing our chores quietly, when she walked in like a phantom. She could not speak, and remained silent for several days. But we learned that minutes before she had gone in front of the firing squad, her execution had been suspended on a point of law. The others were all dead. When she found her voice, she said that the twelve men and four women had sung all the way to Goudi. "They danced like brides and grooms" on the earth where they knew they would fall. *Farewell poor world, Farewell sweet life.*

"Kra, kra, kra."

21
Live your myth in Greece

MAUD

When the telephone rang I was sitting at my desk, staring at dust particles floating in the sunlight. I found myself doing that too much during those days. It was morning, and there were the sounds of delivery men banging their van doors down in the street. Morena was bumping the roaring vacuum cleaner around our apartment. I had shut myself up in my study, partially closed the shutters to keep the sun from dazzling me. I was wondering what might help me tackle the heaps of paper on the desk. One pile consisted of some dull research into how much Greece had suffered financially from hosting the 2004 Olympic Games. I was late with the translation and couldn't face doing it, a state of mind which also applied to another pile, concerning Nikitas' and my finances. There were some semi-intelligible papers concerning the widow's pension. I knew they would require an inordinate amount of traipsing from one public office to another. As it was, the phone rang.

"*Nai?*" – Yes – I answered in the usual Greek manner, the

monosyllable meaning "What do you want?"

"Please could I speak to *Kyria* Perifanis?" The male voice was slow and formal, the Greek spoken with a strong English accent.

"This is she," I replied in Greek, and then tried continuing in English. "Can I help you?"

"Ah. Hello. This is Johnny Fell."

"Oh, how wonderful." I could hardly believe it.

"I received your letter. I am very sorry to hear of your husband's death. I never knew him, but his mother's family were very kind to me. There are many fond memories."

A few moments of conversation indicated that Antigone's old friend was not only alive but very much *compos mentis*. Rashly, I asked if I could visit him. There was a lengthy pause.

"I don't think I can tell you very much. I'm ninety-one, after all."

I ignored the attempted brush-off. "Please. Just to talk. It would mean so much to me."

I found a cheap flight to England, arranged for Tig to stay with Alexandra, and two days later, got up before dawn and took the metro to Eleftherios Venizelos Airport. It sped along the middle of the new motorway, carving through the remnants of olive groves and vineyards. Fresh grass was sprouting lime-green shoots and the first rays of the sun illuminated huge bill-boards that rose from the fields – adverts for bank loans, mobile phones and tourism: *Live your myth in Greece*.

At Gatwick, I hired a car and followed the instructions given by the dull female voice on the satnav. With the two-hour time difference, it was still before midday when I arrived at Claywell, a small village not far from Brighton, tucked under the Downs.

I nosed along a narrow lane, until I came to a crossroads and my irritating guide announced, "You have now reached your destination." Corner House was an L-shaped cottage with terracotta roof tiles and the bare tangles of Virginia creeper and roses on the walls. There was a smell of manure and burning leaves in the chill air and the machine-gun "tat-tat-tat" of magpies. Within seconds of knocking, the door was opened by a stout, middle-aged woman in an apron.

"Mrs Perifanis? Mr Fell is expecting you. Please come in." I followed her through a dim hallway to a spacious, low-ceilinged room lined with books. An elderly dog sprawled on the sofa and eyed me without interest, as his master rose from an armchair by the fire.

"I hope you found the place easily." His voice was measured, placing a distance between us. Tall and thin, with inquisitive, pale eyes, John Fell looked younger than I had imagined. He was surprisingly upright for someone over 90, well turned-out in a tweed jacket and silk tie.

"What can we offer you? Betty could make coffee. Or would you prefer a drink? Whisky? Sherry? Lunch will be later." I hadn't drunk sherry since university, when it was sometimes offered at tutorials, but it seemed to fit the strange occasion.

"Again, please let me express my condolences, Mrs Perifanis."

I asked him to call me Maud, and he repeated the name.

"I had an aunt called Maud. A fine woman. She lived to be over a hundred."

"I always thought it a name for an ancient aunt," I said. "In Greece I'm usually Mond or Mondy, which I think I prefer."

He gave a non-committal smile and asked a few courteous questions, before telling me something of himself. He had spent most of his life teaching classics in a boys' boarding school, and in the 1960s, had written a book based on his research into inscriptions, called *Epigraphy in Ancient Athens*. It had done "modestly well", he said, and had been reprinted. He turned out to have known my grandfather, Desmond ("a notable scholar"), though they were never friends. Johnny had retired in the '80s, but continued writing occasional articles for learned journals until recently.

There was a brief pause, broken only by the snoring of the hairy dog on the sofa.

"I suppose you know your husband contacted me?"

"Nikitas?" I said stupidly, in shock.

"He traced me from the letters, as you did. He said he was writing something about his mother."

"What did he want?"

"There are some papers he thought might be useful. I knew the Perifanis family when I was a student. I never went back after the war, but I often think of them and of Greece. It was such a beautiful place. The purity of the landscape, the light so clear that it brings distant mountains leaping right up to you. And the people – so lively and hospitable. Villagers would give you their food and their bed without asking anything in return. Men like eagles, fiercely handsome…"

"What sort of papers?" I interrupted.

"Some letters. Nothing much."

"Why did you never go back to Greece?" I asked, changing tack.

"Things come to an end. Then I was busy with my work." It

didn't sound very convincing. "It would have been hard to go back after all I saw," he added in a low voice. I asked him if he had ever married and he waved his hand, dismissing the idea. "My life didn't take that direction."

We ate lunch in a burgundy-walled dining room that looked out over a garden with fruit trees and beyond that, a field of Friesian cows. Betty brought in a stew and then apple tart. It presented a picture of an England I thought had disappeared with the Greece of Johnny's memories and it awoke some dormant nostalgia in me for my own country. I was reminded of my grandparents – their ease and comfort, the old books, their measured words (at least on my grandfather's part) and the things they left unsaid. Coffee was served back in the drawing room, in small cups with dark rock sugar like my grandmother used to have. I told Johnny something of recent events and I could see he was intrigued by the story of Antigone's return and of the animosity that still existed between the sisters. He looked sad when I told him about the quarrel over Markos' bones and pointed to a framed picture of an ancient column with a teenage boy leaning against it. The loose-limbed stance and distant gaze reminded me of Orestes and I realised it was Markos.

"So young…" Johnny said, looking at the picture with me and shaking his head. "Such a terrible waste." Moving to his desk, the old man pulled out some letters he said were from Antigone. They were still neatly in their envelopes, tied together with a grey ribbon like a present.

"I was going to give them to Nikitas, so you should have them." I held the small bundle in my hands and stopped myself making the instinctive reaction of sniffing them.

"It was a tragedy, what happened to her," he continued. "It shouldn't have been like that."

"Would you consider coming to Athens?" I asked, before I left. He didn't look as startled as I had imagined. "It will be Nikitas' forty-day memorial soon. It would be a great honour. And significant for everyone involved." His expression told me he understood something of what I was getting at, though he shook his head.

"My travelling days are over. But I promise to think about it, my dear. I never thought I would see Greece again. And I certainly never imagined I would see my old friends."

*　*　*

On the plane back, I read Antigone's letters. The immediacy of this connection to her youth was deeply touching – offering a whole new perspective on a person I only knew as an elderly, buttoned-up victim of war and political movements. On these pages, I found an optimistic girl from a happy, privileged family, who had little to fear. The letters written before the war were in a laborious hand and filled with minor but charming misuses of English. The early ones were signed, *Yours Sincerely, Antigone Perifanis*, with a flourish beneath the signature.

> … *Life is so-and-so in Athens since you left. I wait you again so we can continue our lessons.*

> … *I hope you will not become indisposed from the ugly Oxford weather. Here we have the Alkyonides so it is warm and no breezes. The Myth says that Aeolus, King of winds, stopped all*

wind for 14 days when his daughter, Alkyone, was turned into the alkyonas bird. Now it happens each year in Janury when these birds make its eggs. Someone, presumably Johnny, had pencilled some notes at the side of the page. *Halcyon Days*, it said. *Alkyone = Kingfisher. Ovid.*

… My sister and I are taking French lessons with Mademoiselle Desmarais. It is quite dull, I am sorry to say and she is a "high nose" (is that correct in English?) She looks down at us somewhat.

… I took a walk to the Ilissos. Do you remember our picnic? Now the place is filled with high grass and yellow flowers. I picked some to make a wreath for May day.

A number of letters from Antigone to Johnny were sent from Averoff Prison, on official paper and obviously written with the censor in mind. Her tone veers between cool detachment and affectionate gratitude that Johnny was writing to her and even sending occasional parcels from England. She mentions a correspondence with an English woman, Jennifer Benton, who wrote to her under the auspices of the League for Democracy in Greece, an organisation set up in post-war Britain, which tried to help those mistreated and imprisoned by the new regime in Greece.

Mrs Benton has sent more soap and a box of coloured threads for sewing. She is very kind and I think she hopes to save the world with her goodness. I have a photograph of her and Mr

Benton and two little Bentons having a picnic in a field. It is
like another universe.

Sometimes Antigone opened up to Johnny, despite her mixed feelings about him, and she mentioned Nikitas as an infant. By the time the plane started its descent and the familiar landscape around Athens came into view, I was crying.

I remember how tired we were in the mountains, where you
could hardly stand upright, yet you had to keep on walking.
But the tiredness here is something you cannot imagine. There
is noise all the day and then it continues all the night. Always
people, people. My baby grows while I seem to shrink. Maybe
the whole world has shrunk. It seems like all that exists is the
yard, the lines and lines of beds and our small daily routines.

As I lay in bed that night, unable to sleep, my mind kept worrying away at everything I had read – both the pages of memoir Antigone had given me and the letters. There appeared to be gaps in the story. In particular, I had suspicions about *Kapetan* Eagle and whether he really was Nikitas' father. Antigone did not appear to want to talk about him or to tell me more about their relationship or whether there were any relations left on that side of the family. I began to wonder whether perhaps Johnny might have been responsible for Antigone's pregnancy; an irony, if true, given Nikitas' increasingly jaundiced view of the British. I returned to Johnny's letters when I got home and was intrigued by the continued intimacy between the pair, despite their supposed differences after the war.

The next time I saw Antigone was at Dora's house.

"I would love to know about Nikitas' father," I said, after we had sat down and Dora went to prepare coffee. I didn't ask her if she loved him.

"Nikitas could be proud of him. He was a good man," Antigone said unconvincingly. *Kapetan* Eagle was actually called Haris (short for Haralambos) Papaharalambopoulos, she explained. (No wonder he opted for a short *nom de guerre*; I felt a moment's relief that Nikitas, and consequently Tig and I, had not inherited that unwieldy surname.)

I only felt more confused as Antigone spoke of the *Kapetánios*. The description she gave of her involvement before her arrest with the well-known partisan contradicted everything she had described of the strict moral code in the mountains. It was well known that even the slightest flirtation was forbidden. Full-blown love affairs were treated as treason against the communist principles of comradeship, and sexual relations and marriage (not to mention pregnancy) were utterly incompatible with the practical requirements of guerrilla lifestyle. That side of life was required to be sidelined until after the fight was won.

"Why didn't you get married?" I asked.

"That was impossible. Haris was on the run and I went to Athens. And it wasn't long before he was dead."

When Dora came back into the room, I tried tackling her.

"You must have known Nikitas' father, Dora. I know so little about him – his character, what sort of man he was." Dora flashed a worried glance at Antigone.

"He must have been a wonderful person," I continued disingenuously, as Dora stalled.

"*Kapetan* Eagle," prompted Antigone. "Dora, tell Moody about Haris." It was as though she could hardly be bothered to keep up the pretence. Before I left, I asked the two old comrades whether the name Wasp meant anything to them.

"No!" they both declared without hesitating.

I had not received the promised email from Danae, but following a text message from me, she eventually sent me the details of *Kapetan* Eagle's death. She described how systematic the British had been in trying to annihilate what was left of the resistance in 1946, sending in people to train the army, police and gendarmerie. She had written out pages from a training brochure for gendarmes, which instructed them that partisans should be treated as common brigands:

> *Soldiers will approach dead bandits in groups of three. One will hold his weapon in readiness while the other two cautiously examine the bodies to ensure they are not simulating death and holding grenades or other weapons ... They should then be decapitated and their heads placed in a bag and taken to the nearest command post for public exposure.*

Right-wing murder squads were tolerated and supported by the state and the British, she explained, and *Kapetan* Eagle met his end at the hands of one such group in 1947.

> *He was hunted down by the notorious gang led by Vourlakis, who terrorised the Lamia region. They sliced off his ears and nose before killing him, and then chopped off his head (as recommended) and put it on a stake.*

Not long after, another group of fascist thugs was photographed with the severed heads of several young women hanging from their saddles. The shocking picture reached beyond Greece and was published in the Daily Mail, where the horror of many of its readers led to an enquiry. The British Ambassador in Athens was sent to find out more from the Greek Minister of Justice, whose answer was as simple as it was untrue:

"It is an old custom," he said, "for bandits on whom the State has put a price to be decapitated and have their heads exposed to the public." This was the kind of freedom, justice and democracy that England saw as fitting for their corner of the Mediterranean.

22
I, the undersigned

ANTIGONE

Nikitas grew and although he was behind bars, he was surrounded by love. He really did have hundreds of aunties and grandmothers, and could always play with other children. The little ones didn't know any better than the life they had in prison. Obviously, there were problems. In the summer, we suffered from the heat. You could only open the windows at the top and the concrete walls heated up like an oven. If we poured water on the floors it turned to steam. Then the steam from the "cauldron Marias" below would rise up until we were "like the harem in the *hammám*" (as Dora said, though she'd never been to a Turkish bath in her life).

News of what our brothers and sisters were doing filtered back to our closed community. We learned of the battles up in the mountains, of Vitsi and Grammos, of our newly formed Democratic Army that was fighting the National Army (armed and aided by the British). It was desperately hard for our boys and girls even to survive, let alone win a battle in the intense cold, without proper supplies and with so many weapons having been handed over at Varkiza. Then the villages that supported our side were cleared, their inhabitants taken to the towns "to protect them from the bandits".

When the English ran out of money and left in 1947, the Americans took over. They brought food and built bridges, but the Marshall Plan was not about charity, it was about control. Now American planes swept across the skies and "Greek bandits" became useful guinea pigs for testing new weapons. Napalm was tried out in Greece long before it was used in Vietnam. Stories came back to Averoff of a liquid fire that rained down and stuck to everything it touched. Whole hillsides were charred and the trees have never grown back. Bodies flamed like torches. When a new prisoner arrived, we would learn more details. Little Penelope was eighteen when she came, having lost an ear during a napalm attack. She said, "It just fizzled and dropped off." Penelope had been captured during a raid on a field hospital, where she was being treated for her injuries. She told us how the Democratic Army required her to shout through a bullhorn across the mountains to the boys from the National Army. Her voice was loud and carried well (what my mother called a "shepherdess voice") and a girl's high tones carried better than a man's. They also hoped it would distract the enemy.

"Brother soldiers! Listen to us. We're fighting for justice and freedom. Don't fight us. Come with us. We can't come to you, because they'll kill us..." Unsurprisingly, the National Army had proper megaphones and shouted back threats and abuse.

We wanted to support our brothers and sisters, but the truth was we couldn't. We organised celebrations to mark forbidden anniversaries like the Bolshevik revolution and the founding of our own resistance movement, or to commemorate one of the German mass executions. We read stories and poems, and ate food carefully saved for the occasion. We whispered revolutionary songs and even performed our own silent dance – the secret steps of partisans returning from battle, who could not afford to be heard by the enemy.

By far the worst aspect of being in prison was the pressure to sign the statement of repentance. We were hauled before the officials at regular periods and asked whether we had decided to make the correct decision yet. It was like the Inquisition – we were required to confess to our sin, and as enemies of the family and the state, to make a confession and beg forgiveness. Everyone knew that the results of signing were remarkable – a death sentence would be quashed and you could even be released from prison. It was also a passport to getting a job. Public sector work was closed to anyone who did not have the correct papers and these were unobtainable if you did not denounce the communists. You had to pass through a "loyalty board" that viewed any link to the Party or to our resistance fighters as "treasonous insurrection against the integrity of the country".

The guards tried to get us to sign by promising extra milk for our children. The interrogators veered between brutal threats ("Sign the bloody paper or you'll never leave here alive, you Bulgarian bitch") and wheedling promises ("Sign and become Greek. We'll help you and your son. You'll start a new life"). But for us, signing was the worst possible betrayal, not only of what we had fought for, but of our comrades and of ourselves. Those who signed were expelled from the Party and carried the stigma for life. I knew that. The choice was between Scylla and Charybdis, only we do not all have the luck of Odysseus. The monsters always get you in the end. My time to choose came three years after I had been imprisoned, when the Civil War ended. I have never tried to excuse myself for what I did. I know that each person must take responsibility for his actions and accept the consequences. How do you choose between your honour and your child?

By 1949, the last remaining *andártes* who had not been captured or killed in battle, escaped over the border to Albania. They made their way to Poland, Romania or wherever they could find a welcoming home. The prisons were fuller than ever and the island camps on Makronisos and Youra were used to torture and "reform" anyone who had dared to dream of a better and fairer country. Many died because they didn't "sign the bloody paper". Their deaths hang from me like weights. We knew that our dream was over. But even the more pessimistic didn't imagine two decades of right-wing oppression, followed by the Colonels' seven-year dictatorship. They rolled out many of the same tricks all over again and the same old prisoners were re-arrested, tortured and exiled. After the Junta fell in 1974, the monarchy was finally voted out of existence by the Greek people – at last they'd seen some sense, my compatriots. At that point, many of my old colleagues returned home. But for me, it was too late.

It was in the depressing climate of defeat and pessimism that an announcement was made in Averoff: all children over two years of age were to be taken away. Some went to prisoners' families, some were fostered, but most went to Queen Frederika's Children's Villages. A *Paidopoli* was worse than prison because they pretended to be something else. In effect, they were centres for brain-washing young minds – "political education," it was called. The children were taught that their mother was the Queen and their father King Paul. They sang songs thanking their new mother for saving them from the terrorists and bandits who had betrayed their country. Frederika was born in Germany – a keen member of the Nazi organisation, the League of German Girls, when she was growing up. Her brothers fought in the Wehrmacht. Now, married into the Greek royal family, she was gathering up our Greek children and turning them against their own parents.

I did not have long to decide. It was during this agonising time that my mother came to visit. She looked withered and exhausted, though her will power was undiminished and she lived on for many years. She said, "Do the right thing, Antigone. Save yourself and your child. I will take your son so he is not brought up an orphan. Sign the declaration. They will let you go and you will leave the country." She spoke as though she had learned the words by heart. Her eyes were dull. I watched her through the bars. Agreements had been made, arrangements put in place. I could be free, but humiliated. I could give my son a family, but I must leave him behind. She said, "Your son will live with me. I am his grandmother. I will care for him. You won't have another chance. Give your child some hope." She could never have understood the extent to which this choice tore me apart.

It was only when nurses in white aprons and stiff head-dresses came to take the children that I made my decision. Nikitas was a sturdy boy of three-and-a-half, full of curiosity.

along with the arrangement about where I would "escape". I didn't even tell Dora the truth, though as a mother, she might have understood my dilemma. Spiros knew as well as I that if my comrades had found out about my betrayal of the Party, I would not have been helped out of Greece or given a job on the radio in Moscow. Who knows what would have become of me. Some say my name means "unbending" – *anti* (against) and *gony* (bend or corner) – and flexibility has never been my strength. But a mother can go against her nature for her child.

I tried to empty my mind when Nikitas was taken away. I didn't want to disgrace myself by crying out or collapsing. Our three years locked up together now appeared as a bizarre Eden from which we were now being cast out. I didn't try to explain to him. I just said, "You are going to see your grand-mother." I picked him up and kissed him goodbye without too much fuss, so it seemed as though he was going for the afternoon. And I never saw him again. I had been a curse on my family, as Alexandra said. I had brought them grief, I had been to blame for my brother's death, and now I was forsaking my son.

My departure from Greece is clouded in my mind. It was almost too much to remember. The "escape" went smoothly and I managed to join the last survivors of our Democratic Army without anyone suspecting me as a traitor. We left the country through Albania – a sorry collection of worn out souls. From there we departed by ship, lying sick and defeated in the hold as we passed through the Dardanelles and across the Black Sea. From the Crimea, our journey to Tashkent continued by train. The only things of value I had with me were a lock of hair from my son, a few photographs and the grey button from my brother's jacket, sewn onto my shirt for safe-keeping.

Later, I learned that Alexandra and Spiros had formally adopted my son. In my anguish I sent my sister a "black letter", burnt with a match round the edges and smudged with ash:

> *I, the undersigned Antigone Perifanis, father Petros, mother Maria, born in Athens in the year 1924, declare that I have left my Fatherland and the family who have deceived me and acted as my enemies. I never want to see them again.*

23
The ugly city burns beautifully

MAUD

Johnny rang a few days after my return to Athens.

"I have decided to come. It is probably the foolishness of an old man, but it will be my last journey. Euripides was right to say, 'The life so short, the craft so long to learn.' Perhaps it's not too late to see my old friends…"

"I hope you will stay with us," I said, but he declined.

"I have already booked a room at the Grande Bretagne. For old times' sake. I hear that Athens is somewhat different to the place I knew." He would stay for a week, he said, arriving two days before Nikitas' memorial.

That night was a Saturday and Tig came home very late, again ignoring my attempts to set a reasonable "curfew" ("none of my friends have to be back by midnight"). I rang her mobile several times, leaving messages that got higher in pitch each time: "Tig darling, where are you? Call me." "Tig, it's late. You must come

315

home now." "Why aren't you answering your phone?" She eventually countered with a text: "Home soon. Don't worry." But I did worry. I worried about her going to Exarchia with Orestes and his friends, and about what went on there. The area has an arty, alternative ambience and is brimming with student cafés and myriad small publishing houses. However, it is also the playground for anarchists, junkies and people who think fun is setting fire to rubbish bins and throwing Molotov cocktails at the police. Most nights a bizarre game of cat and mouse is played out between the police and young people in the narrow streets. It wasn't what I had envisaged for my daughter when she was younger.

It was after 2am when I finally heard the click of the door and then whispering. I got out of bed, ready to scold, but when I saw Tig and Orestes I stopped. Tig had evidently been crying – her eyes were swollen and there were streaks of black eyeliner down her face.

"What happened?"

Orestes spoke first. "They killed a boy. The fucking police, they shot him. It happened around the corner from the bar where we were." He slapped his hand against the door in frustration.

"He was a school kid, about my age." Tig was angry as well as upset. "The pigs murdered him. People saw them pass the boy and his friends in their car. They parked and went back on foot. One of the police fired at the boy and then they left. They left him to bleed to death while his friends tried to get help." Her voice was hoarse. "What kind of a country allows the state to murder children?"

"You can imagine what happened when the news got out." Orestes' eyes sparked with fury. "We all gathered at Tzavella

Street where it happened. There was blood on the ground. People sent text messages to their friends, so hundreds, maybe thousands, arrived. It was like a war against the police. Not just the usual thing, but an army of young people fighting, setting things on fire. It was chaos. Tomorrow there's going to be a protest march. The police need to be punished."

The next morning the pair of them set off for the march. They returned some hours later, coughing from the tear gas fired by riot police, but enthused by what was happening. Soon, the whole country would be ablaze in reaction to the murder, they said. The police had to realise they couldn't just murder a schoolboy; they hadn't even apologised. Tig went up to Orestes' terrace to help him make a banner with a quote from Bakunin: *The passion for destruction is a creative passion.*

In the evening, news reports said that Greek youth had taken to the streets in almost every major city. The kids were angry and grief-stricken. They were saying they had had enough. Enough of the endless pressure of school lessons learned by rote and regurgitated for exams, the expensive cramming classes every weekday evening, the chaotic universities, the prospect of unemployment or badly paid jobs. The complaints went on and on. In the meantime, young men, as anonymous as soldiers in their uniform of jeans and hoods, were smashing shop windows, throwing home-made petrol bombs and over-turning cars. Immigrants joined in for the hell of it. The centre of Athens became a war zone and the police and politicians seemed to have gone into hiding. Even the Prime Minister had disappeared. From the terrace, I saw plumes of smoke rising across the city.

The next day was a Monday and the whole country was

in shock. School was out of the question and a large protest gathering was planned, which I agreed to attend with Tig. I didn't approve of children being shot either. We walked to Constitution Square past the Zappeion and through the National Garden, where some emerald-coloured parakeets with scarlet beaks stared down at us from the branches of the trees – incongruous escapees, who had made themselves at home. I recalled Antigone's awful experiences in this place, when she had searched in the dark to identify her brother's body in the ad hoc morgue. It was hard to picture those horrors in a park that was once more orderly and pleasant and along whose well-kept paths animated young people were making their way to the centre.

An enormous crowd of protestors had gathered in Syntagma, most of whom were teenagers and students. Whole classes of thirteen and fourteen-year-olds had come along, some with their teachers, others with parents. Rows of armed riot police stood in the paved area in Amalia Street and in front of the rosy sandstone Parliament building. They were like ancient warriors on a carving, though, instead of elegant bronze helmets and shields, they had white crash helmets and Plexiglas shields, and their faces were hidden by gas masks.

"Cops, pigs, murderers!" The crowds chanted, fuelled by rage. They held banners and large photographs of the dead boy. Fifteen-year-old Alexandros Grigoropoulos was no drop-out or drug addict, but a middle-class kid from the northern suburbs. He had gone for a Saturday night outing with friends and possibly shouted at a passing police car. He had now been elevated from anonymous schoolboy to Alexis, teenage martyr, a curly-haired portrait of innocence destroyed. Behind me, I heard a teenage boy giving an interview to one of the many journalists who were reporting and filming the scene.

"It's not just Alexis' death. The whole system needs changing." He was shouting, his voice breaking.

To my right, a group of school kids were shouting at the lines of police.

"One, two, three, *Na!*" They were making the *moúntza* sign, thrusting their splayed hands in the gesture most likely to offend. Some long-haired girls walked up to the faceless figures and unsmilingly handed them red roses and carnations. The flowers were not taken and fell in front of the sinister, automaton-like figures, whose bodies were tensed, ready to attack like pit-bulls straining on their chains. Other, more daring teenagers sprayed cans of red paint at the lines of the enemy, leaving blood-like patches on the khaki uniforms and shields. As the crowd pushed closer, the police sprayed jets of tear gas at the protestors, thrusting their knees and wielding their truncheons. Tig and I were standing some way back, but I quickly felt my eyes sting and a bitter taste fill my throat. Coughing and trying to wipe away the tears, we pulled our clothes over our noses and edged backwards, trying to distance ourselves. It was clear that things could quickly turn dangerous; there were people on both sides who would welcome some violent action.

"Cops, pigs, murderers! Cops, pigs, murderers!" The crowd's shouting got louder. Some boys pulled a kiosk's refrigerator onto the road, prised the back off and started throwing the cans and plastic bottles of fizzy drinks at the police. They were joined by a sandy-coloured dog that barked at the lines of uniformed men. Later, we noticed his yellow, leonine face appearing on television and in newspaper reports, always on the side of the protestors, rushing fearlessly into clouds of tear gas, his tail flying as he leaped out of the way of baton charges. "Riot Dog" had no owner – he was one of Athens' many street dogs – but he became a celebrity, soon getting his own Facebook page.

As the situation worsened, I told Tig we must leave. Others obviously had the same idea and people were pushing behind us. We were now choking from the acrid tear gas and our eyes streamed. A great wave of bodies carried us along, down the marble steps to the centre of the square. It was clear that if anyone fell, they would be trampled. A man carrying a boy who been overcome by the gas tried unsuccessfully to shove past us, shouting in terror, "Please, space, please."

* * *

The next day, Tig announced she wasn't going to school ("nobody is") and I left her to sleep while I went out on some errands. The centre of Athens was quiet and it turned out there was a general strike in support of the young people's protests. Everything was closed. Shops had been smashed up, buildings burnt and there was hardly a bank in the centre of town that had not had its windows shattered and ATMs destroyed. The huge artificial Christmas tree in the centre of Syntagma Square had been set alight like a pagan sacrifice and was now a blackened metal frame. The place stank of ash and lingering tear gas and there was graffiti sprayed on walls that were normally pristine. *The ugly city burns beautifully*. And someone had written: *My cunt is hotter than your Molotov*. I wondered whether that was the modern version of *Make love not war*.

On the way home, I walked past our local police station.

A group of teenagers was shouting at the officers who had barricaded themselves inside. Their orders were to do nothing: the politicians could not afford another dead child. The kids looked like the sort that hang around our local *frontistíria* cramming classes – well dressed and attractive, but now they were screaming with passionate loathing. I watched as they rocked a patrol car until it turned over onto its roof like an upturned beetle. There was a triumphant roar. It was as if the pent-up frustrations of their generation were coming out all at once and they relished the destruction they were wreaking.

When I got home, I found a note from Tig saying she had gone out and would be back at six. At seven I began to call her, but she didn't answer. At eight I started feeling worried and called Orestes.

"I'm out, but I'll come back," he said, though he had no idea of Tig's whereabouts. He arrived at nine, by which time I was feeling helpless, with no way of locating Tig in the burnt, apparently lawless city. I heard the motorbike in the back alley, the gate opening and Orestes' footsteps pounding up the spiral staircase.

"I have an idea where she might be," he said. "Shall I take you to Exarchia on the bike? I don't know how else you'll manage – you won't find a taxi to go there." He smiled when I asked about a crash helmet (there was a law but like so many, it was not enforced).

"You can have mine. Don't worry, Mondy. The police are all in hiding."

The evening air was chill and damp. I clung to Orestes as strands of his hair whipped my face. He didn't go as fast as I feared, driving steadily past the stadium, along a surprisingly empty King Constantine Avenue, and into Kolonaki. Streets that were normally filled with smart Athenians having drinks or going out to dinner were eerily quiet. We passed several burning cars and overturned wheelie-bins, and there was a crunch of shattered glass under the motorbike's wheels. Orestes slowed as we went down Solon Street, hemmed in by the buildings on either side, with only a thin strip of night sky above. A gang of young men in balaclavas emerged from a wrecked mobile phone shop, laden with looted boxes. They ran down the pavement, shouting and behind them came an old woman in a headscarf, carrying her own booty. She glanced around guiltily, before scuttling away in the opposite direction.

We soon arrived in Exarchia, and the streets were darker than elsewhere. Orestes parked the bike and we walked around the corner into Tzavella Street, where a large crowd of young people had gathered. There were candles everywhere and piles of flowers interspersed with mementoes: T-shirts, cigarettes, cans of Coke and personal notes addressed to the dead boy. The walls of the buildings were covered with posters and cards, and banners hung from balconies: "Let beauty bloom from your blood"; "We won't forget." Somebody had already got a quasi-official blue street sign made and had stuck in on the wall in place of the former one:

Alexandros Grigoropoulos Street, 15 years old, murdered 06/12/2008 by the police.

I walked around, peering at any girl who looked vaguely like Tig, but it was hard to see. There were groups sitting huddled together, talking quietly, like visitors at a shrine and the place smelled of petrol, hot wax and cigarette smoke. Across the road, I heard raised male voices and saw Orestes talking to a group of youths.

"Mod! Come here." He beckoned with the curious Greek gesture that flops the hand forward.

"Tig got hurt. She's gone to hospital." Orestes introduced one of the men as his fellow student, Yangos. "He can tell you more."

"Pleased to meet you." Yangos shook my hand, but I wasn't in the mood for social niceties.

"What happened to my daughter? Where is she?"

"There was some action earlier, down towards the Polytechnic. The police were chasing a group of us and Tig got knocked over. I think that was when she cut her arm. She might have hit her head. But she was OK."

"Why didn't anyone call me?"

"I think she lost her mobile. Our friend, Lena, decided to take her over to Evangelismos Hospital, to get her checked out." I felt nauseous from worry.

"Can we leave right now? Can you take me there?" I tried not to make the panic obvious in my voice but could tell from Orestes' eyes that I was not succeeding. He nodded and we hurried back to the bike. I gripped his leather jacket, digging my nails in hard as we sped straight up the slopes of Lycabettus, then around its pine-filled peripheral road. "Please, God, please," I found myself whispering, though I don't pray or believe in God. It didn't take long to reach the hospital and Orestes parked brazenly on the pavement outside the main entrance.

We found Tig lying on a trolley in A and E, looking tiny and frail, a drip inserted in her hand. A girl in a hippy skirt and floppy hair was standing alongside her – presumably Lena.

"Mum, I'm sorry. I didn't want to worry you and my phone got lost. They said my arm's broken. It really hurts."

I kissed Tig gently and stroked her cheek. "What about your head? What happened?"

"I slipped when the police were chasing us and hit a car. My head was bleeding. There's a big bump on the back." She was trying to be brave, just as she used to when she fell over as a young child and fought her tears. I wondered if I would be able to remain calm; after everything that had happened, this felt like too much. Leaving Tig with Orestes and Lena, who both looked unperturbed by the situation, I went in search of someone who could give me some information. Eventually, a harassed-looking doctor appeared, his skin blotchy under the neon lights.

"We're going to keep her in overnight. We need to do a cranial X-ray and she may need an operation on her arm. The ulna and the radius have multiple fractures and may need plates. You'll have to speak to the surgeon tomorrow."

While Tig was being wheeled around between different departments for X-rays and scans, Orestes sat with me and we talked. He was probably trying to distract me when he asked me how I was getting on with my trawl through Nikitas' office and whether I had uncovered anything interesting about his research. My thoughts went to Danae, and as if wanting to add to my misery, I couldn't resist asking Orestes his opinion.

"Do you think *Babas* was involved with her?"

He laughed. "No. Definitely not!"

"Why are you so sure?" I became even more suspicious. Perhaps Orestes was covering for his father.

"First, because I met her at almost the same time he did, a couple of years ago, and I tried to ask her out. She made it clear she wasn't interested in either of us, and she said she hated older men coming on to her. It was always happening at the newspaper and it had really put her off. Anyway, she was knocked up, and about to get married to another wanker journalist. And after that she was obsessed with the baby – *Babas* told me she was really annoying because she was always late with her work and used the kid as an excuse. He definitely wasn't involved with her."

"She's married and has a child?" I almost smiled. I couldn't believe how much I had misunderstood the woman on the basis of a lipstick she must have just forgotten at Nikitas' office. It was another reminder of how hard it is to arrive at "the truth". So much gets lost, hidden and misinterpreted along the way.

"One less thing to torture yourself with, eh, Mondy?" Orestes must have sensed my train of thought and I felt stupid for having been so suspicious. He laughed again and put his arm around me. "We seem to be making a bad habit of visiting hospitals together. This had better stop."

I don't know what time it was when a technician showed me the X-rays of Tig's skull and explained it was not fractured as they had feared. Orestes kissed me goodnight and left, while a junior doctor put a couple of sutures on the cut, having shaved a portion of the hair. Afterwards, an overly zealous nurse wound bandages all over her head and her right arm. It was the darkest moment before dawn creeps in when Tig was wheeled into a ward. I pulled the flowery curtains round her bed and slumped into an armchair. Tig went straight to sleep and gradually my knees stopped trembling. I watched the drip steadily releasing clear liquid into the plastic tube in Tig's vein and wept from relief and exhaustion. All around were the unfamiliar sounds of a hospital at night: patients coughing, nurses bringing medication on rattling trolleys and the rubbery squeaks of swing doors. Lorries puffed like dragons as they arrived to unload medical supplies in the street below. The view from the window showed the grounds of the British School – the first place I had stayed in Athens as a student.

As it got light, I went in search of a bathroom and passed a room that had been transformed into a shrine. Inside, a regulation metal-framed bed was surrounded by icons, oil lamps, flowers and the photograph of a saint – an old fellow with a white beard and a benevolent expression, who had apparently worked miraculous cures when he was prayed to. Outside the door was a large icon strung with dozens of votive offerings. Each silver rectangle was stamped with the relief image of a torso, a limb, a baby, a heart – whatever fitted the prayer of the supplicant – and was attached to the icon by a ribbon. They looked endearingly innocent. How could any god resist such pretty, shiny entreaties? I entered the room and stood still and exhausted, ready to light any number of candles if that would help.

❋　❋　❋

The surgeon, Mr Sadellakis, was a middle-aged Cretan with sleek black hair and eyes that looked as though they winked their way through life's conspiracies. She required surgery, he confirmed. A plate would be inserted into Tig's arm or it wouldn't mend properly. He was reassuring about the injuries and had a gallant air. By the end of the visit I adored the man and had a strong desire to hug him, but, instead, I shook his hand and thanked him.

"Your daughter will soon be back at school and her arm will be even stronger than before." Addressing Tig, he said:

"And *Despinis* Antigone, once we've operated, you'll make the airport security bleep whenever you pass through." Tig grimaced, and then smiled.

"You'll let me know what the expenses will be," I said, knowing about the unofficial "little envelope" required in state hospitals. Two thousand euros would cover everything, including the anaesthetist, he explained genially, putting his hand on my shoulder. He would ensure that the operation was given top priority. It should be possible to go ahead today. He opened his diary and mumbled, "Let's see, Wednesday, December 10th..." As he said the date, I remembered with horror that Johnny was due to arrive that afternoon. I had promised to collect him at the airport.

As soon as the surgeon left, I rang Orestes in the hope that he could go in my place but his mobile was switched off. My next attempt was Antigone; she might be old, but she could take a taxi to the airport. However, Dora's phone didn't answer and I left a message explaining the problem without being too alarmist about Tig. After half an hour I had heard nothing, so I rang Alexandra.

"My poor little Mondy," she cooed soothingly. That made me cry and I hid the tears from Tig by looking at the people playing tennis in the British School.

"Of course I'll go to meet our old friend," said Alexandra. "It will be my pleasure. And on the way I'll come to see Tig. Don't worry, everything will be all right. What can I bring? Food? Clothes for you?"

I was unable to answer.

"Don't cry, Mondouly. Our little Antigone is going to be fine." It was the first time Aunt Alexandra had used my daughter's name.

"Can you bring a votive offering so I can say a prayer for Tig's arm?" There was a pause as Alexandra wondered whether I was joking – I wasn't sure myself. I turned in time to catch Tig's eye as she furrowed her brow in puzzlement.

"There's a saint's room here," I explained. "A nurse told me the icon really works."

"I'll see what I can do," she replied dubiously. She soon turned up however, en route to the airport, with a package of Chryssa's little cheese pies, some grapes, and miraculously, a gleaming tin oblong stamped with the imprint of an arm.

No sooner had I got off the phone with Alexandra than two policemen appeared in Tig's ward.

"*Kyria* Perifanis?" asked the taller, gum-chewing one. He had acne-scarred cheeks and arms that he held away from his torso like someone emulating a body-builder. "We need to take a statement from your daughter. We have reason to believe that she was involved with an attack on a police bus yesterday." Tig said nothing, eyeing them in disgust.

"My daughter is injured and about to have an operation. She is a child."

"She may be a child, but she is old enough to throw Molotov cocktails at the police. Someone could have been killed. We have reason to believe that she was with Orestes Perifanis, who has been arrested this morning. If your daughter can't speak at the moment, maybe you could answer a few questions about him." I was so shocked I could barely take in what he was saying. I noticed his pistol – stuffed in a leather holster and wedged against the beginnings of a paunch.

"Arrested?" I said. "What happened?"

They wouldn't give much away and insisted that I confirm Orestes' age, address and university department. I refused to name any of his friends and they left, sullenly wishing Tig "Get well soon."

Before I had time to ask Tig for her version of events, a nurse came with some pills for her (sniffing scandal, I sensed) and Yiorgia, Orestes' mother rang.

"They've detained him in the central station on Alexandra Avenue." She used her professional tone, though when I told her about the police visit, she sounded more like a frantic mother.

"Oh, my God! I hope you didn't say anything. You must always say you need a lawyer present – use my name. They're saying he's an anarchist leader, the idiots, and that his friends are part of a terrorist cell. The only evidence they have against Orestes is a film of him organising kids to sell cobblestones at 3 euros each for people to throw at the police! Can you believe it?" From the window I could see the two policemen leaning against their patrol car in the sunshine, smoking and drinking coffee from paper cups. On the wall of the British School behind them, someone had sprayed red graffiti: "A bullet shot our democracy."

24
Anthropos

ANTIGONE

The distant parts of my life are coming ever closer, so that I now remember more about my father and brother than I do about Igor and our decades together in Moscow. My mother's kitchen at Paradise Street and the smells of Aspasia's cooking are clearer to me than all the Russian tastes that dominated my adult life. When I heard Mod's message asking me to meet Johnny at the airport I was surprised, but it made sense to go and see the man I had once loved (I must forget about the hate). He has been in my mind so much recently. Circles are closing. Now, after all these years, I realise that Johnny is just another human like me, reaching the end of his road. *"Anthropos eínai"* [he's human], as they say. What do I expect? Perfection? An angel? Of course we make mistakes, have regrets, let people down, take the wrong road. That is our humanity. It is in our nature to be flawed. People who believe they can be something more end up despots or disappointed. Or plunge to their fate like

Icarus. Worst of all, they become ridiculous.

The taxi to the airport went too fast, and I arrived dizzy and disoriented, just before the first people from the London flight emerged. It occurred to me that I might not recognise Johnny. The image I had was from over sixty years ago – a blondish, freckled young man. But it would have been ridiculous to make a sign like the drivers: "Mr Fell." I stepped back from the throng so I would have time to take a good look before I approached him, but when he appeared through the sliding doors I knew him immediately. Naturally he was old. But he still walked leaning forward, as though he was too tall, though he now had a stick. As I made to go over towards him, I noticed an elderly woman approaching him, holding out her hands in a gesture of welcome. I stopped in shock, squinting over, trying to get a better look. Johnny kissed the woman on both cheeks and she placed her hand on his jacket sleeve. My feet were rooted to the airport floor, my heart hammering and my ears ringing.

As they moved past me, my mother's diamond roses from Constantinople sparkled at Alexandra's ears. She was dressed in her Sunday best and her perfume was so strong it almost gave me a headache

"What a lovely surprise." Johnny's voice was just the same – those elongated vowels we used to mimic as children. "And still so elegant after all this time." He was always chivalrous. I looked at the ground, not wanting to meet his eyes or to confront Alexandra. What would I say? "I'm here too?" Alexandra had not seen me since the last time Johnny was in Greece as part of an occupying force – she would not imagine that the unremarkable old woman within spitting distance was her sister. I looked down in angry bewilderment and noticed that Johnny's trousers were thin at the knees but that his shoes shone.

"After the war I took over my father's business, so clothes have been my business." Alexandra put on her finest English accent. I remembered it from our childhood lessons; it had always annoyed me.

"I've loved clothes since I was young. But, you know, I'm a believer in Plato's theory that simplicity is the foundation stone of style and grace." I felt sick. Why had Mod meddled in our lives and brought Johnny back to Greece?

As they went towards the exit, I plodded after them, wondering what to do. They made their way to the taxi queue and I lurked behind, watching them talking and laughing. My sister was flirting like a girl.

"You shouldn't be staying in a hotel. At least come back to Paradise Street first. Come and see your old home in Mets. It's hardly changed."

I joined the line a few places behind them and, in the muddle of different people hiring taxis, I got into the one after my sister and Johnny.

"Please follow the taxi in front," I said, and the young driver laughed.

"Spying are we?" he said. "I don't want to get into trouble with the police." He laughed some more. "Do you know where we're going, Granny?" I could hardly speak by then. I was sweating and felt weak.

The taxis took ages to get back into Athens as many roads were closed.

"You never know what might hit you," said the driver.

"They're still smashing things up and burning them. Young people have gone crazy and you can see they're enjoying it." We ended up in Paradise Street – Alexandra had evidently worked her ways on Johnny. I asked the driver to park some way behind them and peered out of the window. I watched as they emerged from the car. Johnny took a case from the boot and followed Alexandra up the steps to the house. *My* house – taken by my sister. *My* friend – usurped by her, too. All through my life, she had taken what was mine. She even took my son. That was hard to digest, as they say. It makes your stomach hurt.

I paid the young taxi driver, who continued joking:

"Don't get yourself into trouble now, Granny. This game isn't suitable for a lady of your age." I edged along the pavement, avoiding the low branches, until I was outside number 17. The door was still green. They had gone inside so I was left quite alone. Almost by instinct, I sat on the second step – it had been my favourite as a child. I let my fingers rest on the faint ridges in the stone that I remembered from when I used to wait for the ice man. Once, Markos had found a tortoise on Ardittos hill, under the pine trees, and carried it home. We had put it on the highest step and watched it work its way down to the pavement with surprising ease, though its shell had clunked and it had left a green slick of excrement in its wake. I sat there, thinking about these distant things and longing for my brother. He would have known what to do. A cat slunk past on the other side of the road, looking suspiciously like Misha, and yowled before continuing on its way.

My body was hurting all over and the giddiness was getting worse, so I lay my head down on the step. The fantasies of revenge I had nurtured for my sister when we were younger flooded back. I wanted to hurt her, to make her suffer for everything I had been through. After some time in that position, I heard a voice.

"*Kyria*, are you unwell?" I opened my eyes and took in the black sails of a priest's robe. It seemed like a dream, but then the door opened and I heard a cry. I recognised Chryssa. She sat down next to me, saying my name and asking me questions. Then I heard my sister.

"Antigone?" She sounded horrified. I looked up and our eyes locked in instant recognition, though it had been so many decades since we had last met. Our mutual loathing acted on me like a dose of smelling salts.

"We must phone for an ambulance. She needs a doctor." Alexandra was trying to take charge of the situation before it got out of hand. I suspected she didn't want Johnny to see what was going on.

"No, I'm fine," I said, probably not very convincingly. Raising my head slightly, I saw Alexandra, Chryssa, Johnny and the priest staring down at me.

"I would like to go upstairs to my bedroom, please. Chryssa, will you help me?" I tried to sound dignified, imagining that things would still be as they were and that I would be in the room that looked out at the pines and cypresses of Ardittos.

"But you must come into my house on the ground floor." Alexandra spoke as though this was an entirely normal event, presumably for Johnny's benefit.

"Antigone, it's really you," said Johnny, as though I might be someone else. "Look at us – we're old!" That sounded so funny that, instead of weeping, I began to laugh. And that was how Mod found us when she arrived back from the hospital. I must have looked like a mad woman.

"Shit." Mod sounded exhausted and looked awful. Her hair was uncombed, her clothes crumpled. "What's going on?"

"Don't worry," I said. "It's a sort of family gathering. I was just coming in. May I come with you?"

Mod smiled faintly. "All right. I'm only here to have a shower and change my clothes. Then I must rush back to the hospital. They're operating on Tig's arm. I want to be there when she wakes up." She turned to greet Johnny.

"I'm so sorry I couldn't be there to meet you at the airport. I hope everything went smoothly." The English people shook hands on our doorstep, making polite comments as though they were at a tea party rather than in the middle of a family drama.

"Such a good girl, our *Mondouly*," said my sister patronisingly, addressing Johnny. "She has almost become a Greek, you know. Better than a Greek. She speaks the language so well. And she's such a good mother." Alexandra glanced at me.

The priest hurried off, saying he would call at a more convenient time and Chryssa and Mod helped me up the stairs, step by step. Alexandra disappeared, but Johnny followed, lingering in the doorway as I was put on a bed. Chryssa fetched me a glass of cool water and gradually I felt my strength returning.

"Goodbye, my dear." It was Johnny. He placed his hand on my forehead. "I'll leave you in peace and come to see you tomorrow."

❋ ❋ ❋

I slept the night alone in Mod's apartment. In my home. Before she left for the hospital, she gave me a nightdress and toothbrush.

"Make yourself at home," she said and smiled at the irony. She put me in the spare room, which contained my parents' old bed. It was white cast-iron with brass decoration and creaked every time I moved. Chryssa cared for me, bringing me a plate of soup and sitting on the bed while I ate. We talked for a long time, telling stories of the years and decades that had disappeared. Politics meant nothing to her, she said.

"For us, the 'little people', it doesn't make much difference who is in power. It's always the little people that suffer." She said that Alexandra had been good to her – she couldn't complain, and it wasn't her business what anyone voted. It was the politicians, not the voters, who were to blame for Greece's problems. I told her I was still trying to locate my brother's remains and that Alexandra was refusing to say what had happened.

"I know where he is," she said. "Spiros made an enquiry and they found the grave in the Protestant Cemetery. That was over twenty years ago." So at last, it was dear Chryssa who told me where my brother was. After that I felt a wonderful calmness and fell asleep like a child.

In the morning I woke with the first light and went to the kitchen to find coffee and sugar. Then my grandson, Orestes, walked in. He looked bewilderingly like Markos, in spite of his long hair and the beads and baubles that today's youth decorate themselves with. He was unshaven, with dark shadows under his eyes, but he had the gleeful expression of victory on his face that I remembered from my brother. He had just been released from the police cells. His mother had sorted everything out, he said. "As usual."

I didn't say he was lucky to have a mother like that and he continued, saying that there would be a trial.

"But I should be OK. I'll be luckier than you were... How many years were you put away for?" Orestes kissed me on both cheeks. I wanted to embrace him, but I held back. There's nothing worse than an over-emotional old woman forcing herself on the young.

Instead, I asked him to explain what was going on in Athens. Why was the city tumbling into this chaos?

"What happened to make you all so angry?"

He smiled at my question and said, "If anyone can understand, it's you. The oppression of the weak by the strong isn't only the poor by the rich or the Left by the Right. It's the young by the old."

"And so it has always been."

"Yes. But things can't go on as they are. We're being strangled by a system that we didn't choose and we don't like." He told me that children are treated "like robots" at school. Teenagers are being suffocated by the amount of parrot-style learning they must do to pass their final school exams. Families without the money were having to spend everything they had and more on private lessons.

"We're exhausted and disillusioned before we're even adults," he said. "And now we've reached breaking point. The system has to change."

I told my grandson his anger reminded me of my Uncle

Diamantis, who had been lucky to escape execution as a *Kapetánios* in ELAS. He had remained in prison until the early '60s, and as soon as the Junta came to power in 1967, he had been arrested and taken to Makronisos. And there, on that dreadful island, it began all over again. Torture and the terrible pressure to sign the declaration of repentance. Just the same as in the 1940s and '50s. He wasn't released until the Colonels fell in 1974, by which time he was broken. Within a few months of going home, he died of a heart attack at the age of sixty-five.

As we were speaking, Orestes made coffee and put *koulourákia* on a plate. He seemed less like a revolutionary and more like a good boy, who would become a sensible family man, with his house in order. We sat together companionably and, as the coffee warmed the blood in my veins, I told him my plan.

"There's nobody else I can ask for help."

I hadn't been on the back of a motorbike for decades, but Orestes let me sit side-saddle as girls used to do. The air was chilly, and I felt the warmth from his body as I put my arms around his waist. It only took a couple of minutes to reach the cemetery. A man was polishing a hearse, but otherwise there were few people around. We walked through the gates and turned right, alongside a series of offices and rooms, just as Chryssa had described. Just before a small café that was shut, we came across the ossuary. I had never noticed it in the old days – the only ossuary I knew was the tiny construction in the graveyard at Perivoli, where my father's forebears had always been deposited, some years after their burial. The place in which we found Chryssa after the massacre. This one looked more like one of the filing rooms in the Moscow broadcasting centre, with rows of metal shelving running from one end to another. Only, instead of files or tapes, there were thousands of boxes, each large enough to be filled by a dismantled human skeleton. There was a sickly smell of incense, oil lamps and rooms that have been closed too long, even though the door was open.

"Chryssa said he's right at the back." I peered at the stacks of iron containers, each marked with a number and name, and some decorated by mourners with photographs of the deceased, candles and plastic flowers. A snooty-faced military man was wreathed with artificial roses, into which someone had stuck a cigarette. Elsewhere, an ELAS comrade had fresh lilies next to his small coffer, squeezed onto the utilitarian shelf. Whatever side you fought on, you ended up as neighbours in the ossuary. We continued into the darkest part of the room. Orestes looked closely, reading names and dates, which got older and more illegible.

"Here he is!" He sounded excited. "Look! Markos Perifanis, 1925–1944." My grandson removed the box that was on top and slid ours out. It was closed with wire, but not locked. The number 3782 was scrawled on the lid.

"Shall we open it?" He sounded both reluctant and curious.

"Not here. Not like thieves," I replied. "Let's take him home first."

Nobody questioned us about what we were doing – who would steal old bones? Anyway, a grandmother in a cemetery is hardly suspicious. Orestes walked by my side, carrying the box to the motorbike, where he tied it to the rack on the back.

We were a strange threesome riding the short distance to Paradise Street, me side-saddle again, and what was left of my brother behind me.

Orestes placed the container on a table in Mod's sitting room and I watched, as he untied the twist of wire and lifted the lid. The bones were pale and smaller than what you'd expect for a grown man, but the skull was perfect – completely white and smooth. All the teeth were in place. I didn't lift it out, but placed my hand on the crown, feeling tiny, zigzag lines and a light covering of dust. Undoing the safety pin in my pocket, I took out the button that had been with me all these years. I would put it in Markos' box when it reached its final resting place.

It didn't seem strange when the doorbell went and Orestes ushered Johnny into the room. The old man stared at the young one, and I realised he was seeing Markos in my grandson, with his dark locks and deep brown eyes. Johnny managed to disentangle his gaze to come over and kiss me in a distracted manner, looking down at the mortal remains in their open box. He said, "Markos?"

"We found him today," I replied. "Now, finally, I hope, to do the right thing." Orestes was lurking by the door.

"Sorry, but I've been up all night in the cells and I need to get some sleep. I'll see you later." He spoke in Greek and Johnny tried to answer but stumbled with *"Kalón ýpno"* [sleep well] and switched back to English. He said, "Goodbye, dear boy. God bless."

Johnny and I sat on the sofa, side by side in front of the box. I appreciated that he kept quiet – the most appropriate response to the situation. It gave me time to reflect on our entwined lives and how he had meant so many things to me: teacher and first love, enemy, then someone who offered me help – the only one who did so when I was in prison. Now we were both near the end, dried up skin and bones. The next stage was beneath the earth. I was surprised when I heard a noise like a shuddering, stifled sob and saw that Johnny was crying. He said, "Stupid." Then he shook his head and looked furious with himself for his lapse. "You know, Markos has haunted me since I left Greece. I loved him. I would never have done anything to hurt him. And now... It was my fault, what happened." Johnny brought out a handkerchief and wiped his eyes and nose. His voice was steadier when he spoke again, though he looked drained.

"I was there during the attack." He looked at me for a reaction, but I merely nodded, waiting for him to continue.

"Spiros told Basher and me there were rebels in that house in Kaisariani, but nothing about Markos. I know I said I wasn't involved, but I couldn't face telling you. I hold myself responsible and you have every right to hate me, Antigone. I didn't launch the rockets, but it comes to the same thing."

"We were both responsible for what happened." I knew it was too late now to rage at poor Johnny and, after all, I was well aware that Spiros had followed me up to Kaisariani. I should have done something. My failure to report what I'd seen had been deadly. I put my hand on his – two loose-skinned, liver-spotted toads.

"I loved him," Johnny repeated quietly.

"I used to hate you," I said. "But not any more." For the first time I consciously understood what I had not been able to admit to myself all those years before – that Johnny had truly loved Markos. Although he cared for me, I was never going to be his love. I had kept myself going on a girlish fantasy that had had no foundation in reality. Every show of affection was merely friendship on his part. And in those days there was so much room for misunderstanding. Memories came back, making sense of isolated incidents: even before the war, Johnny and Markos would go off on walking expeditions, leaving Paradise Street with knapsacks for day trips to Mount Parnitha or Pendeli. I was always envious. I recalled the cave in the mountains, where we had all met during the occupation. I had seen Johnny's arm around Markos, but never interpreted it correctly. I had still hoped it was me he wanted. I remembered the comment my sister spat out at a time when Markos and I started doing secret errands for Johnny during the war. "Anyway, he's a poofter."

I didn't say anything. At the time I knew nothing about love between men, though later in Russia I had friends who were that way inclined. Now it seemed too late to question Johnny about long-lost love. It was time to bury the past before we were buried ourselves. It is what it is. I said, "We both loved Markos. And we are just 'little people', as Chryssa says."

"Thank you, Antigone." Johnny looked at me with great gentleness. "Now, please tell me what happened – why you left Greece and Nikitas. And what about all those years in Russia? Were you happy? You were married, weren't you?"

I smiled "That's a lot of questions."

"At least tell me why you came back to Greece. Alexandra said you had made an oath never to return."

"One thing I have learned is that there is never a last word, never a promise which cannot be broken or a belief that continues unaltered. If life has taught me one thing, Johnny, it is that. I came back to mourn my son and there was something else I wanted to do."

Before I could continue, the door of the apartment opened and Mod appeared. At her side was my granddaughter, her arm in a sling and her head swathed in gauze.

"Tig was allowed to leave the hospital, so we came home," Mod explained, supporting her daughter and smiling wanly. "I'll put her to bed and come back." I went over to greet the poor girl, whose face was drawn.

"*Antigonaki mou*, are you all right? *Siderénia* [get strong as iron]."

"Hello *Yiayia*." Never has the word "grandmother" sounded so good.

Johnny stared intently at my granddaughter. "This girl looks just as you did. It's like going back in time." He came over and took Tig's good hand. "I'm very pleased to meet you, Antigone."

"What's that?" asked Tig, peering at the box with Markos' remains. "Is it a head?"

25
Forty days and forty nights

MAUD

When Tig was born, it was Chryssa, childless and probably a virgin, who told me about the forty days when mother and infant must stay at home.

"I know you're a modern girl and times are different." She began diffidently, even though she was usually forthright. "But to do things properly, you should not leave the house unless you have to, and neither should the baby. At the end, you bring in a priest to do a blessing." Nikitas was having none of that, but Chryssa's talk of blood, pollution, unspecified nocturnal dangers and nameless spirits remained with me. I did not take her advice, but I understood the rationale behind the superstition. Long before the advent of baby manuals and childhood experts with all their contradictory teachings on "bonding", village women had found a way of allowing the mother and new baby to be quiet together and to rest before normal life

344

resumed. The forty days were a time of limbo, like Jesus in the wilderness or Moses on Mount Sinai. The number forty also applied to fasting during Lent and to the period between a person's death and the first important memorial service.

The evening before Nikitas' 'forty-day', Chryssa brought wheat, pomegranates and other ingredients for *kólyva,* just as she had for the memorial three days after Nikitas died.

"May God forgive him," she said as she came in, briskly wiping a rheumy eye. "He was like a son to me." She busied herself, letting practicalities take precedence over emotions. Tig was not able to help because of her arm, but sat and watched, smiling bravely. When Antigone got back from a meeting she had arranged with Johnny, she joined them and, from my study, I heard an animated conversation in the kitchen. The words were unintelligible but I could tell it was largely between grandmother and granddaughter, with a few interjections from Chryssa. When I went to see how the *kólyva* was progressing, they abruptly stopped talking.

"Beautiful," I said, taking in the mound of grains and seeds now covered in icing sugar like a shallow, snow-covered volcano.

"And tasty," said Chryssa, friendly but obviously relieved to have found a topic to distract me. "The wheat is good quality and the pomegranates are from a friend's garden. Only the best for our Nikitas." Antigone looked at the floor and Tig glanced at me to see how I reacted.

"I think I'll go and lie down," she said. "My arm's sore. Mum, can I take a Depon?" I went to get her the painkiller and overheard her taking her leave ("Goodnight Chryssa, goodnight *Yiayia*"). It sounded very cosy. I sat on Tig's bed and took in the mix of childhood relics – the teddies and picture books – that sat incongruously with the patchwork of posters, concert tickets, banners and assorted mementoes on the walls. One side of the room was a mural painted by Tig and her friends, depicting a girl spraying graffiti. There were slogans I assumed came from Orestes: "Lifestyle is manic depression, gift-wrapped," and "Buy until you die" (accompanied by the anarchists' A in a circle). Someone had recently added "Cops, pigs, murderers" and "Alexis, that bullet hit us all".

"So, what do you think of your grandmother? You seem to be getting on well." I heard something in my voice that I hoped wasn't jealousy.

"She's nice," Tig replied in non-committal fashion.

❋ ❋ ❋

The winter sun was dazzling. The bitter-orange trees outside the cemetery were laden with ripe fruit, some of which had fallen into the gutters and collected in heaps. The arrangement was that we would meet at the gate and walk to the grave together, locating en route one of the priests who performed memorial rites. I tried to dissuade Tig from coming; it was only the day after her discharge from hospital. But she insisted, walking gingerly alongside her newly acknowledged grandmother. Alexandra proceeded with her head held high, staying next to Johnny, while Orestes (unshaven and in jeans) took my arm on one side and Chryssa's on the other. It felt as though years had passed since we all walked the same way for the funeral, not even six weeks earlier.

Nikos the poet came rushing through the gates, hugging us

all with relief when he found he was not late.

"Meet Konstantina," he said, introducing an attractive, young woman, who looked vaguely familiar. I assumed she was one of the poetry groupies he and Nikitas often joked about, though her straightened, blonde hair and fashionable clothes marked her out from the earnest types who normally pursued the ageing poet.

"Konstantina is an admirer of Nikitas' writing and wanted to come along," Nikos said unconvincingly, as he put an arm around her. I realised she was the television reporter who had interviewed him on the day of the accident.

Danae was lurking awkwardly in the shadows and I called her over. I had rung her the previous day, wanting to make up for my unwarranted suspicions, and invited her to the memorial. I kissed her and she scrubbed at her eyes with one hand.

"Sorry," she tried to smile through watering eyes. "I've been up half the night with my daughter. I'm just tired."

Orestes waved at her casually. "Hi."

"Hi." She gave a small wave back. It was strange how harmless she looked.

The two ex-wives turned up, Kiki draped in a purple scarf and pendants and Yiorgia in a lawyer's suit and heels. They both kissed me politely, but in a manner that said the time for sharing tears and falling into each other's arms was over. In any case, all anyone could talk about was the crisis.

"You can't even walk down University Avenue," Kiki said, throwing out her strong potter's hands in exasperation. "Everywhere is shuttered up and nobody dares go to the centre. You see gangs of 'hooded ones' rampaging along like packs of dogs. They've been attacking policemen. It's unbelievable."

"They deserve it." Orestes never agreed with the opinions of his father's first wife. "The pigs have been beating us up without anyone stopping them for so long, they thought they could start shooting kids in cold blood. The police need to be taught a lesson. This is a war. We're fighting the state. It's more than hooliganism."

Yiorgia joined the debate, taking her son's side.

"I don't know what's going on in this country, when our children are chased by gun-toting policemen in gas masks. There's blood on the pavements in front of the Parliament building. It's like 1944 all over again. It certainly doesn't look like the democracy we fought for." She looked around for support.

"They're already calling it the *Dekemvriana* of 2008," said Kiki, looking pleased with herself. "You know what I saw painted on a wall in the square, near the burnt Christmas tree? *Merry crisis and a happy new fear.* At least they have humour." No one laughed. I saw Antigone listening and watching us, taking in the three wives of the son she didn't know. Her expression was impossible to interpret, her eyes lowered and her lips set. Johnny was standing by her, leaning on a walking stick and far away in his thoughts. He had obviously given up trying to follow the conversation in Greek.

During the short service in the chapel the two sisters stood grimly apart, their faces rigid as though each were a Medusa that had petrified the other. Nothing was given away. The past itself seemed to be set in stone. We walked slowly to the grave. The pathways had become familiar in recent weeks: the prominent corner of the archbishops', the sleeping maiden, and the family tombs with mops and buckets in attendance. Crossing the cemetery's green heart, we made our way up the slope to the "artists' area" and the gravestone made by a local stonemason.

NIKITAS PERIFANIS
1946–2008

You could either sum up a person like that or you could investigate, as I had been doing, not knowing whether you'd ever understand them. A priest was found and he performed the short ritual for my husband, jangling his brass censer enthusiastically, and chanting in a melodious voice. I slipped a 50 euro note into his hand at the end and he nodded his thanks, tucking it into his capacious robes.

The original plan for the reception had been to go to Zonar's in University Avenue. It would have brought back memories for the old people, and Nikitas had favoured the place when it was a more subtle, lugubrious version of its current incarnation. However, the riots in the centre meant it was virtually a no-go area and we decided instead on Café 13, the slightly seedy establishment on Anapafseos Street, where I had first met Antigone. Most of the friends and relations didn't stay long after downing coffee and brandy; they had work and appointments. Within half an hour I was alone with the two old Gorgon sisters, Johnny, Chryssa, Tig and Orestes. Alexandra wasn't exactly flirting with Johnny, but was being as charming as I had ever seen her. When she announced that she had a delicious fish soup and that we should all come home for lunch, it was clearly some kind of challenge to Antigone.

"The past should stay in the past," Alexandra pronounced. "We must all get on with our lives." Her tone was breezy, but she didn't look at Antigone – rather, she silently dared her to protest. She even repeated her words in English for Johnny, who nodded in agreement, evidently not realising the degree to which the sisters were estranged. There was a surprisingly brief pause, during which Antigone caught my eye, then nodded and answered, "Of course."

We sat at the solid mahogany dining-table that Petros and Maria Perifanis had bought for their new house in Paradise Street, almost ninety years before. Alexandra was at the head and served the fragrant fish soup, while the filleted white flesh and boiled vegetables were arranged on a platter, next to a jug of *ladolémono* – whisked oil and lemon. Morena had come to help and fetched and carried from the kitchen. She was prompted by Chryssa who sat with us but had her mind on the practicalities throughout the meal that she had prepared.

"We must drink to Nikitas," said Alexandra, raising a glass of wine. We said his name in unison. Orestes downed his glass in one and poured another. Johnny pronounced Nikitas' name loudly, looking at me and giving a sympathetic smile. Antigone and Tig had mumbled and were concentrating on their drinks.

"May we remember him," said Chryssa, for the hundredth time.

"It's good that your son grew up here, in the same house as you did," said Alexandra, addressing her sister in what was obviously a prepared speech. "He may have been left by his mother, but his roots were here. He had his grandmother. You did the right thing."

"There was not much choice." Antigone spoke softly, but Alexandra did not give up.

"At least he wasn't turned into a little Russian. He stayed in his homeland. It is important for a boy to have a man around, someone who sets him an example. Spiros was like a father to Nikitas." I couldn't tell whether Alexandra was provoking Antigone or whether she believed what she was saying, but it was Orestes who had heard enough.

"I thought Spiros used to beat him. *Babas* told us that he was frightened of him as a child."

Alexandra didn't miss a beat. "Those were different times, my boy, and discipline is an important part of bringing up a child. Spiros believed you should take responsibility for your actions. Crime requires punishment. And a little slap never hurt anyone. Children today could do with more backbone."

Nobody said anything and Alexandra kept going. "Spiros always stuck to his word, which is why he was a good policeman. When he needed to find a criminal, he kept at it with method until he succeeded. That's why he rose to such a high position in the Ministry – he knew when to strike. It wasn't for nothing that his colleagues called him Wasp." Alexandra looked proud as she said that.

"Wasp?" I checked to see whether Antigone and Johnny reacted, but they didn't blink.

"Then what did Spiros do? What happened when Antigone was in prison?" I blurted it out without really thinking and everyone at the table looked at me as if the question didn't make sense. If Spiros was Wasp, what had he done that had shocked Johnny back then? And why did Nikitas have his hated uncle's nickname written on the pad on his desk?

"What do you mean, *Mondouly mou*?" Alexandra asked sweetly, tilting her head to one side.

I should have left it there but I couldn't. It seemed that everyone knew more than I did; even Tig was in league with Antigone. I wanted to know what was going on.

"Johnny, can't you tell me?" I asked in English. "What is it about Spiros? What did he do? I know that Nikitas was puzzling over the name Wasp just before he died? I think you must know. He was my husband. Please." Johnny was embarrassed by my outburst, but I didn't care.

"Maud, my dear…" He fumbled for words. "I think that Antigone should… She is the only one who can speak about this. And I imagine she will want to do so in private." He glanced at Antigone and she nodded with what I now interpret as bleak satisfaction. Tig and Orestes stared at me in bewilderment, as though they were thinking: "Now she really has gone mad."

Alexandra looked furious. "I don't know what you're all talking about, but there's no need to go on about Spiros. He did nothing wrong and you should leave him to rest in peace."

*　*　*

"There are certain things that are better left unsaid. I hoped I wouldn't have to have to re-open these wounds." Antigone and I had retreated upstairs to my sitting room, leaving the others with Alexandra. The winter sun had warmed the air and the street sounds formed an incongruously comfortable, quotidian backing to her words.

"Truth is over-rated as a virtue," she said. "People say they want honesty, but sometimes that's much crueller than a lie and far more destructive." It sounded like a last warning from the oracle: be careful what you wish for.

I nodded. "Yes, but it's too late. I need to know."

"I never told Nikitas, because I wanted my son to grow up with the idea that his father was a brave and good man, a *Kapetánios* who gave his life for his country. It would have been too harsh to tell him that he came from an act of violence. There, I've said it."

"You mean Spiros?"

Her response was a miserable nod.

"How? What happened? Does Alexandra know?"

She gave an empty smile. "Too many questions."

"Did Spiros know he was the father?"

"I don't know. But he must have had a good idea."

"Can you tell me what happened?" I looked at the shrunken old woman in front of me and tried to picture her sixty-two years before – melting brown eyes like her son's, rich dark hair, slender limbs. In photographs she was beautiful and alluring. Perhaps irresistible to Spiros.

"It was not that Spiros wanted me." Antigone was reading my thoughts. "He detested me. What he did was revenge. He disliked me for my beliefs, but what he could never forgive was my part in his humiliation – the time when he was marched out of Athens by me and my comrades. We had stripped him of his power and he had to pay me back. Rape has nothing to do with attraction or desire. It's a weapon, a part of war – an act of hatred."

"How did it happen?" I didn't think that Antigone would describe her attack, but she told me quite fluently, as though it referred to someone else.

353

"When I was first arrested in 1946, I was kept in the police cells. They beat me frequently. They took me up to the top floor and used a blindfold. I presumed that was so I wouldn't know who my tormentors were, and to disorient me. I came to know their voices as they taunted and abused me." Antigone paused, as though realising this was her last chance of not telling me. When she started up again, she spoke quietly and intensely, staring blankly towards the window.

"One day, instead of removing the mattress from the bed where they beat me, they left it in place. While they bound my limbs, I wondered if they were getting soft. As usual, I had been made to strip down to my underclothes – instructed to lie on my front. As usual, they tied me to the bed-frame. I lay there, spread-eagled. I couldn't see anything. But I could hear. Someone came into the room. I sensed a frisson run through the men. Their joking stopped. I heard the door open and close, though I could tell that several people were still in the room. Their boots made a noise. Then, without warning, some-body grabbed my hair so hard I let out a scream. Normally I could keep quiet and I felt humiliated when one of the men shouted, 'Not so brave now, eh?' The man who was holding my hair laughed. And he slapped me. He didn't speak. I never saw him. But I recognised his cologne – it had a strong smell... of nutmeg."

Antigone's voice cracked, and she cleared her throat, looking down at the floor. She rubbed her hand over her forehead, shading her eyes as though she might stop seeing the dreadful images she was conjuring. However, she soon took a breath and kept speaking, her voice dry and almost monotonous. "I was expecting to be beaten. They were shouting... 'Whore! He'll show you how real men do it.' They always called us whores and destroyers of the family... But the irony was that I had never been with a man.

"My underwear was pulled off. I heard it tear. And then I understood. It hurt. But that's not important. I knew about pain. It was the disgust that was much worse. His uniform scratched me. There was a belt-buckle digging into my back. The smell... It was like the attack of a wild beast. Noises of an animal – though no animal takes revenge like that. I saw myself as though looking down on the scene – like a dying person is supposed to do. I have no idea how long it lasted.

"Afterwards, I heard him breathing heavily. He buttoned his clothes. The others congratulated him. 'Bravo, Wasp. You gave her what she needed.' They were like hyenas circling the lion's kill. 'Wasp taught her a lesson.' Spiros didn't speak much, but I heard him mutter that they should take me back to my cell – he didn't want them to share his victim."

Antigone turned to face me, but I was unable to say anything. I was deeply shaken. I put my arm round her shoulder and waited. She looked straight at me, registering the shock on my face, and when she continued, her voice was stronger.

"It happened once more," she said. "I suppose that later, when he learned I was pregnant, he must have known he was the father. Though he didn't let on. From what I understand, he didn't treat Nikitas like a son later, when he knew him. I never told anyone. I let my family believe that I was the immoral woman, the liberated leftist with a lover in the mountains. It was better that way. Better to have a beautiful lie than the ugly truth."

355

I asked Antigone how she could have left her son with the man who raped her.

"Don't forget that it is easy to simplify with hindsight. I didn't have the choice to take him with me. If I hadn't let him go, I would have stayed in prison and he would have been sent to one of Frederika's fascist children's homes. Later, it was impossible to go back and take Nikitas once I was in the Soviet Union. I thought I had done the best thing for him." She paused. "I loved my son, but it was an awful thing to give birth to a child resulting from an abhorrent act of hatred. I wasn't the only woman to suffer that fate. There was a girl at Averoff who lost her mind. She used to hit her baby, shaking it until it screamed. Then she would hug it and kiss it and weep for her brutality. We often had to take it away from her until she calmed down. She wasn't really a bad person … "

I waited for her to continue, not speaking.

"I would never have touched Nikitas, but… " Antigone left the words unsaid. "When my mother offered to take him, it made sense. I knew that Spiros would be there, but I hoped he would be kind to the boy he had fathered."

I thought of telling her what Nikitas had said about Spiros hitting him, calling him "bastard", lying about his mother being dead.

"Nikitas grew up to be a wonderful man," I said. "He was loved, he had two marvellous children, he was successful."

Antigone faced me square-on. "There's something else you should know. "Nikitas found out."

"When? How do you know?"

"The evening before he died, he rang up Dora. She was staying with her sister, down by the sea in Varkiza. Nikitas called her and asked her straight out. He said he knew, and that his assistant had been to the Communist Party archives and found everything there – all the torturers and rapists, with their names and dates. He had worked it out."

"Danae." I groaned. She may not have had an affair with Nikitas, but she had been devastating in another way. I wondered whether she knew how lethal her information had been, whether he had confided in her.

"I don't know the researcher's name," said Antigone. "And it doesn't matter. He would have found it out anyway. You can say that for the communists – they were good at keeping records."

I nodded dismally. It was stupid, if tempting, to search for scapegoats.

"When Nikitas asked Dora to tell him the truth, she did." Antigone looked at me with concern. "She said there wasn't a choice. He said he knew. At the end of the call he said he would drive out to see her. He was upset and sounded as though he'd been drinking."

I didn't say anything. I was wondering why he hadn't told me, whether I could have said something.

"Of course, Dora feels terrible about what happened," continued Antigone. "She only learned about the accident from the television and didn't know what to do. She wanted to call you, but she didn't want to upset you even more. I hope you won't hold it against her. She's a good person."

I would like to say that after Antigone's confession, we went downstairs and confronted Alexandra. I have pictured the scene: Alexandra expressing disbelief then shock, explaining that she had known nothing of the rape, the horror at what she was learning about her late husband. I tried to persuade

Antigone that it was important we should tell her sister, even if Alexandra's crimes were those of omission. Perhaps there could be a reconciliation. I pictured the two elderly women embracing in my apartment, learning to love each other again. My thoughts came out in clichés: working through the trauma, catharsis, closure…

"I won't even discuss that," said Antigone, leaving no room for negotiation. "I told you because you asked. You needed to know. But what will anyone gain at this stage if my sister finds out?" She looked straight at me, challenging, but also with a warmth and openness I hadn't seen before, as though her confession had lightened her. "Who knows? It might kill her to discover that her life was based on lies and that Spiros was a monster. I have kept it to myself until now and I want to keep it between us."

Antigone made me promise that I would not mention the attack to anyone.

"What about Orestes and Tig?" I asked. "I think they should at least know who their grandfather was." Antigone paused, considering the delicacy of her grandchildren's position.

"I don't want the poison to drip on down the generations," she said. "It needs to end. But perhaps you could tell them that Spiros was their grandfather – if that's what you want. Without the details, at least at this stage. It's very delicate, Maud. If my sister finds out, she will turn the subject into another battle between her and me. I can't have this horror as the thing I brought back home. We won't tell Alexandra."

＊　＊　＊

That evening, I consciously thought about my best times with Nikitas. I didn't want everything to be dominated by his end, which threatened to become an obsession. My anger at him had died down, its place taken by a profound sense of loss. Now that I was not plagued by suspicions regarding Danae, I was able to return to what had been there all along – love and tenderness towards a complex man who had his flaws. The fact that he had been unable to share his dreadful discoveries, even with me, was awful, but not something I could hold against him. I realised that I would never know the extent to which he had been affected by finding out that Spiros – the person he had spent his life rejecting – was his father. I had no way of discovering what role it had played in his death, but I was now able to imagine Nikitas' final hours somewhat better than before: the horrible realisation, the drinking, the conversation with Dora, the determination to see her and find out more. It was this last fact that gave some comfort, making me more able to rule out suicide. Not only do I believe that he wouldn't have left us without a word, but I know he wanted information, he was onto a story. And in this verdict, I am backed up by the autopsy's conclusion that his car crash was an accident. This is the version I will choose, though the truth is that nobody will ever be certain.

I disagree with Antigone's favourite expression – "It is what it is." In fact, things frequently turn out to be dramatically different from how they first appear. The past inhabits us, as Nikitas said. It is not something to be put away in a box. Still, at this point, I needed to prise myself away from all the pain and history that threatened to take over my life. Instead of focusing on the horrors that had characterised my husband's early years and his death, I thought about the good parts, above all, our summer trips, which were always unplanned; "spontaneous" is a defining word in Greek and Nikitas was loyal to the principle. One year we travelled around the mountain villages in Epirus and another we went down to Mani, but our favourite was going from island to island in the Aegean, changing location as the mood took us. Because we never booked boat tickets in advance, we often ended up sleeping on deck, using beach mats and towels as bedding, with Tig cocooned between us. We would wake up in the warm glow of the sunrise, with salt and oil smuts on our faces, and Nikitas would fetch coffee from the bar (Nescafé with tinned milk, but it tasted delicious).

One summer, we ended up on a tiny island in the Dodecanese, near Lipsi. It was inhabited by a single family who owned a taverna with a few rented rooms. We were their only visitors. Nobody came to the bay where we went to swim apart from a few goats, their bells sounding as they trotted down to lick the salt from the rocks. The sea was cool despite the burning July heat and shoals of tiny silver fish darted past as we swam. Nikitas spent one afternoon diving down to collect the black urchins that clung to the rocks and he taught me how to recognise the edible females – the larger, browner "priests' wives" – which often have a small "flag" of seaweed speared on their spines. While he amassed a pile of the creatures, Tig, aged three or four, lay curled up asleep under a thin sarong in the shade of a huge, feathery-leafed salt cedar. Its branches dipped into the water and its twisted roots spread along the edge of the stony beach. In the early evening, as the sun slipped down, Nikitas looked to me like Odysseus – strong and quick-witted, making himself at home on a new island. He cut the brittle sea urchins open with a knife to reveal the bright, coral-coloured roe, which we ate straight from the spiky carapace on lumps of bread. The briny substance was like sea made solid, and we washed it down with aniseed ouzo in a tin cup. I pictured us, our bodies warm and salty, groaning with pleasure at the perfect simplicity of the feast we had conjured up.

26
Now it's different

TIG

June 20th 2010
Dear Mr Fell,

I feel really bad that I never answered your letter. And now it's been a year and a half since you were in Greece and since you wrote to me from England. I'm not used to writing letters. In the end, it was my mum who said I should write now. Mum said that now I'm sixteen, school has finished for the summer and I've got plenty of time, I should get writing. She thought you would be interested to hear our news, and that you'd have been sad to have missed the ceremony to bless Markos' bones in the village so I should tell you about that. So finally, you're getting my reply. I'm sorry it's so late.

After the forty-day memorial for *Babas*, when you went back to England, *Yiayia* Antigone and Chryssa told me they'd made a plan. They'd ordered a taxi to take us all the way up to Perivoli. I agreed to go along too – there wasn't any school as they decided to close them down from early December because of the demonstrations, and nobody was going in anyway. It's not the sort of thing I'd usually want to do, especially with my arm in a sling, but after everything that had happened I felt like getting away. We decided not to ask Mum to go. We thought it might put her in an awkward position with *Yiayia* Alexandra, who would probably be annoyed about the plan (it was only later that Orestes told me how he and our grandmother had "stolen" the bones!). I told Mum that I wanted to get to know my new *Yiayia*, especially if she was going to disappear back to Russia. Mum looked a bit worried, but agreed. She took me to the hospital for a check-up and then she kept making sure I had my phone charger and toothpaste etc etc. She even made us some sandwiches for the trip and came to see us off in her embarrassing hippy dressing gown (that she made from an old silk patchwork and is shredding at the edges).

It was very dark and cold that morning. Chryssa carried the metal box with the skeleton and put it in the boot of the taxi along with our bags. And then, just as we were getting into the car, there was this cat hanging around the street, miaowing like mad. It was so funny when *Yiayia* Antigone got excited and started calling to it. I couldn't believe it when she said, "Quick, try and catch him. It's Misha. He's my friend's cat. He came all the way from Moscow with me. We must get him." But the cat didn't want to go to her, and was hissing with his ears flat. She was going "*ksss, ksss*" (the Russian way to call a cat), and Chryssa was going "*psss,*

psss" (the Greek way) and even Mum joined in with "here kitty, kitty," in English. In the end I managed to get him by keeping quiet, moving slowly and picking him up by the scruff of the neck like a kitten. He scratched me a bit on my good arm, but after that we gave him some milk and he calmed down enough for us to put him in a cardboard box with air holes and a blanket.

It took about three hours to get to Perivoli. It rained a lot. I held Misha in the box on my lap and sat with *Yiayia* in the back and Chryssa sat in the front. The driver was a young guy and I don't think he could understand what was going on, what with the bones, the cat, the teenager etc etc. Chryssa had picked some lemons from the tree and handed us quarters to suck, so we didn't feel sick. They really worked.

When we arrived in Perivoli, it was cold but our house was warm and a fire had been lit by one of Chryssa's cousins or nieces. It was strange being there without Mum or *Babas*. The box of bones was placed on a table and Chryssa lit a *kandýli* with oil and there was a framed photo of Markos, who was really young when he died – only a bit older than me. I know he was your friend too. The next day they had organised a service for my "uncle", like a kind of coming home. We were all so surprised when Mum showed up, completely unexpectedly, with *Yiayia* Alexandra and, unbelievably, Orestes. They said they'd just come for the ceremony and would leave for Athens again right after. *Yiayia* Alexandra said, "We are family and we should be able to bury our dead together." And there was lots of hugging and kissing and it was all a bit much really, though it was a relief they weren't quarrelling any more.

Mum had told me and Orestes about Spiros being *Babas'* real father and not *Kapetan* Eagle, like they'd always thought. But I didn't really understand why she got so over-excited about the whole thing. It's so long ago now. As far as I'm concerned, it's "So what the eggs!" as Mum and I used to say. I hardly remember *Papous* Spiros, and "Eagle" died years before even Mum was born. What difference does it make when they're all dead? I don't know why Mum took it so seriously – they weren't *her* fathers. She tried to explain to me about how hard it was sometimes, when life doesn't turn out like the movies, when the baddies don't get punished and the goodies don't live happily ever after. But what did she expect? Did she think that life is fair? It didn't really make sense to me, but she made Orestes and me promise not to tell *Yiayia* Alexandra. It would be hard to learn that your husband cheated on you with your sister. Nobody wanted her to suffer after all that time. I agree about that.

After we had gone to the church with Markos' remains, we took them to the spooky shed in the cemetery with a corrugated iron roof and a window with chicken wire instead of glass. I knew it was the ossuary but I'd never seen inside. I was surprised to find that it was stuffed with boxes. There were newer, shinier ones of metal and really old, crumbling wooden ones, and they all had skeletons in them. They were all people from the village who had been buried and then dug up after some years. So many dead people.

All the bones made me understand better why Mum

says she wants to be cremated when she dies. She told me they recently passed a law allowing it in Greece, but nobody does it because the Church forbids it. Perhaps they think it's a bit lonely being burnt, compared to being part of a big collection of skeletons – like a party for the dead. Chryssa showed me where her parents and brothers' boxes were and said she was glad they were still all there, close together, where she can visit them – Christos Kallos, Lukia Kallos, Panayiotis Kallos, Theodoros Kallos. My grandmother and Chryssa hung around outside the building afterwards, talking and crying. They said that they had "seen things here that nobody should see".

"It's history now," *Yiayia* Antigone said. "It is what it is." And Chryssa said, "Yes, but we will never forget them."

A few days later, I took the train back to Athens on my own. My grandmother told me to look out for the huge, tall viaduct at Gorgopotamos when I passed over it. She explained how you had helped blow it up in the war and told me about the caves and the partisans fighting the Nazis. When the train went over, I looked right down into the gorge and imagined what it was like when you were hiding down there. Awesome.

After our expedition to Perivoli during that strange December in 2008, Chryssa decided not to go back to Athens. She'd been meaning to retire to her village for years, but hadn't wanted to leave *Yiayia* Alexandra alone. Then, once she was actually in Perivoli, she was certain it was the right time. She thought she'd stay with one of her cousins, but Mum said she'd be doing us a favour if she stayed in our house, so she did.

"I keep your house warm," Chryssa told me when I arrived this time. "If a house is cold and kept closed too long, it dies."

Yiayia Antigone decided to stay in the village with Chryssa for a while as she would be lonely back in Russia. I had hoped to go back and see her, to get to know her a bit better. It was fun to get a new grandmother all of a sudden. But then she died. One morning in February, she just didn't wake up. The doctor said it was her heart. Chryssa said she'd been "ready" because she was where she belonged and had finally taken her brother home. We all drove up from Athens (again!) and had yet *another* funeral. We were becoming experts. I can't say it was shattering like losing *Babas*, but it was sad that just when my real grandmother returned, she had to leave again. *Yiayia* Alexandra came and actually looked quite gloomy, even though they didn't get on. She quoted a poem about death only being sweet "When we lie in our fatherland." She also said, "It's my turn next," and we all told her we'd had enough of coffins and she had better keep going for a long time. Luckily, she's been fine, and I often go to lunch with her when I get back from school and sometimes do my homework in her sitting room, because it's much more peaceful and tidy than my room.

Lots of people came to Antigone's funeral at the church in the main square of Perivoli – the whole village turns up when someone dies. We walked past her coffin before they closed it and kissed her on the forehead, which was smooth but hard, like a piece of leather on a cold stone. Orestes and I stopped spending so much time together after that.

I got fed up with his theories and I didn't really like his friends who were always making plans to "kill the pigs". They treated me like a child and I'd had enough of violence and death. Orestes is right that you can't say "please" and wait for the fat politicians who run the country to see the light and do the right thing. You have to fight and make them change. But I was secretly quite glad when Thanasis and Fotis were arrested as I thought they had a bad influence on Orestes and they just hated everything. They were accused of being part of Revolutionary Cell, which has done some really bad things, including blowing up a bank (luckily it was empty) and shooting (and badly wounding) a policeman. They're still awaiting trial, so it's been a tricky time for Orestes. But the good thing is he actually got down to doing some work and he's hoping he'll finally finish his degree this year and stop being "an eternal student". He wants to go to England to do a post-grad thing.

School finished last week and I'm back in Perivoli again, staying with Chryssa. I brought my friend Eurydice. She writes poems that are really good and while I've been writing to you, she's been working on her poetry. Mum didn't want to come as she's finishing her book about *Babas* and *Yiayia* Antigone. She's been using lots of sections that my grandmother wrote. First she translated it and then she put bits of it together with her own writing to turn it into a book. She asked me for a contribution, too, so I might make a copy of this letter for her. I think Mum might be seeing someone, though she hasn't told me. I've noticed her going off in the evenings, without explaining exactly where and looking nicer than usual. Also, she was suspiciously pleased to pack me off to "get some fresh air" in the countryside. The good thing is that she doesn't seem so crazy and obsessed any more, which is a relief as she's not so annoying.

I thought it was going to be boring coming to stay in Perivoli, but in fact it's great. And at least people aren't going on and on about "The Crisis" like they are in Athens, where it's the only topic of conversation and everybody is worried about wages and pensions and Greece going bankrupt. Here, it's like the economy could disappear down the drain and no one would notice. People are just getting on with life. Chryssa spends the time cooking delicious stuff. She bakes massive round loaves of proper *choriátiko* bread in the old wood oven in the yard, like they used to. And she knows how to make yogurt with a creamy skin on the top. *Yiayia*'s cat, Misha, has grown huge and rules the place like an emperor – the neighbours say they've never seen such a fat silky-haired specimen. It's true he's not much like the scrawny cats you see on most Greek streets.

In the early evening, the mountains go yellowy-purple ("like old bruises", said Eurydice) and it's lovely because the air smells of pine, but it's not too hot like in Athens. Most of the villagers go to the square, which is filled with mulberry trees all trained into funny umbrella shapes and joined together at the branches "like a row of Siamese twins" (Eurydice again). The old men play backgammon, the kids run around and eat ice-creams and Chryssa goes to the benches by the memorial and sits there with a group of other grannies, watching everyone and catching up on the gossip. The memorial is a big marble stone covered with a list of the seventy-one people who were killed during the war when Perivoli was burnt. It has all their ages and lots were children.

I've thought about how you said I was almost the exact image of my grandmother, and that she was very beautiful as a girl. Also, that we both have the same straight eyebrows and that you thought I must be as determined as she was. I think I am. During the short time I knew her, my real grandmother often wanted to talk about *Babas* with me, which made me cry (and her too, once). But I was pleased. I liked the way she spoke to me as if I was grown-up. She said how awful it was leaving *Babas* behind when he was a little boy. It was weird, because she seemed to understand how I felt. She said, "Do you think that you are so sad that you'll never be really happy again?" We talked about everything, about being young and about how you suffer because you feel things so strongly. But also you have your life to make something with. "Hope dies last," she said. The way she saw it, *Babas* had been a victim of the war and the Civil War like everyone in Greece. There was so much hatred and pain that people couldn't get away from it. She kept saying: "It is what it is." But then one day she said: "The past is done and there's nothing we can do to change it. But now it's different, you can leave all that behind. You own the future."

This time in Perivoli I told Eurydice about everything that happened after *Babas* died. She thought it was really fun to get a new grandmother. I told her that Antigone admitted she and Markos went pinching fruit from other people's gardens when they were kids. And also how *Babas* used to tell me about the awful stomach aches he had as a boy from all the plums and apples he ate straight from the trees. Yesterday Eurydice and I decided to keep a Perifanis family tradition going. In the afternoon, when it was baking hot and the only living things awake were the cicadas going crazy from their own buzzing, we walked outside the village and found this orchard and vegetable garden filled with different trees. There was a big cloud of yellow butterflies hovering near a row of beans. It was like a hallucination.

"You don't need drugs up here," Eurydice said. We ended up sitting under an apricot tree that was covered with perfectly ripe, golden fruit and pigged out. We threw the stones into the grass and ended up too bloated to move so we went to sleep and got sunburnt on our legs. But it was worth it. As Eurydice said, we had tasted "ambrosia of the gods".

This is probably the longest letter I'll ever write. I hope you reply soon.

Yours sincerely,
Antigone Perifanis

A NOTE ON THE BACKGROUND

A few years ago, some cousins of my husband, Vassilis, told us about a ritual they had recently carried out for a family member. Their aunt, Sophia Vlachou, was born in Dikastro, the same mountain village as Vassilis' father (a place with many similarities to "Perivoli" in *The House on Paradise Street*). As a young woman, Sophia was active in the resistance during the German occupation. Soon after the war, her partisan husband was executed, and following the Civil War, she went into exile in Romania. For many years, her family didn't know what had become of her, but in 1962 they got word that she had died, having suffered badly from her war injuries. They were unable to go to her funeral and it was not until over forty years later that her family brought her remains back from Bucharest. They placed her bones in a beautiful wooden box, organised a priest to make a blessing in the cemetery in Dikastro, and laid her to rest permanently in the ossuary there.

This incident moved me and re-kindled my interest in the legacy of the Greek Civil War. I had first become aware of its significance when I was an anthropology student doing research in the Peloponnese. I read Kevin Andrews' wonderful book, *The Flight of Icaros*, about his travels in a country devastated by war and then ground into despair by hatred and suspicion. Although many decades have passed since those dreadful years, Greeks are still affected by what happened. Some of the problems at the root of the current economic crisis and the intensity of the street protests as a reaction, can be linked back to the oppressive regimes that dominated Greece for so long. Families still carry painful memories of the Colonels' Junta (1967-74), and for many, this dictatorship was a repeat of what had happened in the 1940s; the same people went back to prison or into exile.

If Sophia Vlachou provided some of the inspiration for Antigone, many other people also contributed elements to what became her story. My aunt by marriage, Xanthe Papadimitriou, told me about her life in Athens before the war. Her family was not unlike Antigone's, with its comfortable house, good food, servants and high educational aspirations. The shock of losing everything during the war was deeply felt, and Xanthe described the endless search for food, the negotiations with black-marketeers and the increasing presence of death and starvation on the streets.

"We younger children would go and write slogans on walls," she said. "We were told by the older ones what to write: Down with Germans! Or, Italians – Traitors!

"If the police caught anyone they'd beat them black and blue, but it was more serious if you were older."

For some women I spoke to, the experiences after the war were even worse than during the occupation. Poppy Voliotou, now in her mid-eighties, lives on her own in a small apartment in Exarchia, central Athens. Everything there is orderly, down to the label for "hand towel" in the bathroom, and the plastic bowl in the basin to save and recycle water. I wondered if she had learned these habits as a prisoner, as she spent many years in Averoff Prison, which stood not far from her current home. A village girl who was married at sixteen, Poppy was put on trial for helping the partisans, and was only spared a death sentence because she was pregnant. Her baby was born with prison guards outside the hospital room and she eventually had her two older children brought to live with her in prison as there was nobody else to care for them.

Poppy told me horrific stories about her experiences in Averoff, about women who were pregnant following rape, about a grandmother and her twelve-year-old granddaughter in jail for handing out pro-partisan leaflets. But she also described the camaraderie of this unusual community of women and children, and her energy and optimism and her small, wiry frame all contributed to the character of Dora.

When I met the late Maria Beikou, I was amazed by how much about her life corresponded with what I had envisaged for Antigone. As an attractive, intelligent university student, she had "gone to the mountains" aged eighteen and fought in the resistance. After the Civil War she travelled to Tashkent and she ended up as an announcer on the radio station in Moscow. Unlike Antigone, Maria returned to Greece after the end of the Junta, in 1975. At the time I interviewed her, she was finishing a book about her life and participating in a theatre production of Mauser by the German playwright Heiner Muller, organised by the experimental director Theodoros Terzopoulos. She was eighty-three.

"I was never a fanatical communist," she said, despite having been the Greek voice of communism on Moscow Calling for many years. "But I think people will go back to Marx. After the fall of communism I didn't lose my life. What remained was comradeship, knowledge..." Sadly, she died in 2011, aged eighty-five, but remained active to the end.

Sofka Zinovieff, October 2011

A BRIEF HISTORY OF GREECE

We think of Greece as an ancient country, so it is easy to forget that it only became an independent state in 1830, after the War of Independence against the Ottoman Turks. It wasn't until much later, following the Balkan Wars of 1912-13, that it acquired the territory that gives it its present shape, and the Dodecanese islands were only ceded from Italy in 1947.

After the First World War, Greece was supported by the Great Powers (especially Britain) in invading parts of Asia Minor and taking control of the mainly Greek city of Smyrna. The debacle that followed became known as "the Catastrophe" by Greeks: the Allied Powers stood by as Turkish nationalists under Kemal Ataturk routed the Greek troops and destroyed Smyrna. The resulting population exchange between Greece and Turkey in 1923 was the twentieth century's first example of ethnic cleansing, as 1.4 million Christians (classified as "Greeks") were forced to leave their homes in Turkey. It was as refugees that they arrived in a Greek "homeland" they had never known (that itself had a population of only 4 million). 500,000 Muslims were expelled from Greece and sent to Turkey.

In 1936, following his coup, General Ioannis Metaxas was made Prime Minister by King George II. Metaxas quickly declared a state of emergency, suspended Parliament and made himself into a Mussolini-esque dictator, and self-styled "Saviour of the Nation". He banned communism, established prison camps for political enemies, and banned books that didn't suit the regime's ideology. His finest moment was when he followed the spirit of his nation and refused to allow Italian troops to occupy Greece in 1940. His resounding "No!" is still celebrated in Greece every October 28th.

Greece's brave defence and their counter-attack in Albania was a highly significant early victory for the Allies, at a time when the Nazis were sweeping through much of Europe and morale was low. The Greek defeat of the Italians forced the Nazis to step in, defeat the Greek army and join the subsequent occupation of the country by Germany, Italy and Bulgaria. The King, the Greek government and British troops in Greece were forced to flee, making their base in Egypt.

The Greeks suffered particularly badly during the war. Over 250,000 people died of starvation, the Jewish community was almost completely destroyed by the Nazis, and by the end, the country was physically devastated and divided along political lines. British secret agents of SOE (Secret Operations Executive) fought alongside resistance groups during the occupation, but the British army quickly sided with the more right-wing factions following liberation in October 1944. By December the British were fighting the largest, most popular resistance group, ELAS, in the streets of Athens. The seeds of the Civil War had been sown. From 1946-49, the British and then the Americans, supported the National Army in its struggle to destroy the communist-controlled Democratic army. Much of the fighting took place in the mountains of northern Greece.

Atrocities took place on both sides during the Civil War, but by 1949, the left-wing had been destroyed, its remaining members imprisoned, exiled or forced to flee to neighbouring communist countries. The following 25 years saw a series of right-wing governments, mostly headed by Constantine Karamanlis.

These were supported by the US, which also helped reconstruct the country under the Marshall Plan and simultaneously tried to keep "the threat of Communism at bay". In 1967, a group of military officers, known as "the Colonels", made a coup d'état and established a military dictatorship. Supported by the CIA, they were signed in by King Constantine, who later made an abortive attempt to oust them and was forced to flee the country.

In 1973, a mass demonstration of students took place in Athens' Polytechnic, the Junta sent in the army with tanks and many young people were injured and killed. The shock of this brutality, combined with the abortive attempt by the Colonels to instigate a coup in Cyprus in order to get rid of President Makarios (which was followed by the Turkish invasion), led to the collapse of the dictatorship in 1974. Democracy was restored, Constantine Karamanlis returned from exile in Paris as the Prime Minister, and Greece became a republic after a referendum vote rejected the return of King Constantine.

Some political exiles began to return from eastern bloc countries after the end of the Junta, but it was not until 1981 that Greece had its first socialist government since the war. Under the policy of National Reconciliation, the left-wing national resistance during the Nazi occupation was recognised for the first time. It has only been since then – 30 years – that political and social integration has allowed Greece to create a fully functional democracy.

ACKNOWLEDGEMENTS

Many of the incidents in this book are inspired by actual events. I am profoundly indebted to those who talked to me about their often difficult experiences during and after the war: Sylvia Ioannidou, Katina Latifi, Maria Beikou, Mairy Aroni, Poppy Voliotou, Yiorgos Votsis, Themis Marinos, Kostas Vlachos, Dimitris Vlachos, Nikos Belloyiannis, Xanthe Papadimitriou and Irini Raya.

I am particularly grateful to two friends: Stelios Kouloglou helped me understand more about the Civil War when I started the project and introduced me to some extraordinary people; and Paul Johnston gave invaluable advice all the way through.

Many books were useful for my research, but several provided crucial details: Olympia Papadouka, *Geinaikeiai Filakai Averoff* (Averoff Women's Prison); P. Aronis and V. Vardinogiannis, *Oi Misoi Sta Sidera* (Half of Them Behind Bars); Dominiqe Eudes, *The Kapetánios: Partisans and Civil War in Greece, 1943-1949*; Stelios Kouloglou, Martiries gia ton Emfilio kai tin Elliniki Aristera (Witnesses of the Civil War and the Greek Left); and for the great title, Akis Gavriilidis, *I Atherapefti Nekrofilia tou Rizospastikou Patriostismou* (The Incurable Necrophilia of Radical Patriotism).

Thank you for a variety of good things to my dear friends, Amalia Zepou, Katya Michos and Tessa Charlton. I would also like to thank Yiorgos Alexopoulos for information about Athenian archaeology, Sotiris Glykofridis for conversations about Parmenides, Yanis Varoufakis who talked about students, Lee

Sarafis for information about the Civil War, and Ioanna Haritatou for showing me her inspiring house in Mets. Phivos Karzis and Mark Dragoumis helped with historical tips Thanks also to my stepmother, Jenny Zinovieff, and to my father, Peter Zinovieff, the only person who read tender parts of work-in-progress.

George Miller, Effie Basdra and Jacoline Vinke gave immensely helpful, intelligent comments on the manuscript. Thank you.

Huge thanks to my editor, Aurea Carpenter. Also to everyone at Short Books.

I am deeply grateful to my agent, Caroline Dawnay, for all her help. Also to her assistant, Olivia Hunt.

Vassilis Papadimitriou, my husband, gave unstinting love and support and helped me believe it was possible. The book is dedicated to our daughters, whose Greek grandparents, Photini and Kostas Papadimitriou, lived through the horrors of the German occupation and the Civil War.